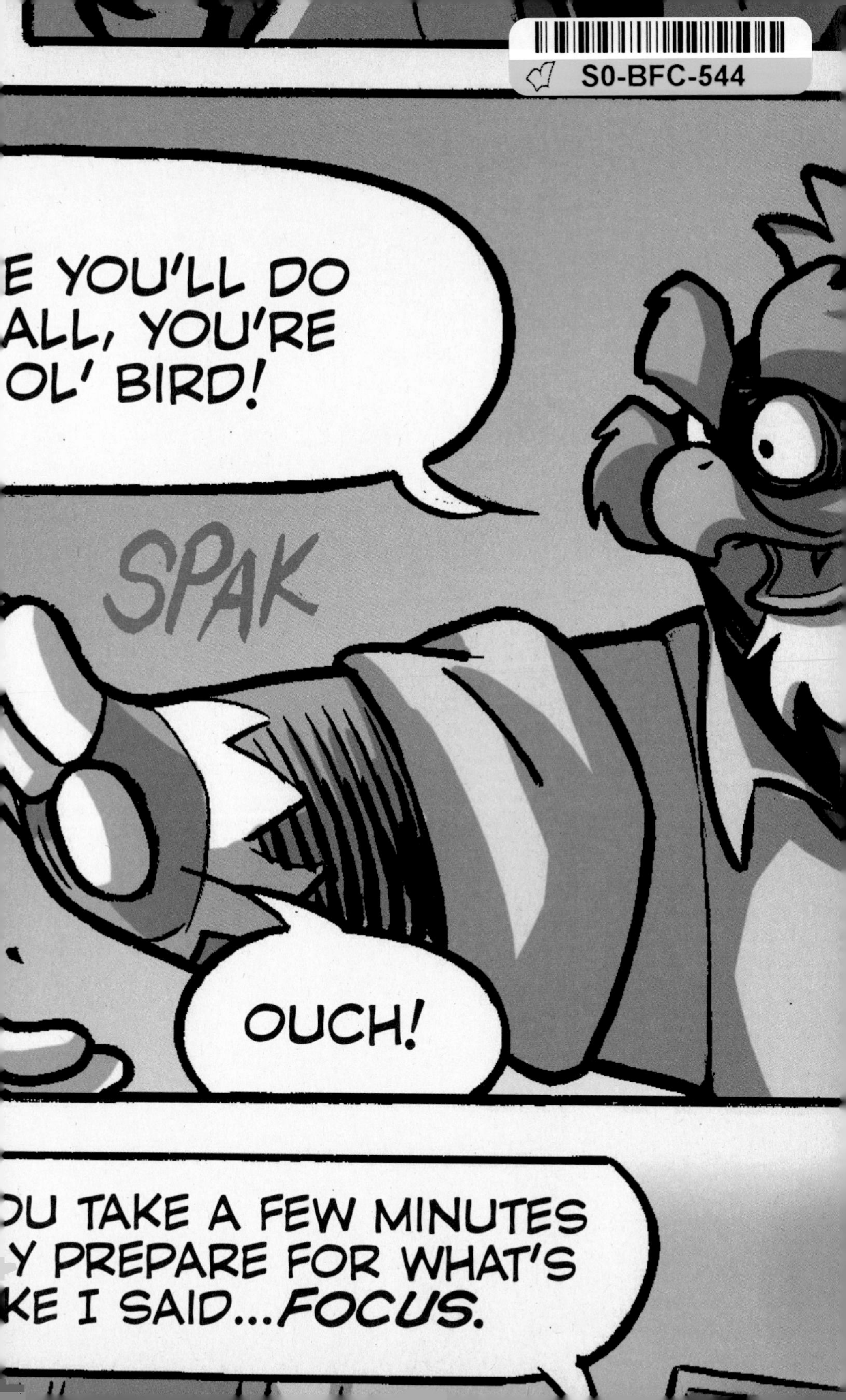
E YOU'LL DO
ALL, YOU'RE
OL' BIRD!
SPAK
OUCH!
OU TAKE A FEW MINUTES
Y PREPARE FOR WHAT'S
KE I SAID...*FOCUS.*

DOUBLE
DUCK

ROSS RICHIE
chief executive officer

MARK WAID
editor-in-chief

ADAM FORTIER
vice president,
publishing

CHIP MOSHER
marketing director

MATT GAGNON
managing editor

JENNY CHRISTOPHER
sales director

FIRST EDITION: JANUARY 2010

10 9 8 7 6 5 4 3 2 1
PRINTED BY WORLD COLOR PRESS, INC.
ST ROMUALD, QC., CANADA.

DONALD DUCK AND FRIENDS: DOUBLE DUCK – published by BOOM Kids!, a division of Boom Entertainment, Inc. All contents © 2010 Walt Disney Company. BOOM Kids! and the BOOM Kids! logo are trademarks of Boom Entertainment, Inc., registered in various countries and categories. All rights reserved.

Office of publication: 6310 San Vicente Blvd Ste 404, Los Angeles, CA 90048-5457.

A catalog record for this book is available from OCLC and on our website www.boom-kids.com on the Librarians page.

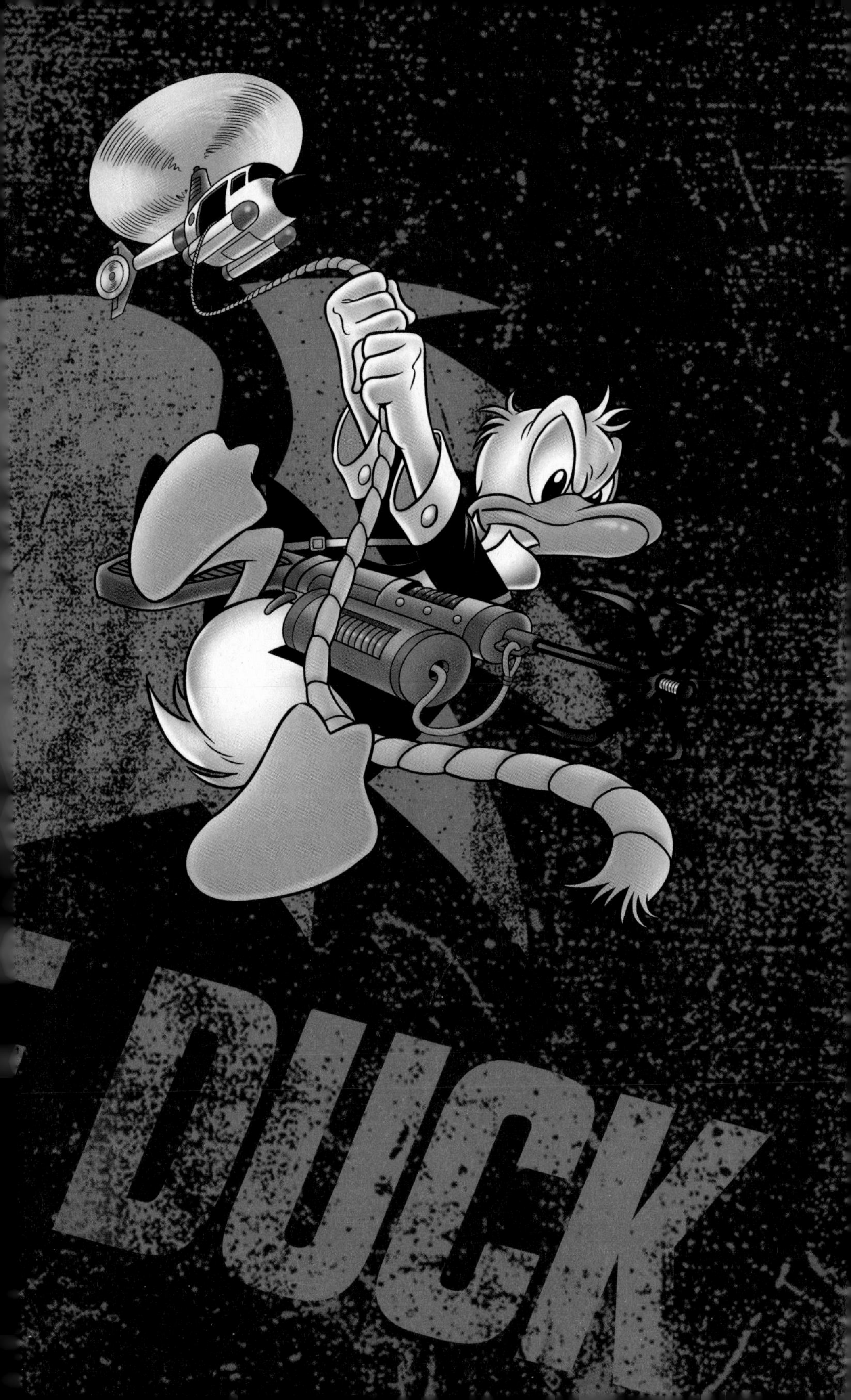
DUCK

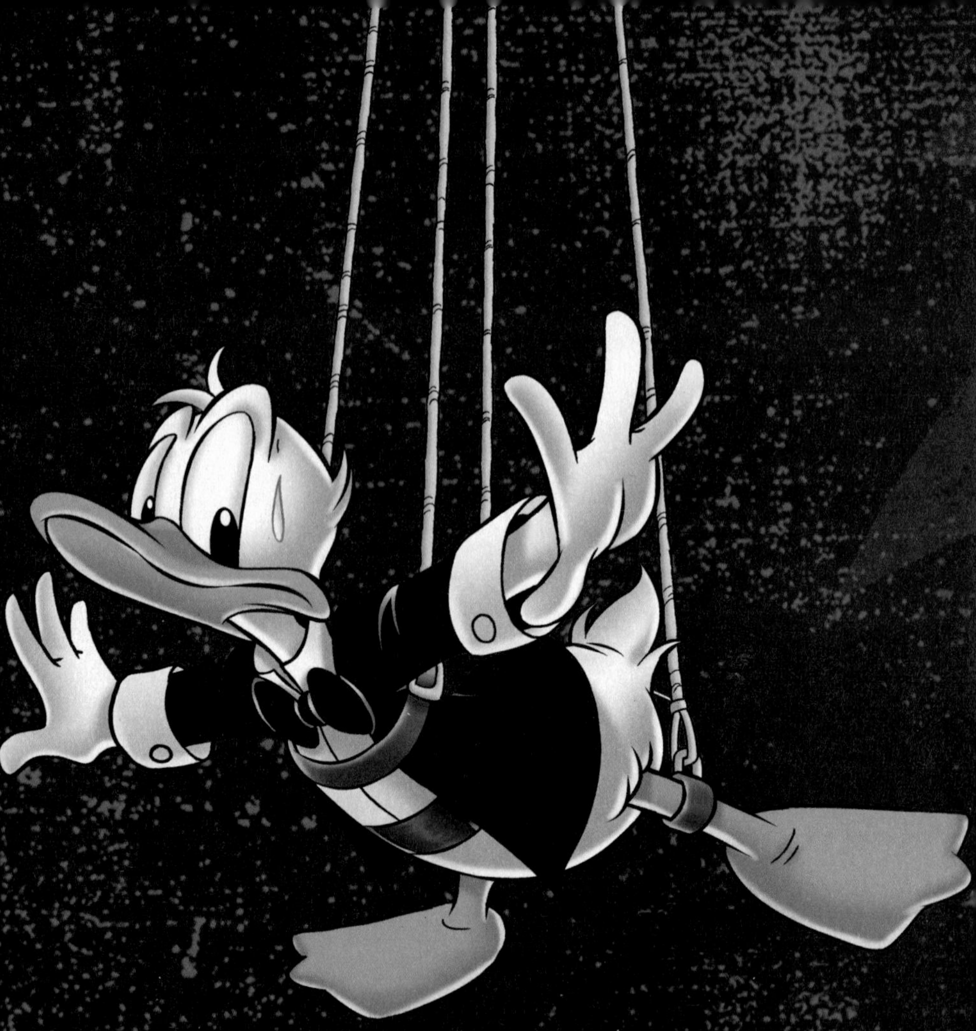

WRITTEN BY:
FAUSTO VITALIANO & MARCO BOSCO

ART BY:
ALESSANDRO FRECCERO,
VITALE MANGIATORDI, MARCO MAZZARELLO
& FRANCESCO D'IPPOLITO

EDITOR:
AARON SPARROW

ASSISTANT EDITOR:
CHRISTOPHER BURNS

COVER:
MAGIC EYE STUDIOS

HARDCOVER CASE WRAP:
ANDREA FRECCERO

TRANSLATORS:
SAIDA TEMOFONTE &
STEFANIA BRONZONI

LETTERER:
JOSE MACASOCOL JR.

DESIGNER:
ERIKA TERRIQUEZ

SPECIAL THANKS TO:
JESSE POST, LAUREN KRESSEL
& ELENA GARBO

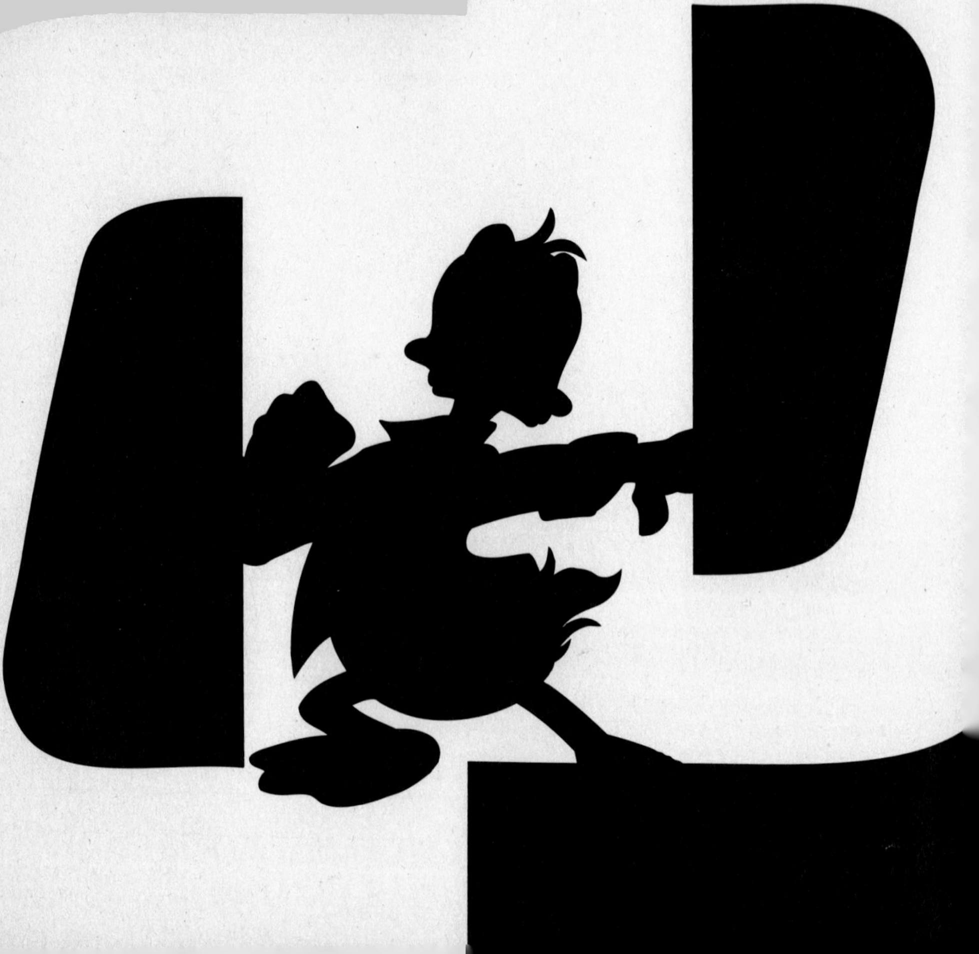

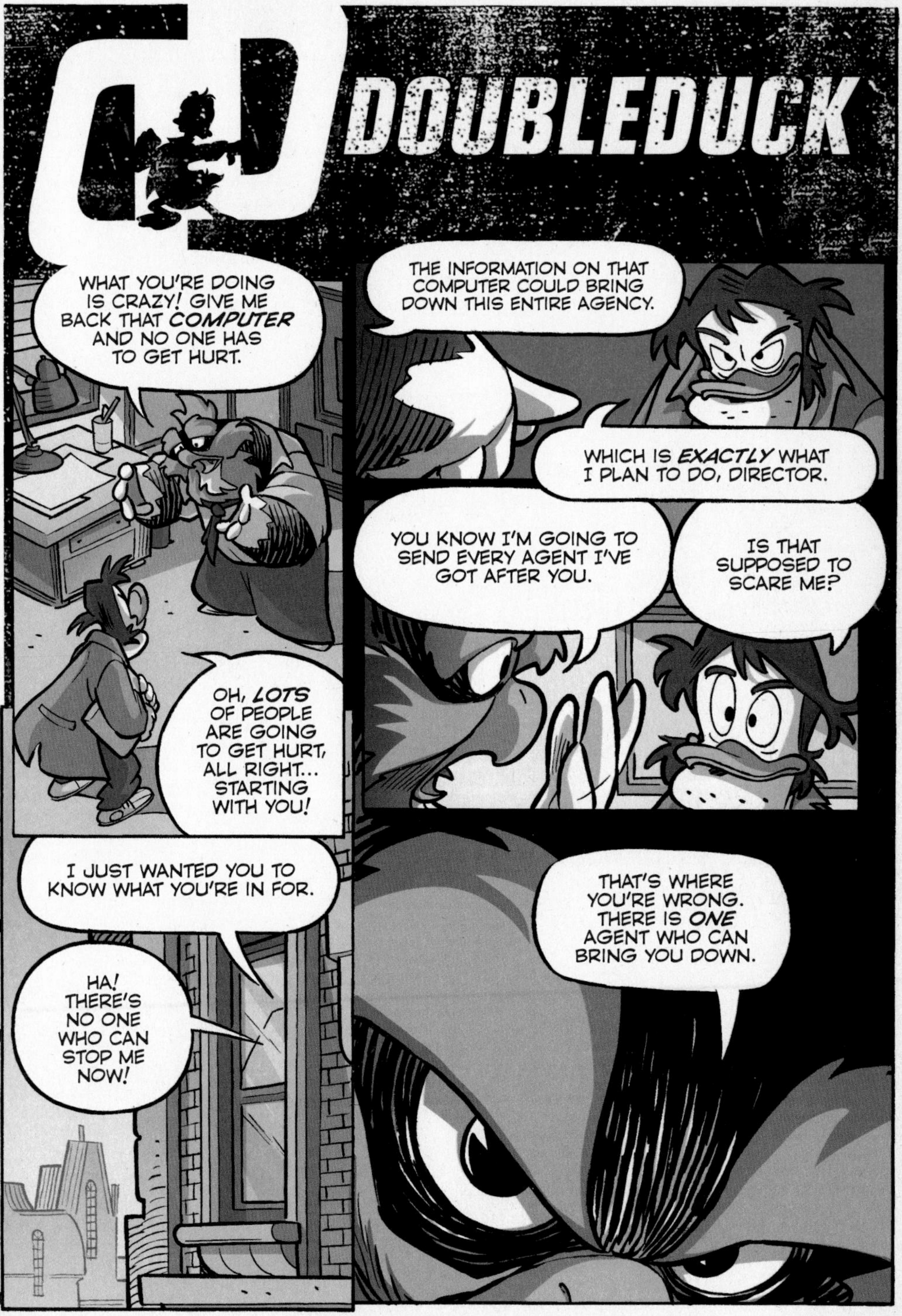
DOUBLEDUCK
WHAT YOU'RE DOING IS CRAZY! GIVE ME BACK THAT COMPUTER AND NO ONE HAS TO GET HURT.
THE INFORMATION ON THAT COMPUTER COULD BRING DOWN THIS ENTIRE AGENCY.
WHICH IS EXACTLY WHAT I PLAN TO DO, DIRECTOR.
YOU KNOW I'M GOING TO SEND EVERY AGENT I'VE GOT AFTER YOU.
IS THAT SUPPOSED TO SCARE ME?
OH, LOTS OF PEOPLE ARE GOING TO GET HURT, ALL RIGHT... STARTING WITH YOU!
I JUST WANTED YOU TO KNOW WHAT YOU'RE IN FOR.
HA! THERE'S NO ONE WHO CAN STOP ME NOW!
THAT'S WHERE YOU'RE WRONG. THERE IS ONE AGENT WHO CAN BRING YOU DOWN.

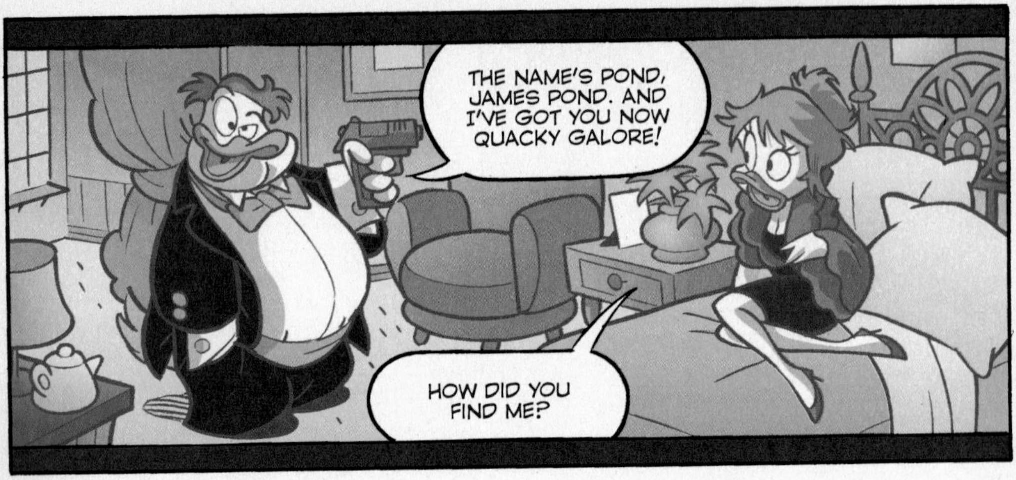
THE NAME'S POND, JAMES POND. AND I'VE GOT YOU NOW QUACKY GALORE!
HOW DID YOU FIND ME?

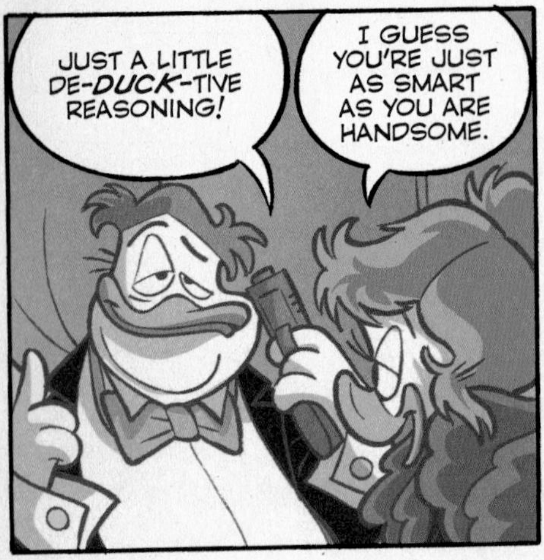
JUST A LITTLE DE-DUCK-TIVE REASONING!
I GUESS YOU'RE JUST AS SMART AS YOU ARE HANDSOME.

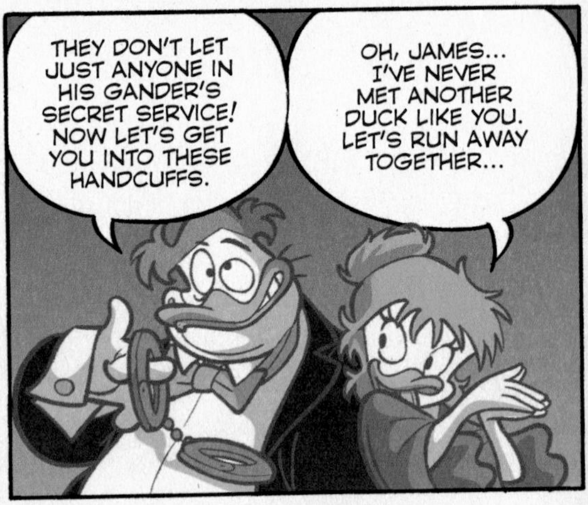
THEY DON'T LET JUST ANYONE IN HIS GANDER'S SECRET SERVICE! NOW LET'S GET YOU INTO THESE HANDCUFFS.
OH, JAMES... I'VE NEVER MET ANOTHER DUCK LIKE YOU. LET'S RUN AWAY TOGETHER...

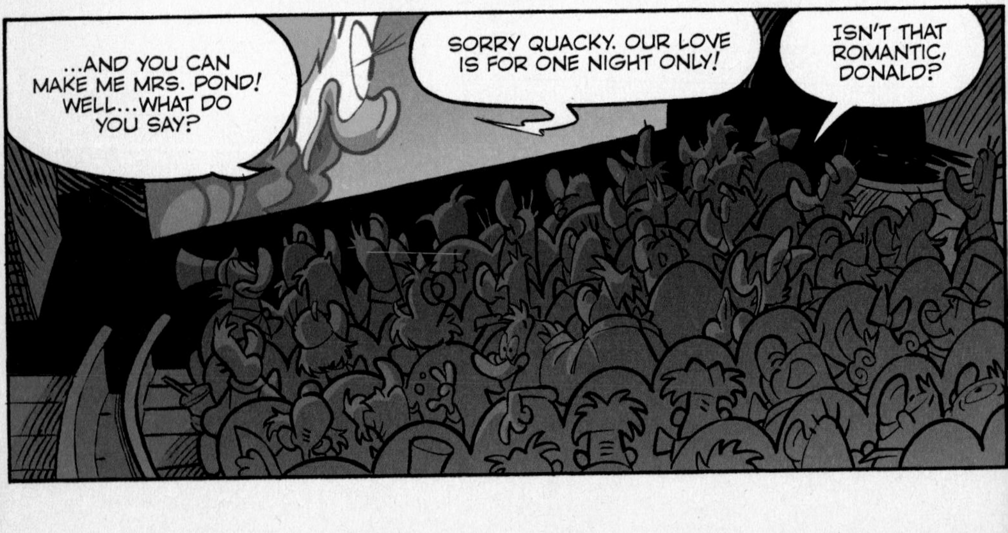
...AND YOU CAN MAKE ME MRS. POND! WELL...WHAT DO YOU SAY?
SORRY QUACKY. OUR LOVE IS FOR ONE NIGHT ONLY!
ISN'T THAT ROMANTIC, DONALD?

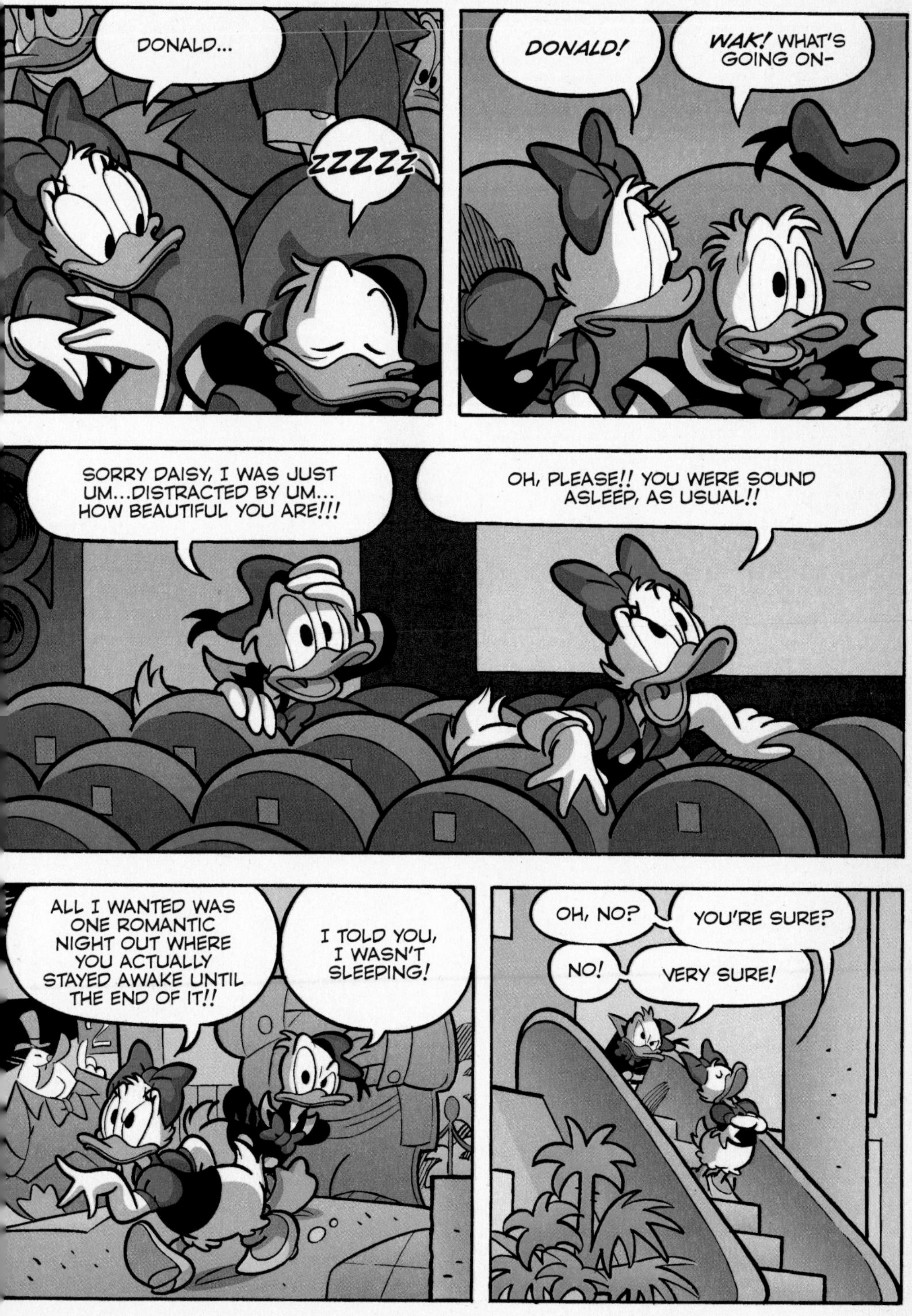
DONALD...
ZZZZZ
DONALD!
WAK! WHAT'S GOING ON-
SORRY DAISY, I WAS JUST UM...DISTRACTED BY UM... HOW BEAUTIFUL YOU ARE!!!
OH, PLEASE!! YOU WERE SOUND ASLEEP, AS USUAL!!
ALL I WANTED WAS ONE ROMANTIC NIGHT OUT WHERE YOU ACTUALLY STAYED AWAKE UNTIL THE END OF IT!!
I TOLD YOU, I WASN'T SLEEPING!
OH, NO?
NO!
YOU'RE SURE?
VERY SURE!

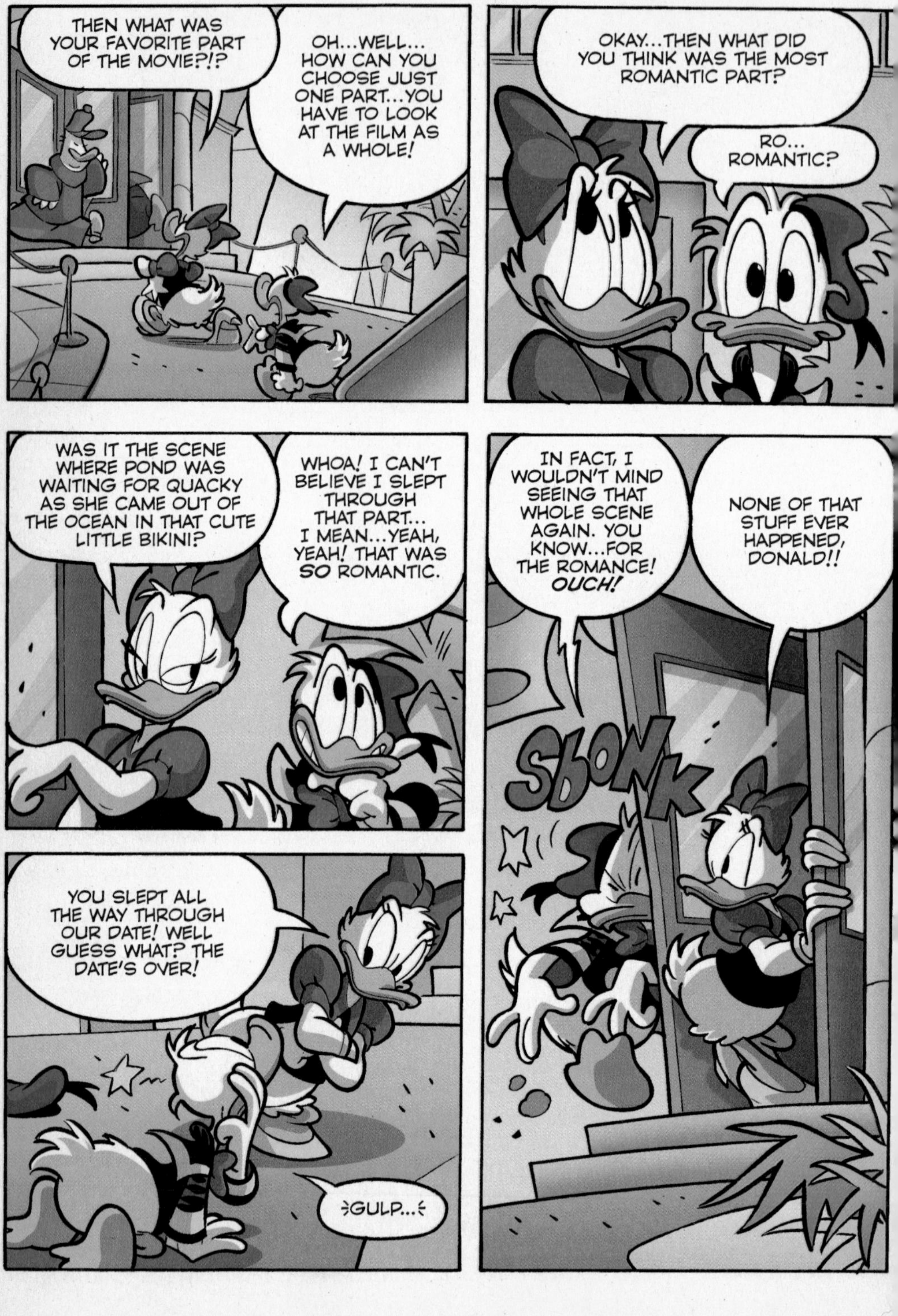
THEN WHAT WAS YOUR FAVORITE PART OF THE MOVIE?!?
OH...WELL... HOW CAN YOU CHOOSE JUST ONE PART...YOU HAVE TO LOOK AT THE FILM AS A WHOLE!
OKAY...THEN WHAT DID YOU THINK WAS THE MOST ROMANTIC PART?
RO... ROMANTIC?
WAS IT THE SCENE WHERE POND WAS WAITING FOR QUACKY AS SHE CAME OUT OF THE OCEAN IN THAT CUTE LITTLE BIKINI?
WHOA! I CAN'T BELIEVE I SLEPT THROUGH THAT PART... I MEAN...YEAH, YEAH! THAT WAS SO ROMANTIC.
IN FACT, I WOULDN'T MIND SEEING THAT WHOLE SCENE AGAIN. YOU KNOW...FOR THE ROMANCE! OUCH!
NONE OF THAT STUFF EVER HAPPENED, DONALD!!
SBONK
YOU SLEPT ALL THE WAY THROUGH OUR DATE! WELL GUESS WHAT? THE DATE'S OVER!
GULP...

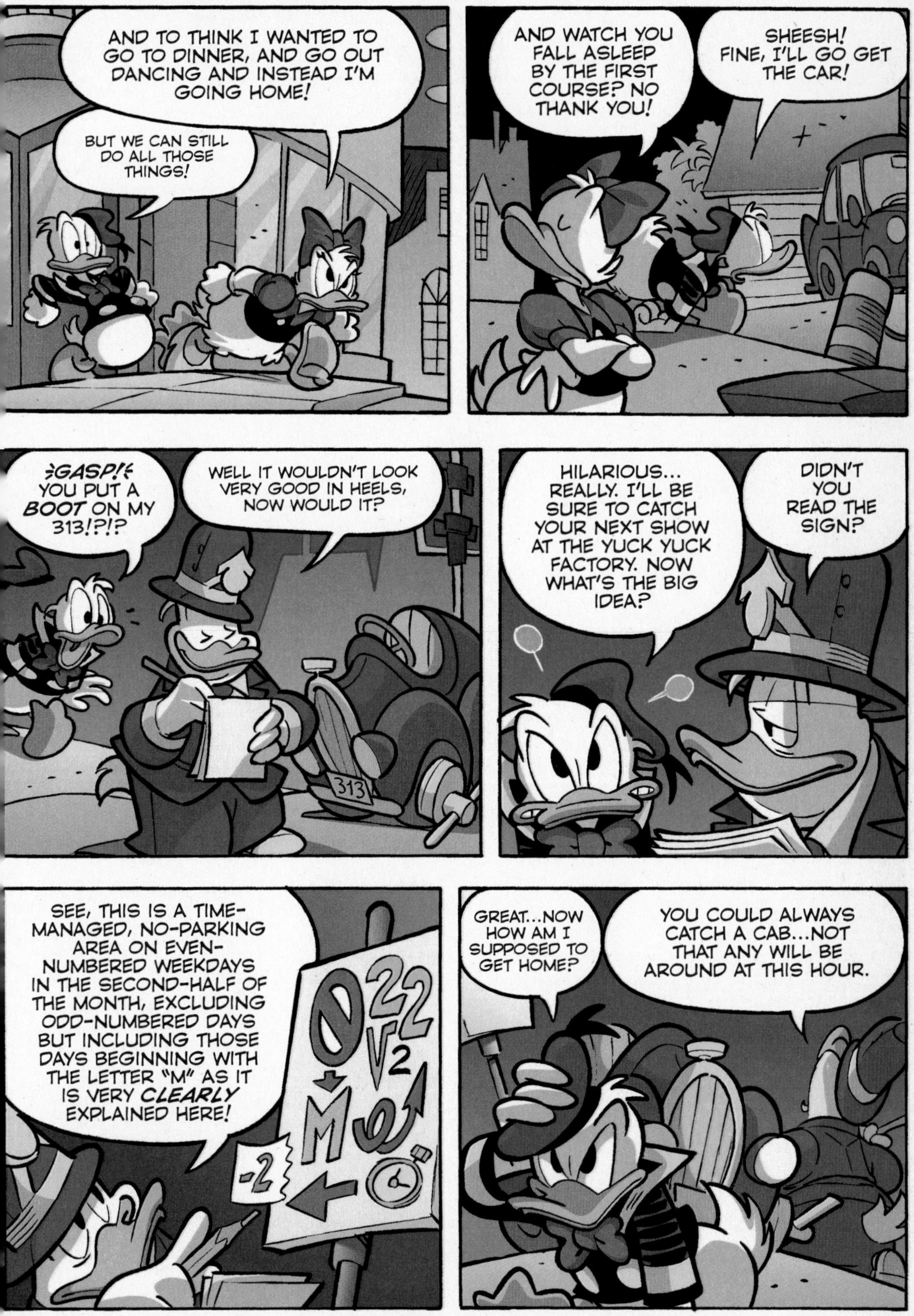
AND TO THINK I WANTED TO GO TO DINNER, AND GO OUT DANCING AND INSTEAD I'M GOING HOME!
BUT WE CAN STILL DO ALL THOSE THINGS!
AND WATCH YOU FALL ASLEEP BY THE FIRST COURSE? NO THANK YOU!
SHEESH! FINE, I'LL GO GET THE CAR!
GASP! YOU PUT A BOOT ON MY 313!?!?
WELL IT WOULDN'T LOOK VERY GOOD IN HEELS, NOW WOULD IT?
313
HILARIOUS... REALLY. I'LL BE SURE TO CATCH YOUR NEXT SHOW AT THE YUCK YUCK FACTORY. NOW WHAT'S THE BIG IDEA?
DIDN'T YOU READ THE SIGN?
SEE, THIS IS A TIME-MANAGED, NO-PARKING AREA ON EVEN-NUMBERED WEEKDAYS IN THE SECOND-HALF OF THE MONTH, EXCLUDING ODD-NUMBERED DAYS BUT INCLUDING THOSE DAYS BEGINNING WITH THE LETTER "M" AS IT IS VERY CLEARLY EXPLAINED HERE!
22
V2
M
-2
GREAT...NOW HOW AM I SUPPOSED TO GET HOME?
YOU COULD ALWAYS CATCH A CAB...NOT THAT ANY WILL BE AROUND AT THIS HOUR.

UM... DAISY, MY SWEET... SMALL PROBLEM.
DONALD, IF YOU DON'T HAVE ME HOME IN TEN MINUTES YOU'RE GOING TO HAVE A *BIG* PROBLEM.
I JUST NEED TO CALL A TAXI AND THEN I'LL GET YOU HOME.
A TAXI?? IT WILL TAKE FOREVER TO GET A CAB OUT HERE AT THIS HOUR!
PERHAPS I COULD BE OF SERVICE!
I'D BE HAPPY TO GET YOU A TAXI, DAISY.
OH NO YOU DON'T, GLADSTONE! YOU MAY HAVE A REPUTATION FOR BEING LUCKY, BUT THERE IS NO WAY, NO HOW... THAT YOU'RE GETTING A CAB *BEFORE ME!*
TAXI
THERE'S ONLY ONE GUY TAKING DAISY HOME, AND THAT GUY IS... *ULP!*
GLADSTONE GANDER!? HAVEN'T SEEN YOU IN YEARS! NEED A LIFT?
WELL, WELL. ISN'T THAT LUCKY?
SKREEEK
I'LL BE YOUR PERSONAL CHAUFFEUR FOR THE REST OF THE EVENING. AND I'VE GOT FREE PASSES TO PLACES ALL OVER TOWN. DINNER, DANCING...YOU NAME IT!
TAXI
DAISY, MY DEAR, LOOKS LIKE THIS IS YOUR LUCKY NIGHT!
ROOOAR

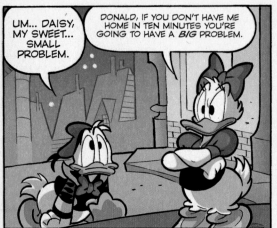

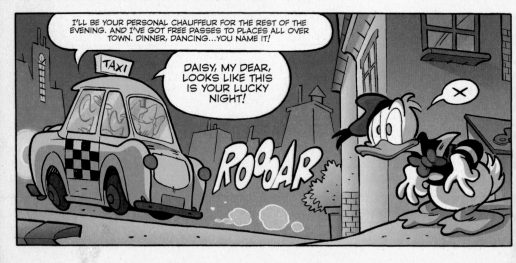

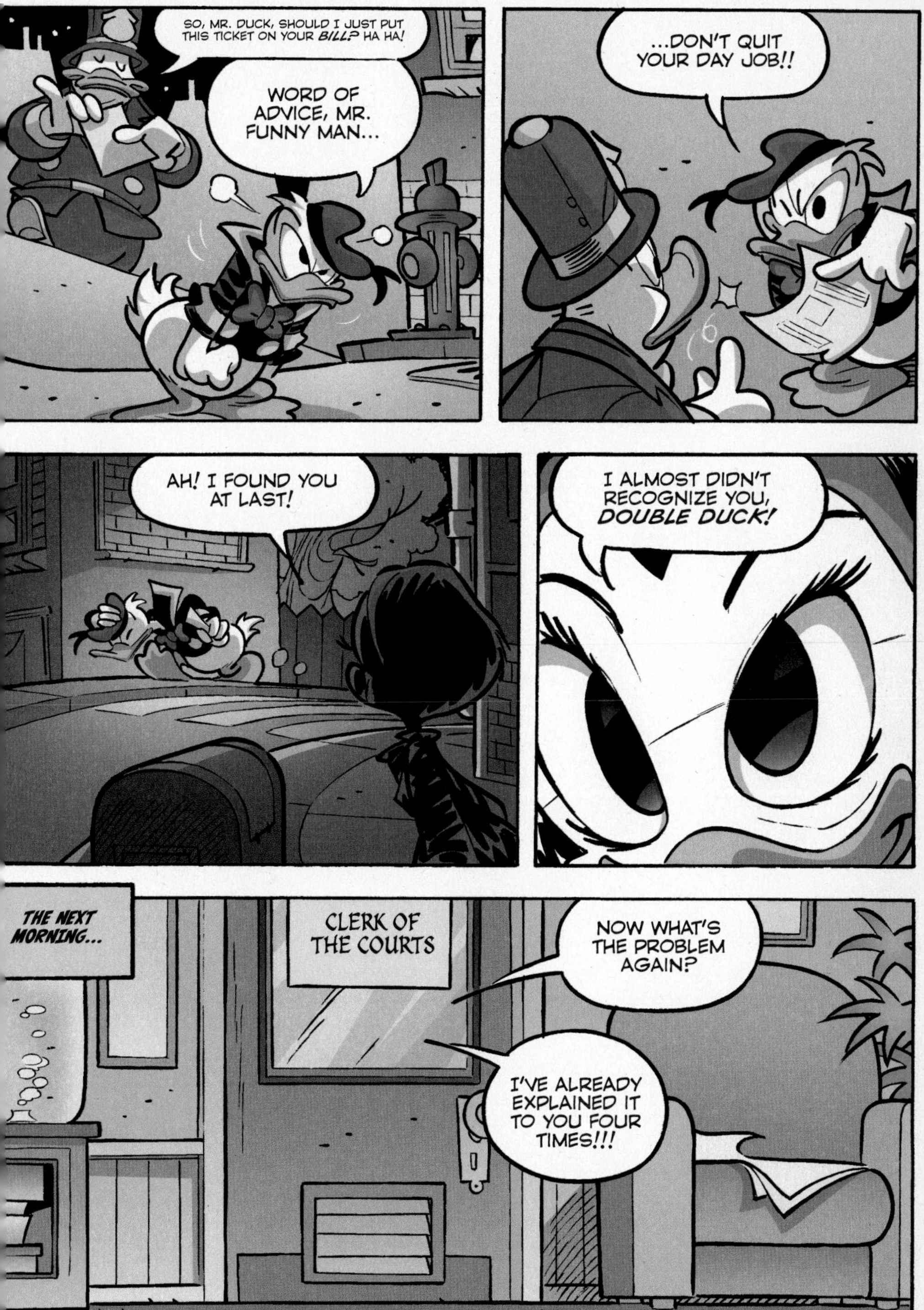

SO, MR. DUCK, SHOULD I JUST PUT THIS TICKET ON YOUR BILL? HA HA!
WORD OF ADVICE, MR. FUNNY MAN...
...DON'T QUIT YOUR DAY JOB!!
AH! I FOUND YOU AT LAST!
I ALMOST DIDN'T RECOGNIZE YOU, DOUBLE DUCK!
THE NEXT MORNING...
CLERK OF THE COURTS
NOW WHAT'S THE PROBLEM AGAIN?
I'VE ALREADY EXPLAINED IT TO YOU FOUR TIMES!!!

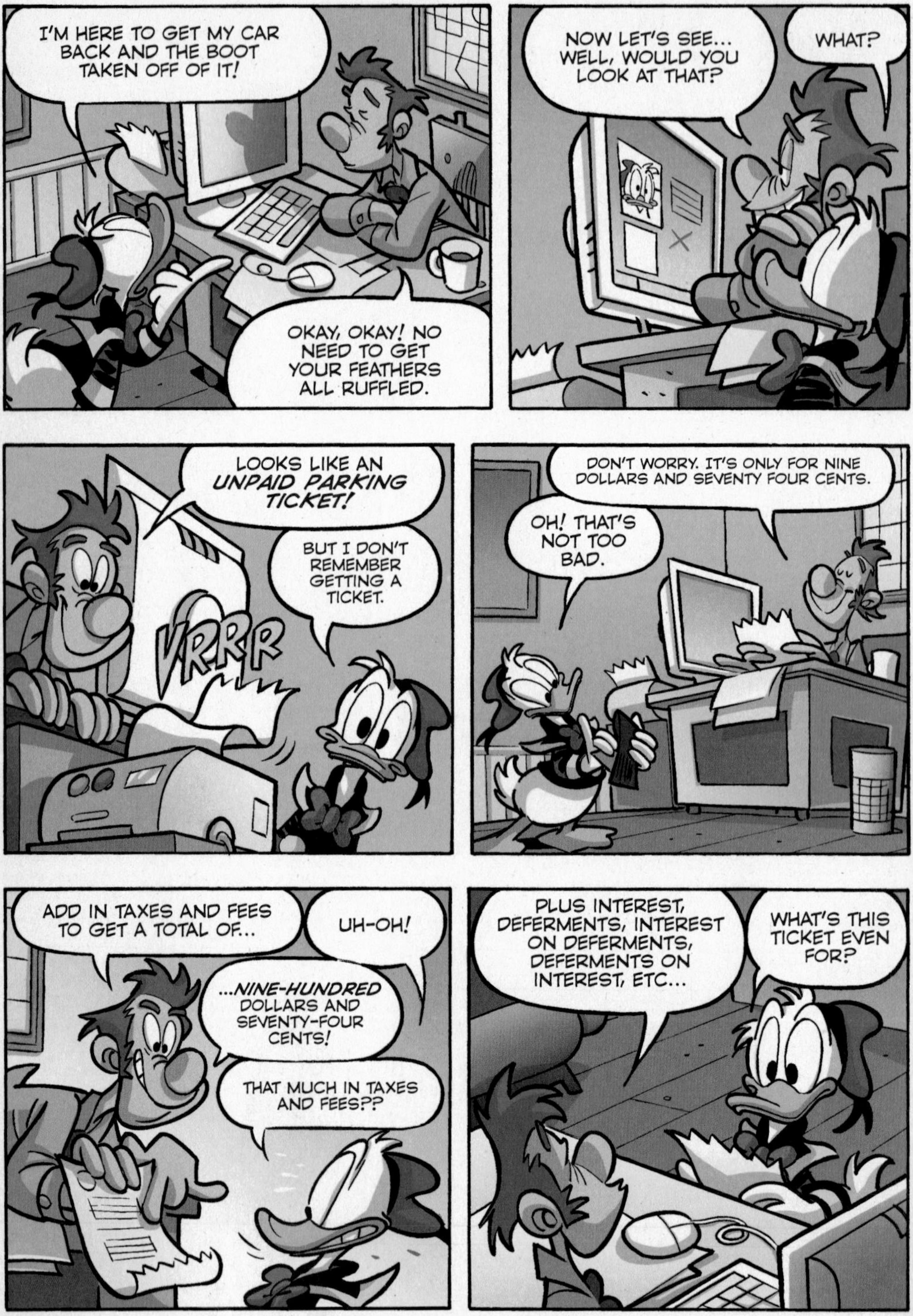
I'M HERE TO GET MY CAR BACK AND THE BOOT TAKEN OFF OF IT!
OKAY, OKAY! NO NEED TO GET YOUR FEATHERS ALL RUFFLED.
NOW LET'S SEE... WELL, WOULD YOU LOOK AT THAT?
WHAT?
LOOKS LIKE AN UNPAID PARKING TICKET!
VRRR
BUT I DON'T REMEMBER GETTING A TICKET.
DON'T WORRY. IT'S ONLY FOR NINE DOLLARS AND SEVENTY FOUR CENTS.
OH! THAT'S NOT TOO BAD.
ADD IN TAXES AND FEES TO GET A TOTAL OF...
UH-OH!
...NINE-HUNDRED DOLLARS AND SEVENTY-FOUR CENTS!
THAT MUCH IN TAXES AND FEES??
PLUS INTEREST, DEFERMENTS, INTEREST ON DEFERMENTS, DEFERMENTS ON INTEREST, ETC...
WHAT'S THIS TICKET EVEN FOR?

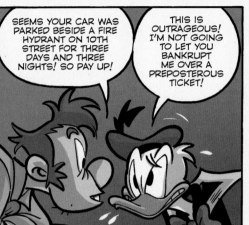

SEEMS YOUR CAR WAS PARKED BESIDE A FIRE HYDRANT ON 10TH STREET FOR THREE DAYS AND THREE NIGHTS! SO PAY UP!

THIS IS OUTRAGEOUS! I'M NOT GOING TO LET YOU BANKRUPT ME OVER A PREPOSTEROUS TICKET!

HEY!! YOU'VE ONLY GOT THREE DAYS TO PAY THIS!!!

OR WHAT?

OR YOU'LL HAVE A *REAL* REASON TO HAVE YOUR FEATHERS RUFFLED!!!

I'VE *NEVER* EVEN PARKED ON 10TH ST, I'M SURE OF THAT!

WHAT *WAS* I DOING ON THOSE *THREE DAYS?*

MON- HAMMOCK
TUE- HAMMOCK
WED- X
THU- X
FRI- X
SAT- HAMMOCK
SUN- OFF

NOTHING ON THE CALENDAR... MAYBE SOMEONE ELSE KNOWS WHERE I WAS...

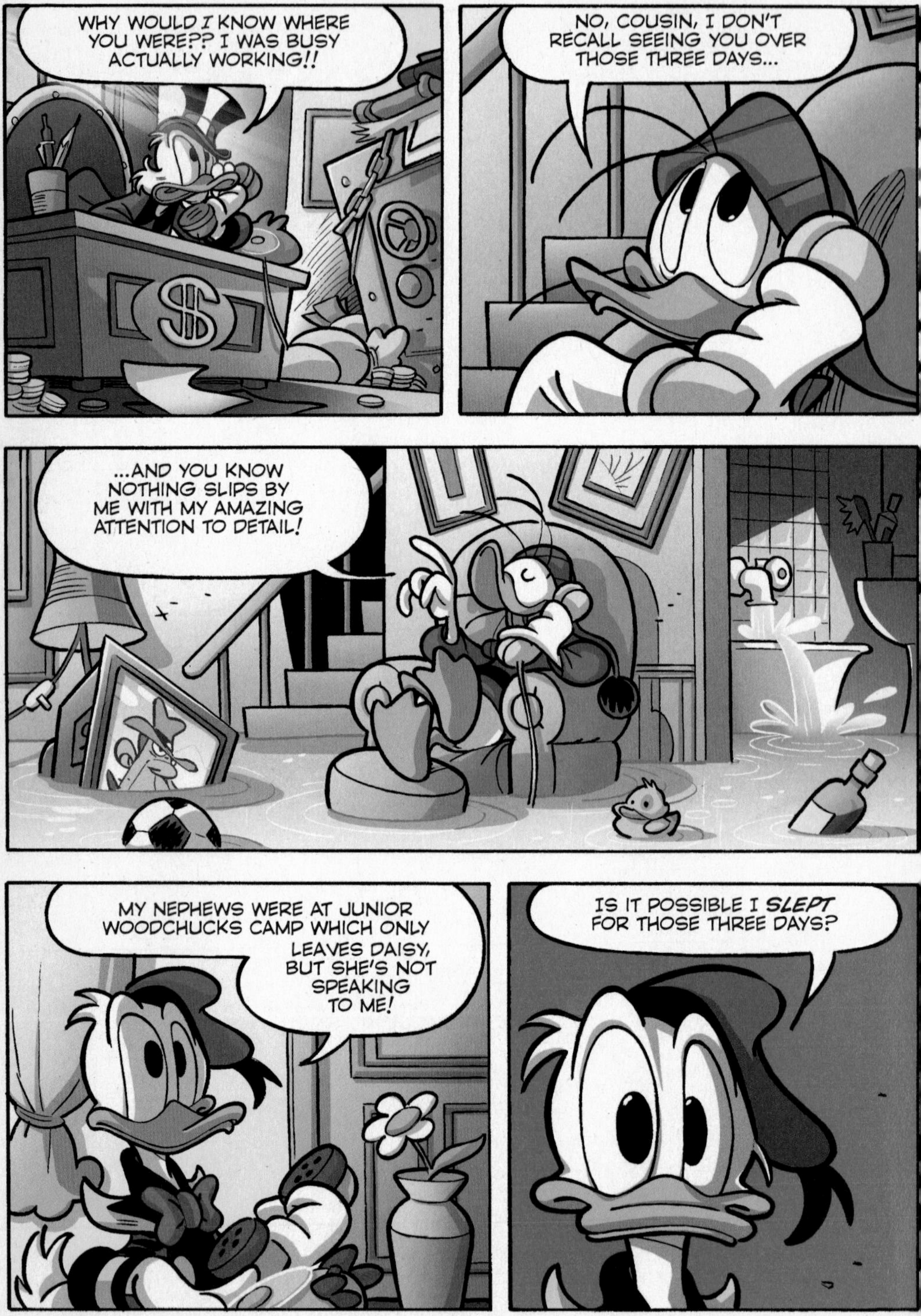
WHY WOULD I KNOW WHERE YOU WERE?? I WAS BUSY ACTUALLY WORKING!!
NO, COUSIN, I DON'T RECALL SEEING YOU OVER THOSE THREE DAYS...
...AND YOU KNOW NOTHING SLIPS BY ME WITH MY AMAZING ATTENTION TO DETAIL!
MY NEPHEWS WERE AT JUNIOR WOODCHUCKS CAMP WHICH ONLY LEAVES DAISY, BUT SHE'S NOT SPEAKING TO ME!
IS IT POSSIBLE I SLEPT FOR THOSE THREE DAYS?

THE NEXT DAY...

I'M TELLING YOU, IT'S A MISTAKE!

I WASN'T EVEN IN THAT PART OF TOWN THAT DAY!

OH REALLY. WELL, IF YOU CAN PROVE IT, YOU MAY HAVE A CASE.

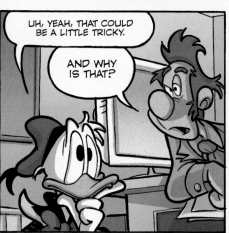

UH, YEAH, THAT COULD BE A LITTLE TRICKY.

AND WHY IS THAT?

IT'S LIKE THOSE DAYS DON'T EVEN EXIST! I CAN'T REMEMBER ANYTHING ABOUT THEM!!

THEN HOW DO YOU KNOW YOU WEREN'T THERE?!?

WHAT DO YOU TAKE ME FOR, AN IDIOT?

OF COURSE NOT! I HOLD IDIOTS IN *MUCH* HIGHER REGARD!!

IF YOU DON'T PAY THIS TICKET BY THE DAY-AFTER-TOMORROW, I'M GOING TO ISSUE A WARRANT FOR YOUR ARREST AND EVERY COP IN TOWN WILL BE LOOKING FOR YOU!

≥GRUNT!≤

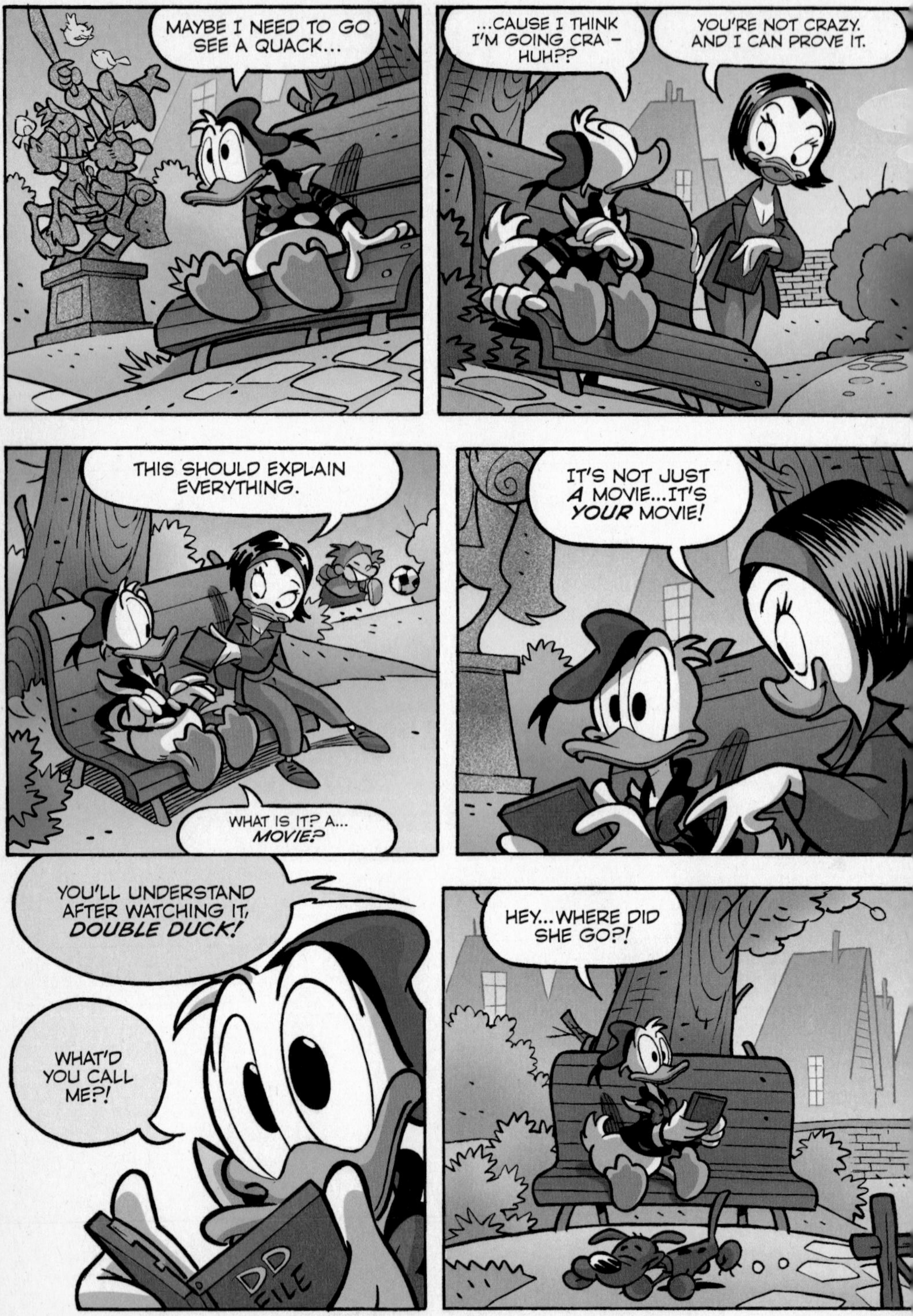
MAYBE I NEED TO GO SEE A QUACK...
...CAUSE I THINK I'M GOING CRA – HUH??
YOU'RE NOT CRAZY. AND I CAN PROVE IT.
THIS SHOULD EXPLAIN EVERYTHING.
WHAT IS IT? A... *MOVIE?*
IT'S NOT JUST *A* MOVIE...IT'S *YOUR* MOVIE!
YOU'LL UNDERSTAND AFTER WATCHING IT, *DOUBLE DUCK!*
WHAT'D YOU CALL ME?!
DD FILE
HEY...WHERE DID SHE GO?!

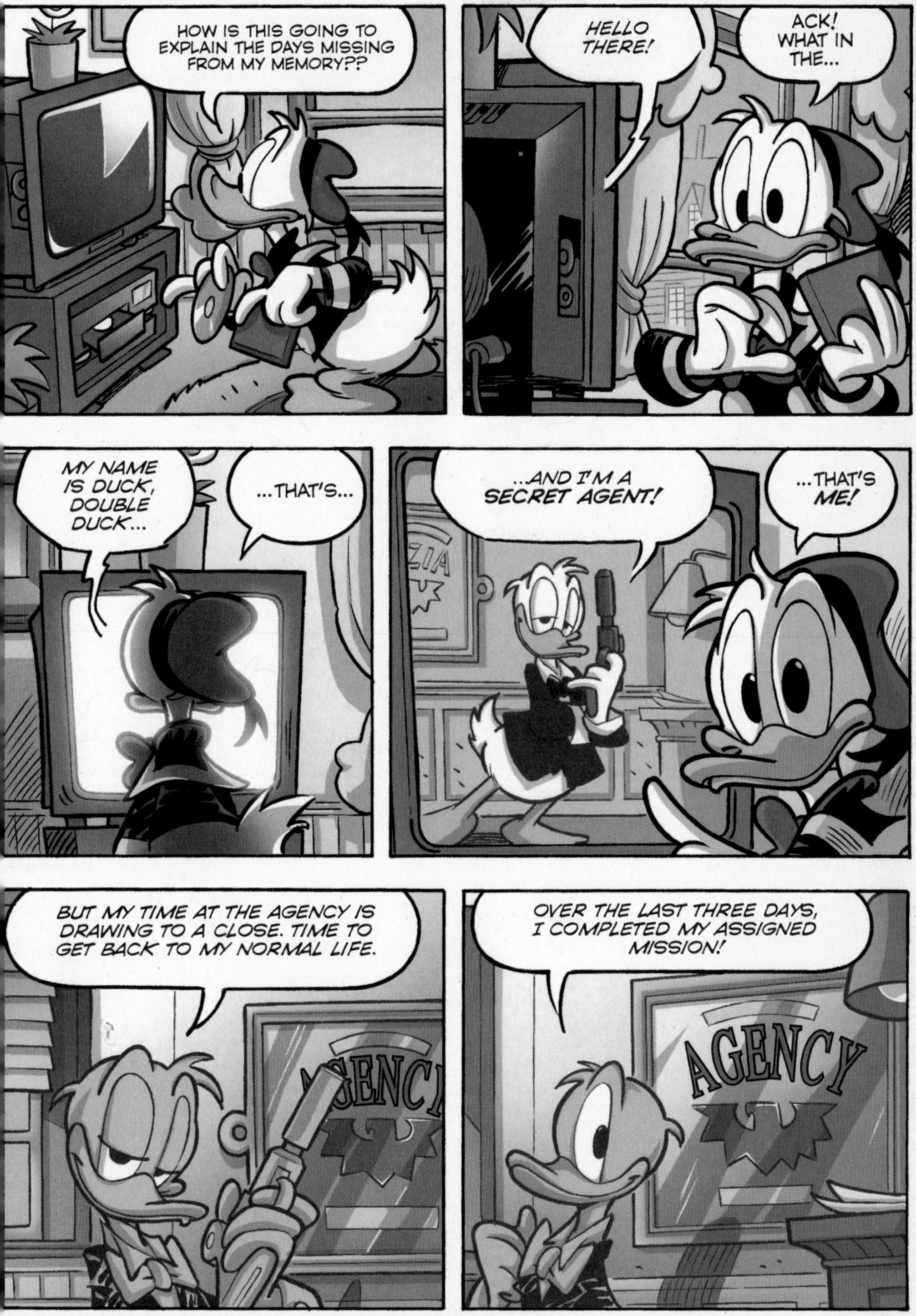
HOW IS THIS GOING TO EXPLAIN THE DAYS MISSING FROM MY MEMORY??
HELLO THERE!
ACK! WHAT IN THE...
MY NAME IS DUCK, DOUBLE DUCK...
...THAT'S...
...AND I'M A SECRET AGENT!
...THAT'S ME!
BUT MY TIME AT THE AGENCY IS DRAWING TO A CLOSE. TIME TO GET BACK TO MY NORMAL LIFE.
AGENCY
OVER THE LAST THREE DAYS, I COMPLETED MY ASSIGNED MISSION!
AGENCY

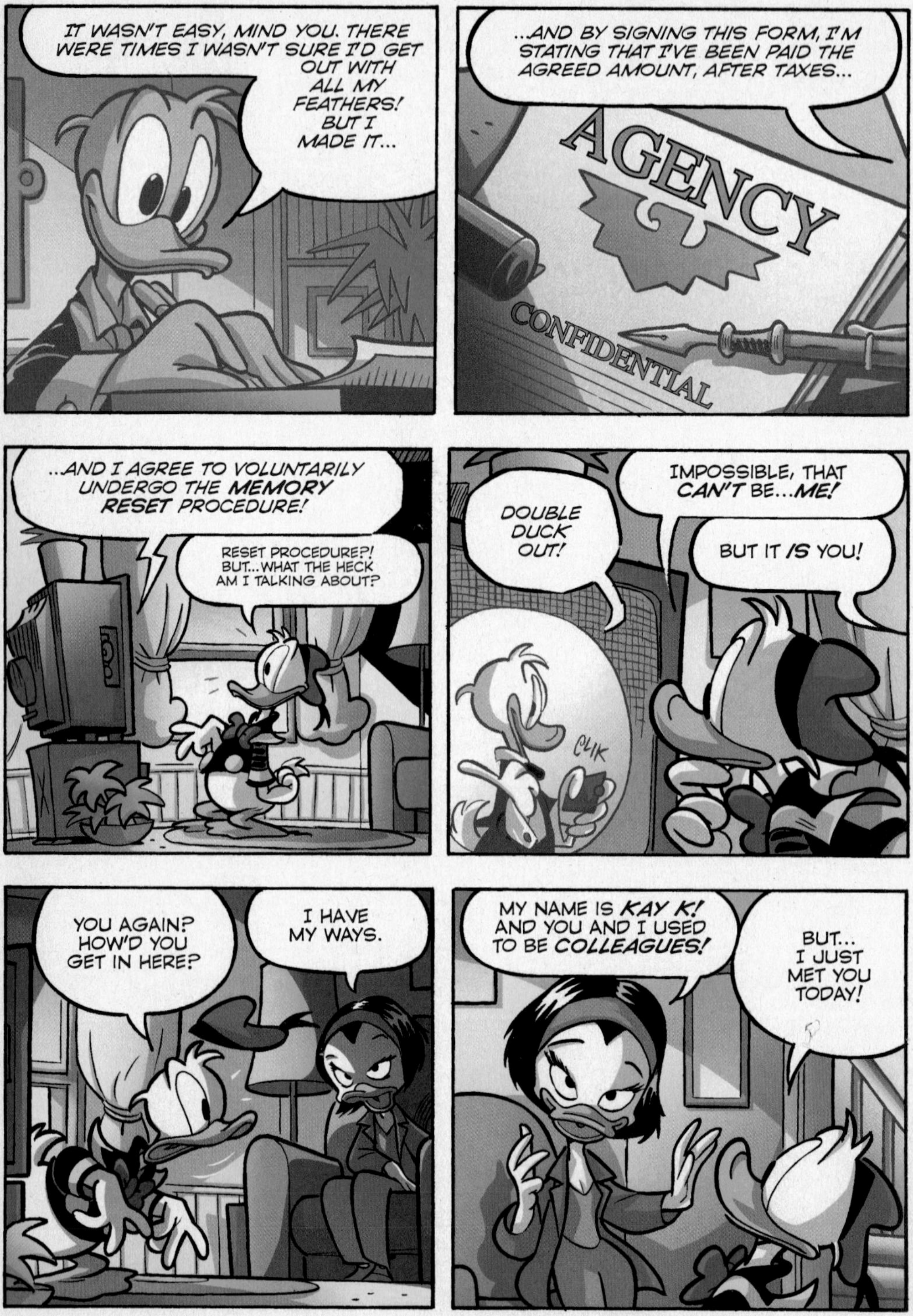
IT WASN'T EASY, MIND YOU. THERE WERE TIMES I WASN'T SURE I'D GET OUT WITH ALL MY FEATHERS! BUT I MADE IT...
...AND BY SIGNING THIS FORM, I'M STATING THAT I'VE BEEN PAID THE AGREED AMOUNT, AFTER TAXES...
AGENCY
CONFIDENTIAL
...AND I AGREE TO VOLUNTARILY UNDERGO THE MEMORY RESET PROCEDURE!
RESET PROCEDURE?! BUT...WHAT THE HECK AM I TALKING ABOUT?
DOUBLE DUCK OUT!
IMPOSSIBLE, THAT CAN'T BE...ME!
BUT IT IS YOU!
CLIK
YOU AGAIN? HOW'D YOU GET IN HERE?
I HAVE MY WAYS.
MY NAME IS KAY K! AND YOU AND I USED TO BE COLLEAGUES!
BUT... I JUST MET YOU TODAY!

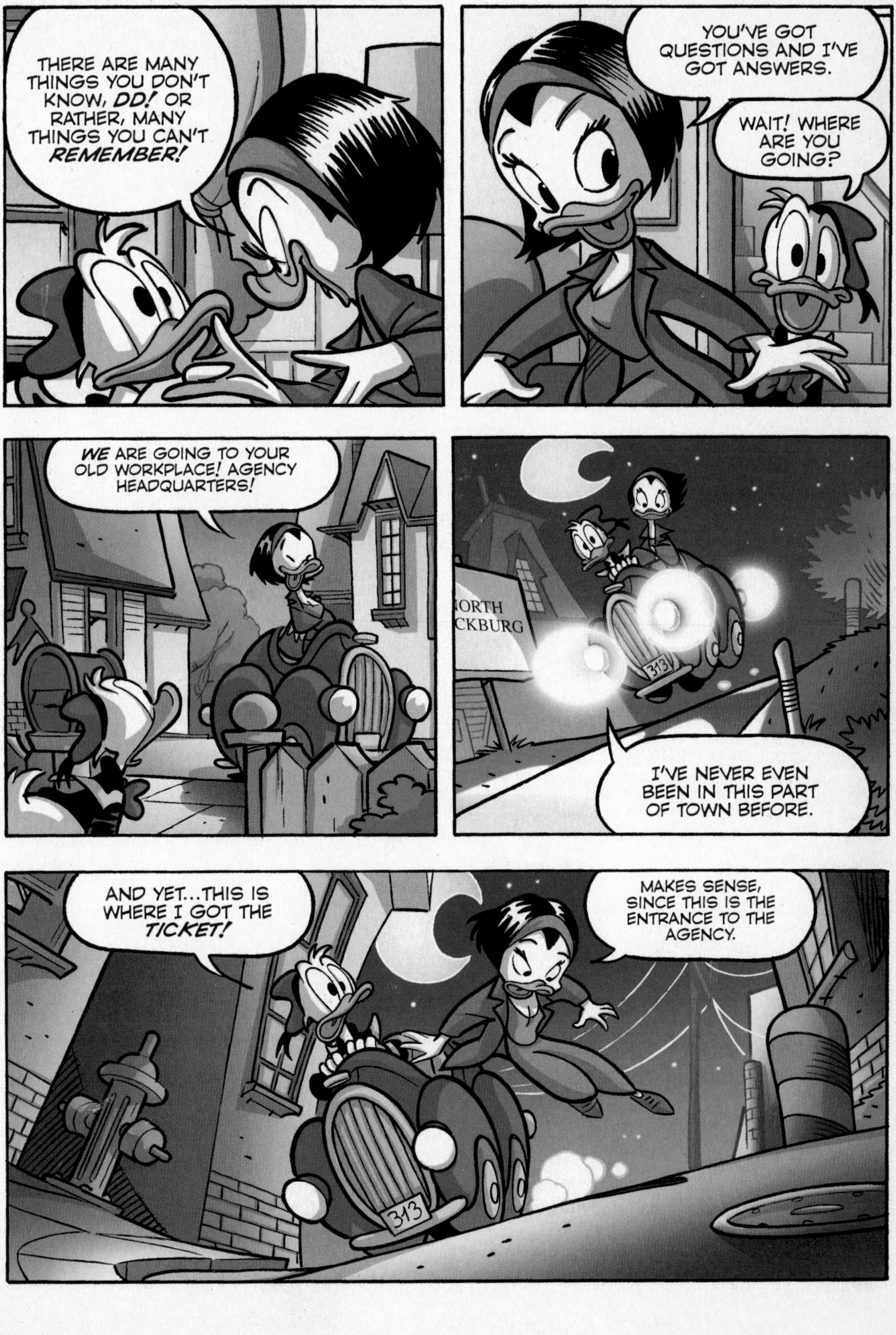
THERE ARE MANY THINGS YOU DON'T KNOW, DD! OR RATHER, MANY THINGS YOU CAN'T REMEMBER!
YOU'VE GOT QUESTIONS AND I'VE GOT ANSWERS.
WAIT! WHERE ARE YOU GOING?
WE ARE GOING TO YOUR OLD WORKPLACE! AGENCY HEADQUARTERS!
ORTH
CKBURG
313
I'VE NEVER EVEN BEEN IN THIS PART OF TOWN BEFORE.
AND YET...THIS IS WHERE I GOT THE TICKET!
MAKES SENSE, SINCE THIS IS THE ENTRANCE TO THE AGENCY.
313

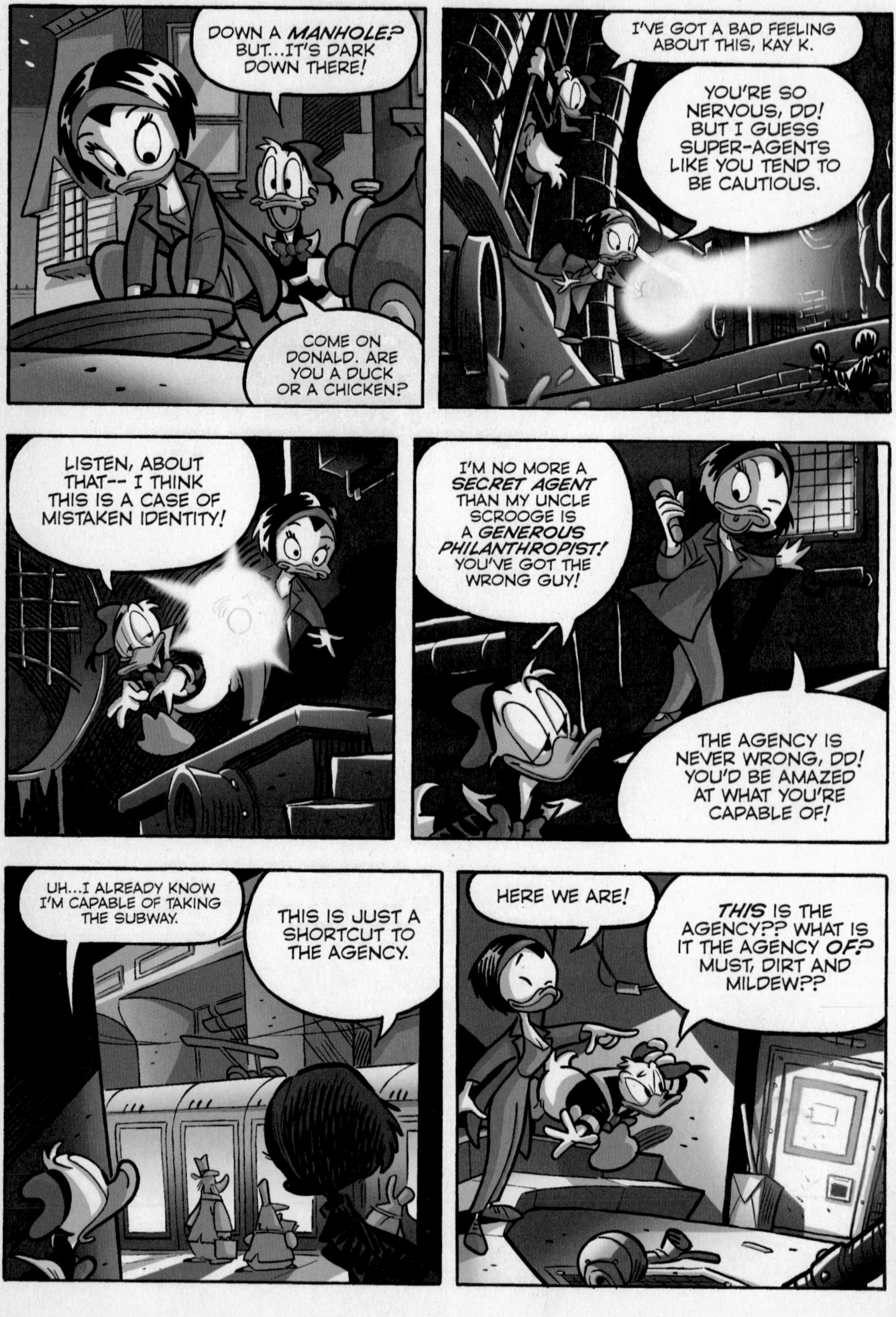
DOWN A *MANHOLE?* BUT...IT'S DARK DOWN THERE!
COME ON DONALD. ARE YOU A DUCK OR A CHICKEN?
I'VE GOT A BAD FEELING ABOUT THIS, KAY K.
YOU'RE SO NERVOUS, DD! BUT I GUESS SUPER-AGENTS LIKE YOU TEND TO BE CAUTIOUS.
LISTEN, ABOUT THAT-- I THINK THIS IS A CASE OF MISTAKEN IDENTITY!
I'M NO MORE A *SECRET AGENT* THAN MY UNCLE SCROOGE IS A *GENEROUS PHILANTHROPIST!* YOU'VE GOT THE WRONG GUY!
THE AGENCY IS NEVER WRONG, DD! YOU'D BE AMAZED AT WHAT YOU'RE CAPABLE OF!
UH...I ALREADY KNOW I'M CAPABLE OF TAKING THE SUBWAY.
THIS IS JUST A SHORTCUT TO THE AGENCY.
HERE WE ARE!
THIS IS THE AGENCY?? WHAT IS IT THE AGENCY *OF?* MUST, DIRT AND MILDEW??

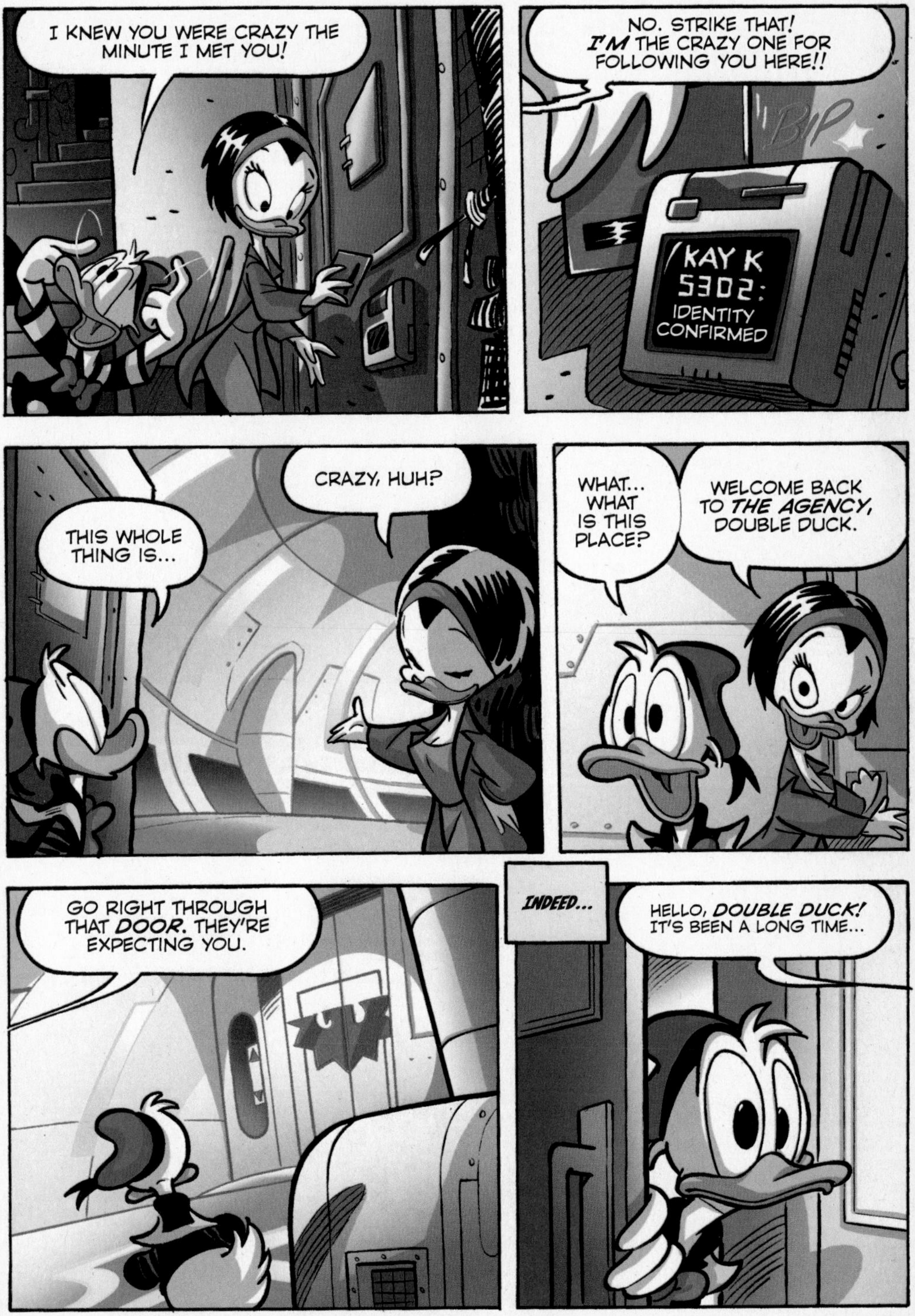
I KNEW YOU WERE CRAZY THE MINUTE I MET YOU!
NO. STRIKE THAT! I'M THE CRAZY ONE FOR FOLLOWING YOU HERE!!
BIP
KAY K 5302: IDENTITY CONFIRMED
THIS WHOLE THING IS...
CRAZY, HUH?
WHAT... WHAT IS THIS PLACE?
WELCOME BACK TO THE AGENCY, DOUBLE DUCK.
GO RIGHT THROUGH THAT DOOR. THEY'RE EXPECTING YOU.
INDEED...
HELLO, DOUBLE DUCK! IT'S BEEN A LONG TIME...

...BUT I REMEMBER YOU WELL!

I WISH I COULD SAY THE SAME THING!

OF COURSE! I'M *LIZ ZAGO*, THE *NEW DIRECTOR'S* ASSISTANT. HE'LL BE WITH YOU SHORTLY.

THE NEW... DIRECTOR?

MR. JAY J!

⸮SIGH⸮ I GUESS I'M SUPPOSED TO REMEMBER HIM, TOO?

MR. JAY

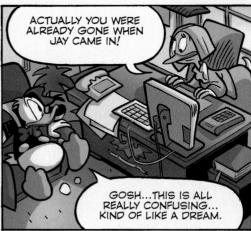

ACTUALLY YOU WERE ALREADY GONE WHEN JAY CAME IN!

GOSH...THIS IS ALL REALLY CONFUSING... KIND OF LIKE A DREAM.

WAIT A MINUTE! MAYBE THIS *IS* A DREAM!! MAYBE I'M STILL ASLEEP AT THE THEATER!

AND ALL THIS SPY STUFF IS BROUGHT ON BY THE JAMES POND MOVIE THAT DAISY MADE ME GO TO!

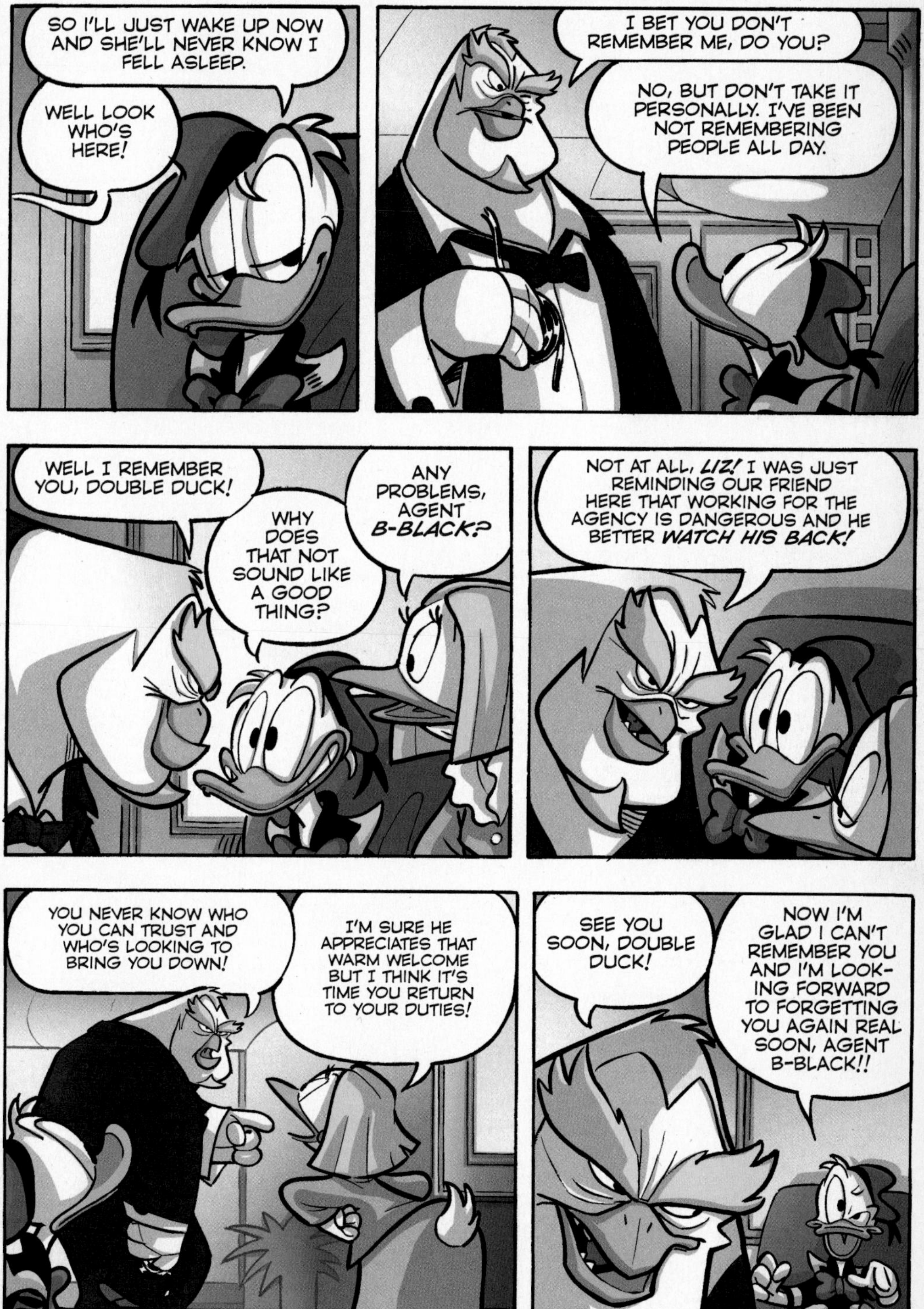
SO I'LL JUST WAKE UP NOW AND SHE'LL NEVER KNOW I FELL ASLEEP.
WELL LOOK WHO'S HERE!
I BET YOU DON'T REMEMBER ME, DO YOU?
NO, BUT DON'T TAKE IT PERSONALLY. I'VE BEEN NOT REMEMBERING PEOPLE ALL DAY.
WELL I REMEMBER YOU, DOUBLE DUCK!
WHY DOES THAT NOT SOUND LIKE A GOOD THING?
ANY PROBLEMS, AGENT B-BLACK?
NOT AT ALL, LIZ! I WAS JUST REMINDING OUR FRIEND HERE THAT WORKING FOR THE AGENCY IS DANGEROUS AND HE BETTER WATCH HIS BACK!
YOU NEVER KNOW WHO YOU CAN TRUST AND WHO'S LOOKING TO BRING YOU DOWN!
I'M SURE HE APPRECIATES THAT WARM WELCOME BUT I THINK IT'S TIME YOU RETURN TO YOUR DUTIES!
SEE YOU SOON, DOUBLE DUCK!
NOW I'M GLAD I CAN'T REMEMBER YOU AND I'M LOOKING FORWARD TO FORGETTING YOU AGAIN REAL SOON, AGENT B-BLACK!!

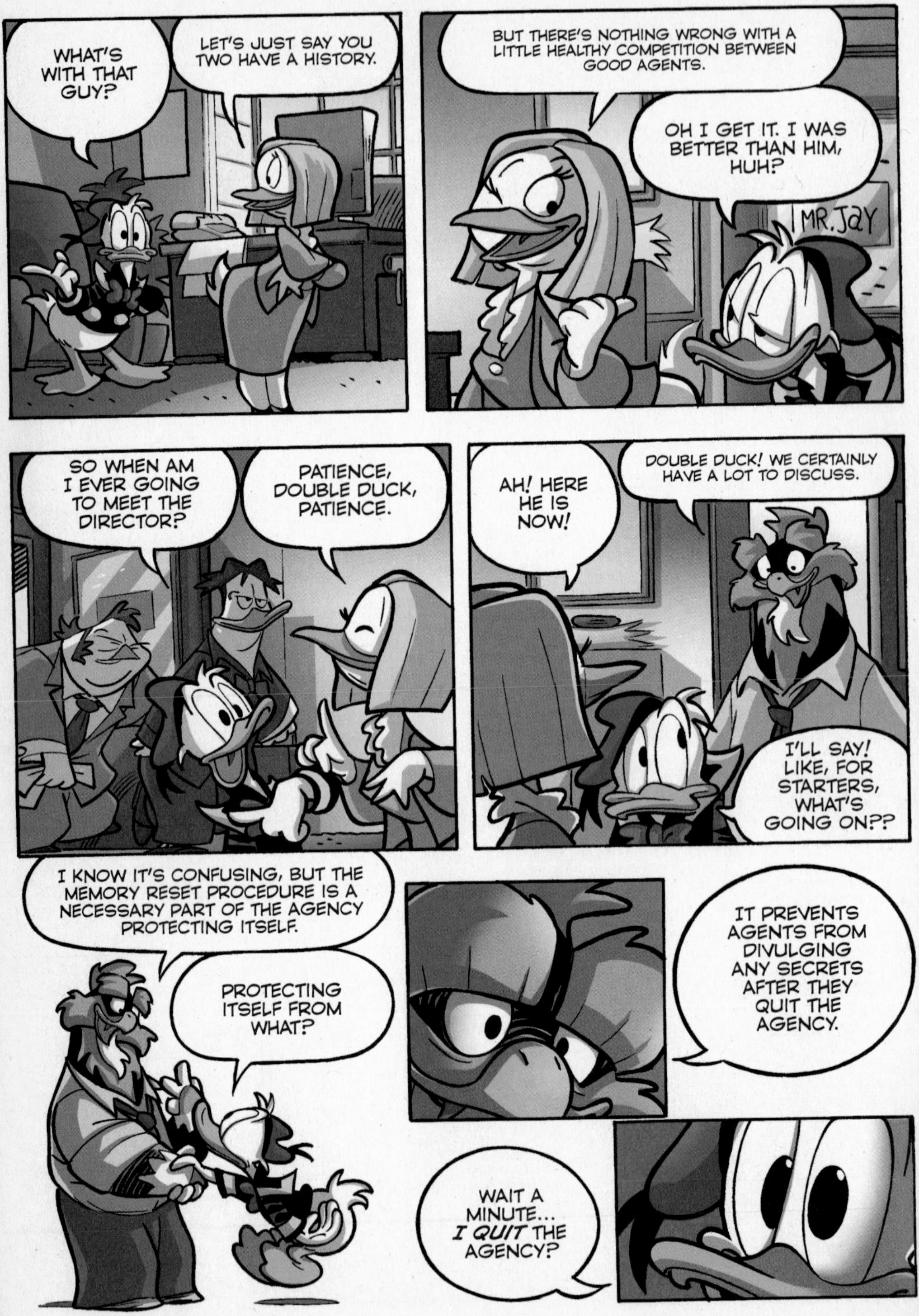
WHAT'S WITH THAT GUY?
LET'S JUST SAY YOU TWO HAVE A HISTORY.
BUT THERE'S NOTHING WRONG WITH A LITTLE HEALTHY COMPETITION BETWEEN GOOD AGENTS.
OH I GET IT. I WAS BETTER THAN HIM, HUH?
MR. JAY
SO WHEN AM I EVER GOING TO MEET THE DIRECTOR?
PATIENCE, DOUBLE DUCK, PATIENCE.
AH! HERE HE IS NOW!
DOUBLE DUCK! WE CERTAINLY HAVE A LOT TO DISCUSS.
I'LL SAY! LIKE, FOR STARTERS, WHAT'S GOING ON??
I KNOW IT'S CONFUSING, BUT THE MEMORY RESET PROCEDURE IS A NECESSARY PART OF THE AGENCY PROTECTING ITSELF.
PROTECTING ITSELF FROM WHAT?
IT PREVENTS AGENTS FROM DIVULGING ANY SECRETS AFTER THEY QUIT THE AGENCY.
WAIT A MINUTE... *I QUIT* THE AGENCY?

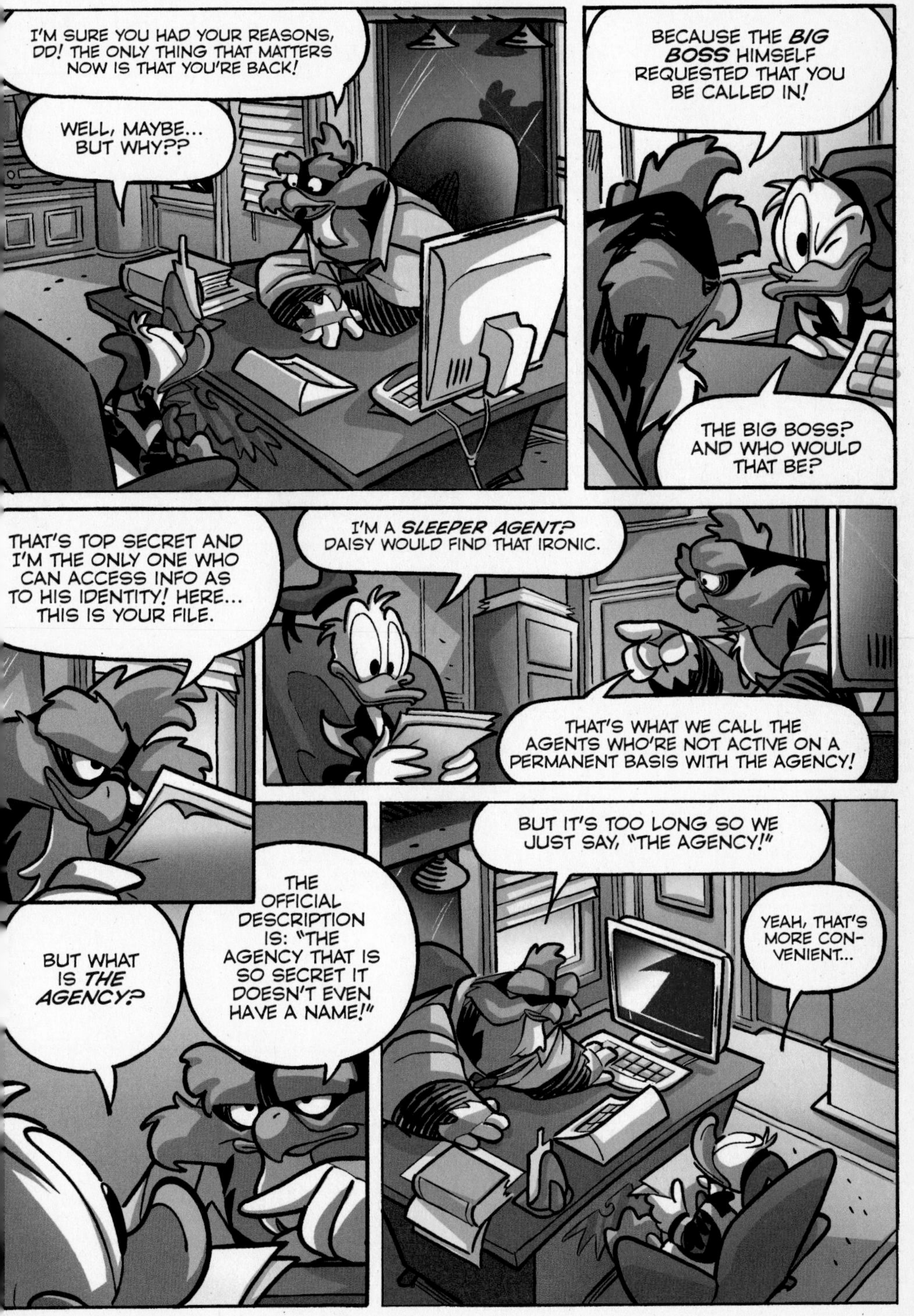
I'M SURE YOU HAD YOUR REASONS, DD! THE ONLY THING THAT MATTERS NOW IS THAT YOU'RE BACK!
WELL, MAYBE... BUT WHY??
BECAUSE THE *BIG BOSS* HIMSELF REQUESTED THAT YOU BE CALLED IN!
THE BIG BOSS? AND WHO WOULD THAT BE?
THAT'S TOP SECRET AND I'M THE ONLY ONE WHO CAN ACCESS INFO AS TO HIS IDENTITY! HERE... THIS IS YOUR FILE.
I'M A *SLEEPER AGENT?* DAISY WOULD FIND THAT IRONIC.
THAT'S WHAT WE CALL THE AGENTS WHO'RE NOT ACTIVE ON A PERMANENT BASIS WITH THE AGENCY!
BUT WHAT IS *THE AGENCY?*
THE OFFICIAL DESCRIPTION IS: "THE AGENCY THAT IS SO SECRET IT DOESN'T EVEN HAVE A NAME!"
BUT IT'S TOO LONG SO WE JUST SAY, "THE AGENCY!"
YEAH, THAT'S MORE CON- VENIENT...

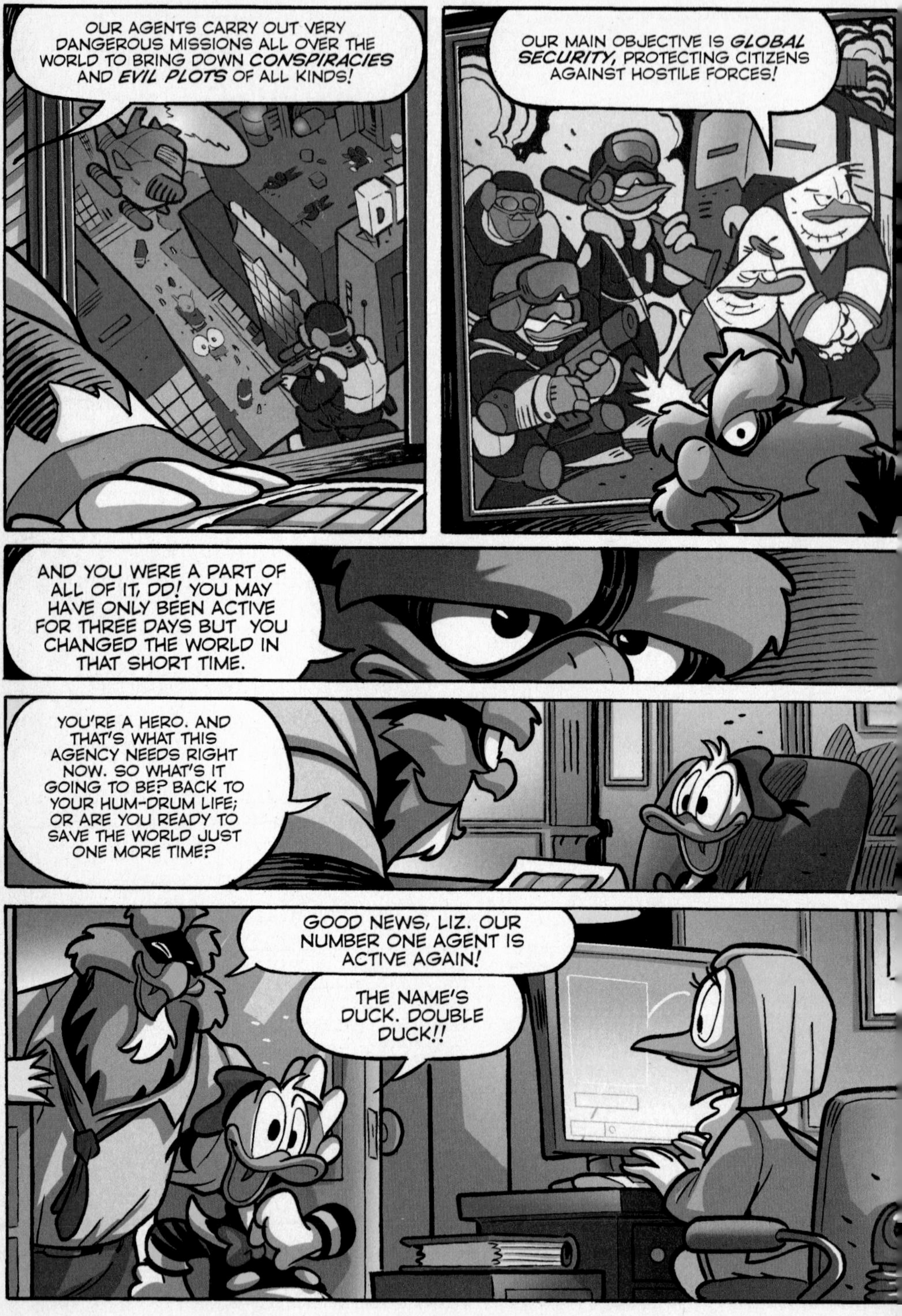

OUR AGENTS CARRY OUT VERY DANGEROUS MISSIONS ALL OVER THE WORLD TO BRING DOWN *CONSPIRACIES* AND *EVIL PLOTS* OF ALL KINDS!
OUR MAIN OBJECTIVE IS *GLOBAL SECURITY,* PROTECTING CITIZENS AGAINST HOSTILE FORCES!
AND YOU WERE A PART OF ALL OF IT, DD! YOU MAY HAVE ONLY BEEN ACTIVE FOR THREE DAYS BUT YOU CHANGED THE WORLD IN THAT SHORT TIME.
YOU'RE A HERO. AND THAT'S WHAT THIS AGENCY NEEDS RIGHT NOW. SO WHAT'S IT GOING TO BE? BACK TO YOUR HUM-DRUM LIFE; OR ARE YOU READY TO SAVE THE WORLD JUST ONE MORE TIME?
GOOD NEWS, LIZ. OUR NUMBER ONE AGENT IS ACTIVE AGAIN!
THE NAME'S DUCK. DOUBLE DUCK!!

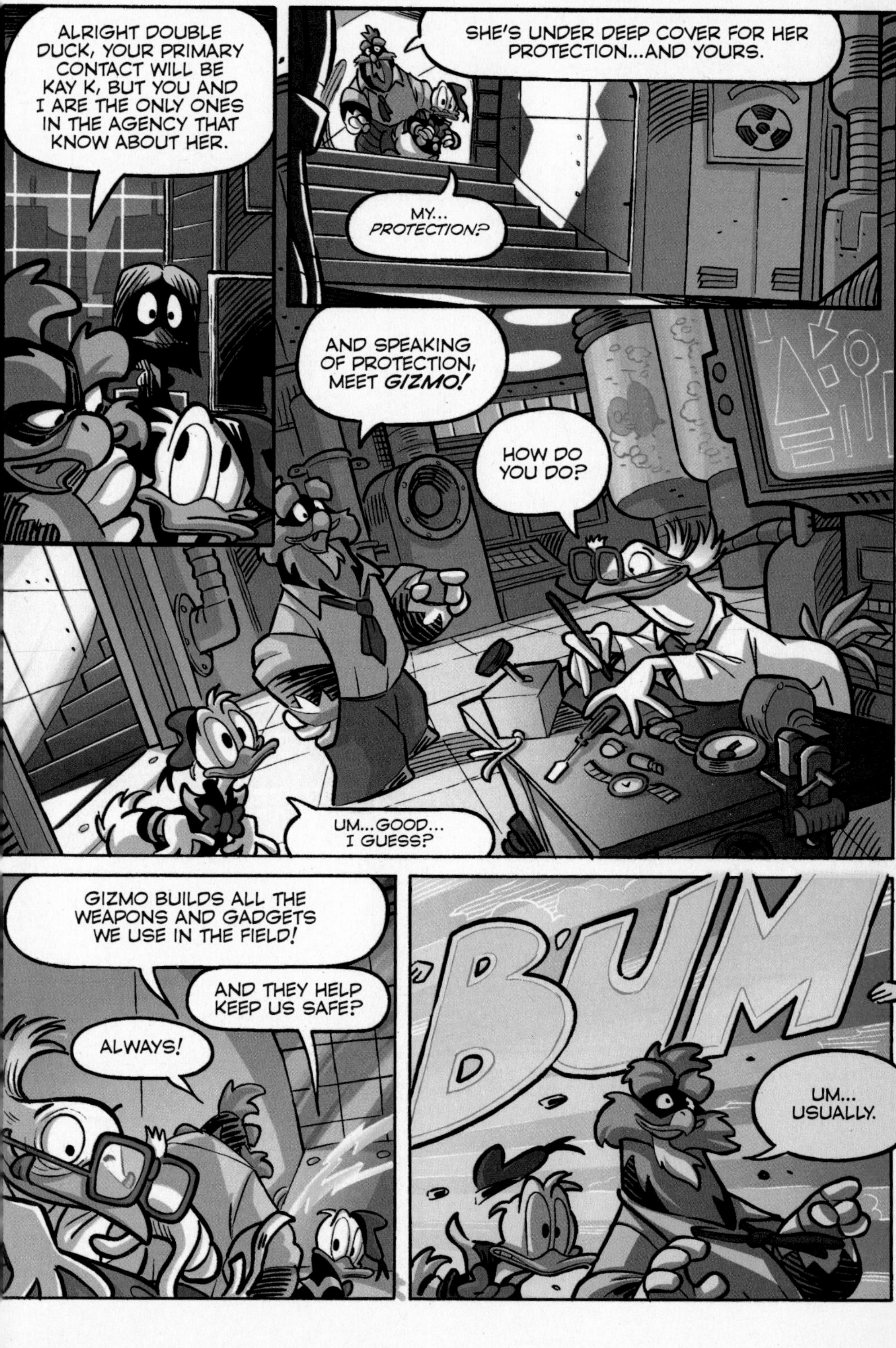
ALRIGHT DOUBLE DUCK, YOUR PRIMARY CONTACT WILL BE KAY K, BUT YOU AND I ARE THE ONLY ONES IN THE AGENCY THAT KNOW ABOUT HER.
SHE'S UNDER DEEP COVER FOR HER PROTECTION...AND YOURS.
MY... PROTECTION?
AND SPEAKING OF PROTECTION, MEET GIZMO!
HOW DO YOU DO?
UM...GOOD... I GUESS?
GIZMO BUILDS ALL THE WEAPONS AND GADGETS WE USE IN THE FIELD!
AND THEY HELP KEEP US SAFE?
ALWAYS!
BUM
UM... USUALLY.

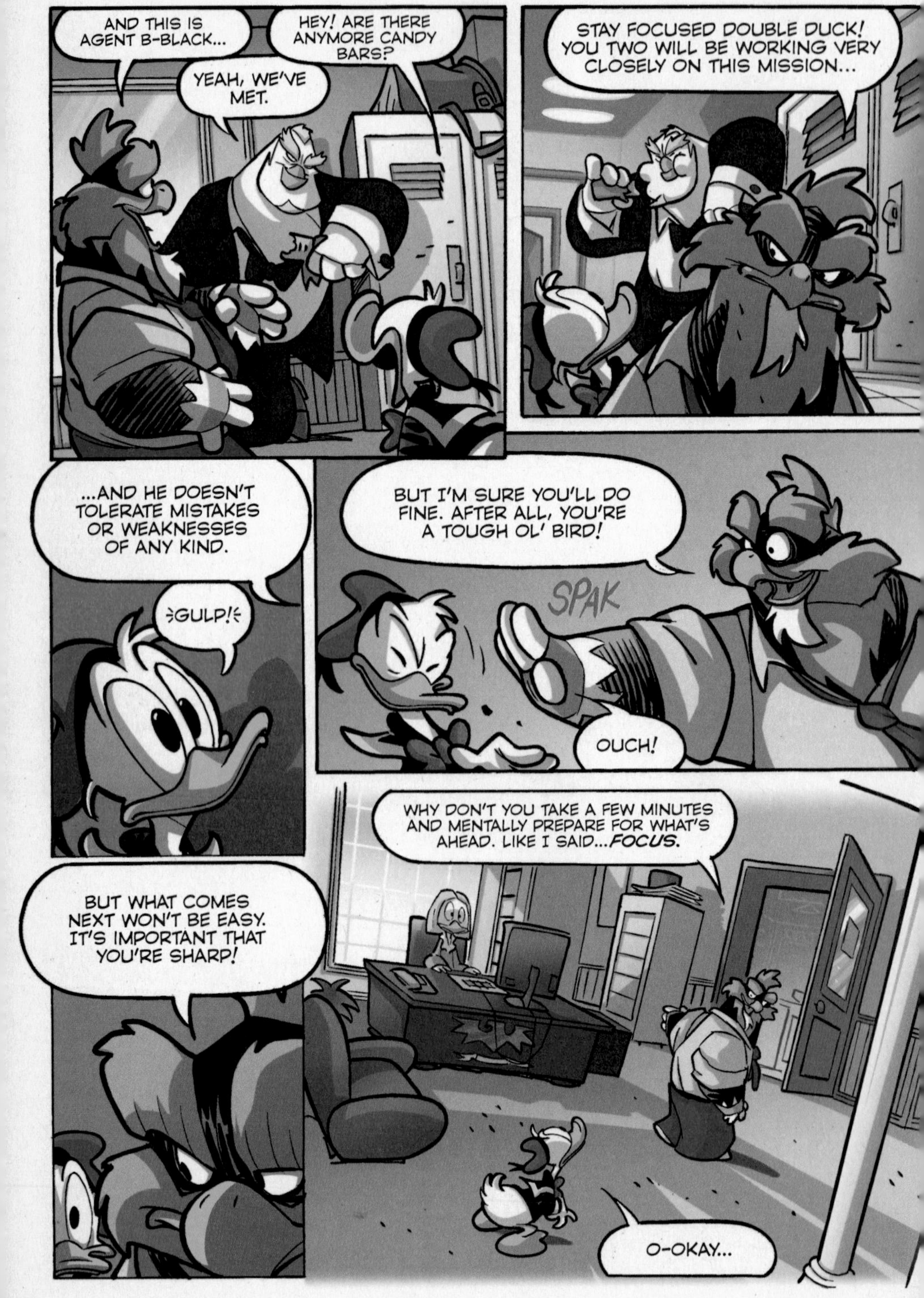
AND THIS IS AGENT B-BLACK...
HEY! ARE THERE ANYMORE CANDY BARS?
YEAH, WE'VE MET.
STAY FOCUSED DOUBLE DUCK! YOU TWO WILL BE WORKING VERY CLOSELY ON THIS MISSION...
...AND HE DOESN'T TOLERATE MISTAKES OR WEAKNESSES OF ANY KIND.
GULP!
BUT I'M SURE YOU'LL DO FINE. AFTER ALL, YOU'RE A TOUGH OL' BIRD!
SPAK
OUCH!
BUT WHAT COMES NEXT WON'T BE EASY. IT'S IMPORTANT THAT YOU'RE SHARP!
WHY DON'T YOU TAKE A FEW MINUTES AND MENTALLY PREPARE FOR WHAT'S AHEAD. LIKE I SAID...FOCUS.
O-OKAY...

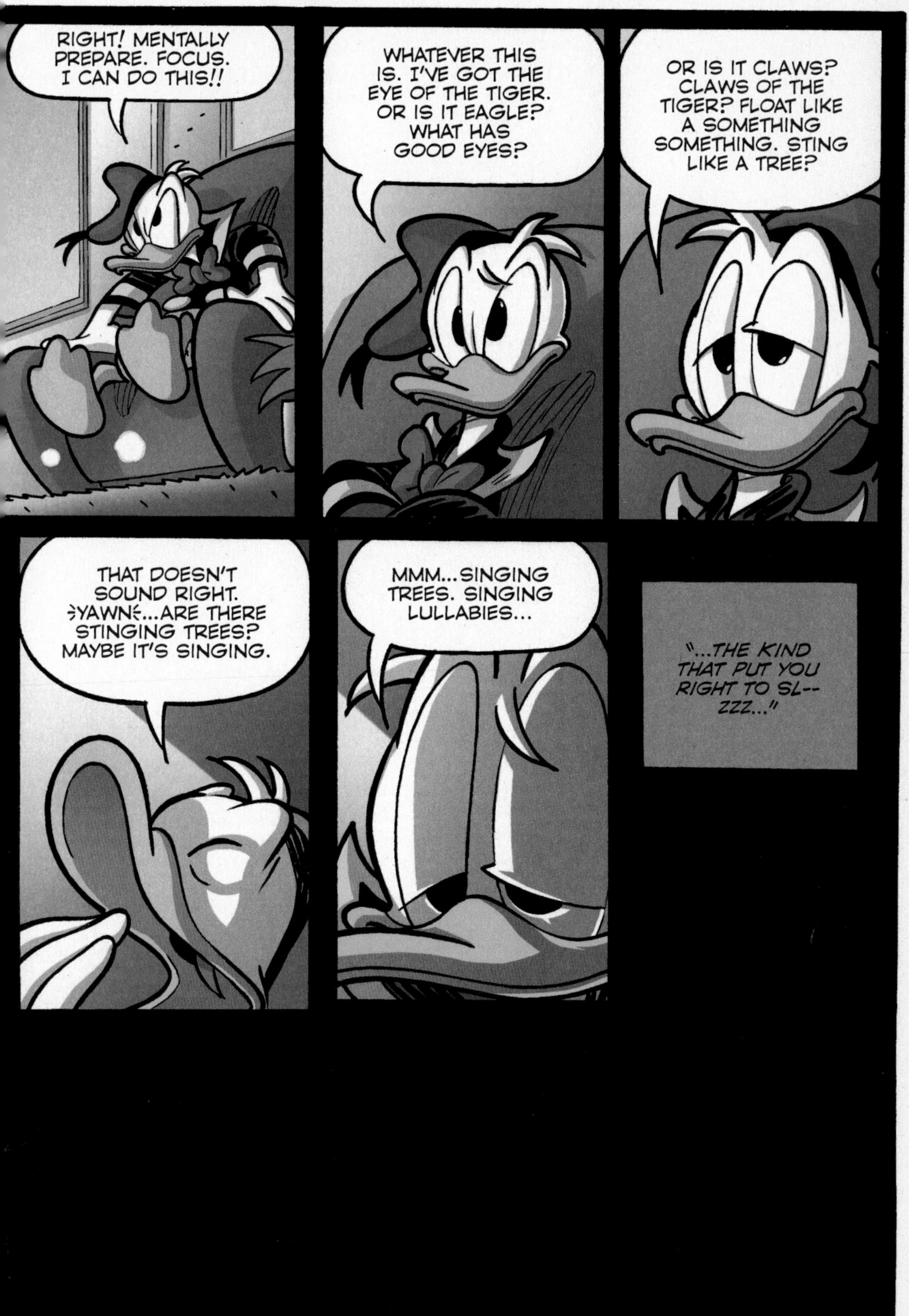
RIGHT! MENTALLY PREPARE. FOCUS. I CAN DO THIS!!
WHATEVER THIS IS. I'VE GOT THE EYE OF THE TIGER. OR IS IT EAGLE? WHAT HAS GOOD EYES?
OR IS IT CLAWS? CLAWS OF THE TIGER? FLOAT LIKE A SOMETHING SOMETHING. STING LIKE A TREE?
THAT DOESN'T SOUND RIGHT. ≷YAWN≶...ARE THERE STINGING TREES? MAYBE IT'S SINGING.
MMM...SINGING TREES. SINGING LULLABIES...
"...THE KIND THAT PUT YOU RIGHT TO SL--ZZZ..."

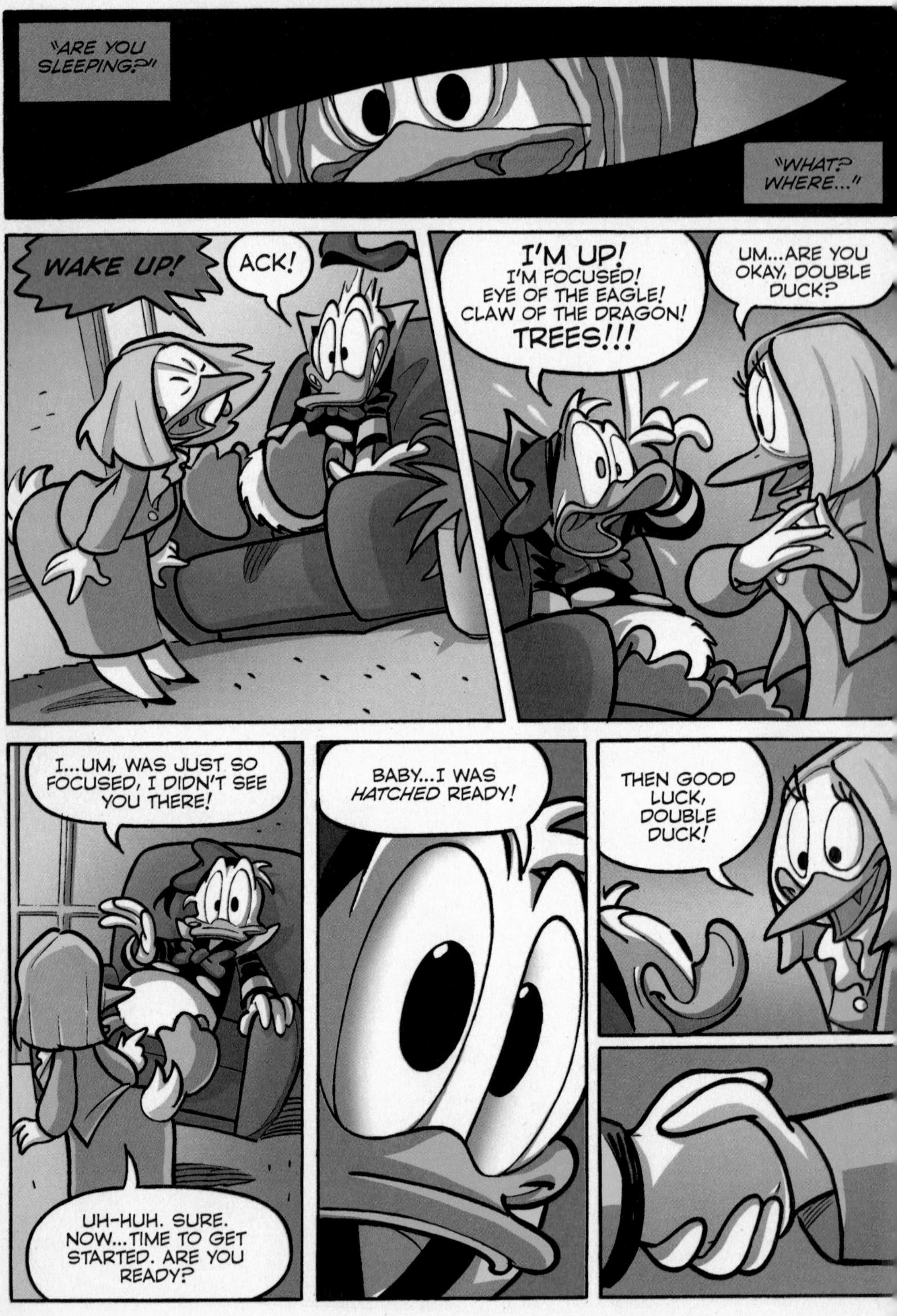
"ARE YOU SLEEPING?"
"WHAT? WHERE..."
WAKE UP!
ACK!
I'M UP! I'M FOCUSED! EYE OF THE EAGLE! CLAW OF THE DRAGON! TREES!!!
UM...ARE YOU OKAY, DOUBLE DUCK?
I...UM, WAS JUST SO FOCUSED, I DIDN'T SEE YOU THERE!
UH-HUH. SURE. NOW...TIME TO GET STARTED. ARE YOU READY?
BABY...I WAS HATCHED READY!
THEN GOOD LUCK, DOUBLE DUCK!

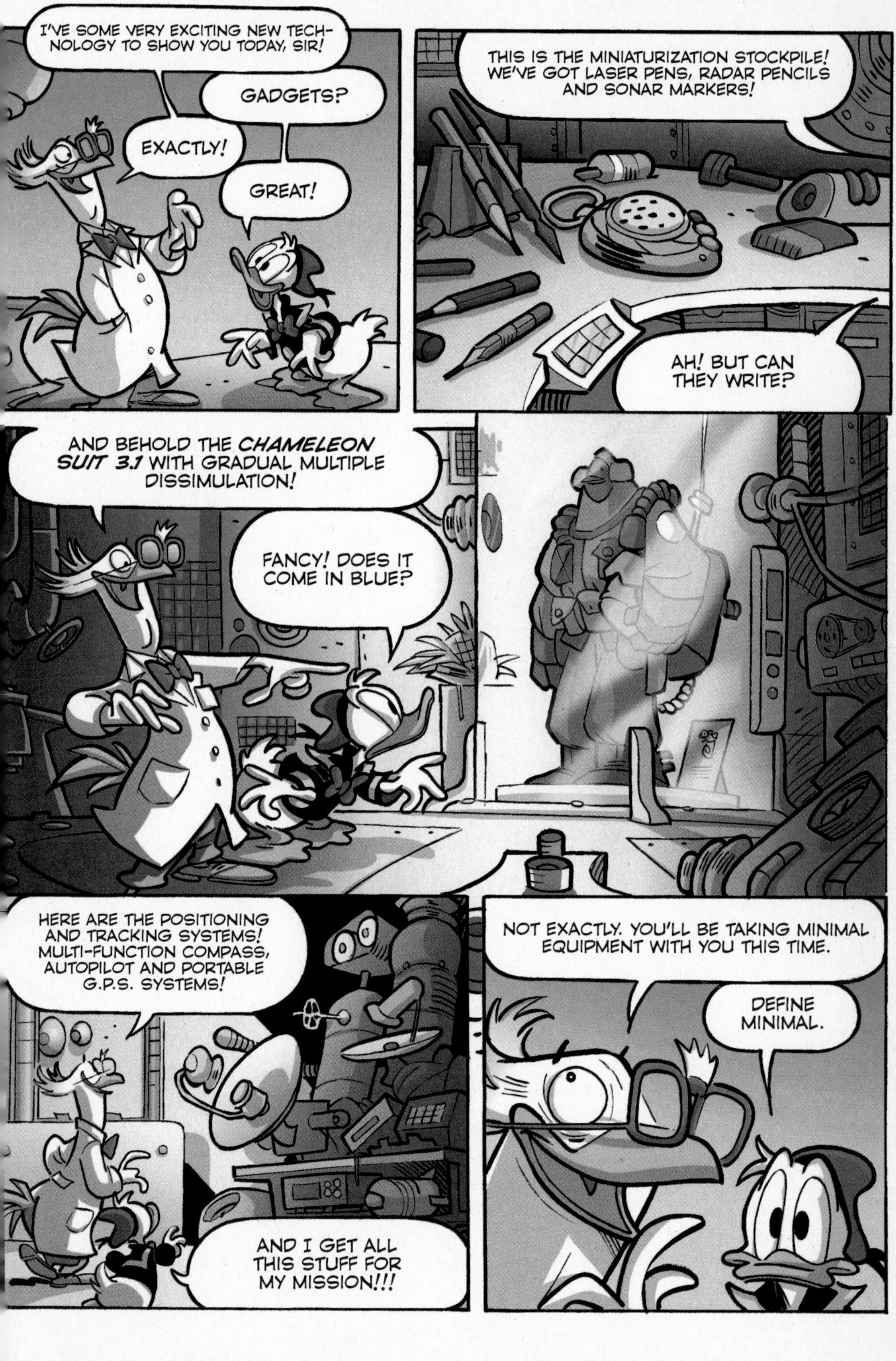
I'VE SOME VERY EXCITING NEW TECH-NOLOGY TO SHOW YOU TODAY, SIR!
GADGETS?
EXACTLY!
GREAT!
THIS IS THE MINIATURIZATION STOCKPILE! WE'VE GOT LASER PENS, RADAR PENCILS AND SONAR MARKERS!
AH! BUT CAN THEY WRITE?
AND BEHOLD THE CHAMELEON SUIT 3.1 WITH GRADUAL MULTIPLE DISSIMULATION!
FANCY! DOES IT COME IN BLUE?
HERE ARE THE POSITIONING AND TRACKING SYSTEMS! MULTI-FUNCTION COMPASS, AUTOPILOT AND PORTABLE G.P.S. SYSTEMS!
AND I GET ALL THIS STUFF FOR MY MISSION!!!
NOT EXACTLY. YOU'LL BE TAKING MINIMAL EQUIPMENT WITH YOU THIS TIME.
DEFINE MINIMAL.

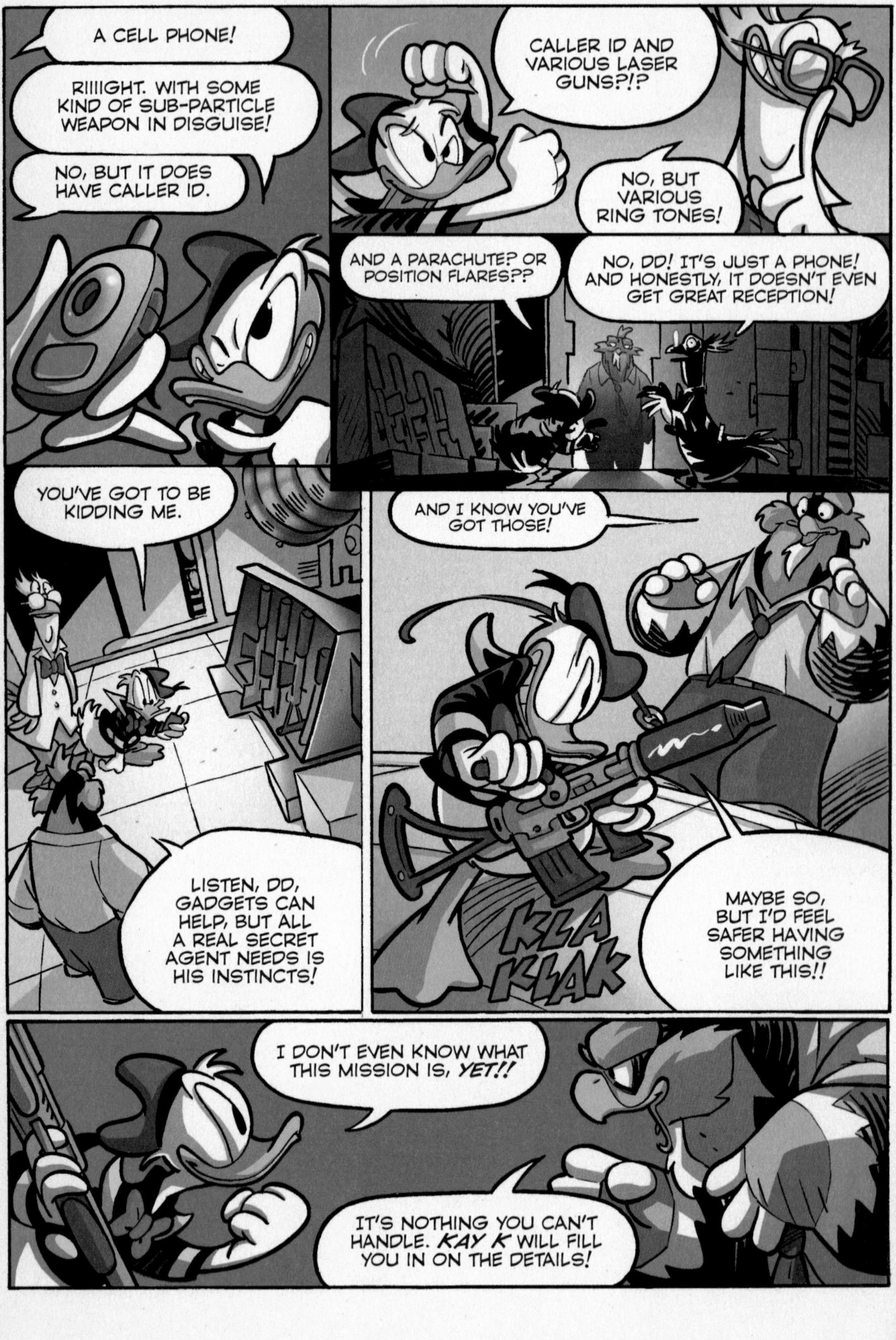
A CELL PHONE!
RIIIIGHT. WITH SOME KIND OF SUB-PARTICLE WEAPON IN DISGUISE!
NO, BUT IT DOES HAVE CALLER ID.
CALLER ID AND VARIOUS LASER GUNS?!?
NO, BUT VARIOUS RING TONES!
AND A PARACHUTE? OR POSITION FLARES??
NO, DD! IT'S JUST A PHONE! AND HONESTLY, IT DOESN'T EVEN GET GREAT RECEPTION!
YOU'VE GOT TO BE KIDDING ME.
LISTEN, DD, GADGETS CAN HELP, BUT ALL A REAL SECRET AGENT NEEDS IS HIS INSTINCTS!
AND I KNOW YOU'VE GOT THOSE!
KLA KLAK
MAYBE SO, BUT I'D FEEL SAFER HAVING SOMETHING LIKE THIS!!
I DON'T EVEN KNOW WHAT THIS MISSION IS, YET!!
IT'S NOTHING YOU CAN'T HANDLE. KAY K WILL FILL YOU IN ON THE DETAILS!

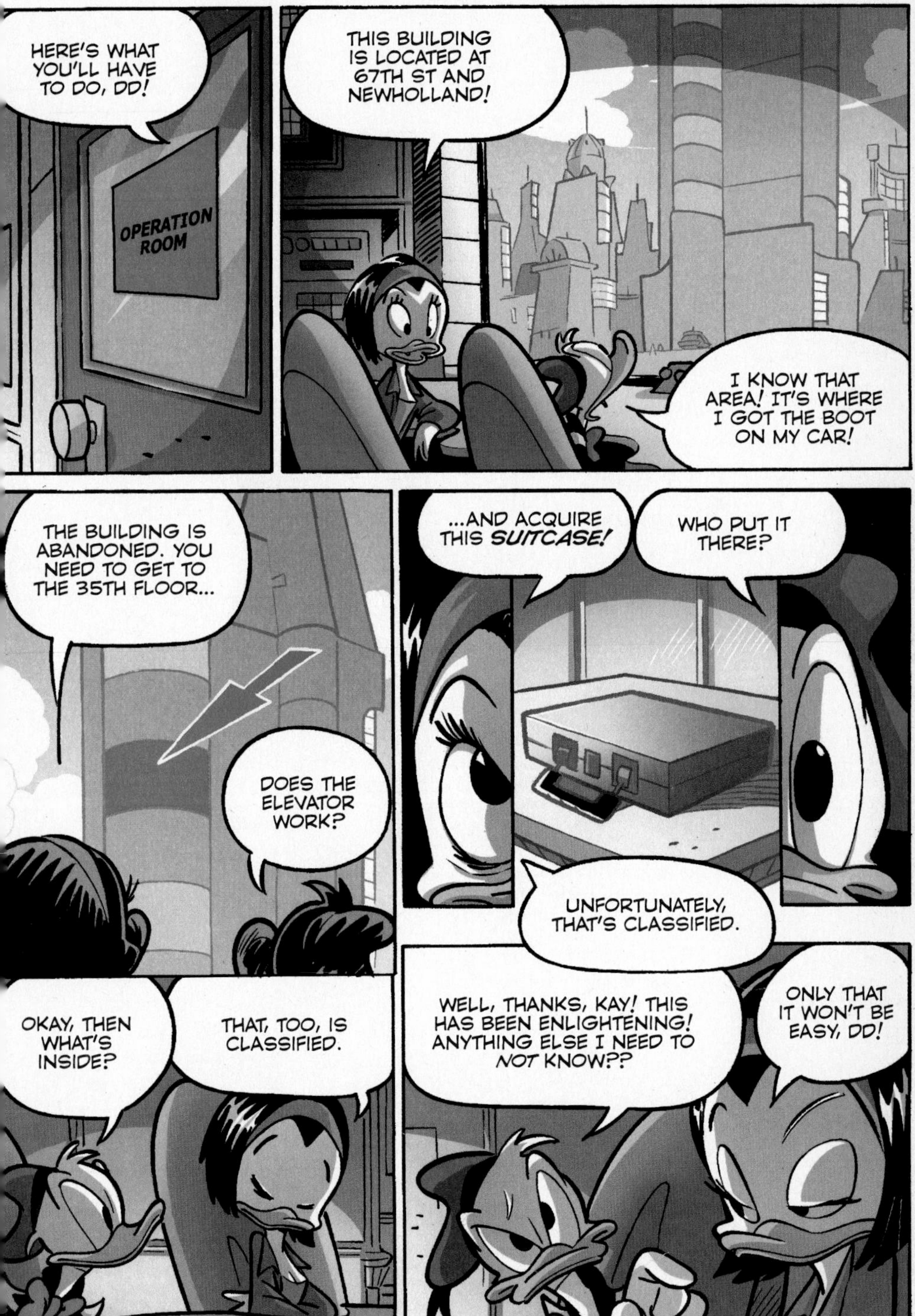
HERE'S WHAT YOU'LL HAVE TO DO, DD!
OPERATION ROOM
THIS BUILDING IS LOCATED AT 67TH ST AND NEWHOLLAND!
I KNOW THAT AREA! IT'S WHERE I GOT THE BOOT ON MY CAR!
THE BUILDING IS ABANDONED. YOU NEED TO GET TO THE 35TH FLOOR...
DOES THE ELEVATOR WORK?
...AND ACQUIRE THIS SUITCASE!
WHO PUT IT THERE?
UNFORTUNATELY, THAT'S CLASSIFIED.
OKAY, THEN WHAT'S INSIDE?
THAT, TOO, IS CLASSIFIED.
WELL, THANKS, KAY! THIS HAS BEEN ENLIGHTENING! ANYTHING ELSE I NEED TO NOT KNOW??
ONLY THAT IT WON'T BE EASY, DD!

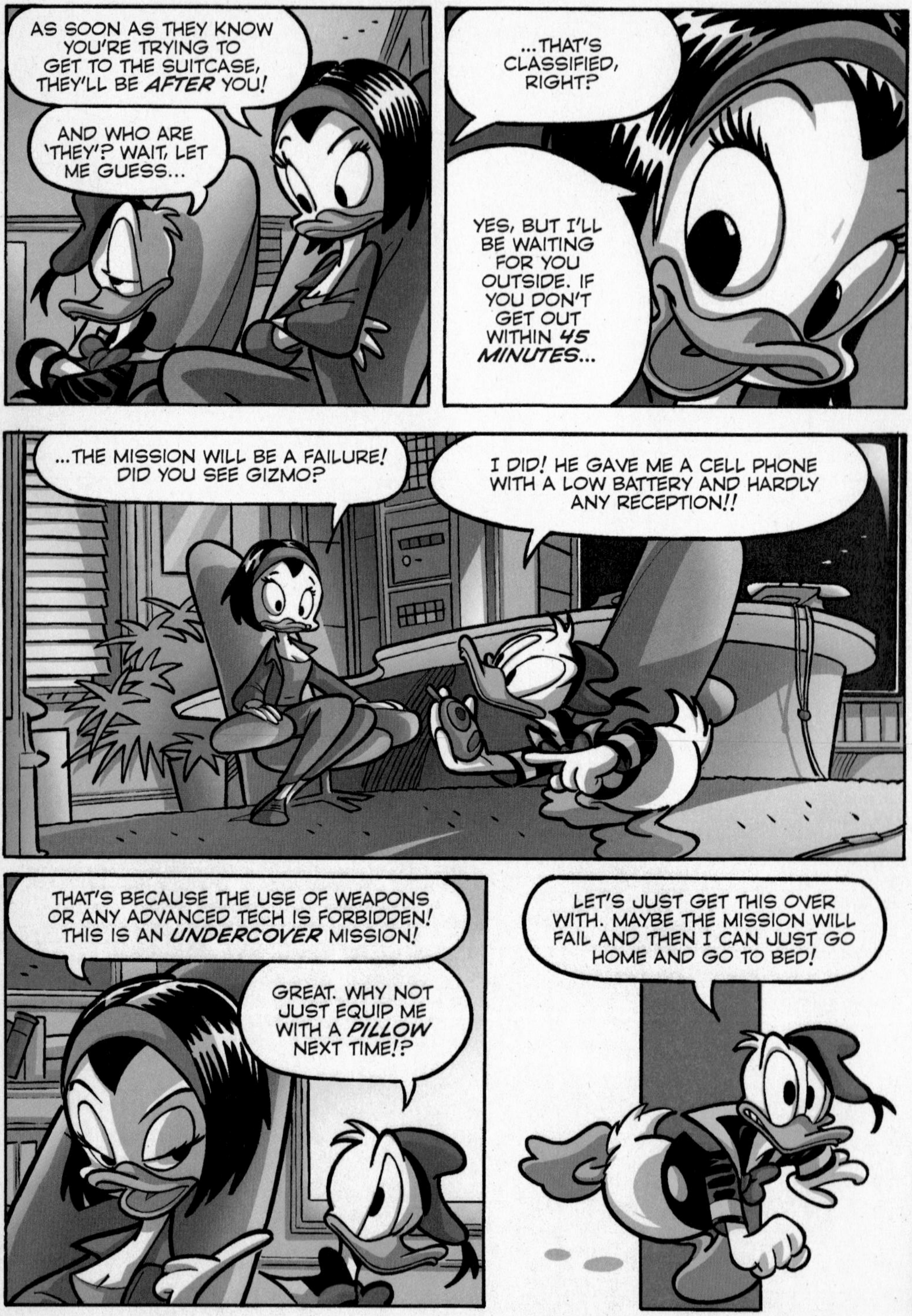
AS SOON AS THEY KNOW YOU'RE TRYING TO GET TO THE SUITCASE, THEY'LL BE *AFTER* YOU!
AND WHO ARE 'THEY'? WAIT, LET ME GUESS...
...THAT'S CLASSIFIED, RIGHT?
YES, BUT I'LL BE WAITING FOR YOU OUTSIDE. IF YOU DON'T GET OUT WITHIN *45 MINUTES*...
...THE MISSION WILL BE A FAILURE! DID YOU SEE GIZMO?
I DID! HE GAVE ME A CELL PHONE WITH A LOW BATTERY AND HARDLY ANY RECEPTION!!
THAT'S BECAUSE THE USE OF WEAPONS OR ANY ADVANCED TECH IS FORBIDDEN! THIS IS AN *UNDERCOVER* MISSION!
GREAT. WHY NOT JUST EQUIP ME WITH A *PILLOW* NEXT TIME!?
LET'S JUST GET THIS OVER WITH. MAYBE THE MISSION WILL FAIL AND THEN I CAN JUST GO HOME AND GO TO BED!

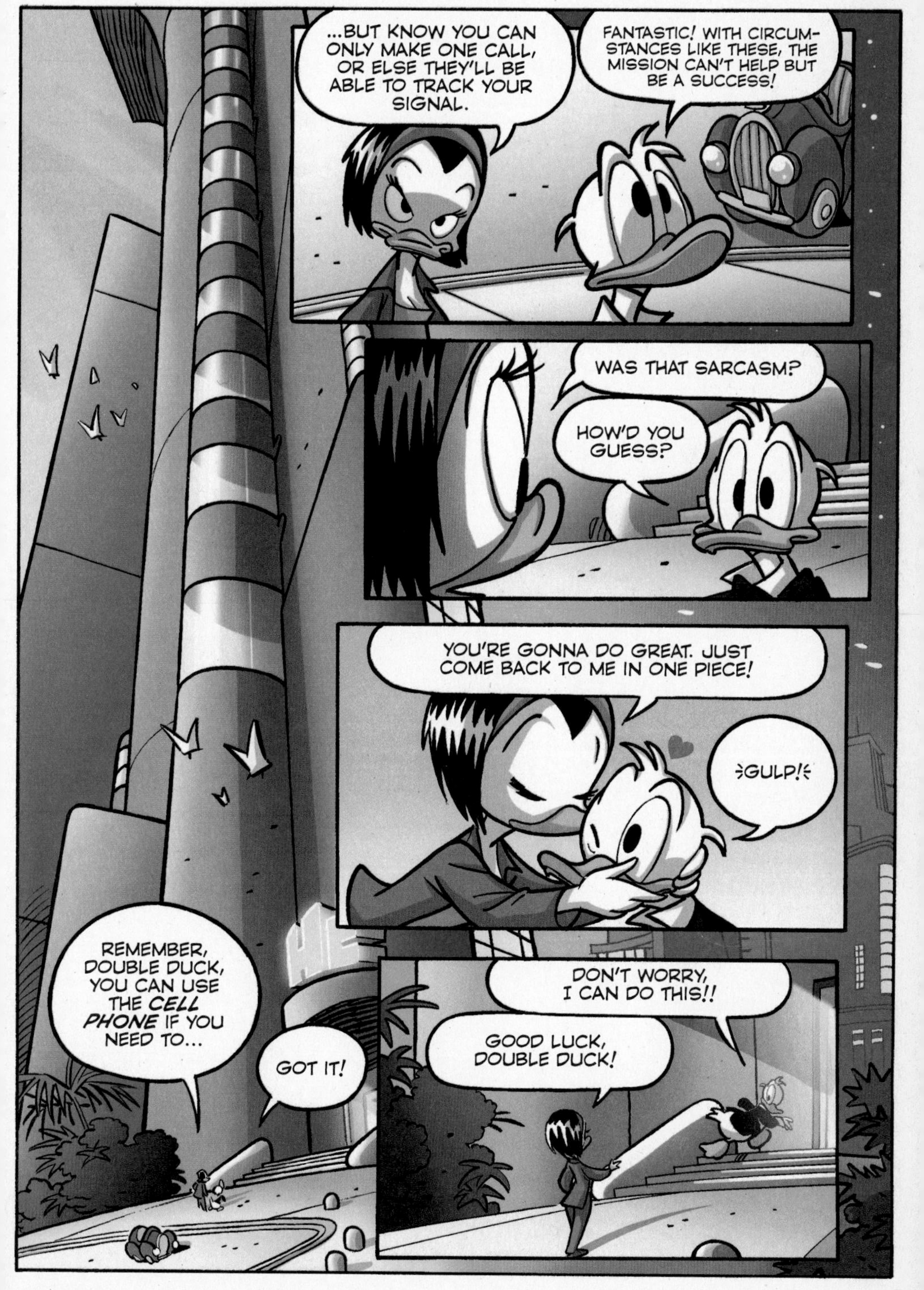
...BUT KNOW YOU CAN ONLY MAKE ONE CALL, OR ELSE THEY'LL BE ABLE TO TRACK YOUR SIGNAL.
FANTASTIC! WITH CIRCUM-STANCES LIKE THESE, THE MISSION CAN'T HELP BUT BE A SUCCESS!
WAS THAT SARCASM?
HOW'D YOU GUESS?
YOU'RE GONNA DO GREAT. JUST COME BACK TO ME IN ONE PIECE!
GULP!
REMEMBER, DOUBLE DUCK, YOU CAN USE THE *CELL PHONE* IF YOU NEED TO...
GOT IT!
DON'T WORRY, I CAN DO THIS!!
GOOD LUCK, DOUBLE DUCK!

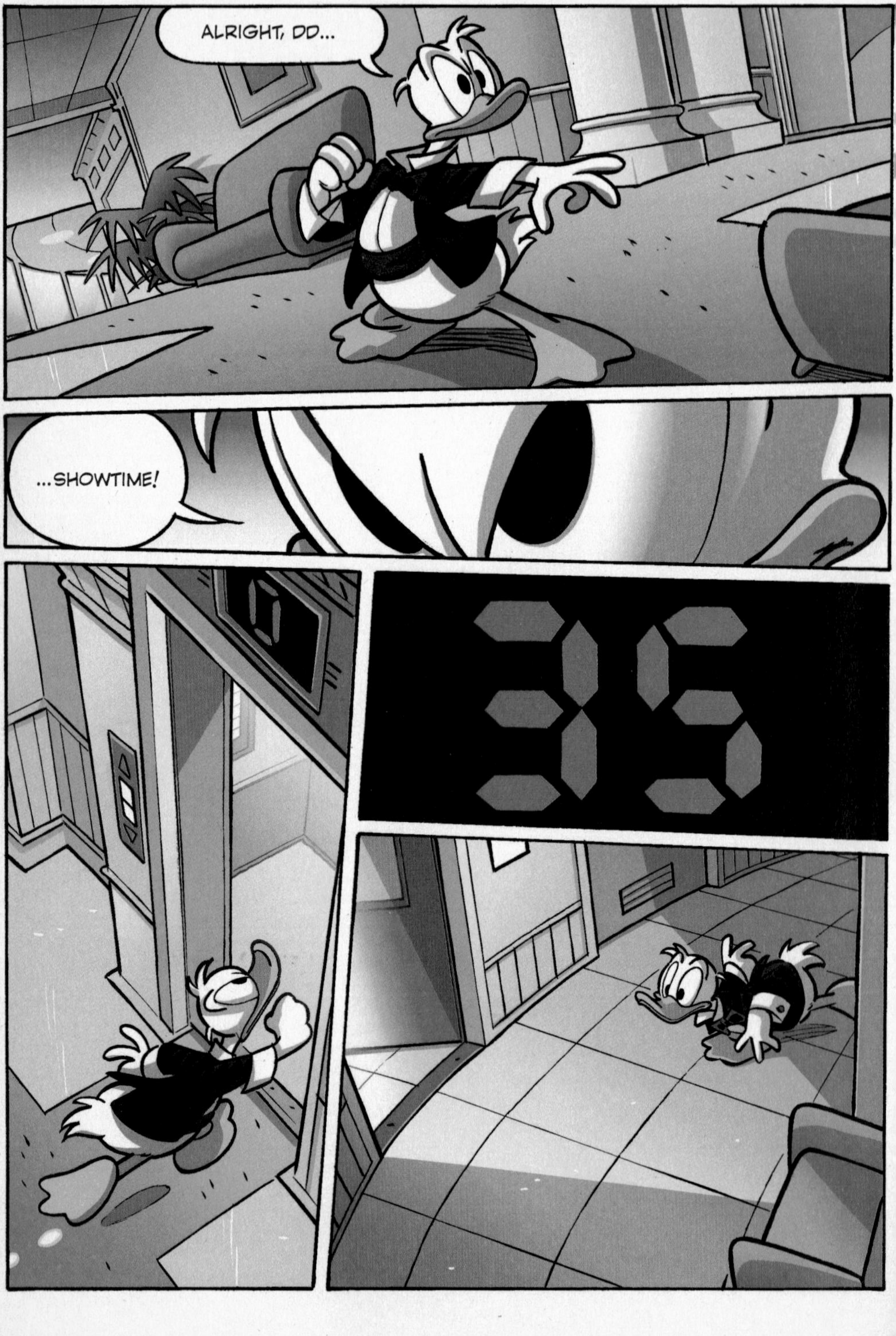
ALRIGHT, DD...
...SHOWTIME!

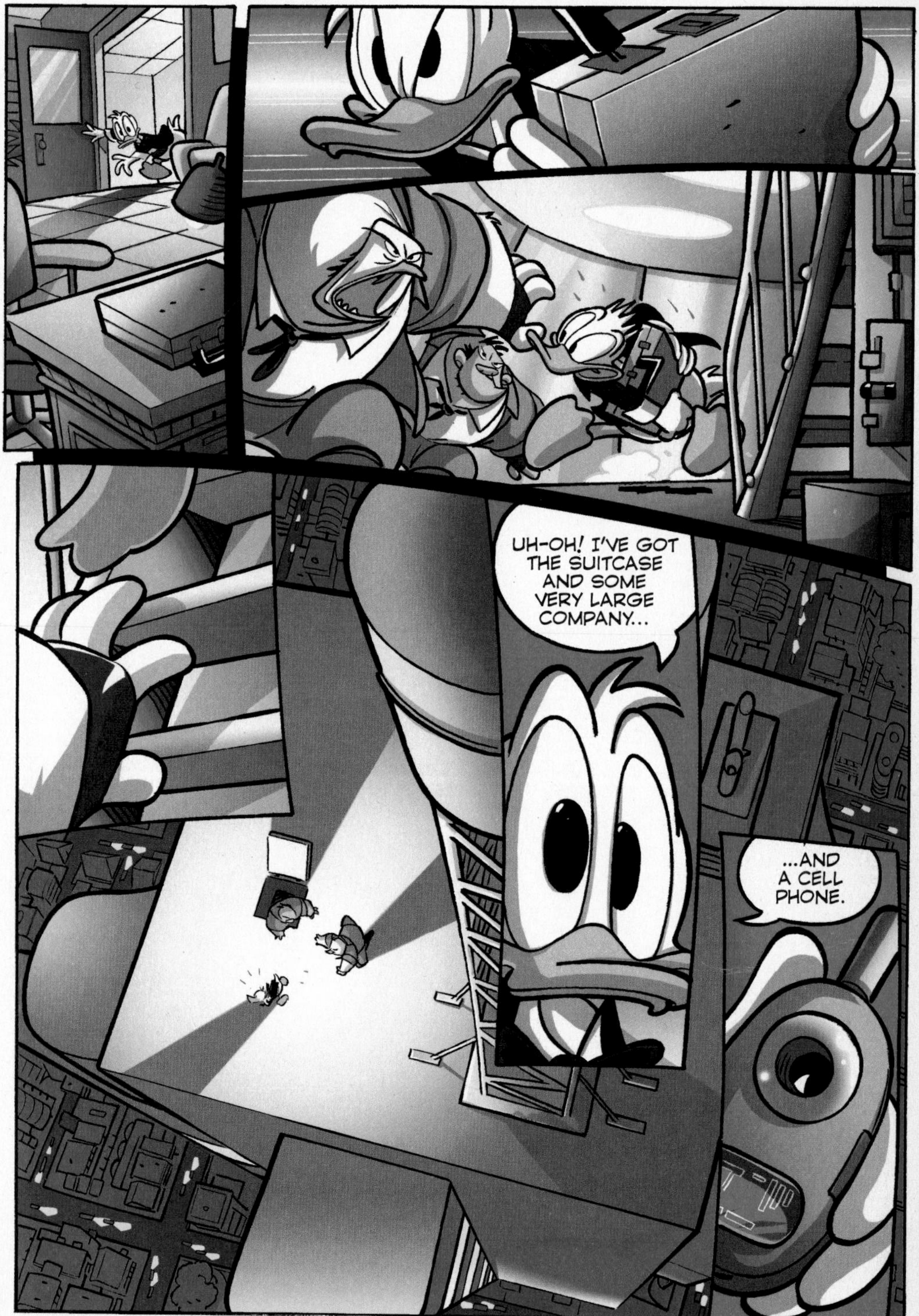
UH-OH! I'VE GOT THE SUITCASE AND SOME VERY LARGE COMPANY...
...AND A CELL PHONE.

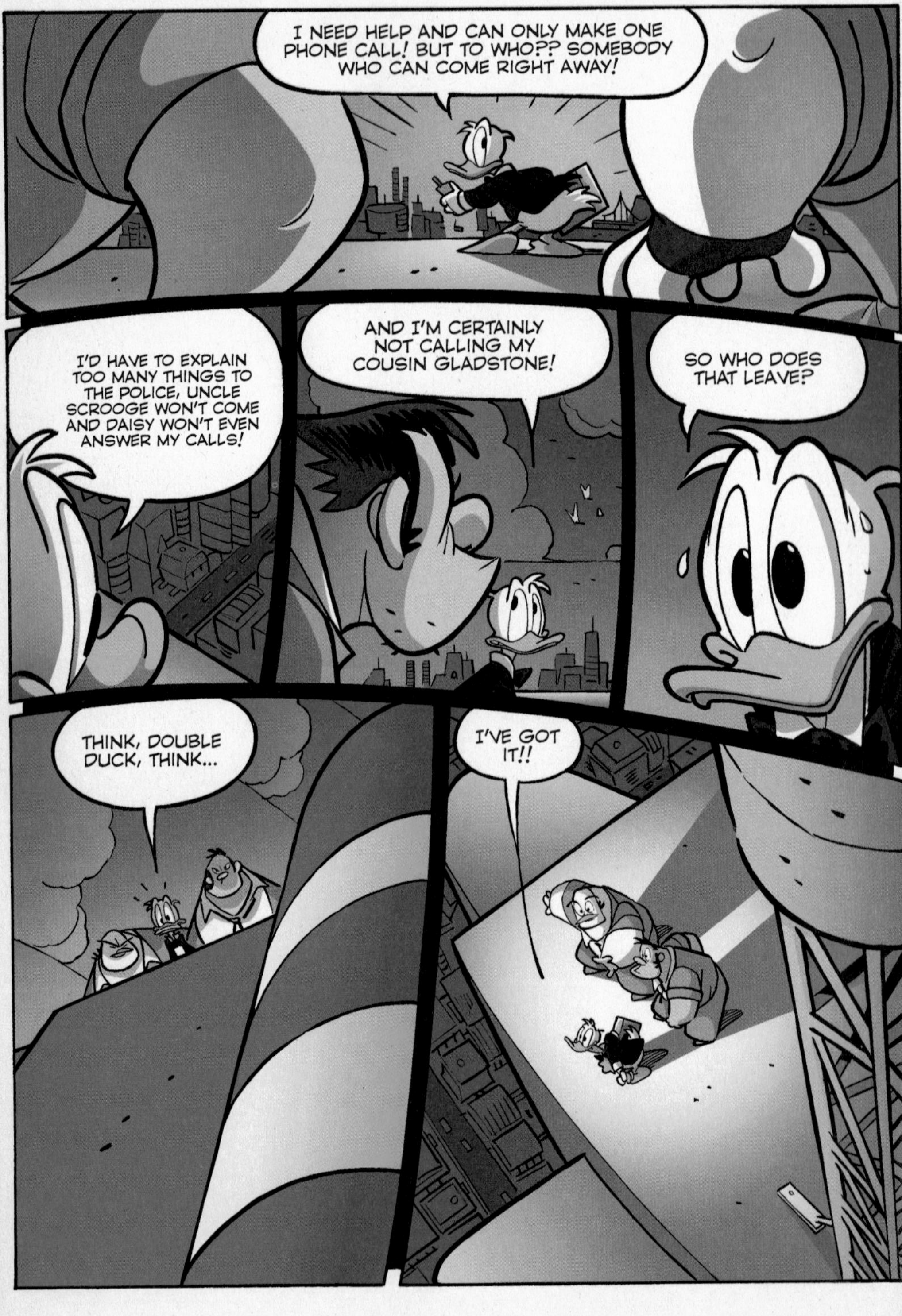
I NEED HELP AND CAN ONLY MAKE ONE PHONE CALL! BUT TO WHO?? SOMEBODY WHO CAN COME RIGHT AWAY!
I'D HAVE TO EXPLAIN TOO MANY THINGS TO THE POLICE, UNCLE SCROOGE WON'T COME AND DAISY WON'T EVEN ANSWER MY CALLS!
AND I'M CERTAINLY NOT CALLING MY COUSIN GLADSTONE!
SO WHO DOES THAT LEAVE?
THINK, DOUBLE DUCK, THINK...
I'VE GOT IT!!

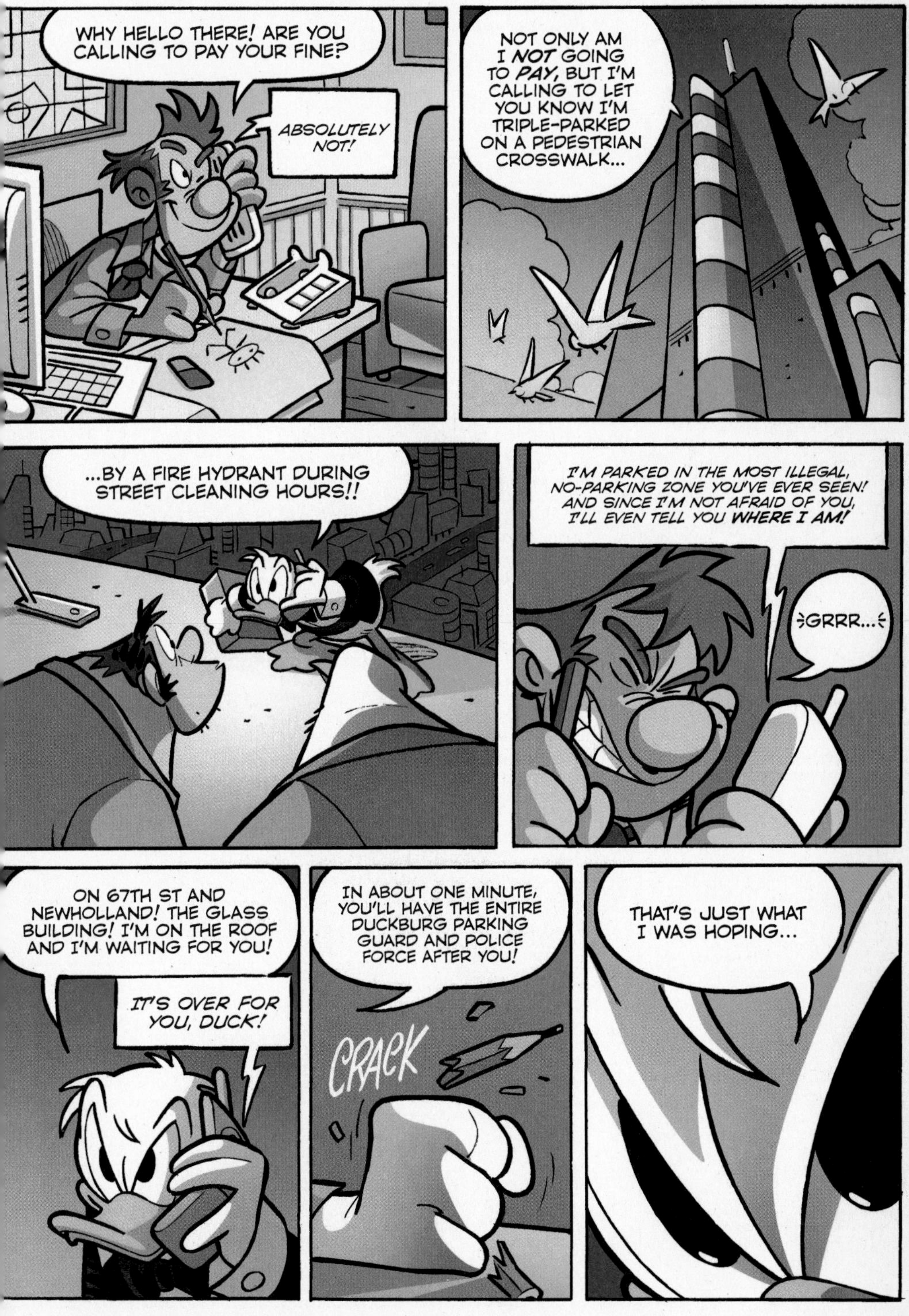
WHY HELLO THERE! ARE YOU CALLING TO PAY YOUR FINE?
ABSOLUTELY NOT!
NOT ONLY AM I NOT GOING TO PAY, BUT I'M CALLING TO LET YOU KNOW I'M TRIPLE-PARKED ON A PEDESTRIAN CROSSWALK...
...BY A FIRE HYDRANT DURING STREET CLEANING HOURS!!
I'M PARKED IN THE MOST ILLEGAL, NO-PARKING ZONE YOU'VE EVER SEEN! AND SINCE I'M NOT AFRAID OF YOU, I'LL EVEN TELL YOU WHERE I AM!
GRRR...
ON 67TH ST AND NEWHOLLAND! THE GLASS BUILDING! I'M ON THE ROOF AND I'M WAITING FOR YOU!
IT'S OVER FOR YOU, DUCK!
IN ABOUT ONE MINUTE, YOU'LL HAVE THE ENTIRE DUCKBURG PARKING GUARD AND POLICE FORCE AFTER YOU!
CRACK
THAT'S JUST WHAT I WAS HOPING...

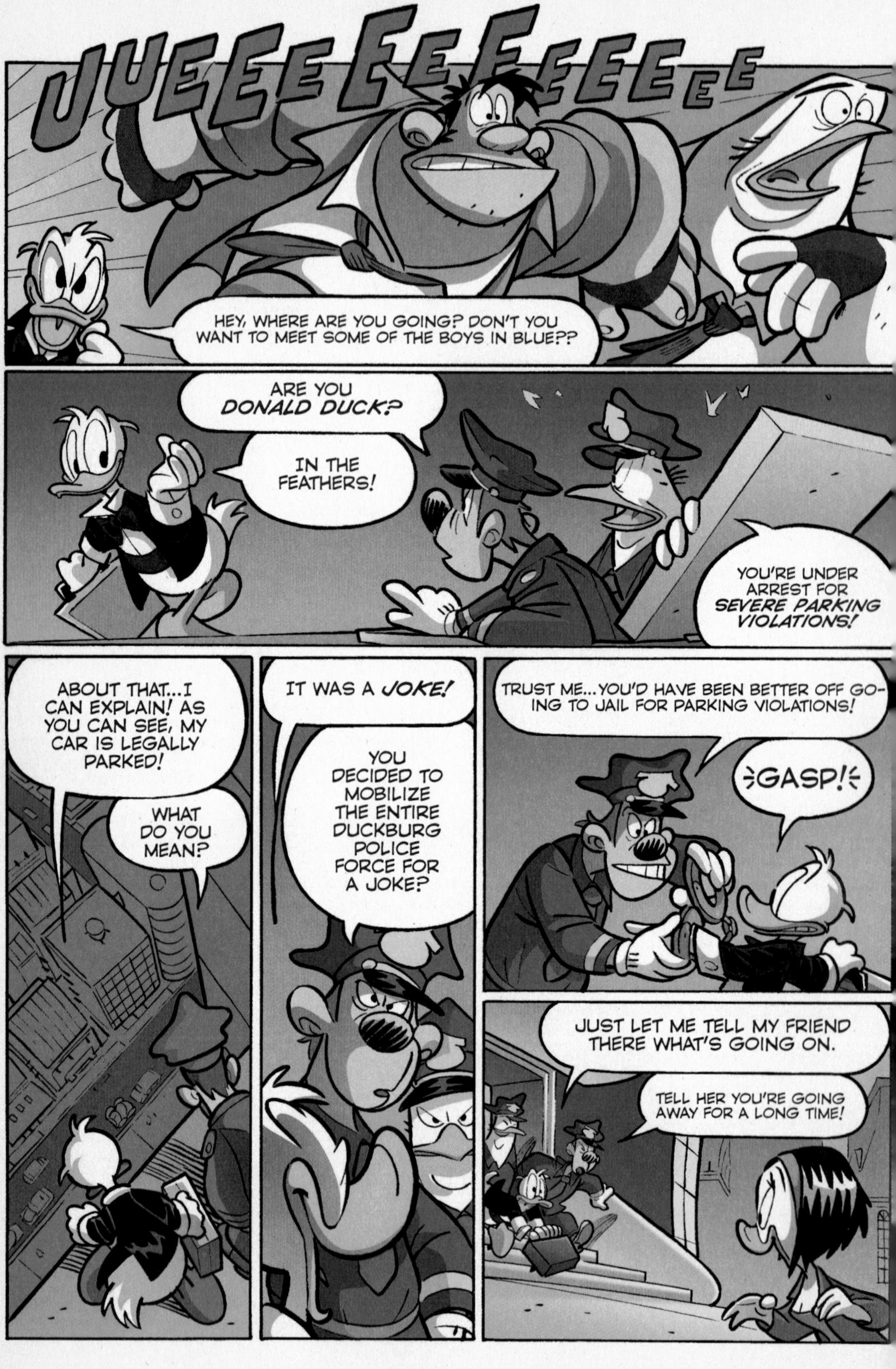
JUEEEEEEEEEEEEEE
HEY, WHERE ARE YOU GOING? DON'T YOU WANT TO MEET SOME OF THE BOYS IN BLUE??
ARE YOU DONALD DUCK?
IN THE FEATHERS!
YOU'RE UNDER ARREST FOR SEVERE PARKING VIOLATIONS!
ABOUT THAT...I CAN EXPLAIN! AS YOU CAN SEE, MY CAR IS LEGALLY PARKED!
WHAT DO YOU MEAN?
IT WAS A JOKE!
YOU DECIDED TO MOBILIZE THE ENTIRE DUCKBURG POLICE FORCE FOR A JOKE?
TRUST ME...YOU'D HAVE BEEN BETTER OFF GO-ING TO JAIL FOR PARKING VIOLATIONS!
GASP!
JUST LET ME TELL MY FRIEND THERE WHAT'S GOING ON.
TELL HER YOU'RE GOING AWAY FOR A LONG TIME!

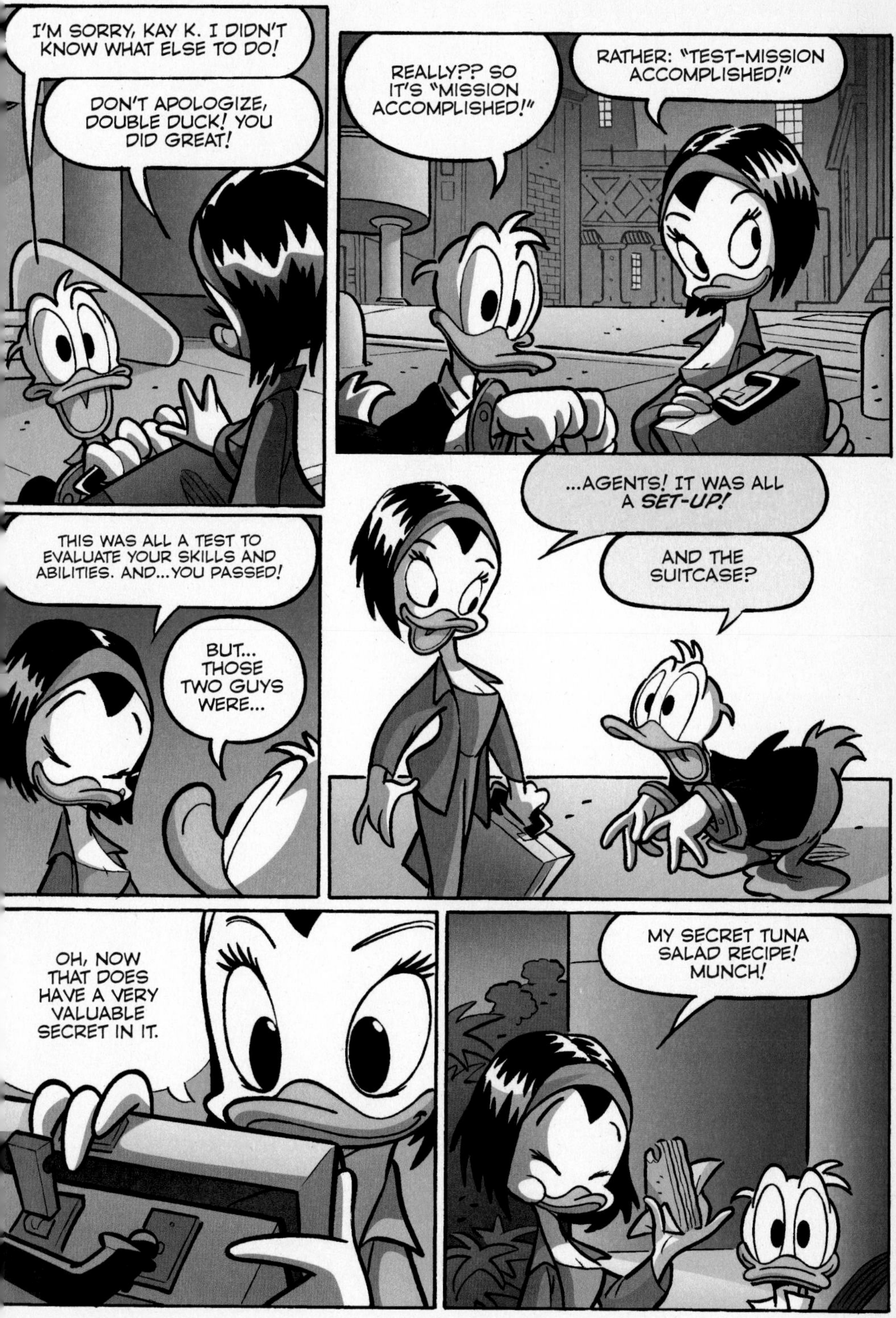
I'M SORRY, KAY K. I DIDN'T KNOW WHAT ELSE TO DO!
DON'T APOLOGIZE, DOUBLE DUCK! YOU DID GREAT!
REALLY?? SO IT'S "MISSION ACCOMPLISHED!"
RATHER: "TEST-MISSION ACCOMPLISHED!"
THIS WAS ALL A TEST TO EVALUATE YOUR SKILLS AND ABILITIES. AND...YOU PASSED!
BUT... THOSE TWO GUYS WERE...
...AGENTS! IT WAS ALL A SET-UP!
AND THE SUITCASE?
OH, NOW THAT DOES HAVE A VERY VALUABLE SECRET IN IT.
MY SECRET TUNA SALAD RECIPE! MUNCH!

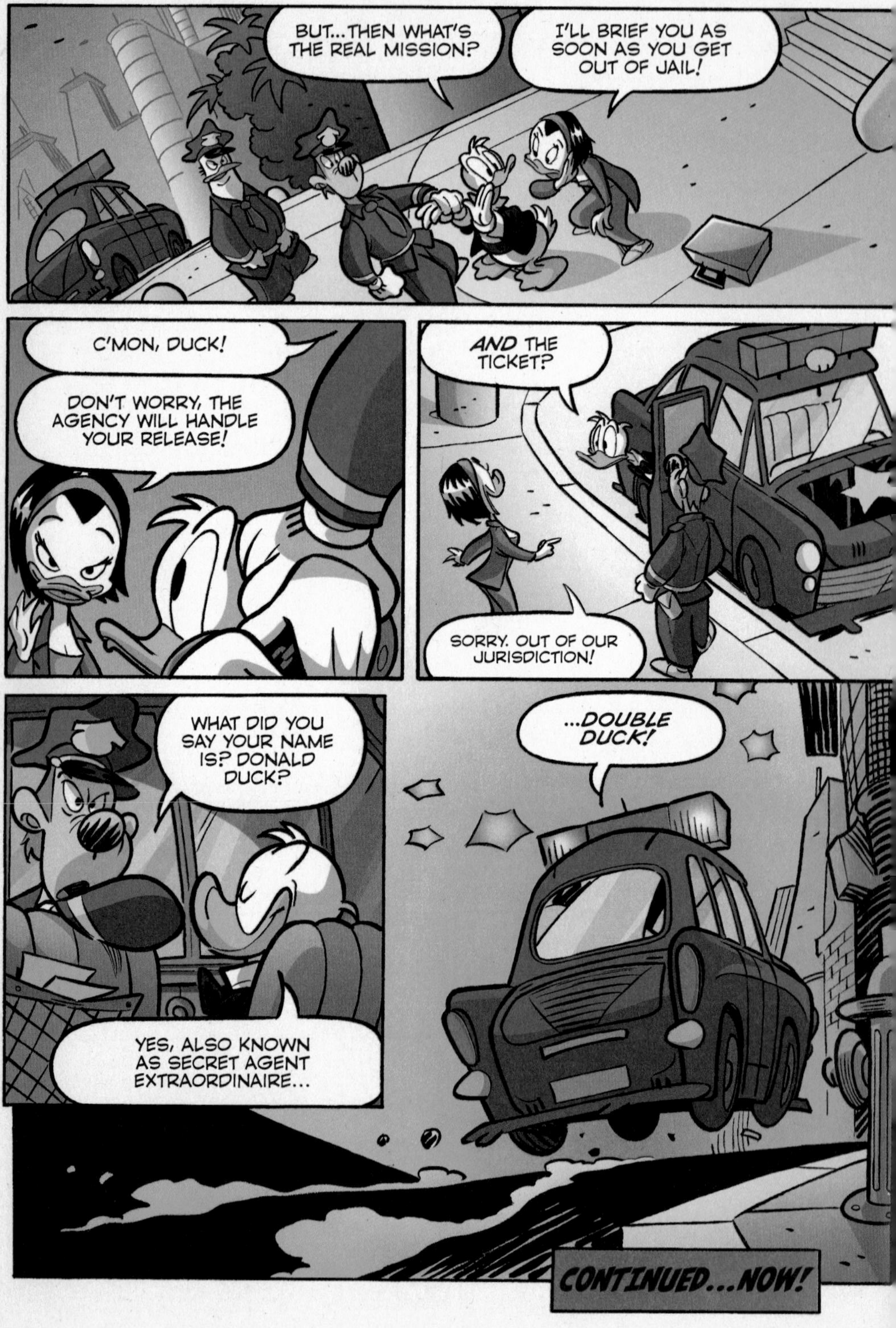
BUT...THEN WHAT'S THE REAL MISSION?
I'LL BRIEF YOU AS SOON AS YOU GET OUT OF JAIL!
C'MON, DUCK!
DON'T WORRY, THE AGENCY WILL HANDLE YOUR RELEASE!
AND THE TICKET?
SORRY. OUT OF OUR JURISDICTION!
WHAT DID YOU SAY YOUR NAME IS? DONALD DUCK?
YES, ALSO KNOWN AS SECRET AGENT EXTRAORDINAIRE...
...DOUBLE DUCK!
CONTINUED...NOW!

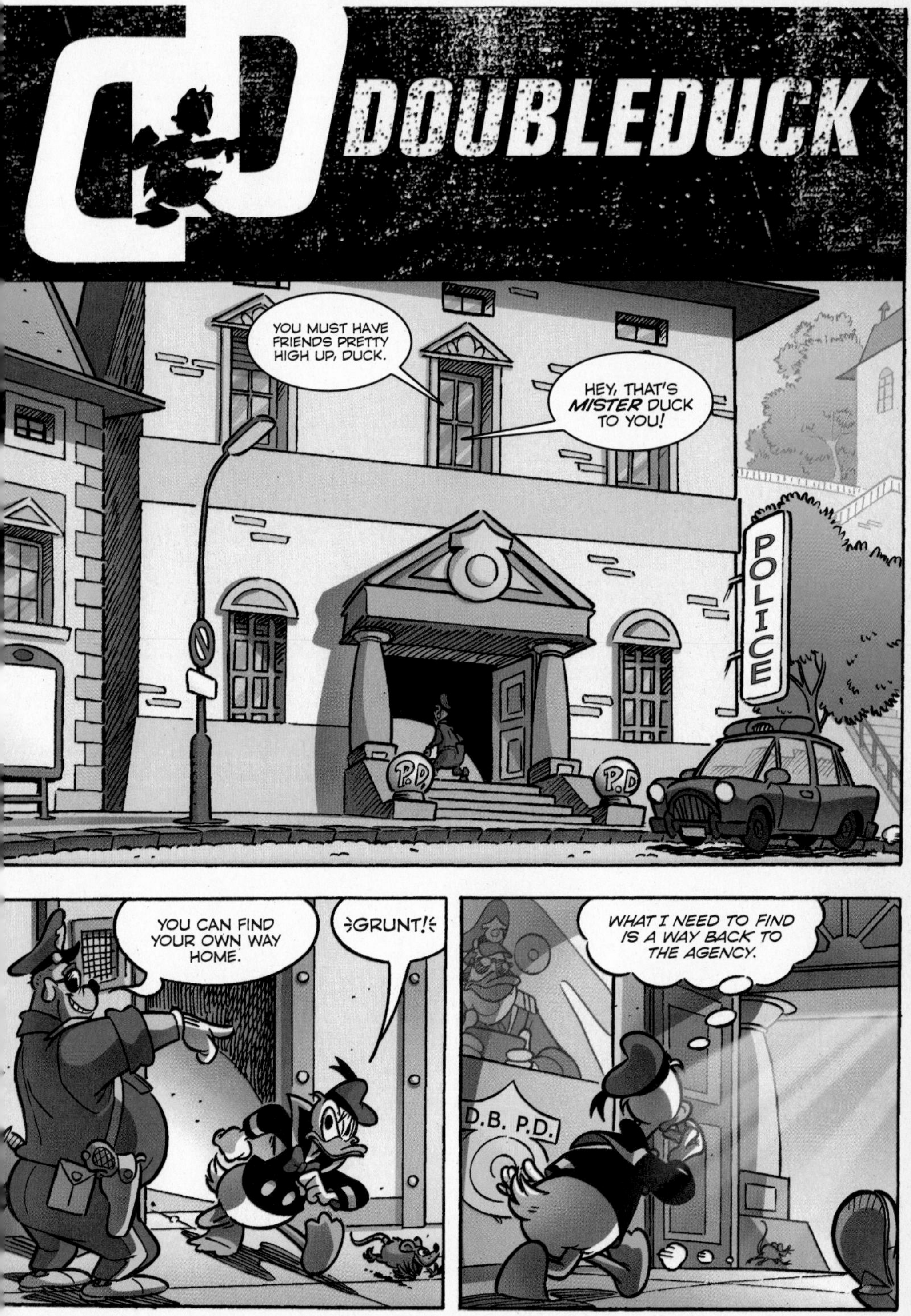
DOUBLEDUCK
YOU MUST HAVE FRIENDS PRETTY HIGH UP, DUCK.
HEY, THAT'S MISTER DUCK TO YOU!
POLICE
P.D.
P.D
YOU CAN FIND YOUR OWN WAY HOME.
GRUNT!
WHAT I NEED TO FIND IS A WAY BACK TO THE AGENCY.
D.B. P.D.

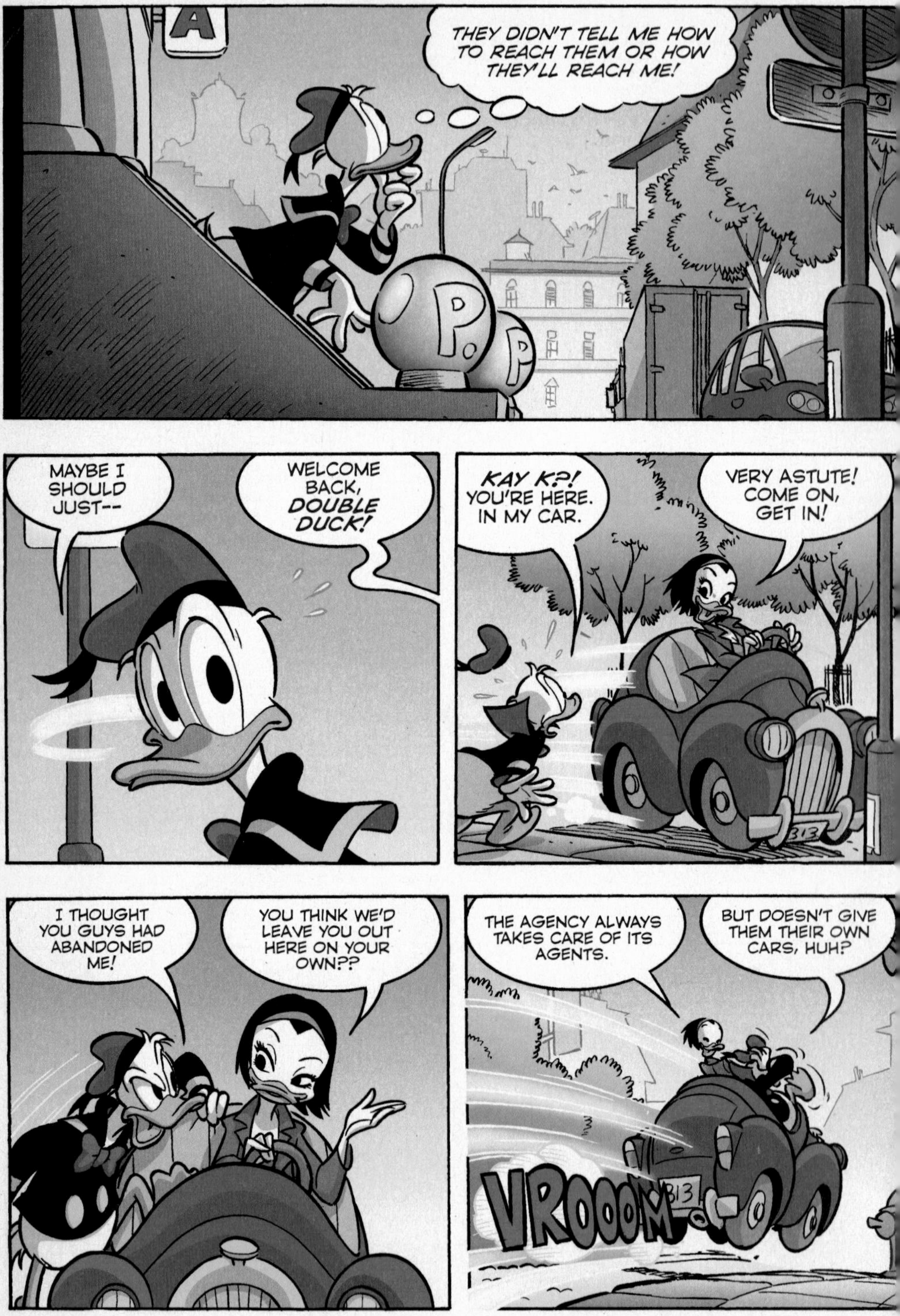

THEY DIDN'T TELL ME HOW TO REACH THEM OR HOW THEY'LL REACH ME!
MAYBE I SHOULD JUST--
WELCOME BACK, DOUBLE DUCK!
KAY K?! YOU'RE HERE. IN MY CAR.
VERY ASTUTE! COME ON, GET IN!
I THOUGHT YOU GUYS HAD ABANDONED ME!
YOU THINK WE'D LEAVE YOU OUT HERE ON YOUR OWN??
THE AGENCY ALWAYS TAKES CARE OF ITS AGENTS.
BUT DOESN'T GIVE THEM THEIR OWN CARS, HUH?
VROOOM
313

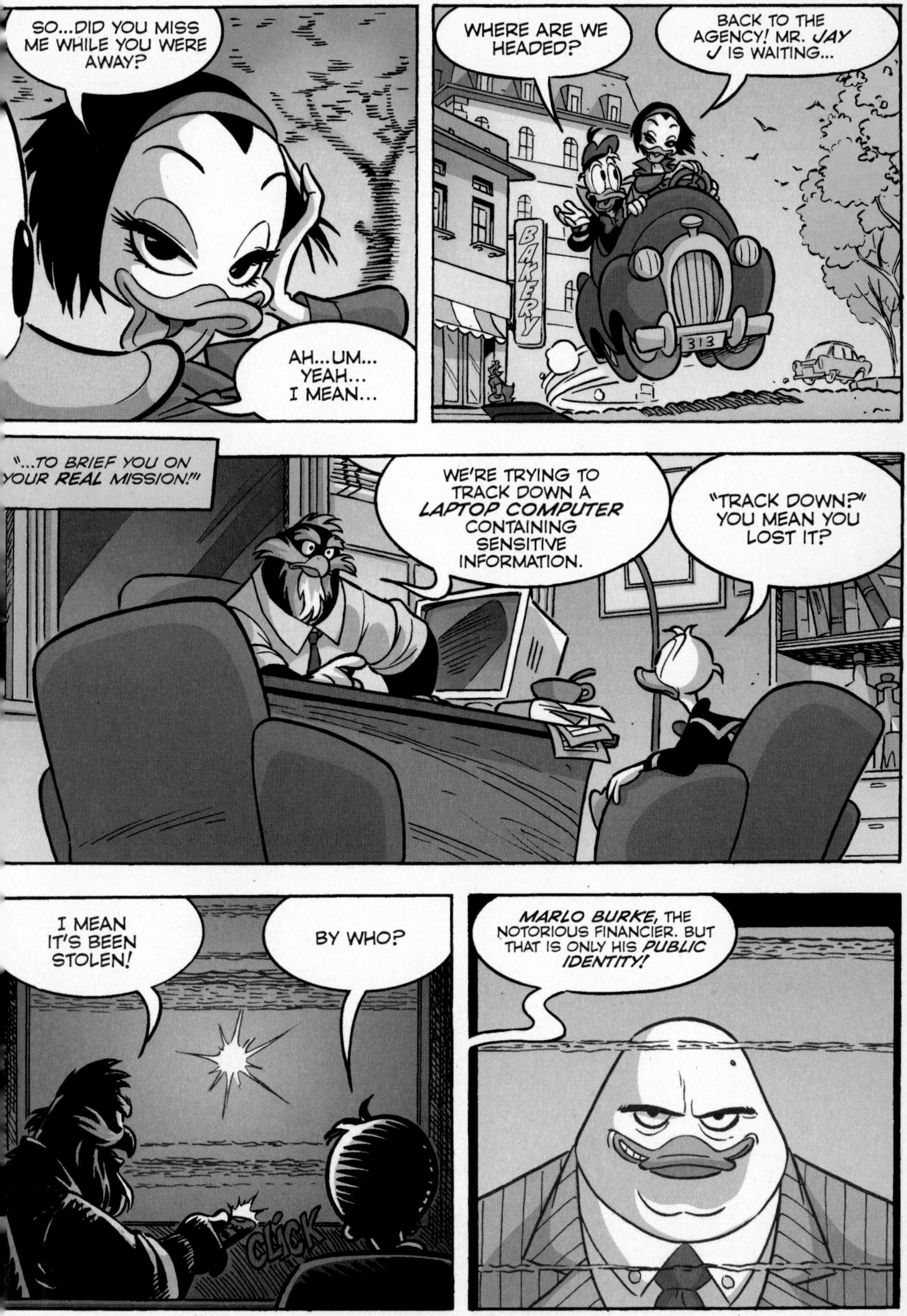
SO...DID YOU MISS ME WHILE YOU WERE AWAY?
AH...UM... YEAH... I MEAN...
WHERE ARE WE HEADED?
BACK TO THE AGENCY! MR. JAY J IS WAITING...
BAKERY
313
"...TO BRIEF YOU ON YOUR REAL MISSION!"
WE'RE TRYING TO TRACK DOWN A LAPTOP COMPUTER CONTAINING SENSITIVE INFORMATION.
"TRACK DOWN?" YOU MEAN YOU LOST IT?
I MEAN IT'S BEEN STOLEN!
BY WHO?
CLICK
MARLO BURKE, THE NOTORIOUS FINANCIER. BUT THAT IS ONLY HIS PUBLIC IDENTITY!

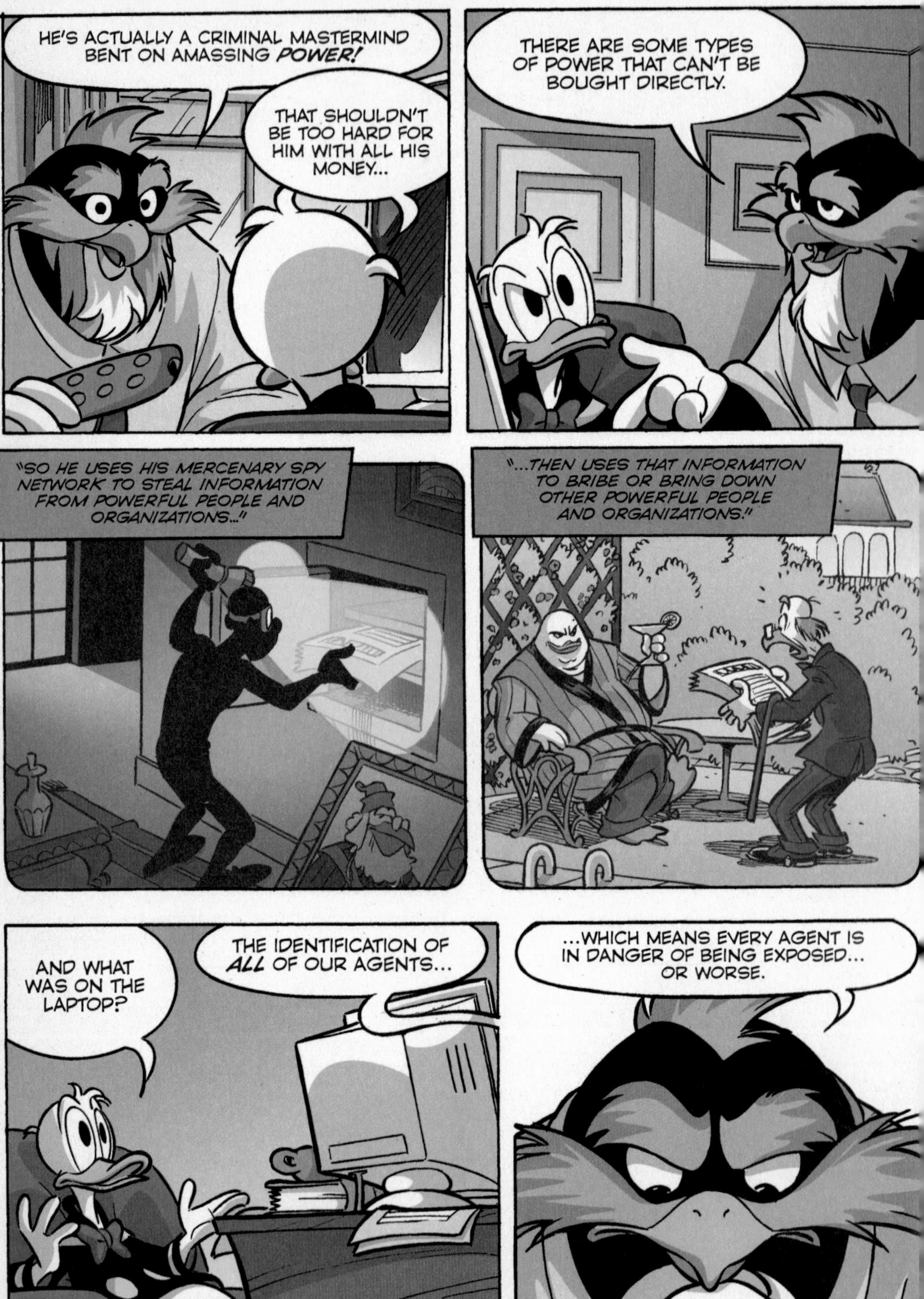
HE'S ACTUALLY A CRIMINAL MASTERMIND BENT ON AMASSING *POWER!*
THAT SHOULDN'T BE TOO HARD FOR HIM WITH ALL HIS MONEY...
THERE ARE SOME TYPES OF POWER THAT CAN'T BE BOUGHT DIRECTLY.
"SO HE USES HIS MERCENARY SPY NETWORK TO STEAL INFORMATION FROM POWERFUL PEOPLE AND ORGANIZATIONS..."
"...THEN USES THAT INFORMATION TO BRIBE OR BRING DOWN OTHER POWERFUL PEOPLE AND ORGANIZATIONS."
AND WHAT WAS ON THE LAPTOP?
THE IDENTIFICATION OF *ALL* OF OUR AGENTS...
...WHICH MEANS EVERY AGENT IS IN DANGER OF BEING EXPOSED... OR WORSE.

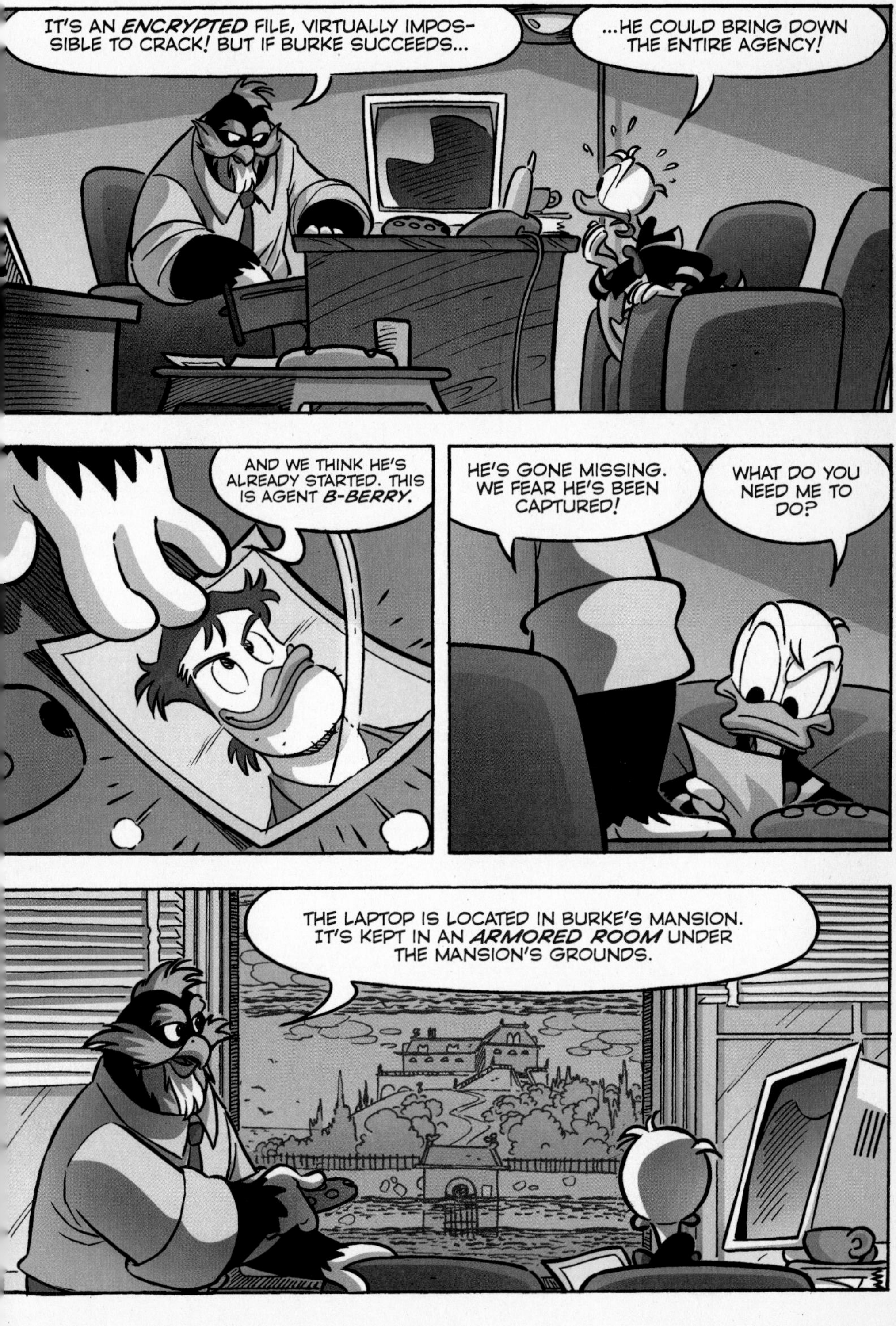
IT'S AN ENCRYPTED FILE, VIRTUALLY IMPOSSIBLE TO CRACK! BUT IF BURKE SUCCEEDS...
...HE COULD BRING DOWN THE ENTIRE AGENCY!
AND WE THINK HE'S ALREADY STARTED. THIS IS AGENT B-BERRY.
HE'S GONE MISSING. WE FEAR HE'S BEEN CAPTURED!
WHAT DO YOU NEED ME TO DO?
THE LAPTOP IS LOCATED IN BURKE'S MANSION. IT'S KEPT IN AN ARMORED ROOM UNDER THE MANSION'S GROUNDS.

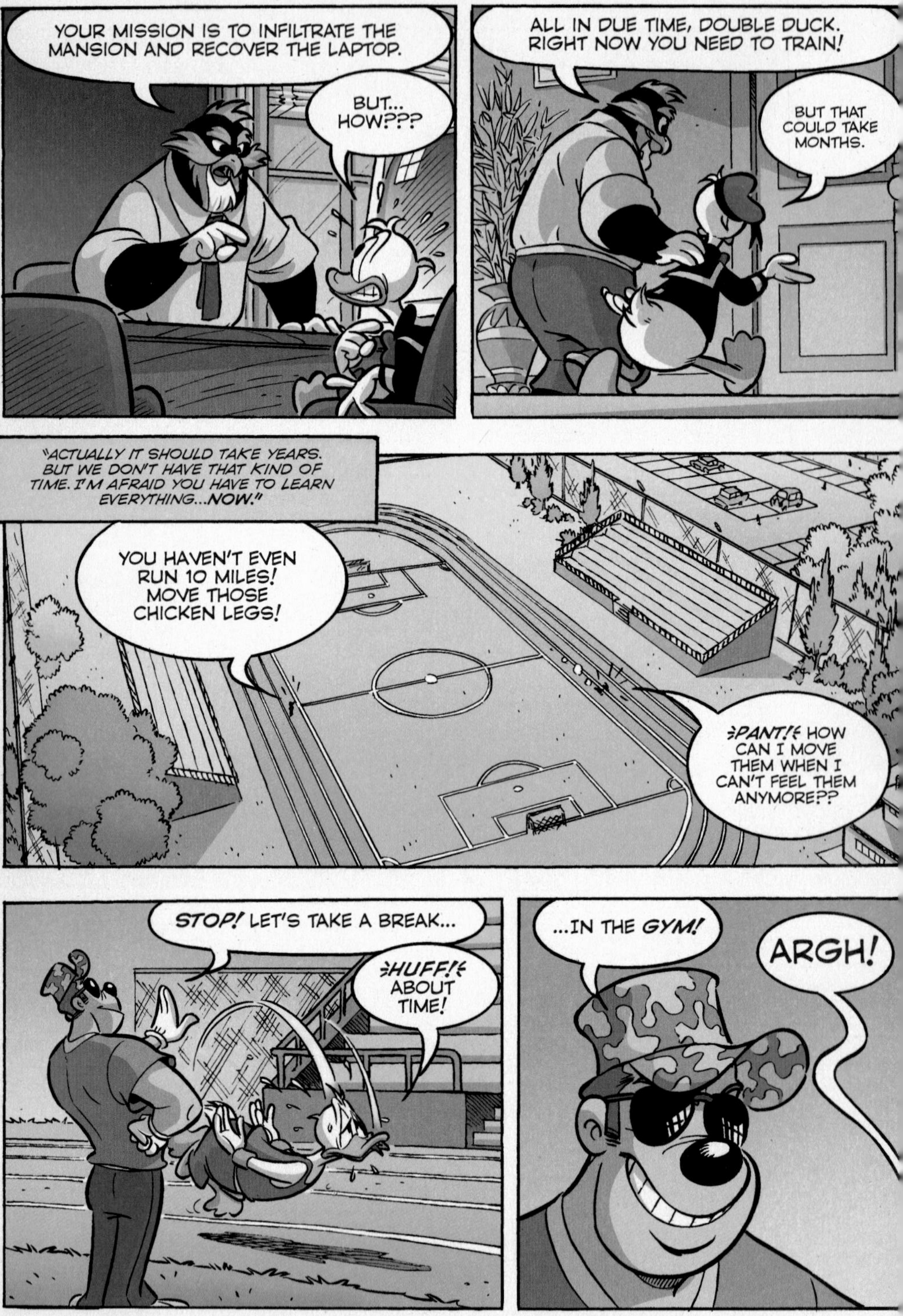
YOUR MISSION IS TO INFILTRATE THE MANSION AND RECOVER THE LAPTOP.
BUT... HOW???
ALL IN DUE TIME, DOUBLE DUCK. RIGHT NOW YOU NEED TO TRAIN!
BUT THAT COULD TAKE MONTHS.
"ACTUALLY IT SHOULD TAKE YEARS. BUT WE DON'T HAVE THAT KIND OF TIME. I'M AFRAID YOU HAVE TO LEARN EVERYTHING...NOW."
YOU HAVEN'T EVEN RUN 10 MILES! MOVE THOSE CHICKEN LEGS!
PANT! HOW CAN I MOVE THEM WHEN I CAN'T FEEL THEM ANYMORE??
STOP! LET'S TAKE A BREAK...
HUFF! ABOUT TIME!
...IN THE GYM!
ARGH!

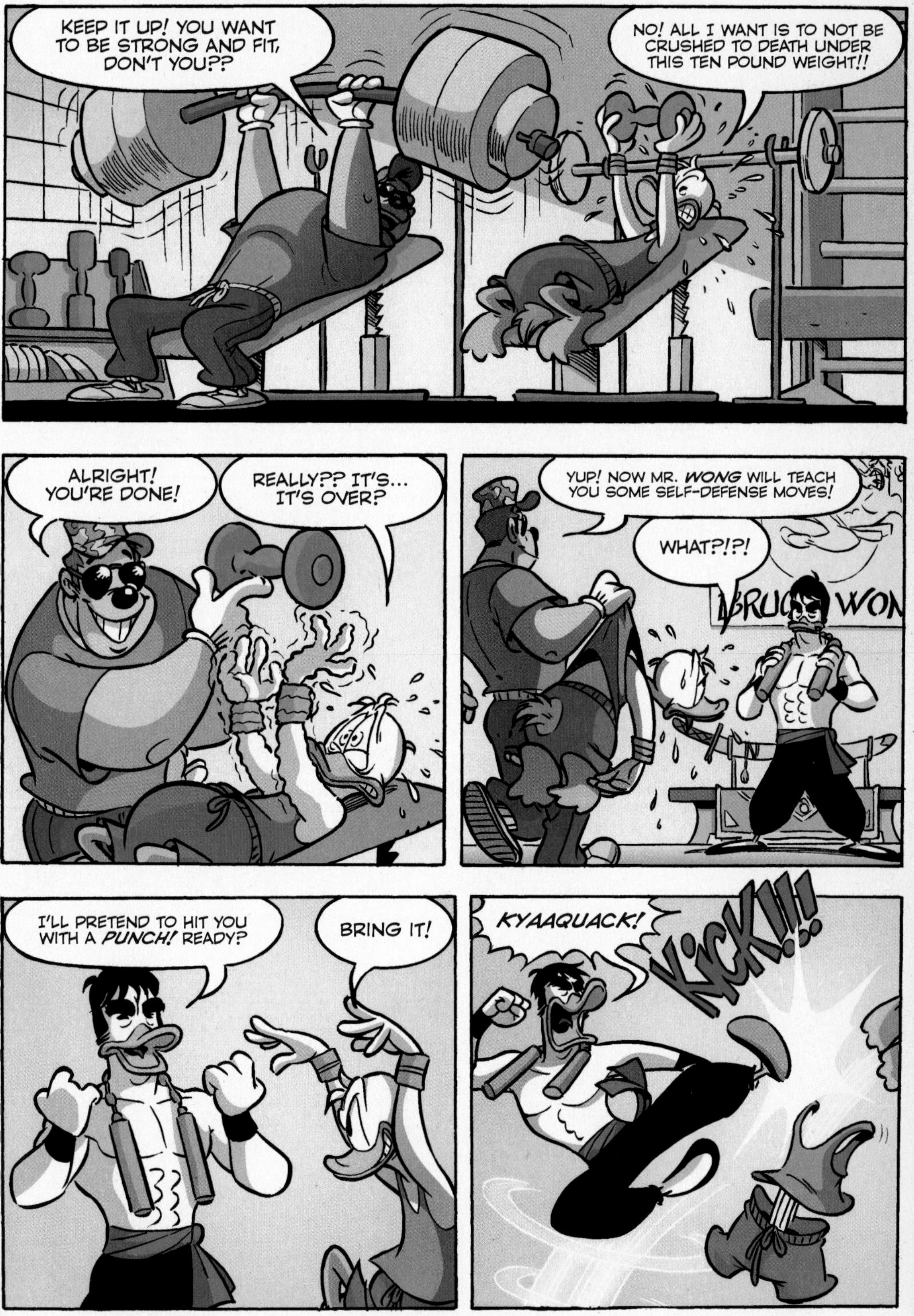
KEEP IT UP! YOU WANT TO BE STRONG AND FIT, DON'T YOU??
NO! ALL I WANT IS TO NOT BE CRUSHED TO DEATH UNDER THIS TEN POUND WEIGHT!!
ALRIGHT! YOU'RE DONE!
REALLY?? IT'S... IT'S OVER?
YUP! NOW MR. WONG WILL TEACH YOU SOME SELF-DEFENSE MOVES!
WHAT?!?!
I'LL PRETEND TO HIT YOU WITH A PUNCH! READY?
BRING IT!
KYAAQUACK!
KICK!!!

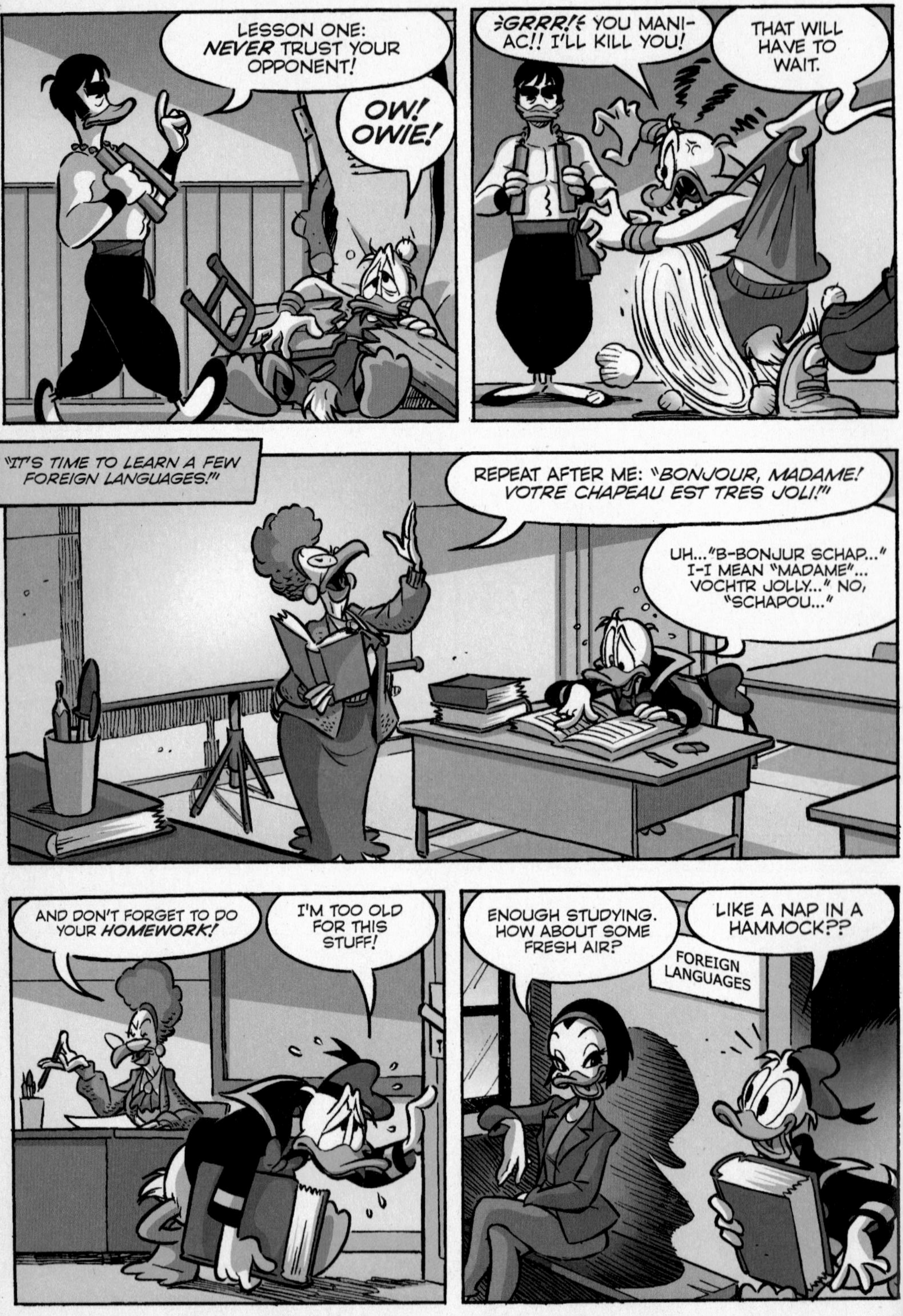

LESSON ONE: NEVER TRUST YOUR OPPONENT!
OW! OWIE!
GRRR! YOU MANI-AC!! I'LL KILL YOU!
THAT WILL HAVE TO WAIT.
"IT'S TIME TO LEARN A FEW FOREIGN LANGUAGES!"
REPEAT AFTER ME: "BONJOUR, MADAME! VOTRE CHAPEAU EST TRES JOLI!"
UH..."B-BONJUR SCHAP..." I-I MEAN "MADAME"... VOCHTR JOLLY..." NO, "SCHAPOU..."
AND DON'T FORGET TO DO YOUR HOMEWORK!
I'M TOO OLD FOR THIS STUFF!
ENOUGH STUDYING. HOW ABOUT SOME FRESH AIR?
LIKE A NAP IN A HAMMOCK??
FOREIGN LANGUAGES

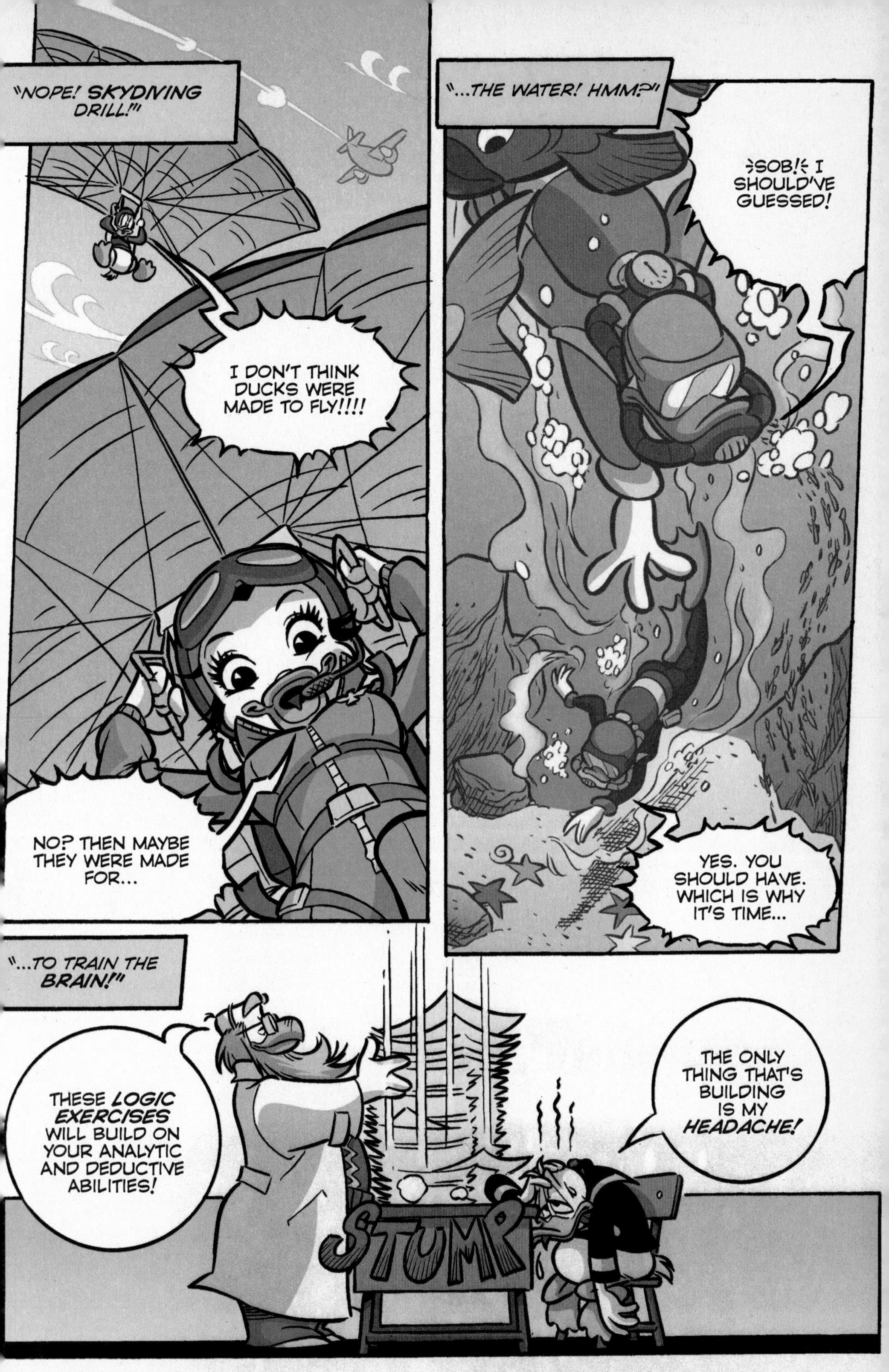
"NOPE! SKYDIVING DRILL!"
I DON'T THINK DUCKS WERE MADE TO FLY!!!!
NO? THEN MAYBE THEY WERE MADE FOR...
"...THE WATER! HMM?"
SOB! I SHOULD'VE GUESSED!
YES. YOU SHOULD HAVE. WHICH IS WHY IT'S TIME...
"...TO TRAIN THE BRAIN!"
THESE LOGIC EXERCISES WILL BUILD ON YOUR ANALYTIC AND DEDUCTIVE ABILITIES!
THE ONLY THING THAT'S BUILDING IS MY HEADACHE!
STUMP

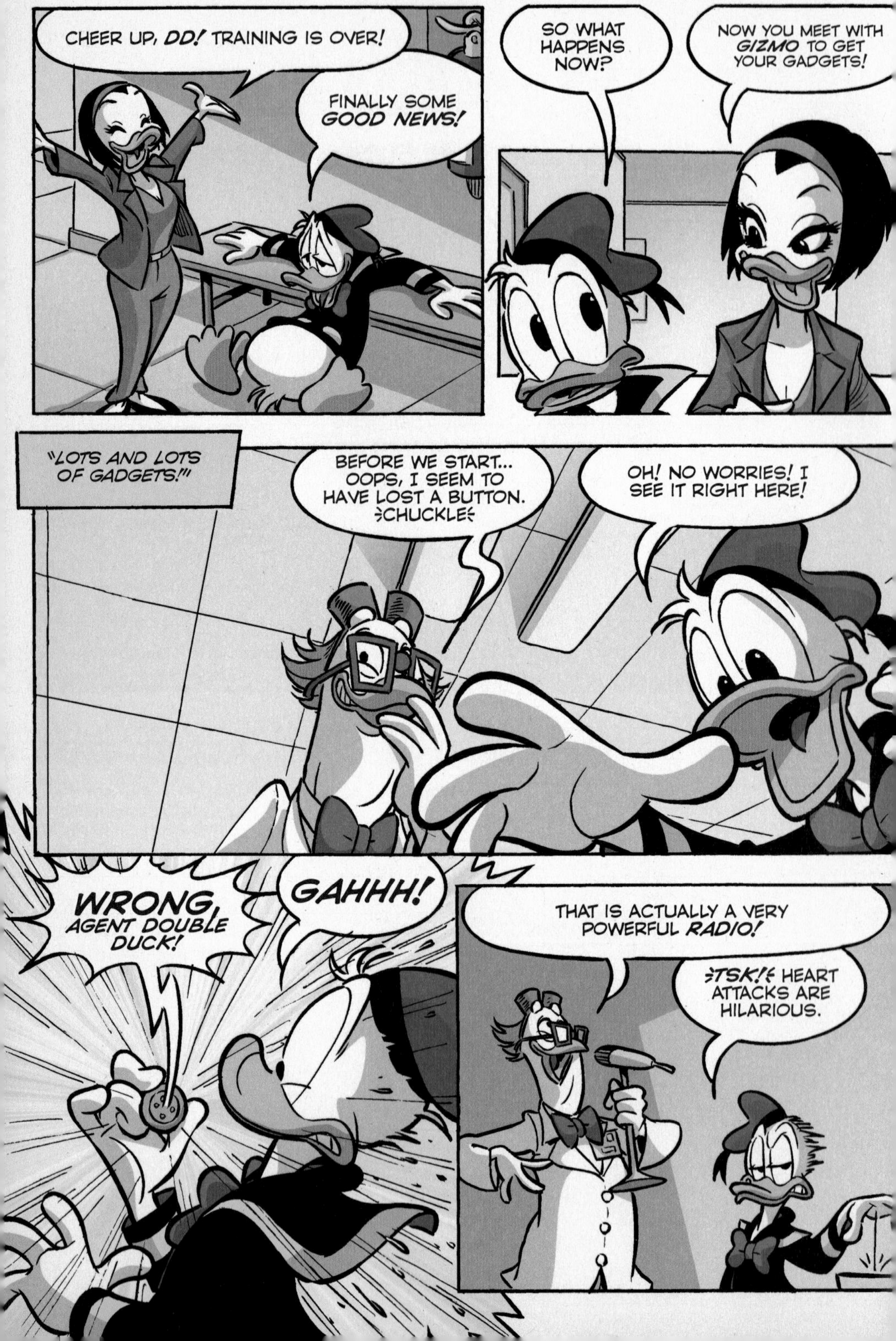
CHEER UP, DD! TRAINING IS OVER!
FINALLY SOME GOOD NEWS!
SO WHAT HAPPENS NOW?
NOW YOU MEET WITH GIZMO TO GET YOUR GADGETS!
"LOTS AND LOTS OF GADGETS!"
BEFORE WE START... OOPS, I SEEM TO HAVE LOST A BUTTON. ⁝CHUCKLE⁝
OH! NO WORRIES! I SEE IT RIGHT HERE!
WRONG, AGENT DOUBLE DUCK!
GAHHH!
THAT IS ACTUALLY A VERY POWERFUL RADIO!
⁝TSK!⁝ HEART ATTACKS ARE HILARIOUS.

AND THIS DEVICE HERE, IS A DIGITAL *PICKLOCK*...

...CAPABLE OF DISABLING ANY COMBINATION LOCK!

CLUNK

I'VE GOT AN *UNCLE* WHO WOULDN'T APPROVE!

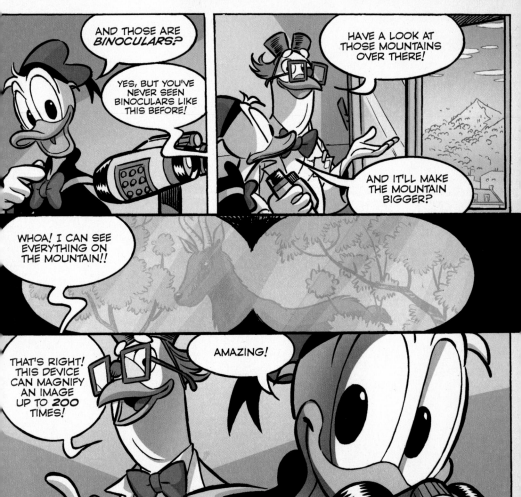

AND THOSE ARE *BINOCULARS?*

YES, BUT YOU'VE NEVER SEEN BINOCULARS LIKE THIS BEFORE!

HAVE A LOOK AT THOSE MOUNTAINS OVER THERE!

AND IT'LL MAKE THE MOUNTAIN BIGGER?

WHOA! I CAN SEE EVERYTHING ON THE MOUNTAIN!!

THAT'S RIGHT! THIS DEVICE CAN MAGNIFY AN IMAGE UP TO *200* TIMES!

AMAZING!

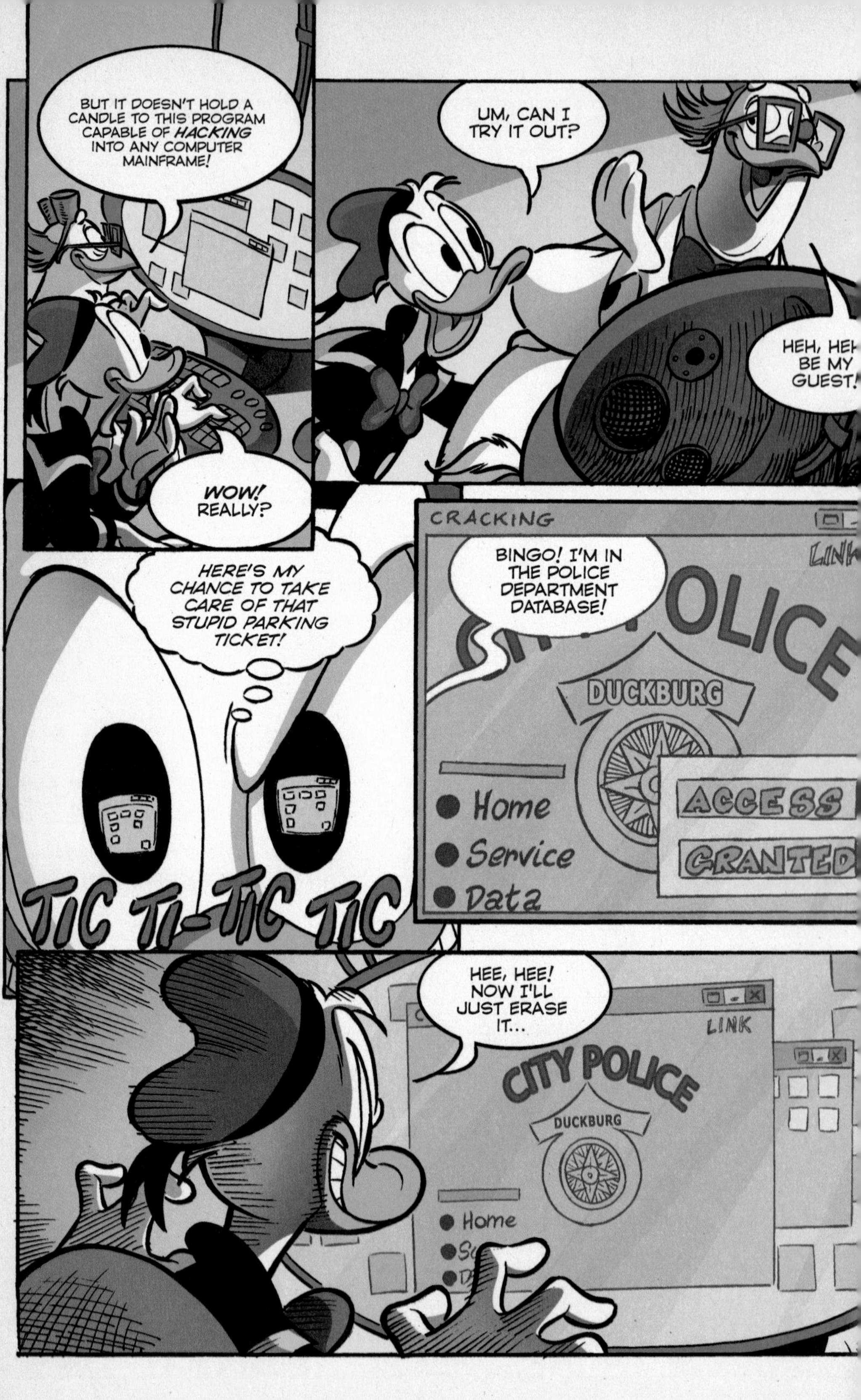
BUT IT DOESN'T HOLD A CANDLE TO THIS PROGRAM CAPABLE OF HACKING INTO ANY COMPUTER MAINFRAME!
WOW! REALLY?
UM, CAN I TRY IT OUT?
HEH, HEH BE MY GUEST!
HERE'S MY CHANCE TO TAKE CARE OF THAT STUPID PARKING TICKET!
TIC TI-TIC TIC
CRACKING
BINGO! I'M IN THE POLICE DEPARTMENT DATABASE!
LINK
DUCKBURG
Home
Service
Data
ACCESS
GRANTED
HEE, HEE! NOW I'LL JUST ERASE IT...
LINK
CITY POLICE
DUCKBURG
Home

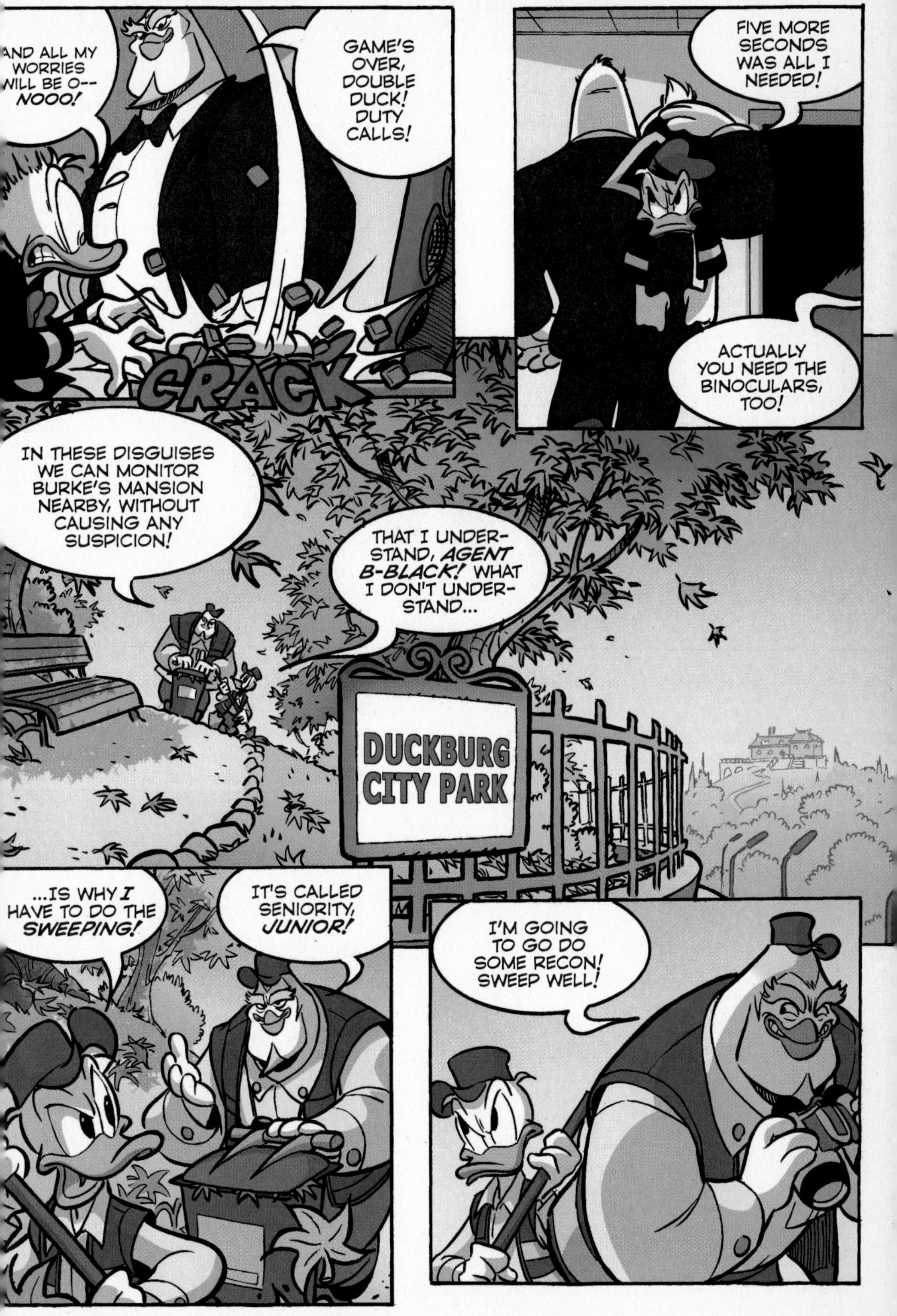
AND ALL MY WORRIES WILL BE O-- NOOO!
GAME'S OVER, DOUBLE DUCK! DUTY CALLS!
CRACK
FIVE MORE SECONDS WAS ALL I NEEDED!
ACTUALLY YOU NEED THE BINOCULARS, TOO!
IN THESE DISGUISES WE CAN MONITOR BURKE'S MANSION NEARBY, WITHOUT CAUSING ANY SUSPICION!
THAT I UNDER-STAND, AGENT B-BLACK! WHAT I DON'T UNDER-STAND...
DUCKBURG CITY PARK
...IS WHY I HAVE TO DO THE SWEEPING!
IT'S CALLED SENIORITY, JUNIOR!
I'M GOING TO GO DO SOME RECON! SWEEP WELL!

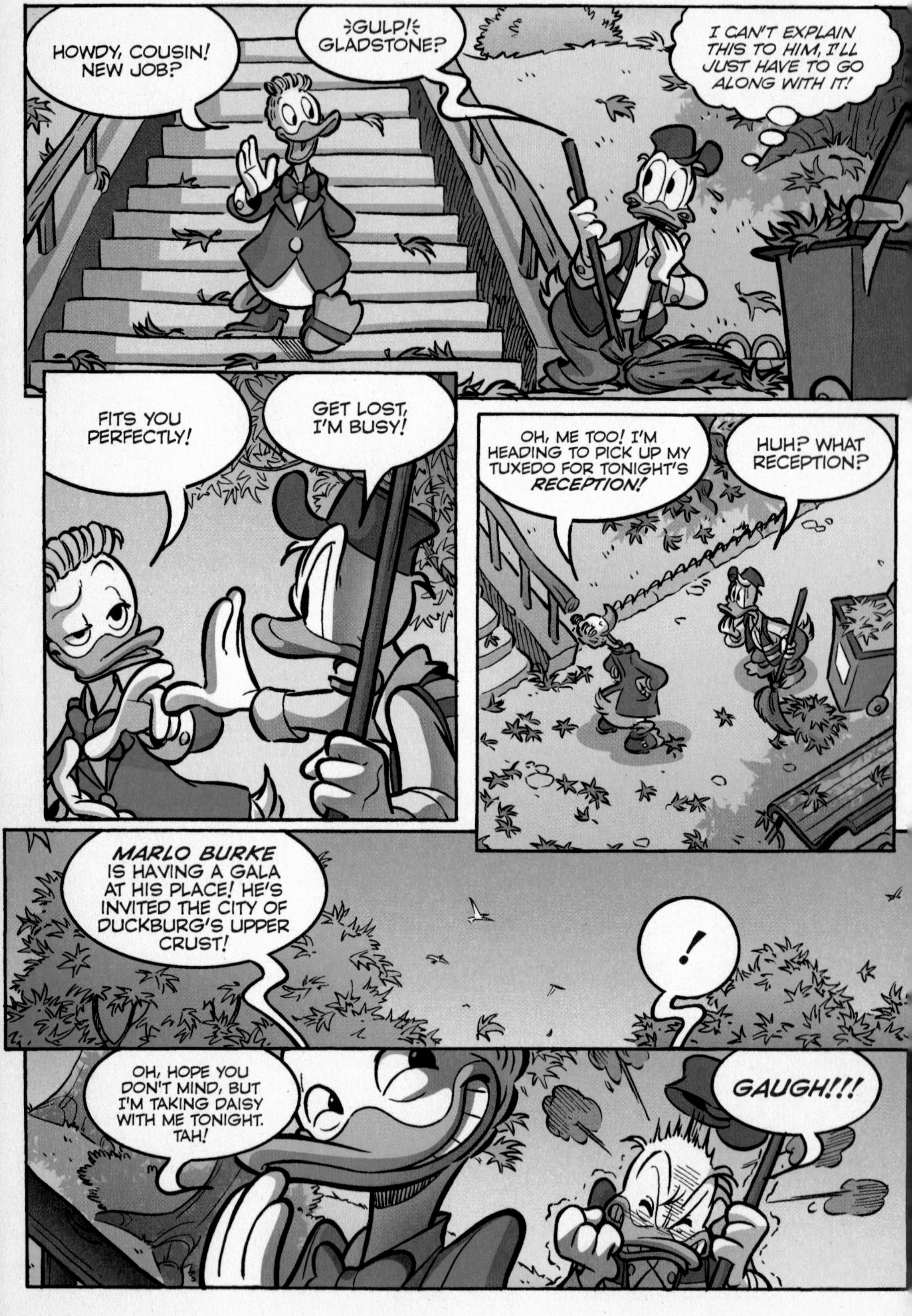
HOWDY, COUSIN! NEW JOB?
GULP! GLADSTONE?
I CAN'T EXPLAIN THIS TO HIM, I'LL JUST HAVE TO GO ALONG WITH IT!
FITS YOU PERFECTLY!
GET LOST, I'M BUSY!
OH, ME TOO! I'M HEADING TO PICK UP MY TUXEDO FOR TONIGHT'S RECEPTION!
HUH? WHAT RECEPTION?
MARLO BURKE IS HAVING A GALA AT HIS PLACE! HE'S INVITED THE CITY OF DUCKBURG'S UPPER CRUST!
!
OH, HOPE YOU DON'T MIND, BUT I'M TAKING DAISY WITH ME TONIGHT. TAH!
GAUGH!!!

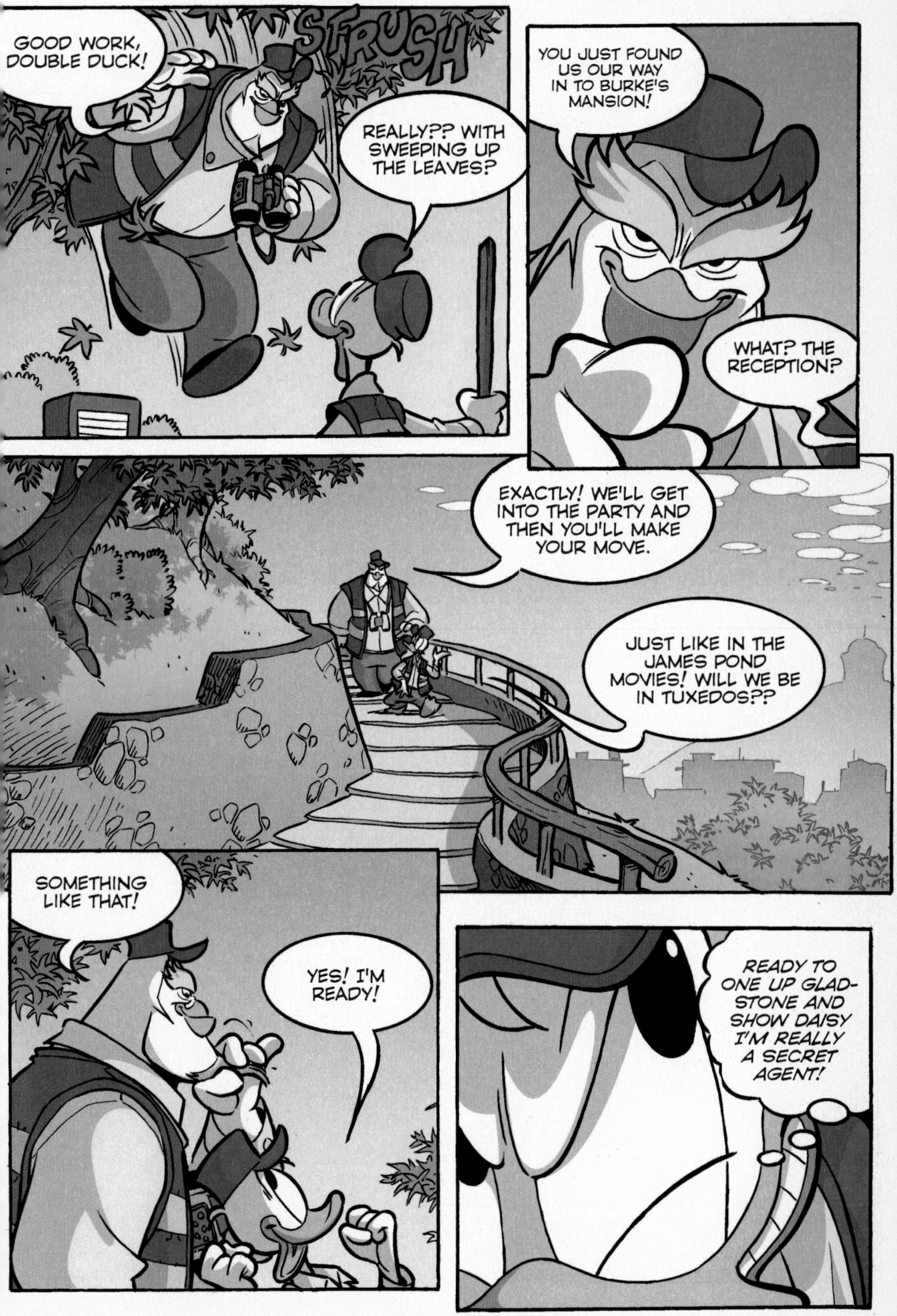
STRUSH
GOOD WORK, DOUBLE DUCK!
REALLY?? WITH SWEEPING UP THE LEAVES?
YOU JUST FOUND US OUR WAY IN TO BURKE'S MANSION!
WHAT? THE RECEPTION?
EXACTLY! WE'LL GET INTO THE PARTY AND THEN YOU'LL MAKE YOUR MOVE.
JUST LIKE IN THE JAMES POND MOVIES! WILL WE BE IN TUXEDOS??
SOMETHING LIKE THAT!
YES! I'M READY!
READY TO ONE UP GLAD-STONE AND SHOW DAISY I'M REALLY A SECRET AGENT!

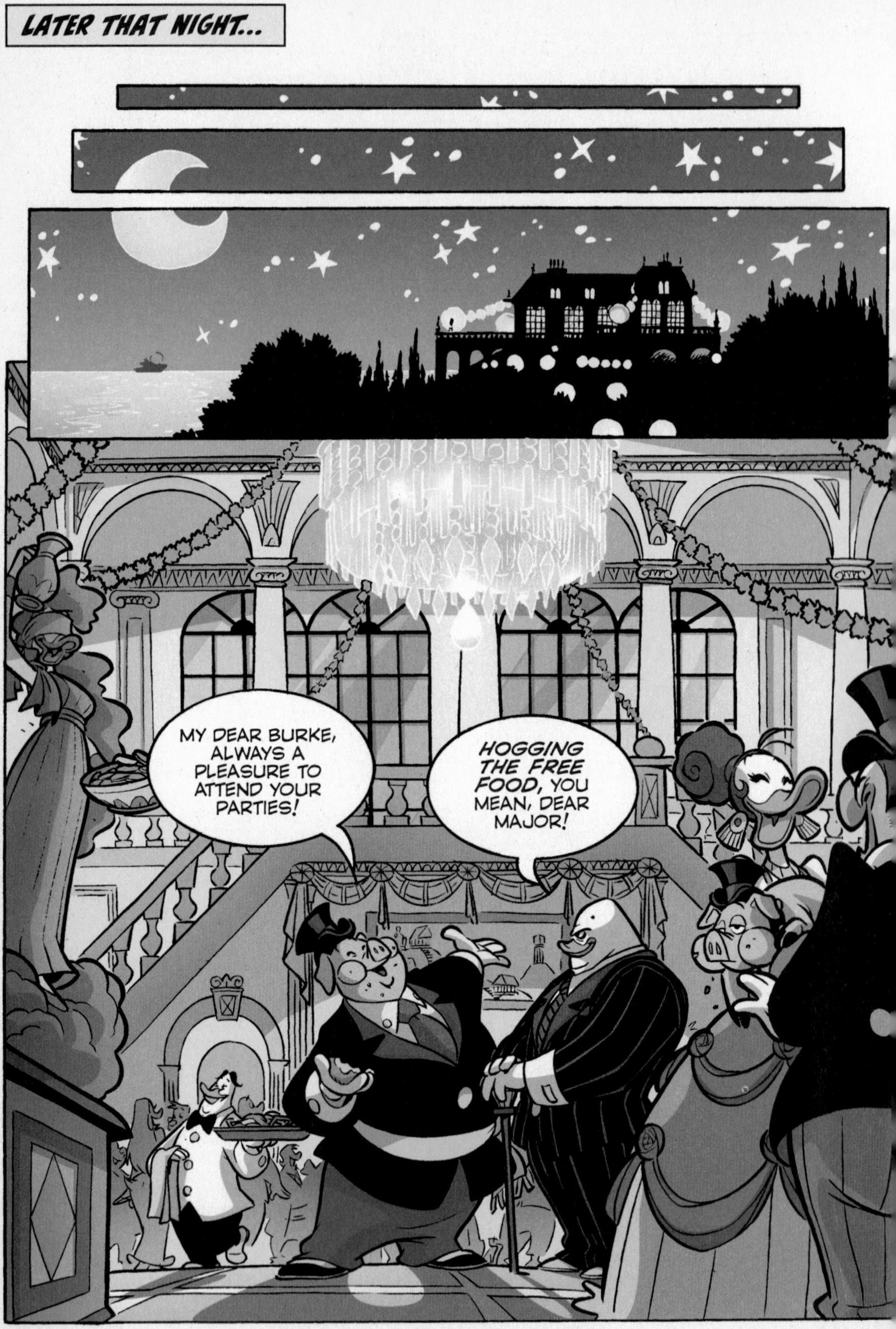
LATER THAT NIGHT...
MY DEAR BURKE, ALWAYS A PLEASURE TO ATTEND YOUR PARTIES!
HOGGING THE FREE FOOD, YOU MEAN, DEAR MAJOR!

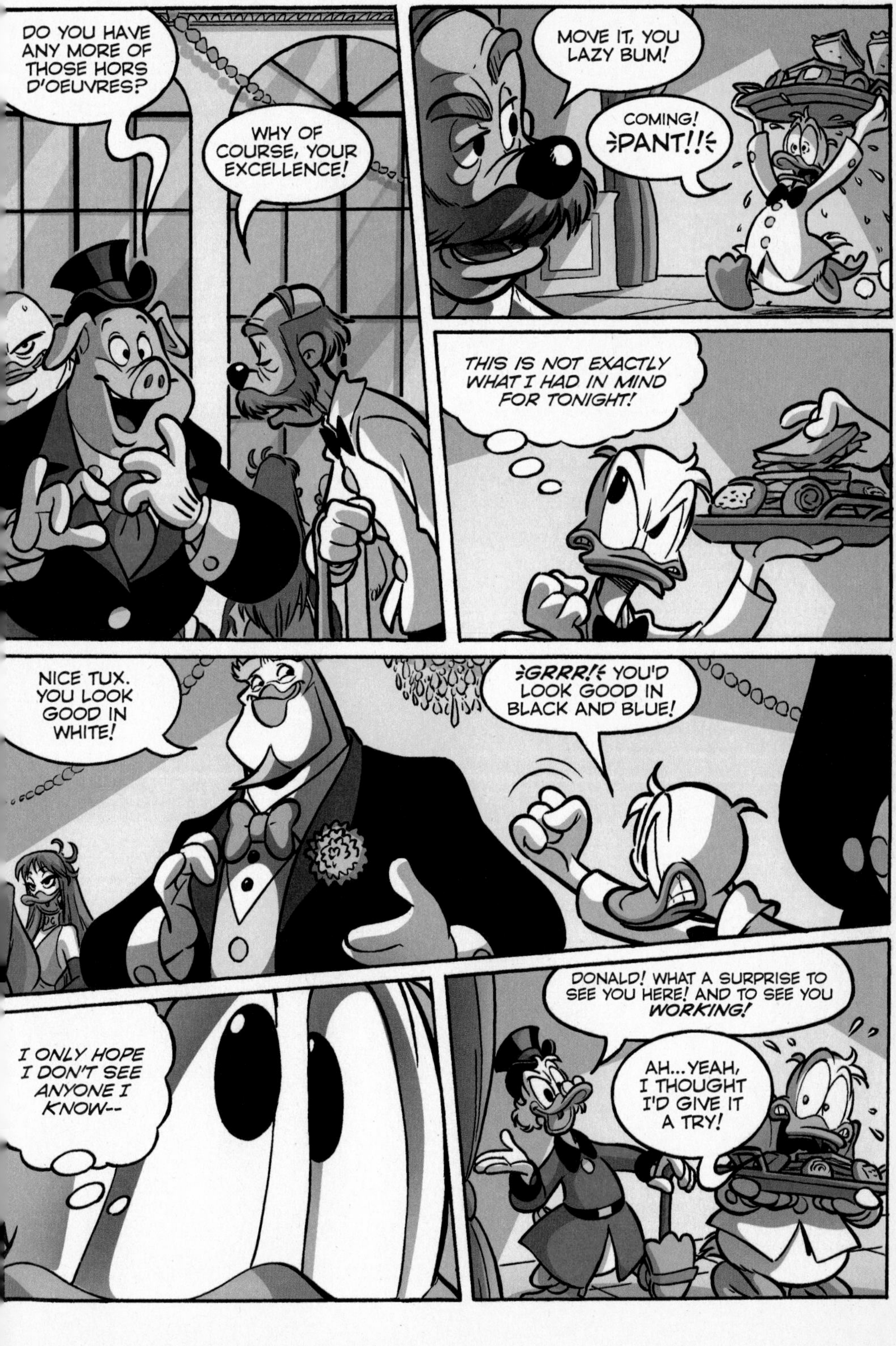
DO YOU HAVE ANY MORE OF THOSE HORS D'OEUVRES?
WHY OF COURSE, YOUR EXCELLENCE!
MOVE IT, YOU LAZY BUM!
COMING! PANT!!
THIS IS NOT EXACTLY WHAT I HAD IN MIND FOR TONIGHT!
NICE TUX. YOU LOOK GOOD IN WHITE!
GRRR! YOU'D LOOK GOOD IN BLACK AND BLUE!
I ONLY HOPE I DON'T SEE ANYONE I KNOW--
DONALD! WHAT A SURPRISE TO SEE YOU HERE! AND TO SEE YOU WORKING!
AH...YEAH, I THOUGHT I'D GIVE IT A TRY!

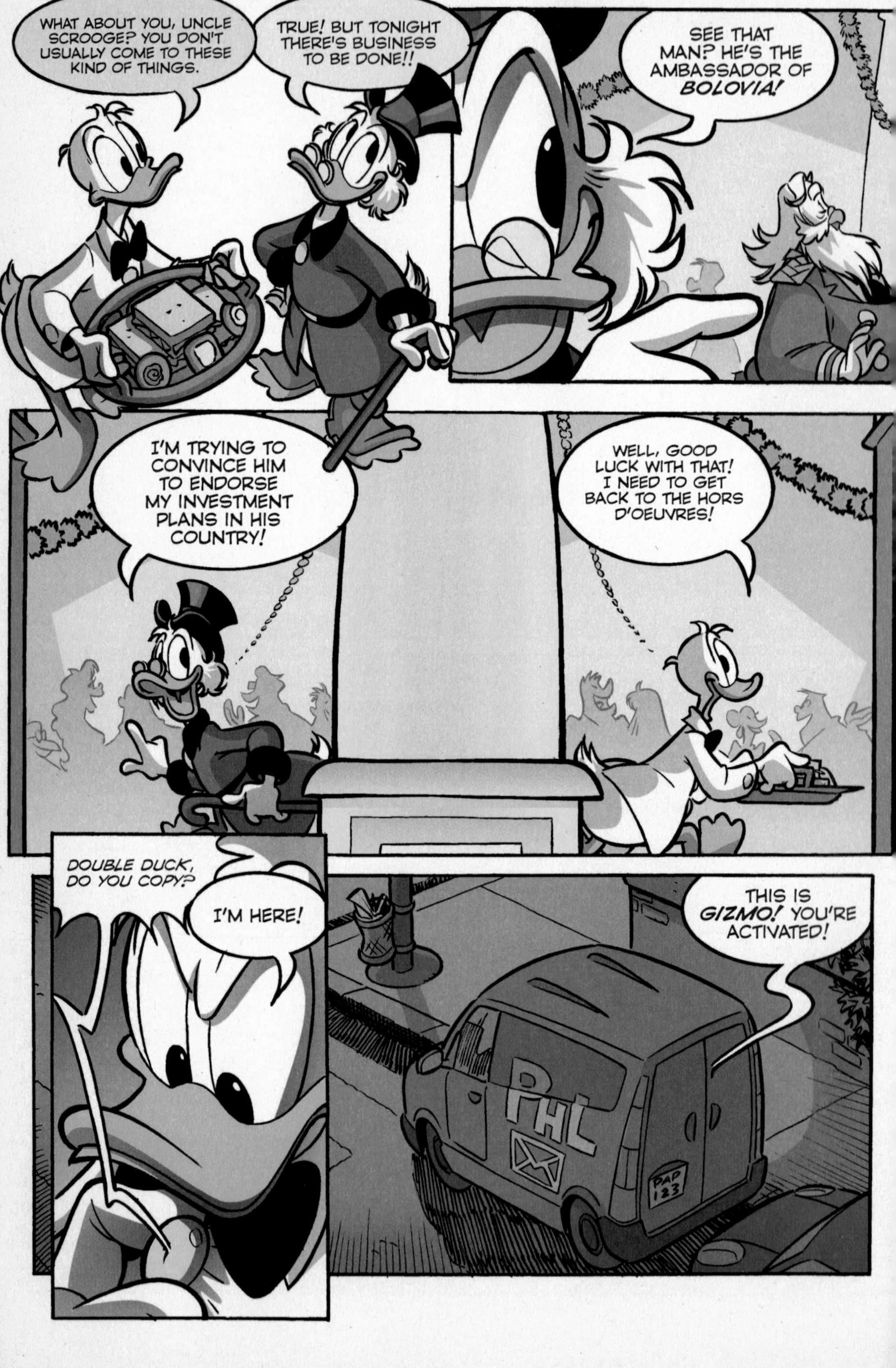
WHAT ABOUT YOU, UNCLE SCROOGE? YOU DON'T USUALLY COME TO THESE KIND OF THINGS.
TRUE! BUT TONIGHT THERE'S BUSINESS TO BE DONE!!
SEE THAT MAN? HE'S THE AMBASSADOR OF BOLOVIA!
I'M TRYING TO CONVINCE HIM TO ENDORSE MY INVESTMENT PLANS IN HIS COUNTRY!
WELL, GOOD LUCK WITH THAT! I NEED TO GET BACK TO THE HORS D'OEUVRES!
DOUBLE DUCK, DO YOU COPY?
I'M HERE!
THIS IS GIZMO! YOU'RE ACTIVATED!
PHL
PAP 123

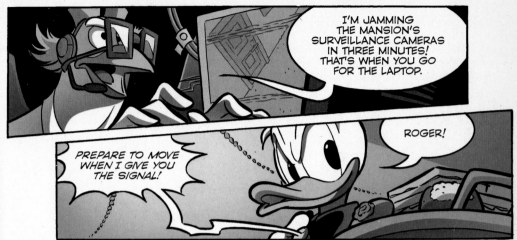

I'M JAMMING THE MANSION'S SURVEILLANCE CAMERAS IN THREE MINUTES! THAT'S WHEN YOU GO FOR THE LAPTOP.

ROGER!

PREPARE TO MOVE WHEN I GIVE YOU THE SIGNAL!

DONALD?! WHAT ARE *YOU* DOING HERE?

FAILING AS A WAITER, APPARENTLY.

ARGH!

WHAT'S THE MATTER? COULDN'T HACK IT AS A STREET SWEEPER?

I CAN SWEEP THE FLOOR WITH YOUR FACE!

COME ON, GLADSTONE! DONALD'S WORKING!

OF COURSE. I'LL LET YOU GET BACK TO YOUR JOB!

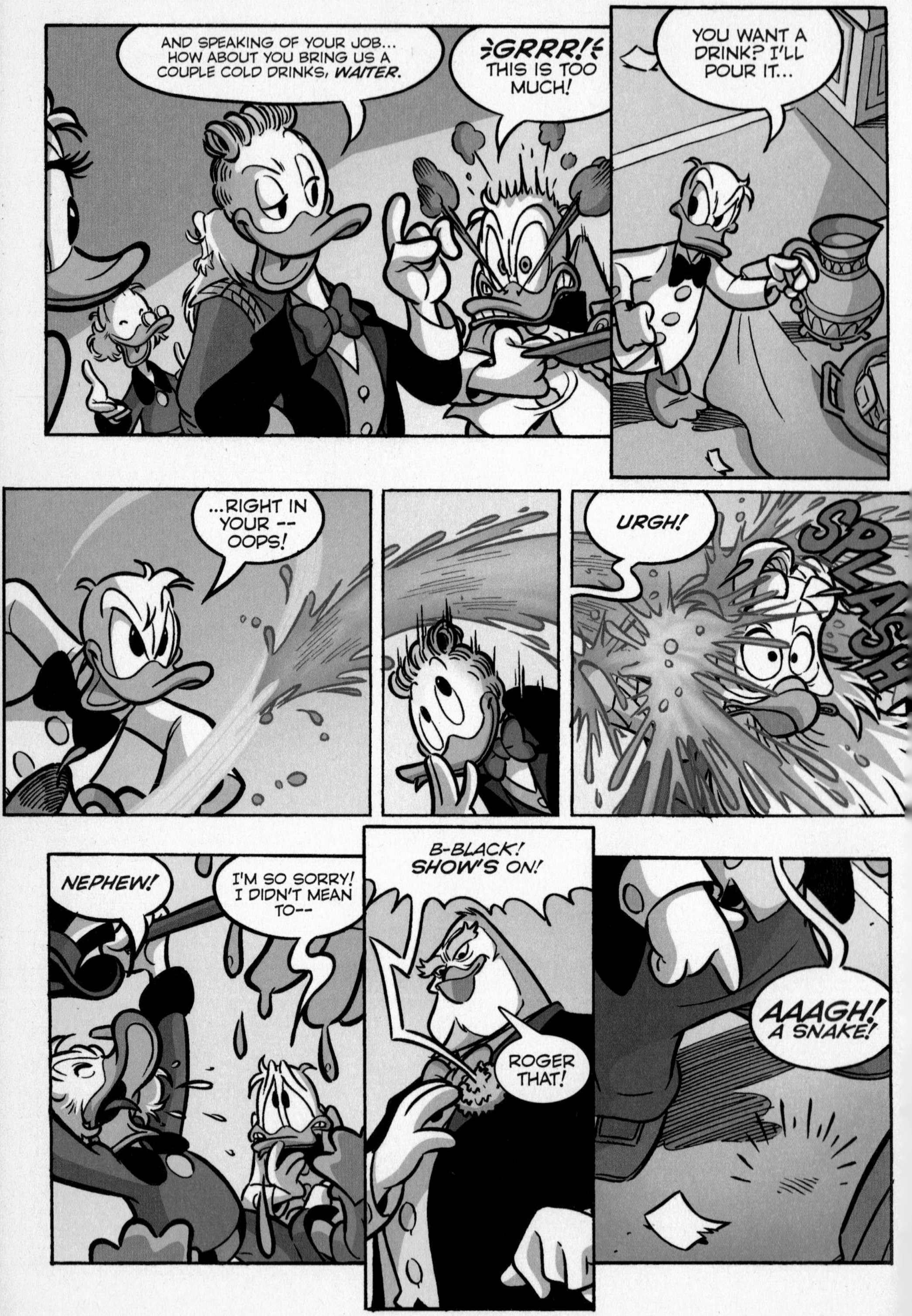
AND SPEAKING OF YOUR JOB... HOW ABOUT YOU BRING US A COUPLE COLD DRINKS, WAITER.
GRRR! THIS IS TOO MUCH!
YOU WANT A DRINK? I'LL POUR IT...
...RIGHT IN YOUR -- OOPS!
URGH!
SPLASH
NEPHEW!
I'M SO SORRY! I DIDN'T MEAN TO--
B-BLACK! SHOW'S ON!
ROGER THAT!
AAAGH! A SNAKE!

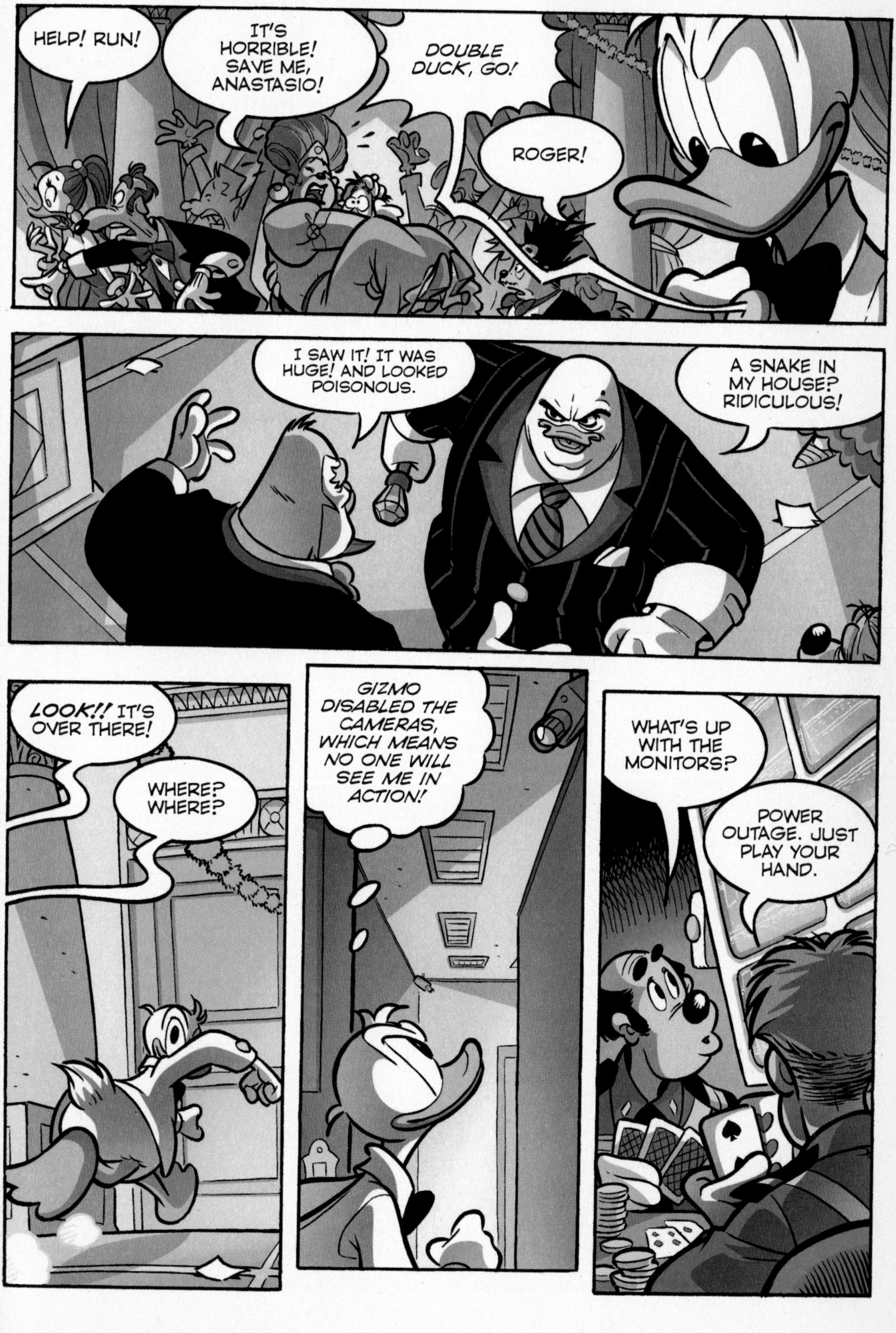
HELP! RUN!
IT'S HORRIBLE! SAVE ME, ANASTASIO!
DOUBLE DUCK, GO!
ROGER!
I SAW IT! IT WAS HUGE! AND LOOKED POISONOUS.
A SNAKE IN MY HOUSE? RIDICULOUS!
LOOK!! IT'S OVER THERE!
WHERE? WHERE?
GIZMO DISABLED THE CAMERAS, WHICH MEANS NO ONE WILL SEE ME IN ACTION!
WHAT'S UP WITH THE MONITORS?
POWER OUTAGE. JUST PLAY YOUR HAND.

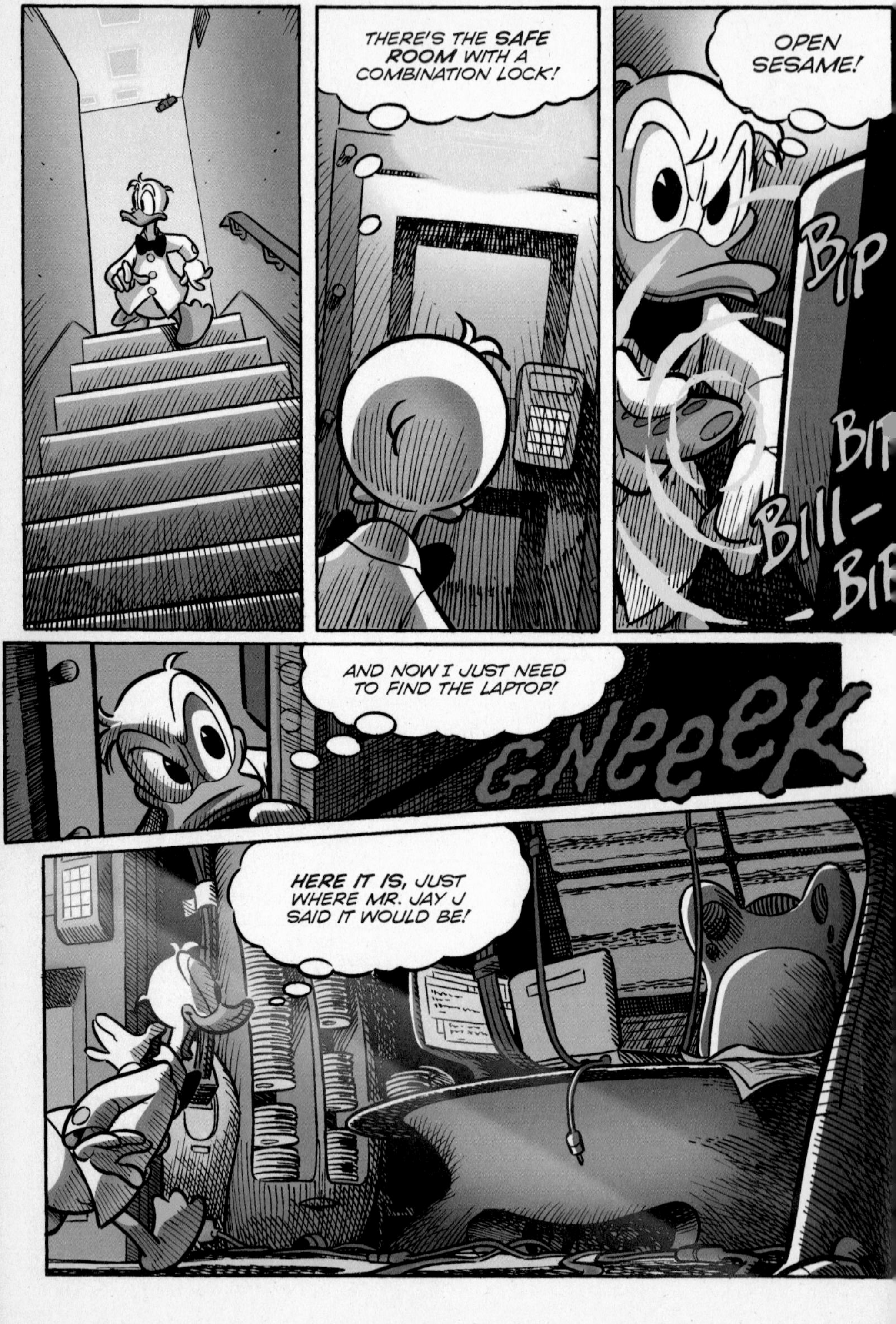
THERE'S THE SAFE ROOM WITH A COMBINATION LOCK!
OPEN SESAME!
BIP
BIT
BIII-
BIP
AND NOW I JUST NEED TO FIND THE LAPTOP!
GNEEEK
HERE IT IS, JUST WHERE MR. JAY J SAID IT WOULD BE!

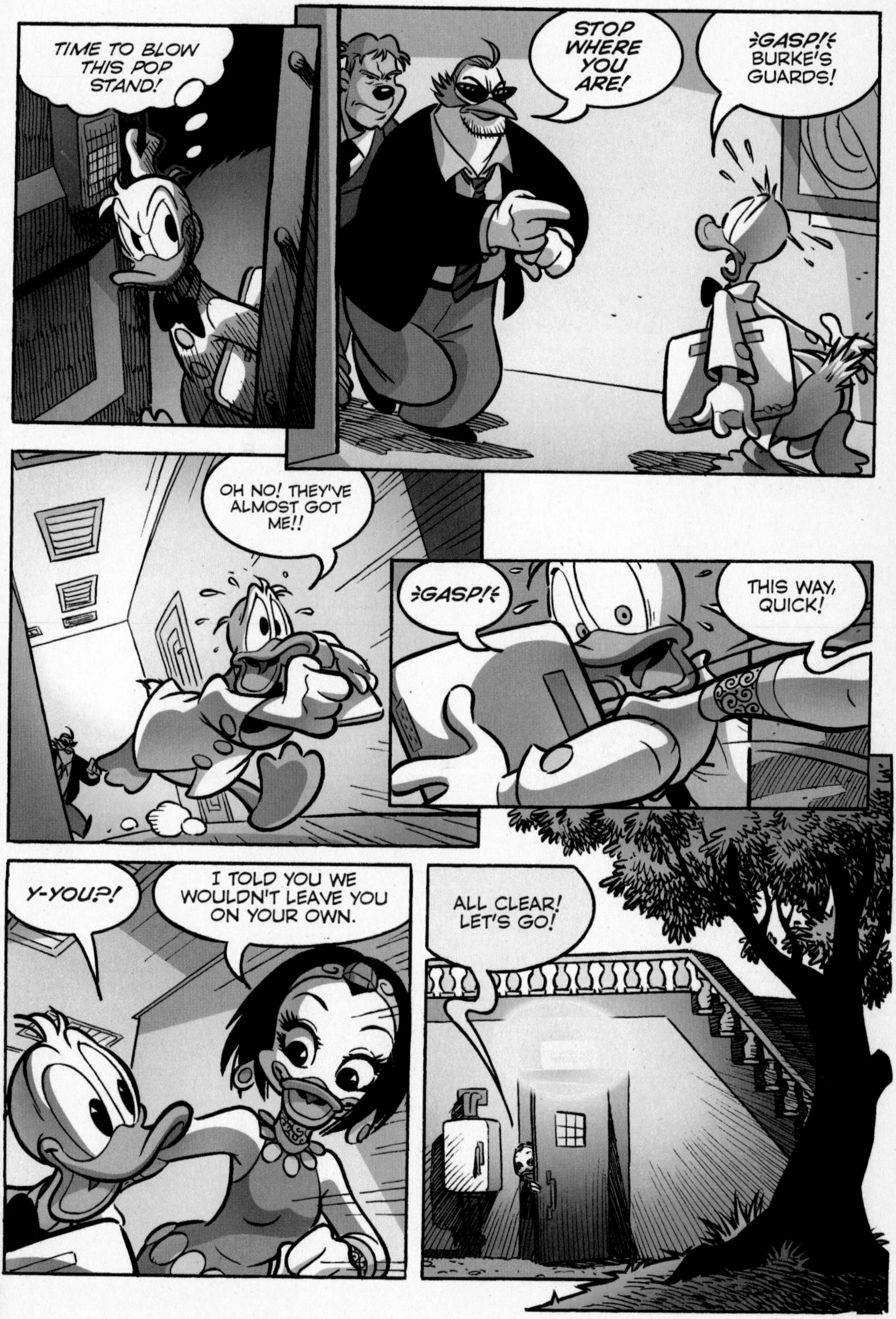
TIME TO BLOW THIS POP STAND!
STOP WHERE YOU ARE!
GASP! BURKE'S GUARDS!
OH NO! THEY'VE ALMOST GOT ME!!
GASP!
THIS WAY, QUICK!
Y-YOU?!
I TOLD YOU WE WOULDN'T LEAVE YOU ON YOUR OWN.
ALL CLEAR! LET'S GO!

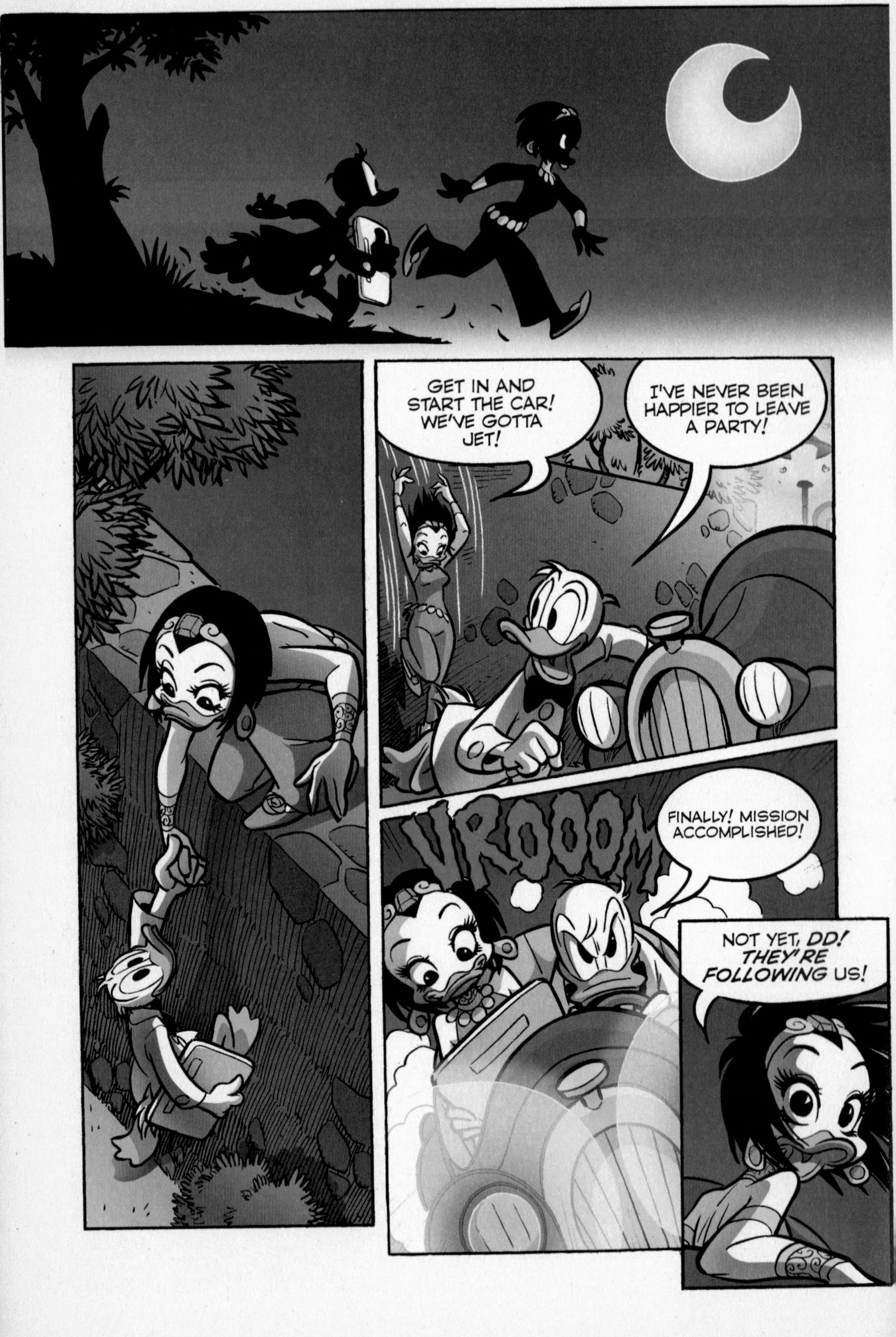
GET IN AND START THE CAR! WE'VE GOTTA JET!
I'VE NEVER BEEN HAPPIER TO LEAVE A PARTY!
VROOOM
FINALLY! MISSION ACCOMPLISHED!
NOT YET, *DD! THEY'RE FOLLOWING* US!

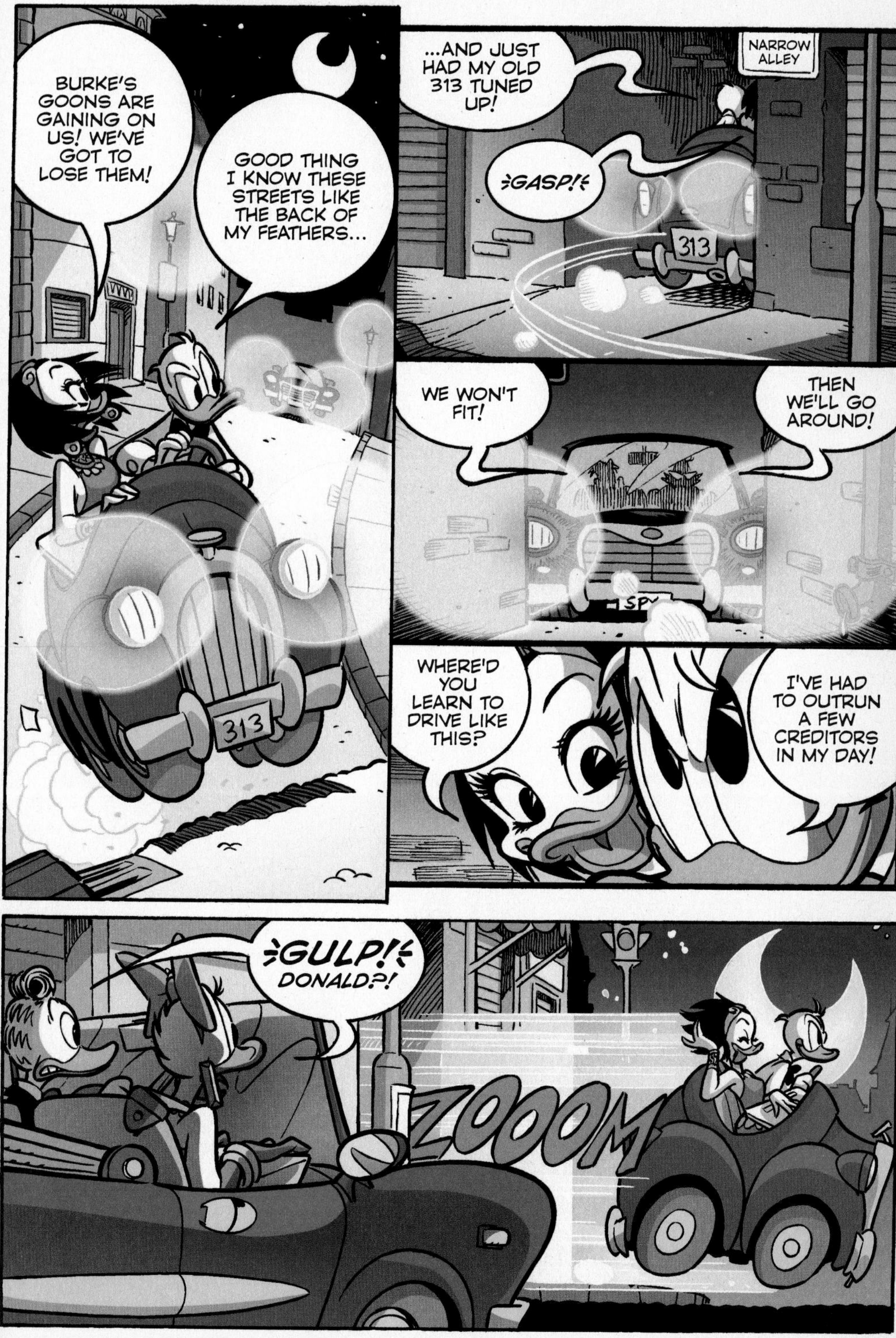
BURKE'S GOONS ARE GAINING ON US! WE'VE GOT TO LOSE THEM!
GOOD THING I KNOW THESE STREETS LIKE THE BACK OF MY FEATHERS...
...AND JUST HAD MY OLD 313 TUNED UP!
NARROW ALLEY
GASP!
313
WE WON'T FIT!
THEN WE'LL GO AROUND!
WHERE'D YOU LEARN TO DRIVE LIKE THIS?
I'VE HAD TO OUTRUN A FEW CREDITORS IN MY DAY!
GULP! DONALD?!
ZOOOM

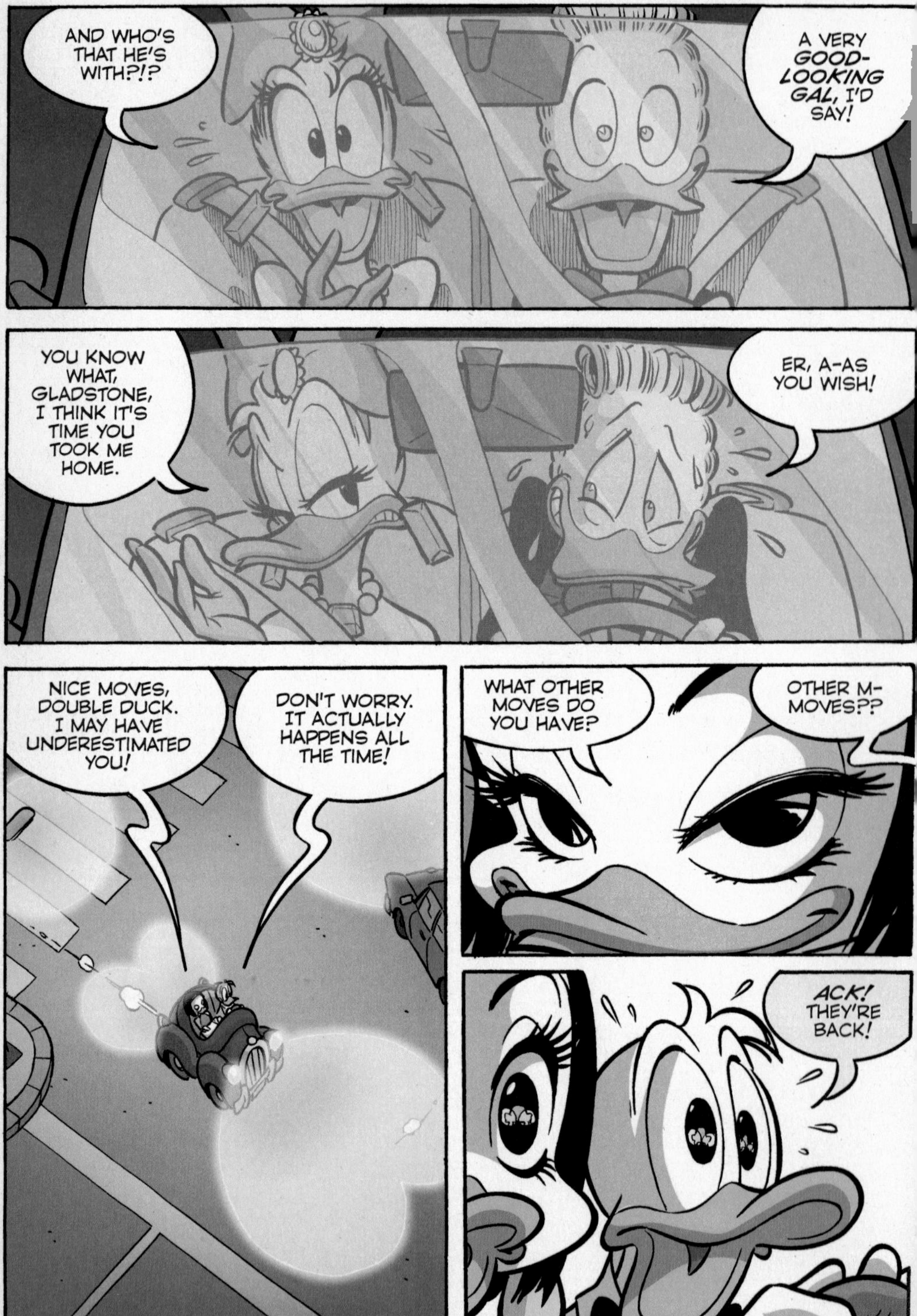
AND WHO'S THAT HE'S WITH?!?
A VERY *GOOD-LOOKING GAL*, I'D SAY!
YOU KNOW WHAT, GLADSTONE, I THINK IT'S TIME YOU TOOK ME HOME.
ER, A-AS YOU WISH!
NICE MOVES, DOUBLE DUCK. I MAY HAVE UNDERESTIMATED YOU!
DON'T WORRY. IT ACTUALLY HAPPENS ALL THE TIME!
WHAT OTHER MOVES DO YOU HAVE?
OTHER M-MOVES??
ACK! THEY'RE BACK!

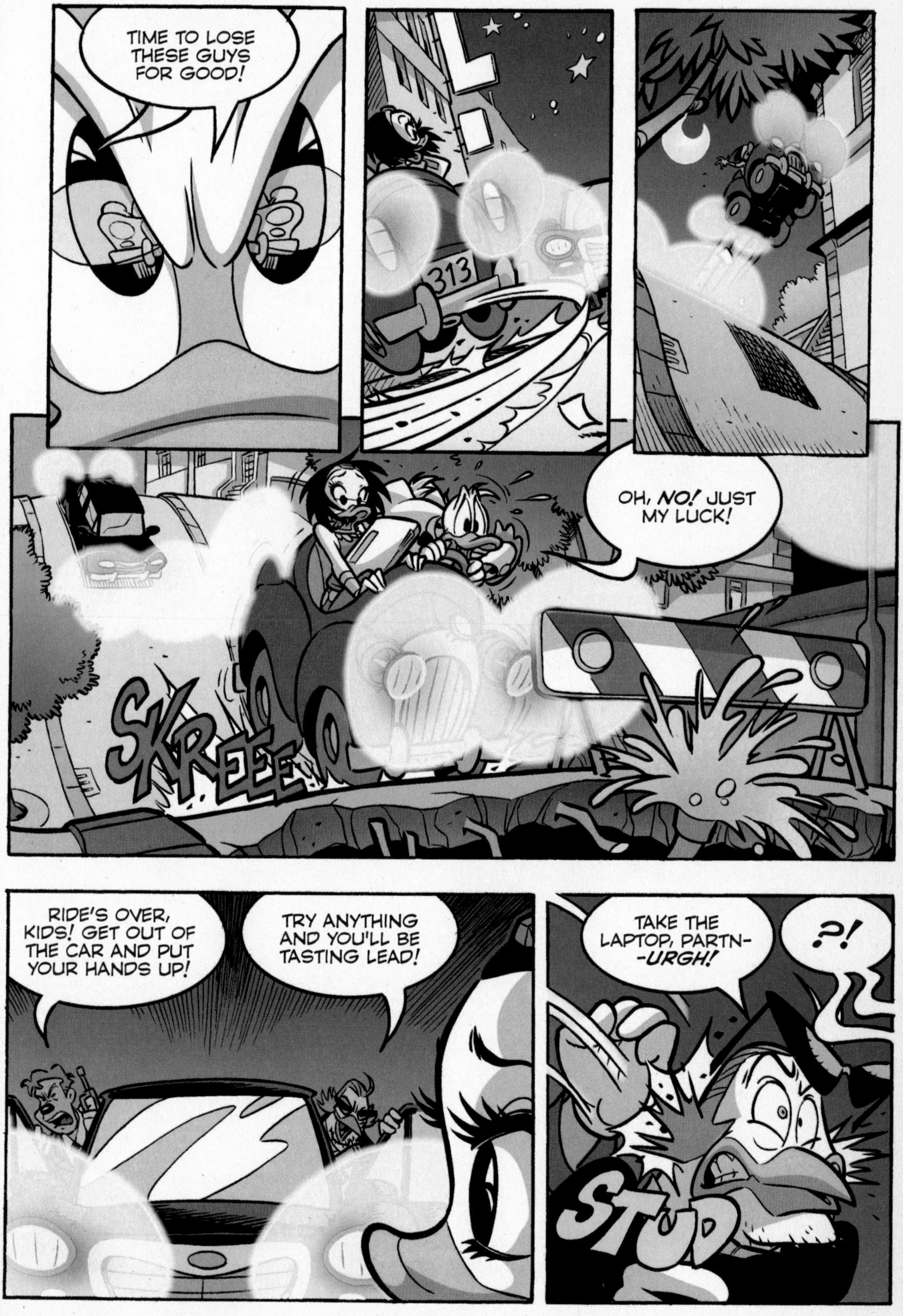
TIME TO LOSE THESE GUYS FOR GOOD!
313
OH, NO! JUST MY LUCK!
SKREEEE
RIDE'S OVER, KIDS! GET OUT OF THE CAR AND PUT YOUR HANDS UP!
TRY ANYTHING AND YOU'LL BE TASTING LEAD!
TAKE THE LAPTOP, PARTN- -URGH!
?!
STUD

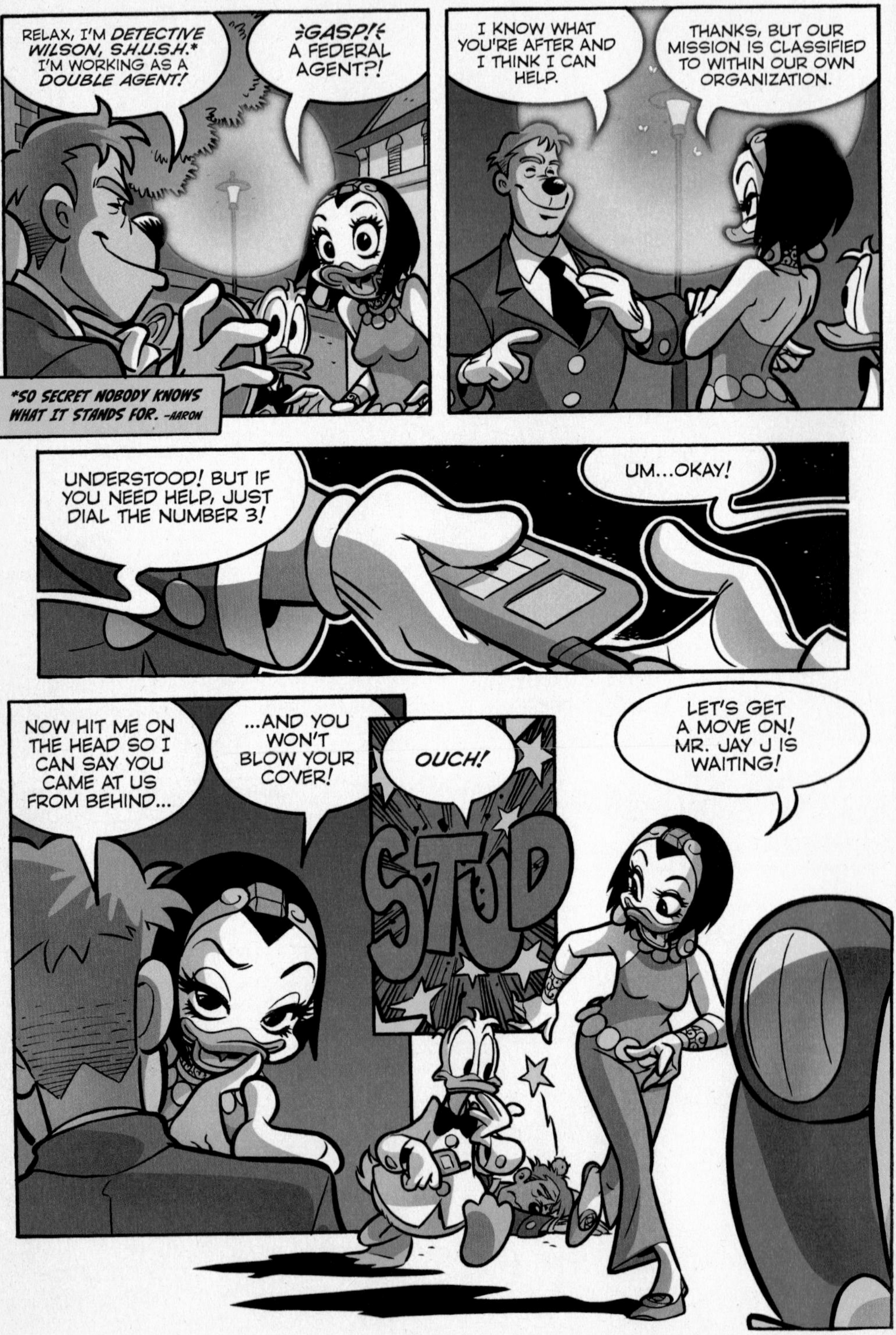

RELAX, I'M DETECTIVE WILSON, S.H.U.S.H.* I'M WORKING AS A DOUBLE AGENT!
GASP! A FEDERAL AGENT?!
*SO SECRET NOBODY KNOWS WHAT IT STANDS FOR. -AARON
I KNOW WHAT YOU'RE AFTER AND I THINK I CAN HELP.
THANKS, BUT OUR MISSION IS CLASSIFIED TO WITHIN OUR OWN ORGANIZATION.
UNDERSTOOD! BUT IF YOU NEED HELP, JUST DIAL THE NUMBER 3!
UM...OKAY!
NOW HIT ME ON THE HEAD SO I CAN SAY YOU CAME AT US FROM BEHIND...
...AND YOU WON'T BLOW YOUR COVER!
OUCH!
STUD
LET'S GET A MOVE ON! MR. JAY J IS WAITING!

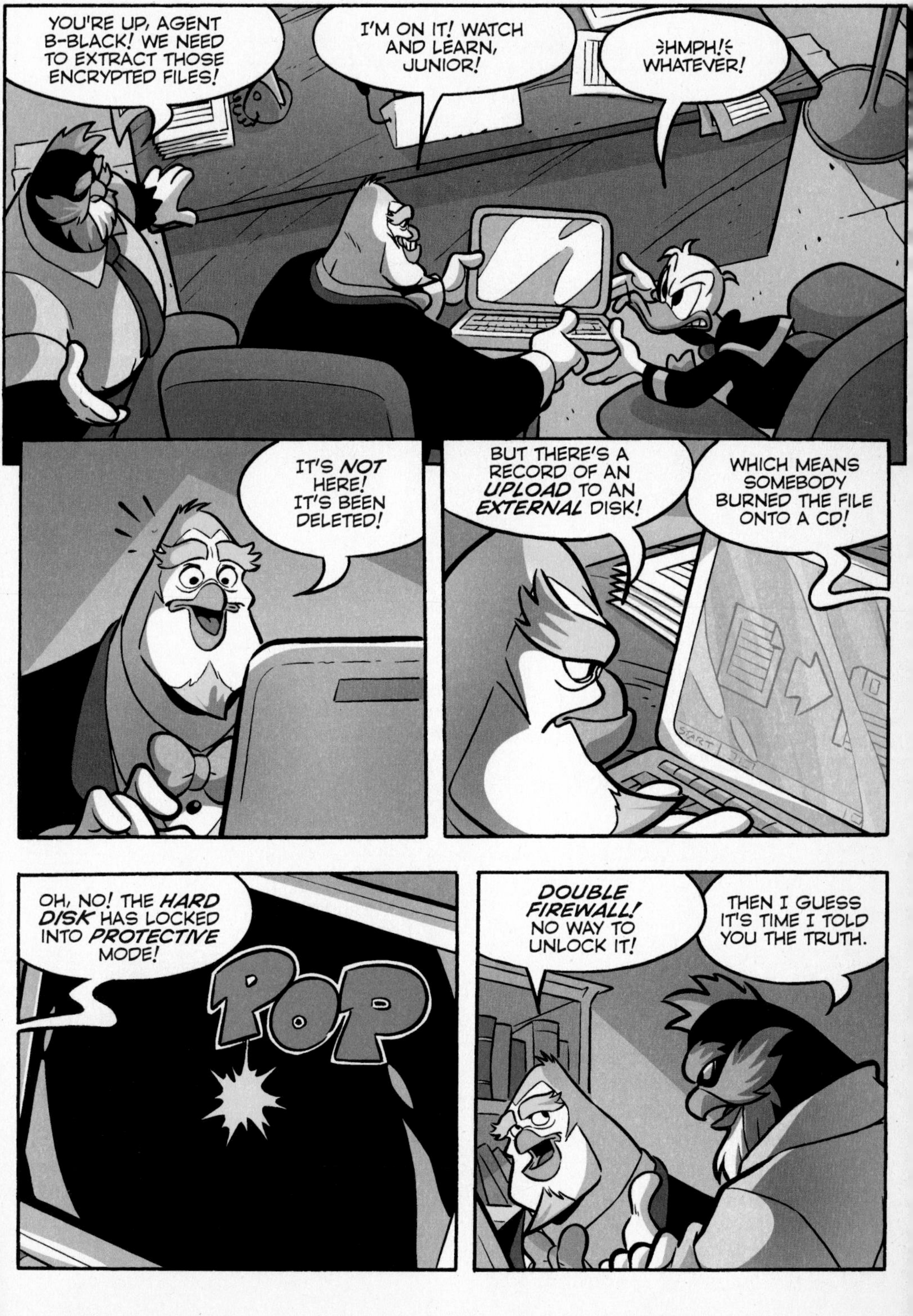
YOU'RE UP, AGENT B-BLACK! WE NEED TO EXTRACT THOSE ENCRYPTED FILES!
I'M ON IT! WATCH AND LEARN, JUNIOR!
HMPH! WHATEVER!
IT'S NOT HERE! IT'S BEEN DELETED!
BUT THERE'S A RECORD OF AN UPLOAD TO AN EXTERNAL DISK!
WHICH MEANS SOMEBODY BURNED THE FILE ONTO A CD!
START
OH, NO! THE HARD DISK HAS LOCKED INTO PROTECTIVE MODE!
POP
DOUBLE FIREWALL! NO WAY TO UNLOCK IT!
THEN I GUESS IT'S TIME I TOLD YOU THE TRUTH.

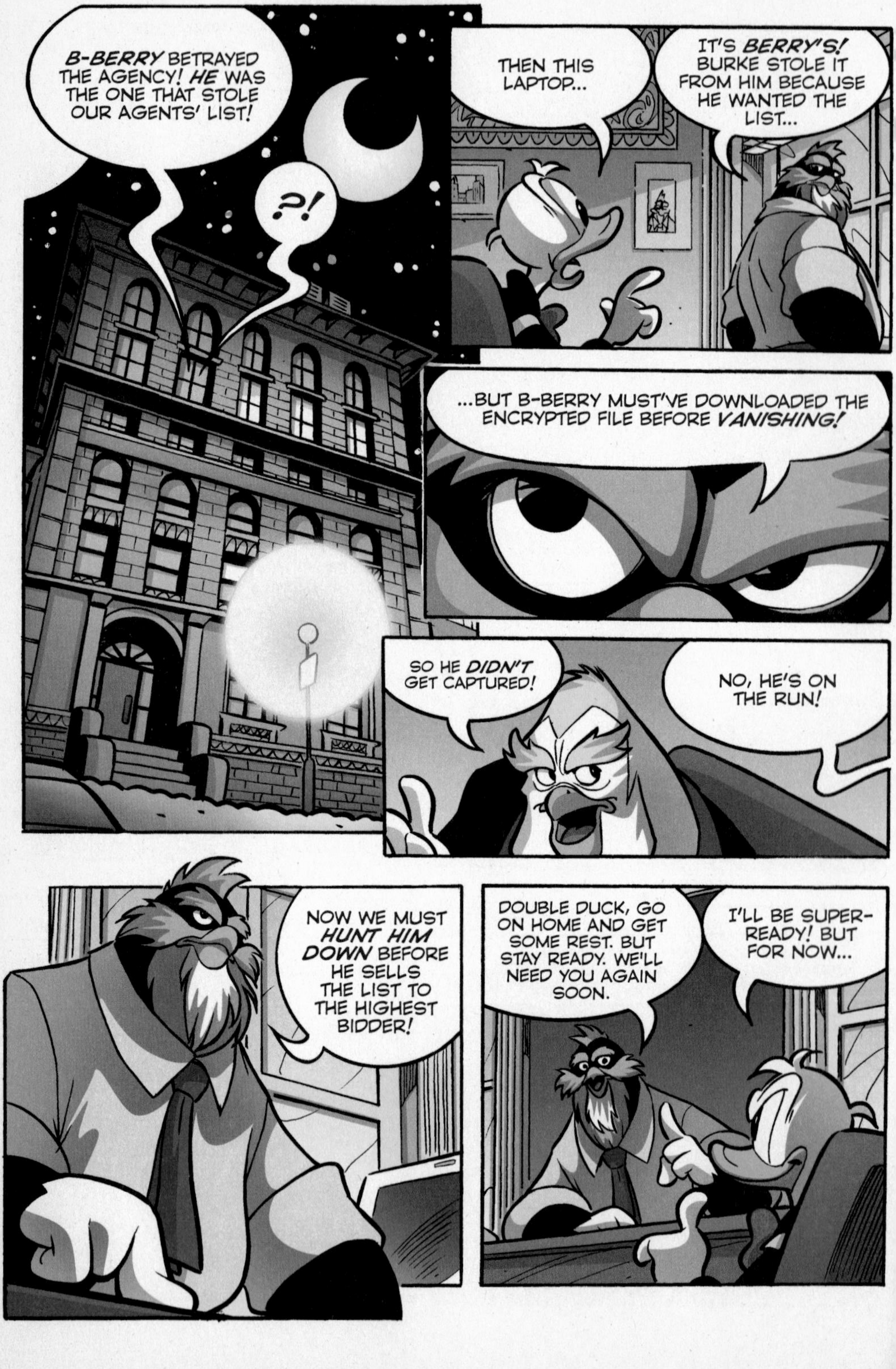
B-BERRY BETRAYED THE AGENCY! HE WAS THE ONE THAT STOLE OUR AGENTS' LIST!
?!
THEN THIS LAPTOP...
IT'S BERRY'S! BURKE STOLE IT FROM HIM BECAUSE HE WANTED THE LIST...
...BUT B-BERRY MUST'VE DOWNLOADED THE ENCRYPTED FILE BEFORE VANISHING!
SO HE DIDN'T GET CAPTURED!
NO, HE'S ON THE RUN!
NOW WE MUST HUNT HIM DOWN BEFORE HE SELLS THE LIST TO THE HIGHEST BIDDER!
DOUBLE DUCK, GO ON HOME AND GET SOME REST. BUT STAY READY. WE'LL NEED YOU AGAIN SOON.
I'LL BE SUPER-READY! BUT FOR NOW...

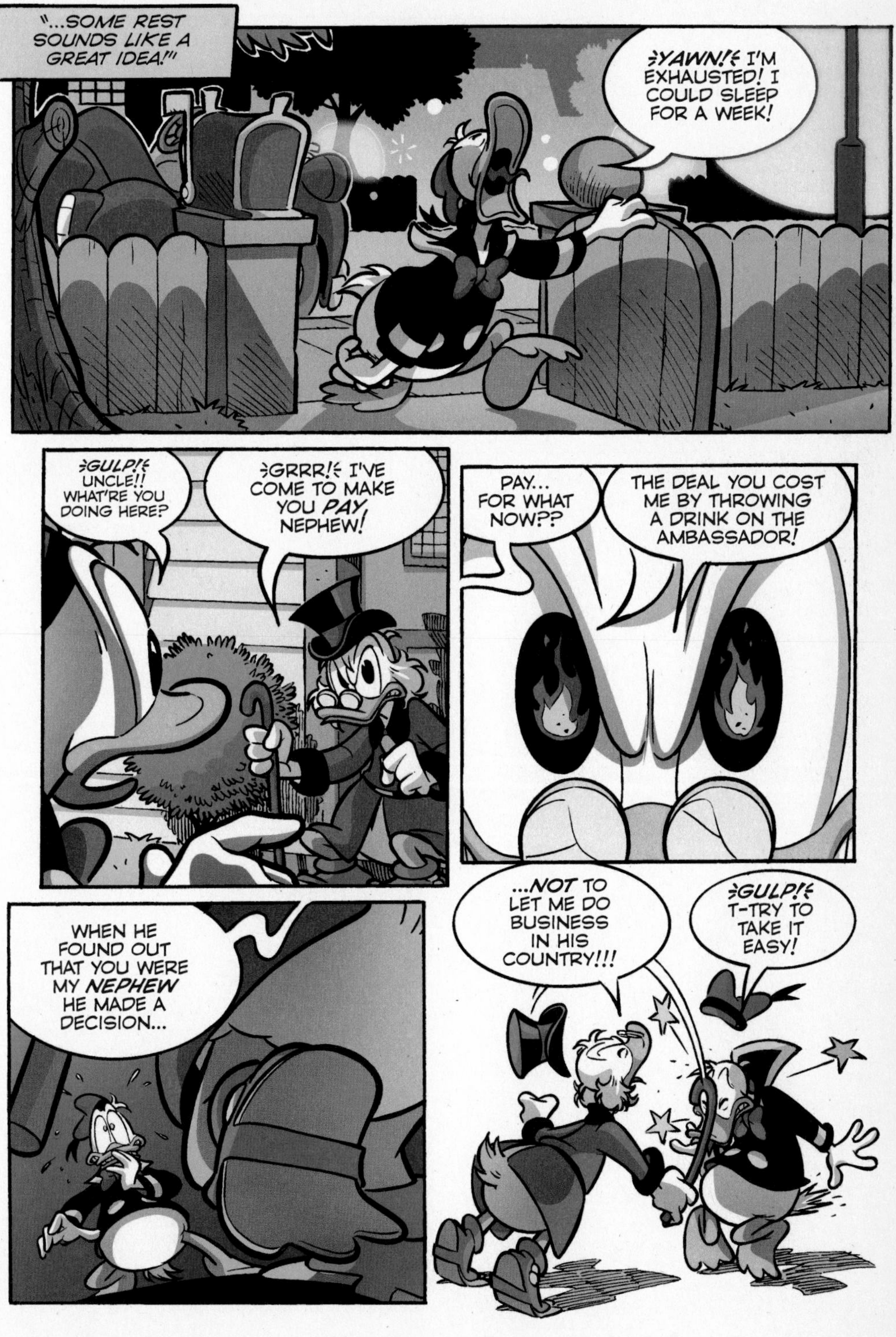
"...SOME REST SOUNDS LIKE A GREAT IDEA!"
YAWN! I'M EXHAUSTED! I COULD SLEEP FOR A WEEK!
GULP! UNCLE!! WHAT'RE YOU DOING HERE?
GRRR! I'VE COME TO MAKE YOU PAY, NEPHEW!
PAY... FOR WHAT NOW??
THE DEAL YOU COST ME BY THROWING A DRINK ON THE AMBASSADOR!
WHEN HE FOUND OUT THAT YOU WERE MY NEPHEW HE MADE A DECISION...
...NOT TO LET ME DO BUSINESS IN HIS COUNTRY!!!
GULP! T-TRY TO TAKE IT EASY!

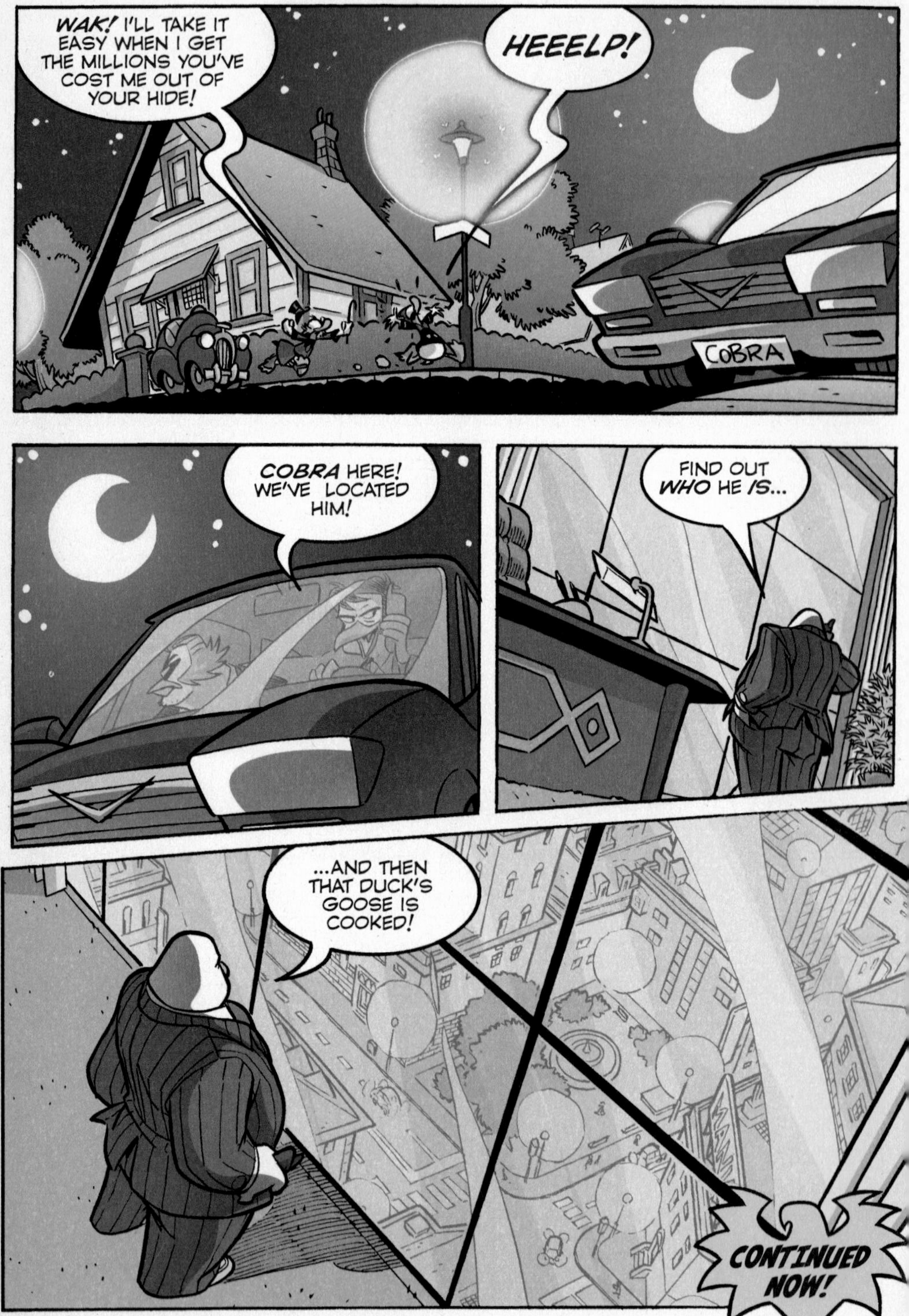
WAK! I'LL TAKE IT EASY WHEN I GET THE MILLIONS YOU'VE COST ME OUT OF YOUR HIDE!
HEEELP!
COBRA
COBRA HERE! WE'VE LOCATED HIM!
FIND OUT WHO HE IS...
...AND THEN THAT DUCK'S GOOSE IS COOKED!
CONTINUED NOW!

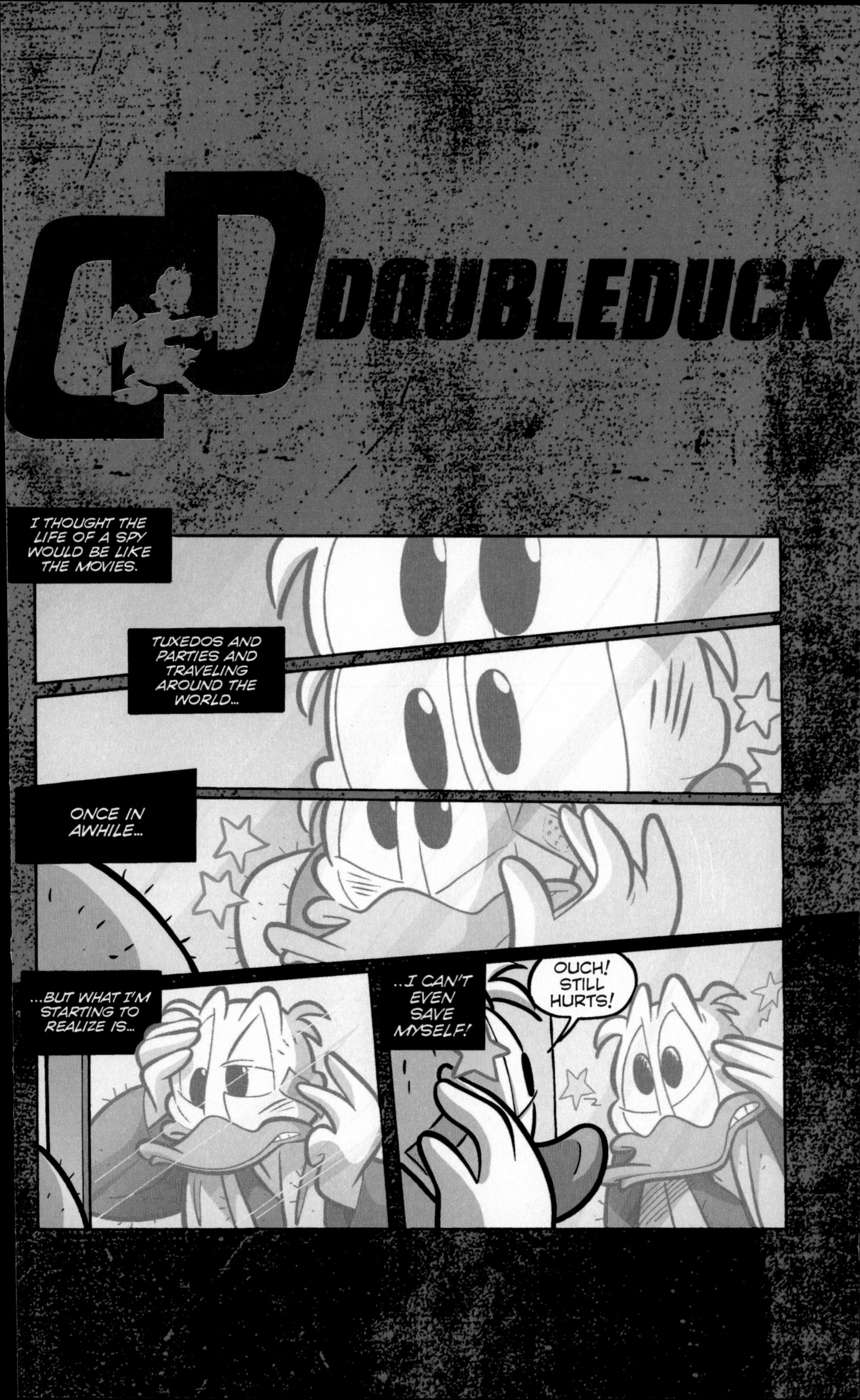
DOUBLEDUCK
I THOUGHT THE LIFE OF A SPY WOULD BE LIKE THE MOVIES.
TUXEDOS AND PARTIES AND TRAVELING AROUND THE WORLD...
ONCE IN AWHILE...
...BUT WHAT I'M STARTING TO REALIZE IS...
...I CAN'T EVEN SAVE MYSELF!
OUCH! STILL HURTS!

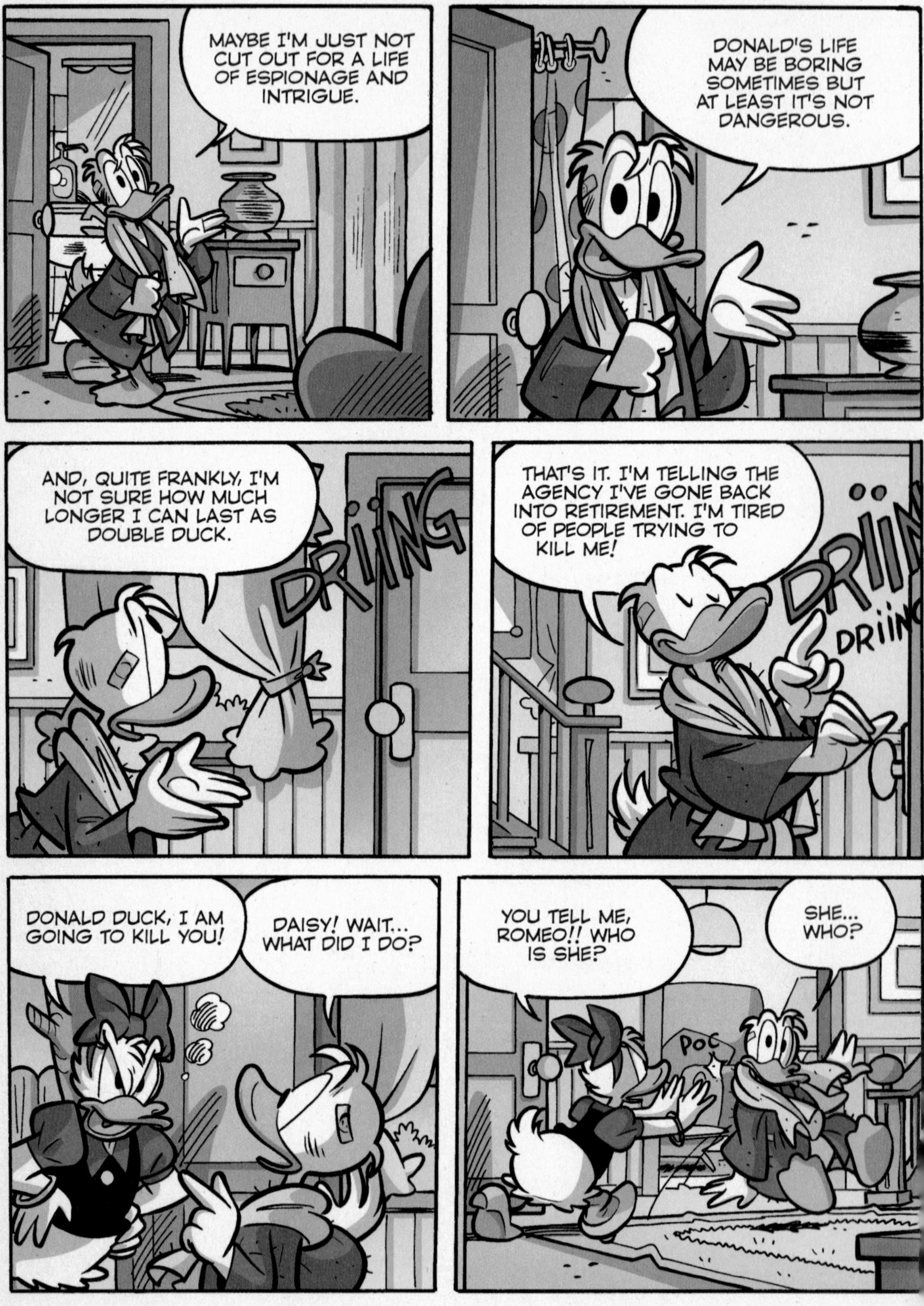

MAYBE I'M JUST NOT CUT OUT FOR A LIFE OF ESPIONAGE AND INTRIGUE.
DONALD'S LIFE MAY BE BORING SOMETIMES BUT AT LEAST IT'S NOT DANGEROUS.
AND, QUITE FRANKLY, I'M NOT SURE HOW MUCH LONGER I CAN LAST AS DOUBLE DUCK.
DRIING
THAT'S IT. I'M TELLING THE AGENCY I'VE GONE BACK INTO RETIREMENT. I'M TIRED OF PEOPLE TRYING TO KILL ME!
DONALD DUCK, I AM GOING TO KILL YOU!
DAISY! WAIT... WHAT DID I DO?
YOU TELL ME, ROMEO!! WHO IS SHE?
SHE... WHO?
POC

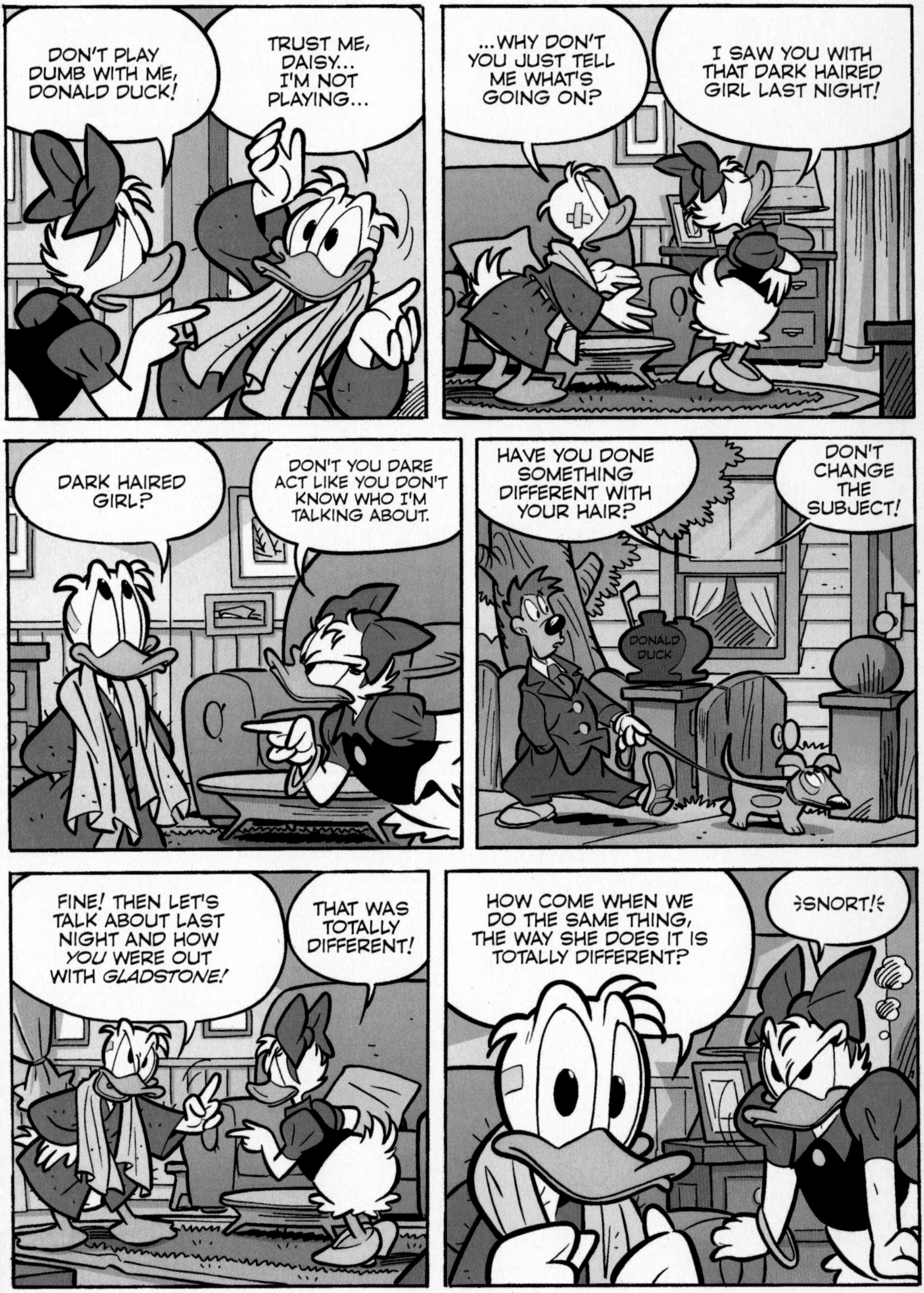
DON'T PLAY DUMB WITH ME, DONALD DUCK!
TRUST ME, DAISY... I'M NOT PLAYING...
...WHY DON'T YOU JUST TELL ME WHAT'S GOING ON?
I SAW YOU WITH THAT DARK HAIRED GIRL LAST NIGHT!
DARK HAIRED GIRL?
DON'T YOU DARE ACT LIKE YOU DON'T KNOW WHO I'M TALKING ABOUT.
HAVE YOU DONE SOMETHING DIFFERENT WITH YOUR HAIR?
DON'T CHANGE THE SUBJECT!
DONALD DUCK
FINE! THEN LET'S TALK ABOUT LAST NIGHT AND HOW YOU WERE OUT WITH GLADSTONE!
THAT WAS TOTALLY DIFFERENT!
HOW COME WHEN WE DO THE SAME THING, THE WAY SHE DOES IT IS TOTALLY DIFFERENT?
SNORT!

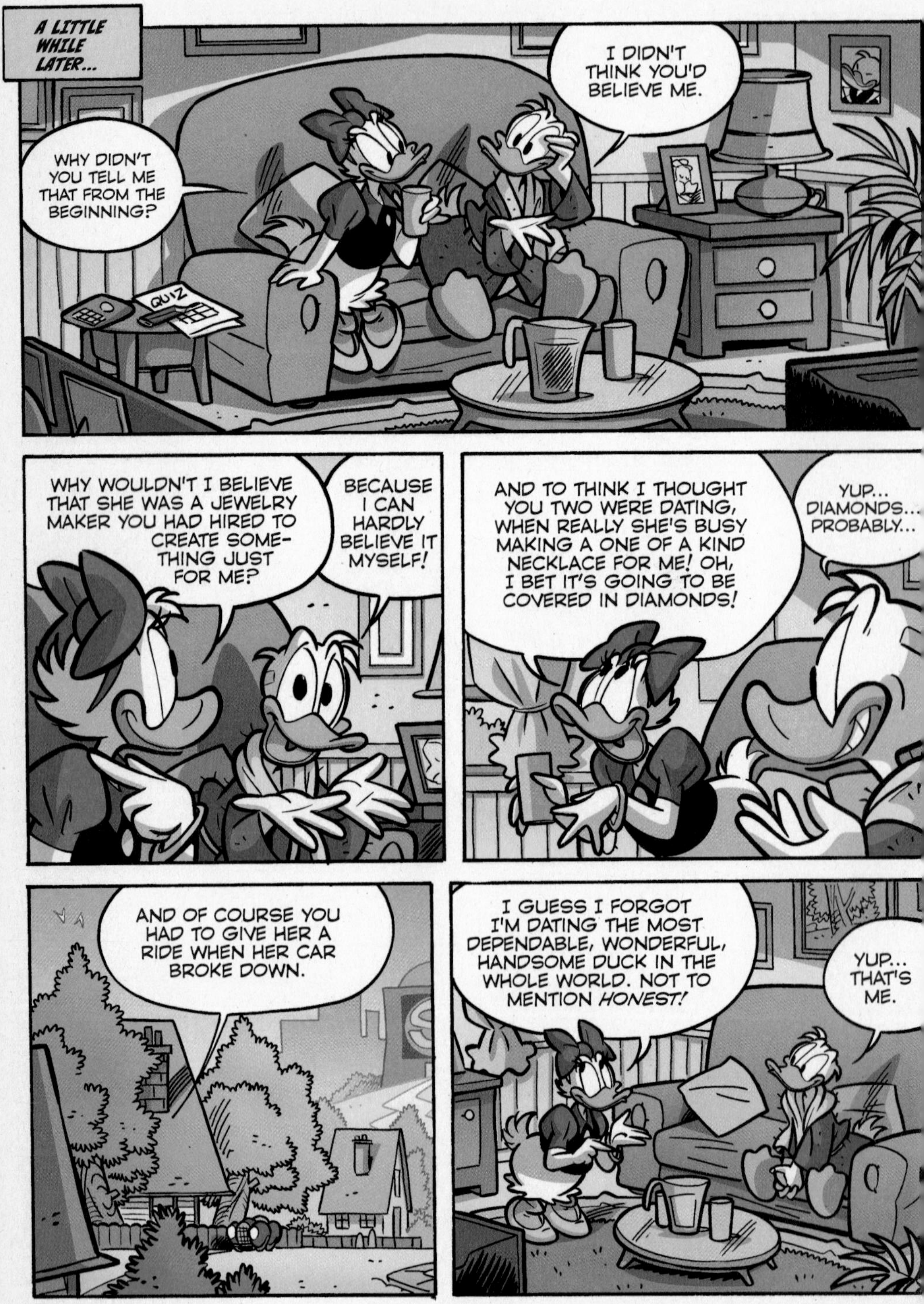
A LITTLE WHILE LATER...
WHY DIDN'T YOU TELL ME THAT FROM THE BEGINNING?
I DIDN'T THINK YOU'D BELIEVE ME.
QUIZ
WHY WOULDN'T I BELIEVE THAT SHE WAS A JEWELRY MAKER YOU HAD HIRED TO CREATE SOME-THING JUST FOR ME?
BECAUSE I CAN HARDLY BELIEVE IT MYSELF!
AND TO THINK I THOUGHT YOU TWO WERE DATING, WHEN REALLY SHE'S BUSY MAKING A ONE OF A KIND NECKLACE FOR ME! OH, I BET IT'S GOING TO BE COVERED IN DIAMONDS!
YUP... DIAMONDS... PROBABLY...
AND OF COURSE YOU HAD TO GIVE HER A RIDE WHEN HER CAR BROKE DOWN.
I GUESS I FORGOT I'M DATING THE MOST DEPENDABLE, WONDERFUL, HANDSOME DUCK IN THE WHOLE WORLD. NOT TO MENTION *HONEST!*
YUP... THAT'S ME.

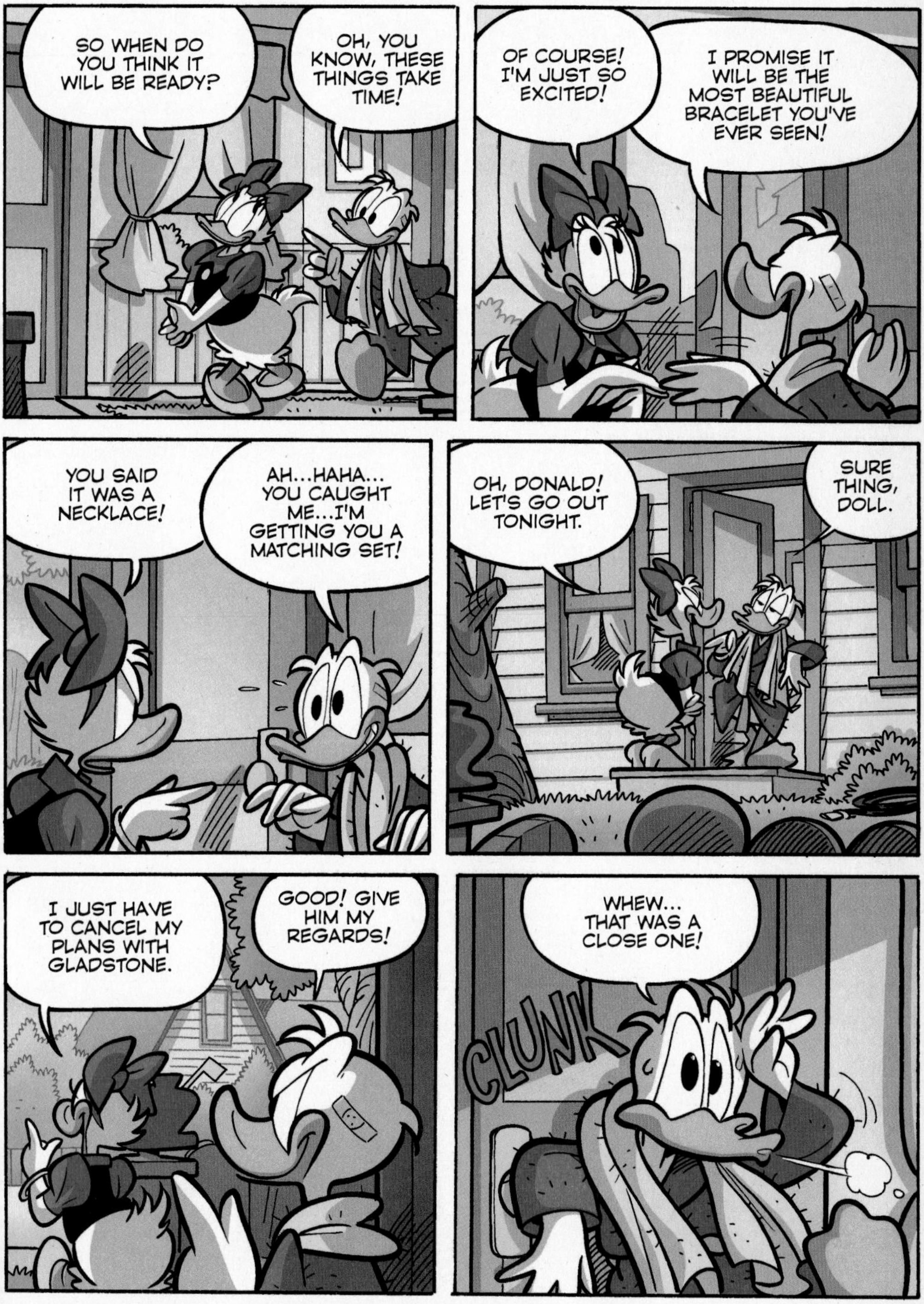

SO WHEN DO YOU THINK IT WILL BE READY?
OH, YOU KNOW, THESE THINGS TAKE TIME!
OF COURSE! I'M JUST SO EXCITED!
I PROMISE IT WILL BE THE MOST BEAUTIFUL BRACELET YOU'VE EVER SEEN!
YOU SAID IT WAS A NECKLACE!
AH...HAHA... YOU CAUGHT ME...I'M GETTING YOU A MATCHING SET!
OH, DONALD! LET'S GO OUT TONIGHT.
SURE THING, DOLL.
I JUST HAVE TO CANCEL MY PLANS WITH GLADSTONE.
GOOD! GIVE HIM MY REGARDS!
WHEW... THAT WAS A CLOSE ONE!
CLUNK

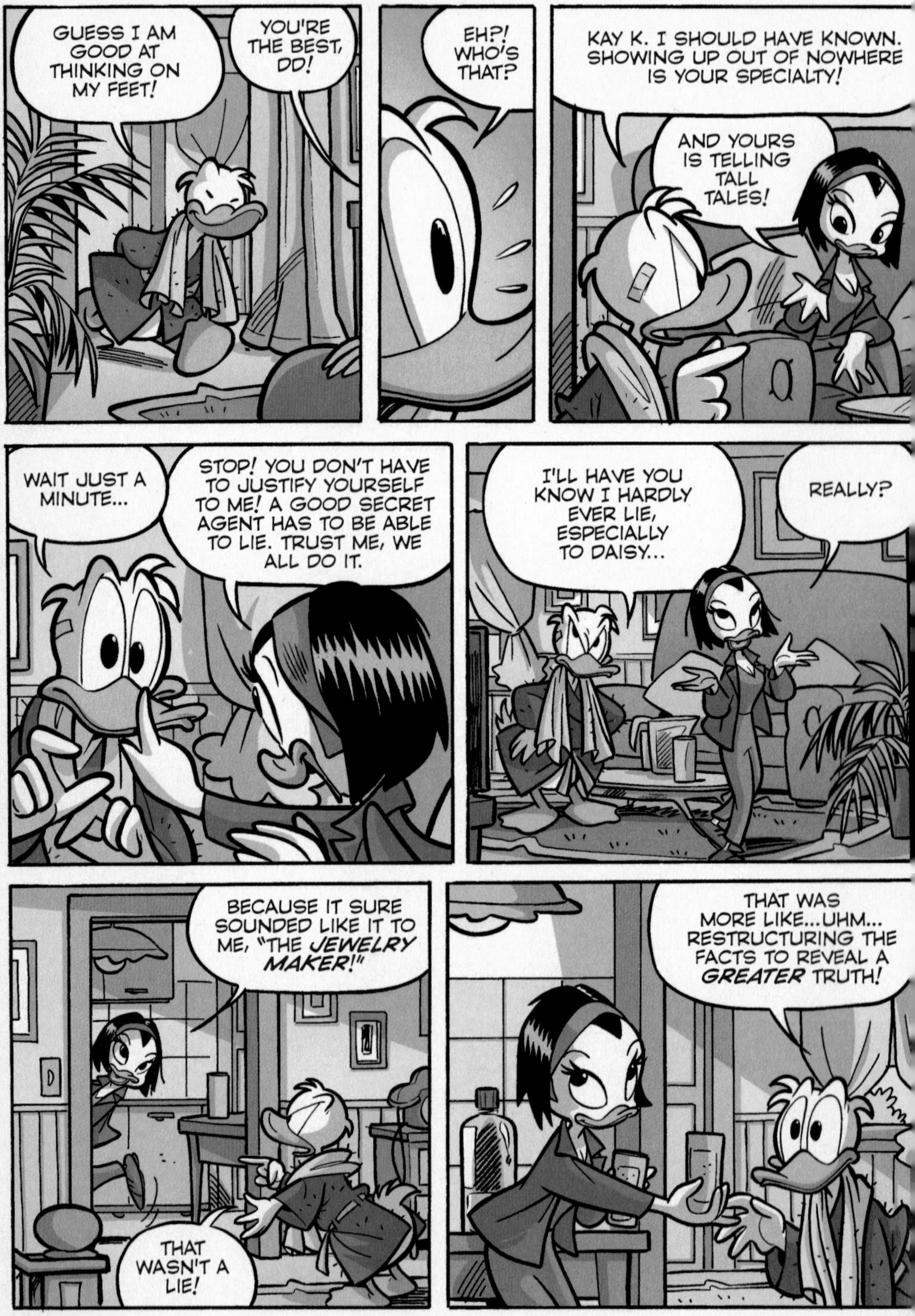
GUESS I AM GOOD AT THINKING ON MY FEET!
YOU'RE THE BEST, DD!
EH?! WHO'S THAT?
KAY K. I SHOULD HAVE KNOWN. SHOWING UP OUT OF NOWHERE IS YOUR SPECIALTY!
AND YOURS IS TELLING TALL TALES!
WAIT JUST A MINUTE...
STOP! YOU DON'T HAVE TO JUSTIFY YOURSELF TO ME! A GOOD SECRET AGENT HAS TO BE ABLE TO LIE. TRUST ME, WE ALL DO IT.
I'LL HAVE YOU KNOW I HARDLY EVER LIE, ESPECIALLY TO DAISY...
REALLY?
BECAUSE IT SURE SOUNDED LIKE IT TO ME, "THE *JEWELRY MAKER!*"
THAT WASN'T A LIE!
THAT WAS MORE LIKE...UHM... RESTRUCTURING THE FACTS TO REVEAL A *GREATER* TRUTH!

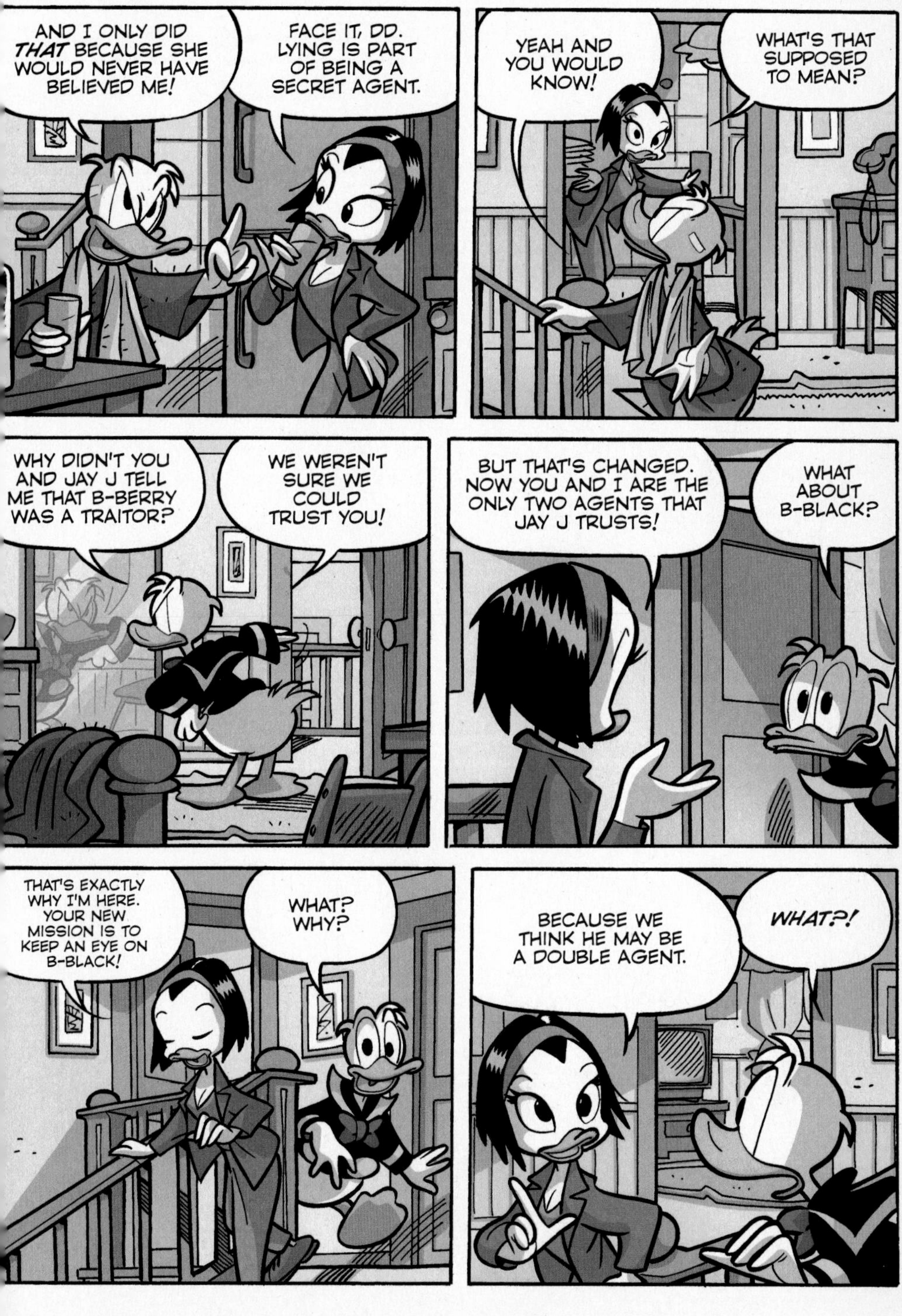
AND I ONLY DID *THAT* BECAUSE SHE WOULD NEVER HAVE BELIEVED ME!
FACE IT, DD. LYING IS PART OF BEING A SECRET AGENT.
YEAH AND YOU WOULD KNOW!
WHAT'S THAT SUPPOSED TO MEAN?
WHY DIDN'T YOU AND JAY J TELL ME THAT B-BERRY WAS A TRAITOR?
WE WEREN'T SURE WE COULD TRUST YOU!
BUT THAT'S CHANGED. NOW YOU AND I ARE THE ONLY TWO AGENTS THAT JAY J TRUSTS!
WHAT ABOUT B-BLACK?
THAT'S EXACTLY WHY I'M HERE. YOUR NEW MISSION IS TO KEEP AN EYE ON B-BLACK!
WHAT? WHY?
BECAUSE WE THINK HE MAY BE A DOUBLE AGENT.
WHAT?!

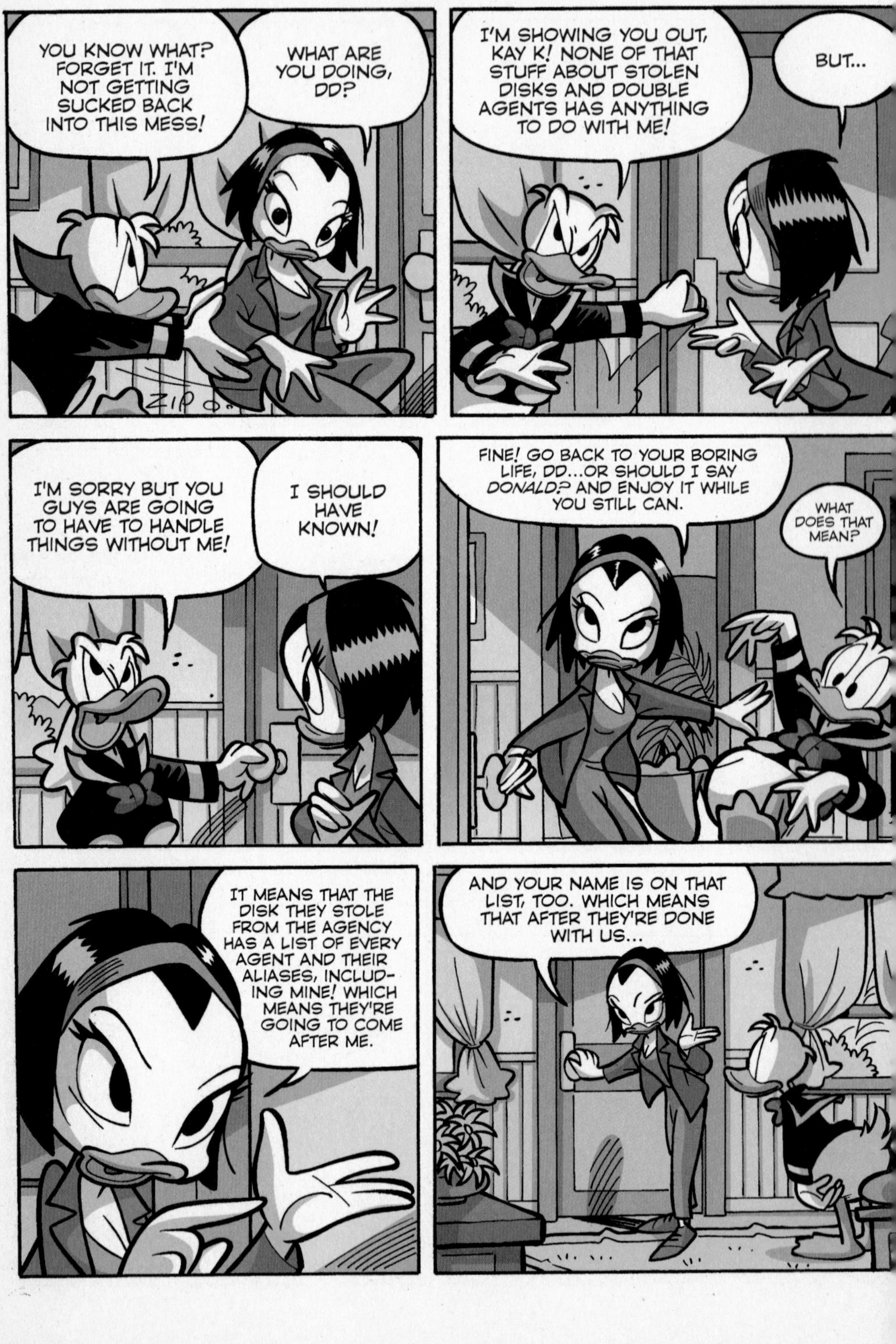
YOU KNOW WHAT? FORGET IT. I'M NOT GETTING SUCKED BACK INTO THIS MESS!
WHAT ARE YOU DOING, DD?
ZIP
I'M SHOWING YOU OUT, KAY K! NONE OF THAT STUFF ABOUT STOLEN DISKS AND DOUBLE AGENTS HAS ANYTHING TO DO WITH ME!
BUT...
I'M SORRY BUT YOU GUYS ARE GOING TO HAVE TO HANDLE THINGS WITHOUT ME!
I SHOULD HAVE KNOWN!
FINE! GO BACK TO YOUR BORING LIFE, DD...OR SHOULD I SAY *DONALD*? AND ENJOY IT WHILE YOU STILL CAN.
WHAT DOES THAT MEAN?
IT MEANS THAT THE DISK THEY STOLE FROM THE AGENCY HAS A LIST OF EVERY AGENT AND THEIR ALIASES, INCLUDING MINE! WHICH MEANS THEY'RE GOING TO COME AFTER ME.
AND YOUR NAME IS ON THAT LIST, TOO. WHICH MEANS THAT AFTER THEY'RE DONE WITH US...

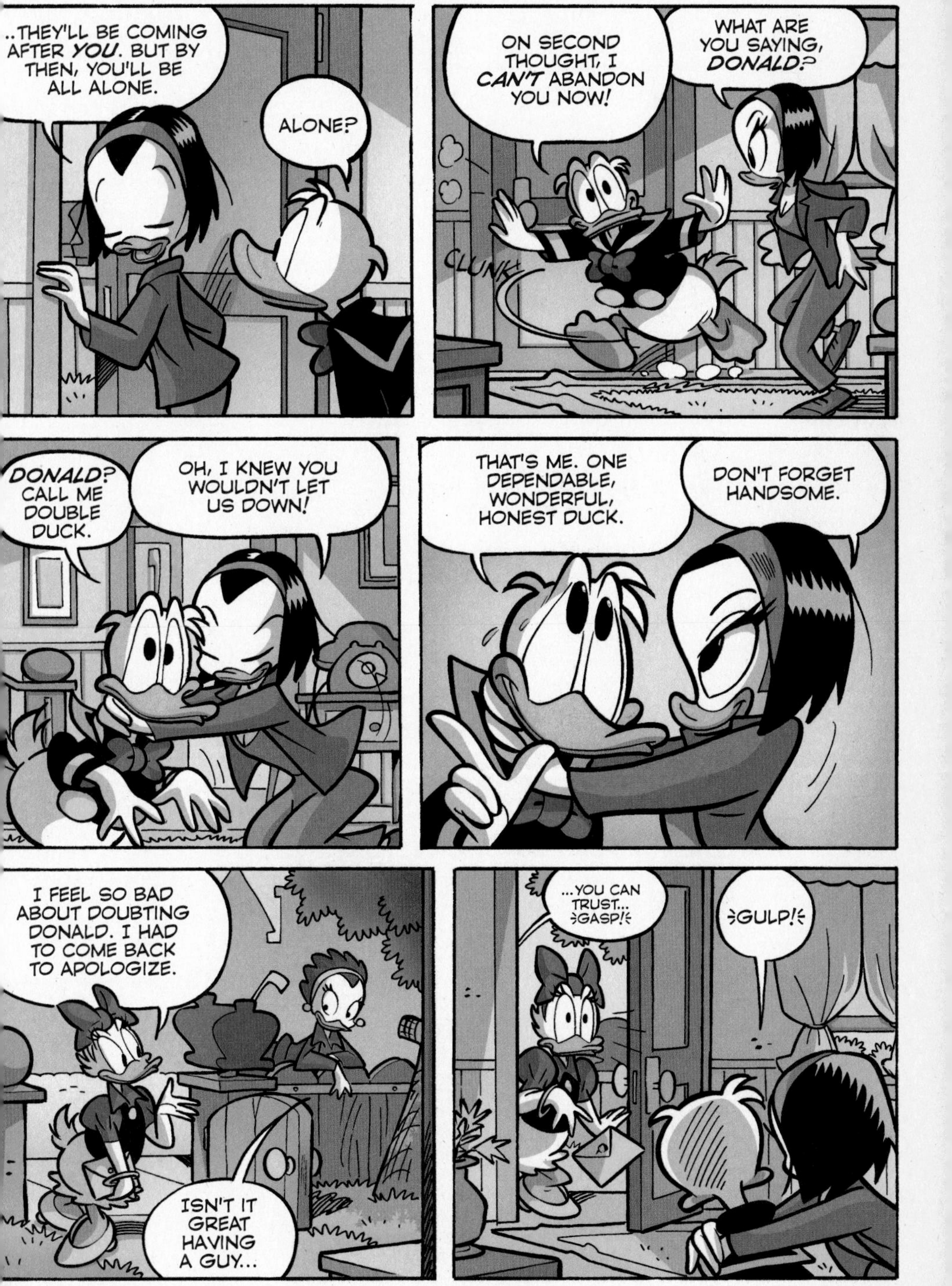
..THEY'LL BE COMING AFTER *YOU*. BUT BY THEN, YOU'LL BE ALL ALONE.
ALONE?
ON SECOND THOUGHT, I *CAN'T* ABANDON YOU NOW!
CLUNK
WHAT ARE YOU SAYING, *DONALD?*
DONALD? CALL ME DOUBLE DUCK.
OH, I KNEW YOU WOULDN'T LET US DOWN!
THAT'S ME. ONE DEPENDABLE, WONDERFUL, HONEST DUCK.
DON'T FORGET HANDSOME.
I FEEL SO BAD ABOUT DOUBTING DONALD. I HAD TO COME BACK TO APOLOGIZE.
ISN'T IT GREAT HAVING A GUY...
...YOU CAN TRUST... GASP!
GULP!

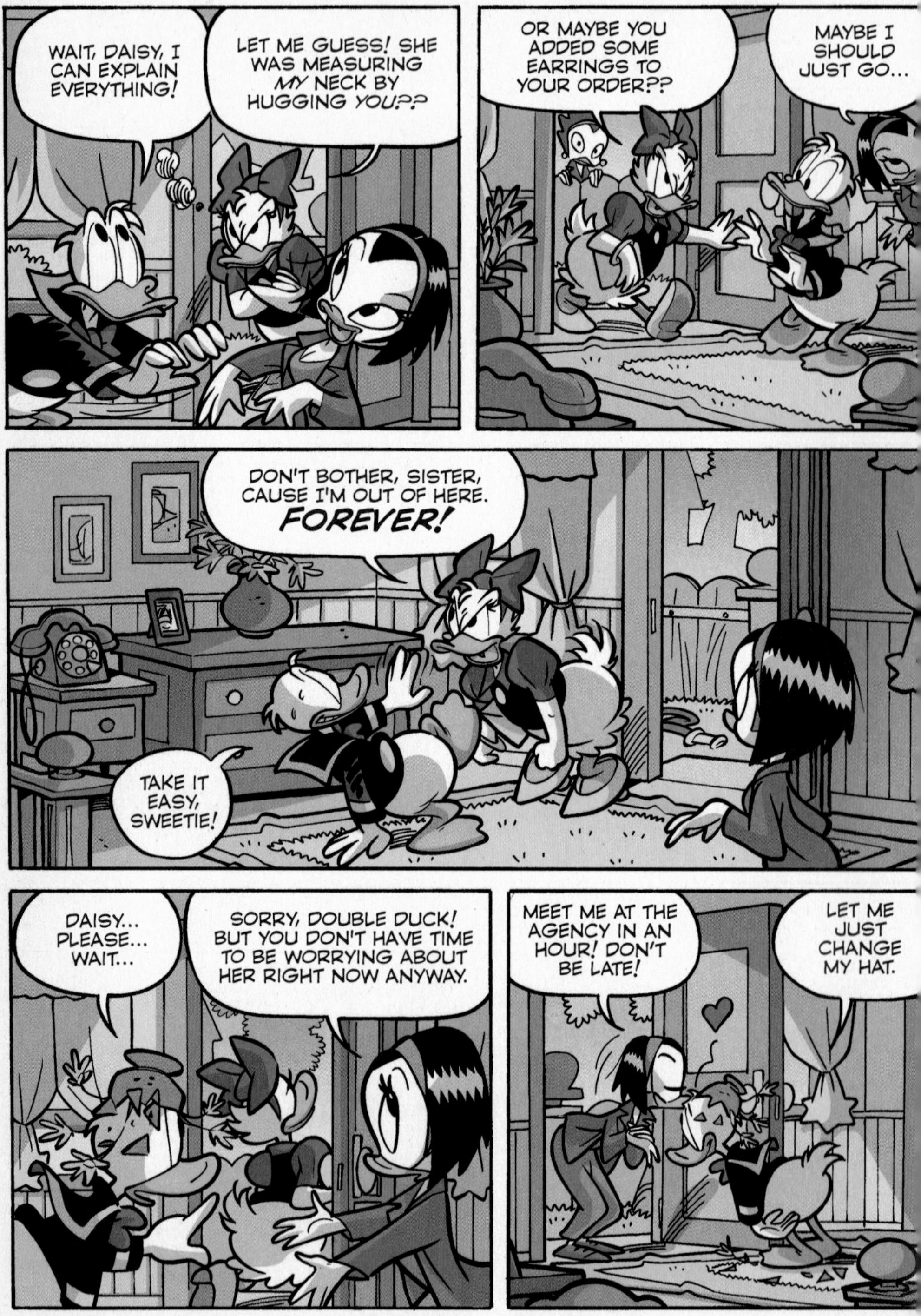
WAIT, DAISY, I CAN EXPLAIN EVERYTHING!
LET ME GUESS! SHE WAS MEASURING MY NECK BY HUGGING YOU??
OR MAYBE YOU ADDED SOME EARRINGS TO YOUR ORDER??
MAYBE I SHOULD JUST GO...
DON'T BOTHER, SISTER, CAUSE I'M OUT OF HERE. FOREVER!
TAKE IT EASY, SWEETIE!
DAISY... PLEASE... WAIT...
SORRY, DOUBLE DUCK! BUT YOU DON'T HAVE TIME TO BE WORRYING ABOUT HER RIGHT NOW ANYWAY.
MEET ME AT THE AGENCY IN AN HOUR! DON'T BE LATE!
LET ME JUST CHANGE MY HAT.

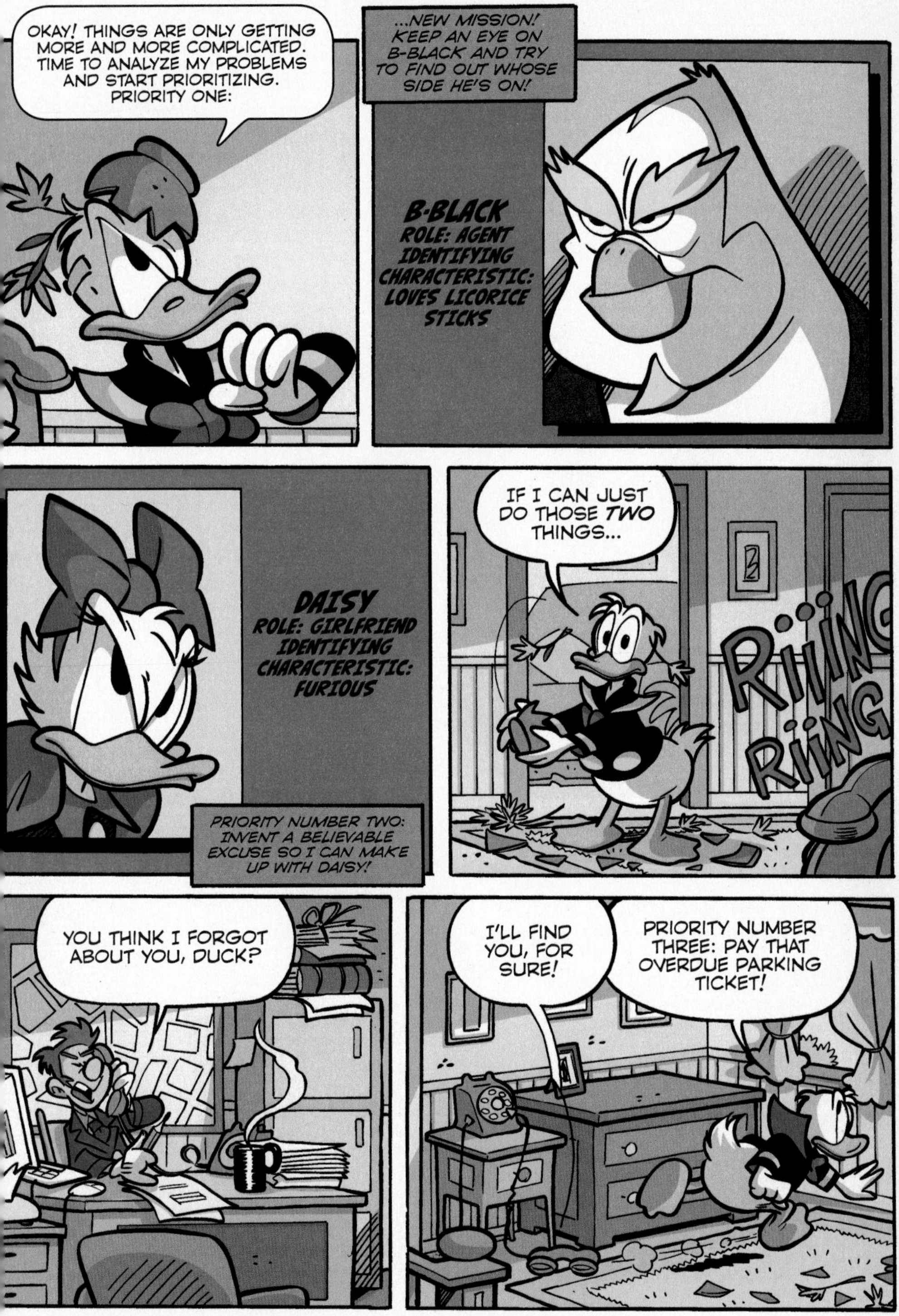
OKAY! THINGS ARE ONLY GETTING MORE AND MORE COMPLICATED. TIME TO ANALYZE MY PROBLEMS AND START PRIORITIZING. PRIORITY ONE:
...NEW MISSION! KEEP AN EYE ON B-BLACK AND TRY TO FIND OUT WHOSE SIDE HE'S ON!
B-BLACK
ROLE: AGENT
IDENTIFYING CHARACTERISTIC: LOVES LICORICE STICKS
DAISY
ROLE: GIRLFRIEND
IDENTIFYING CHARACTERISTIC: FURIOUS
PRIORITY NUMBER TWO: INVENT A BELIEVABLE EXCUSE SO I CAN MAKE UP WITH DAISY!
IF I CAN JUST DO THOSE *TWO* THINGS...
RIIING
RIING
YOU THINK I FORGOT ABOUT YOU, DUCK?
I'LL FIND YOU, FOR SURE!
PRIORITY NUMBER THREE: PAY THAT OVERDUE PARKING TICKET!

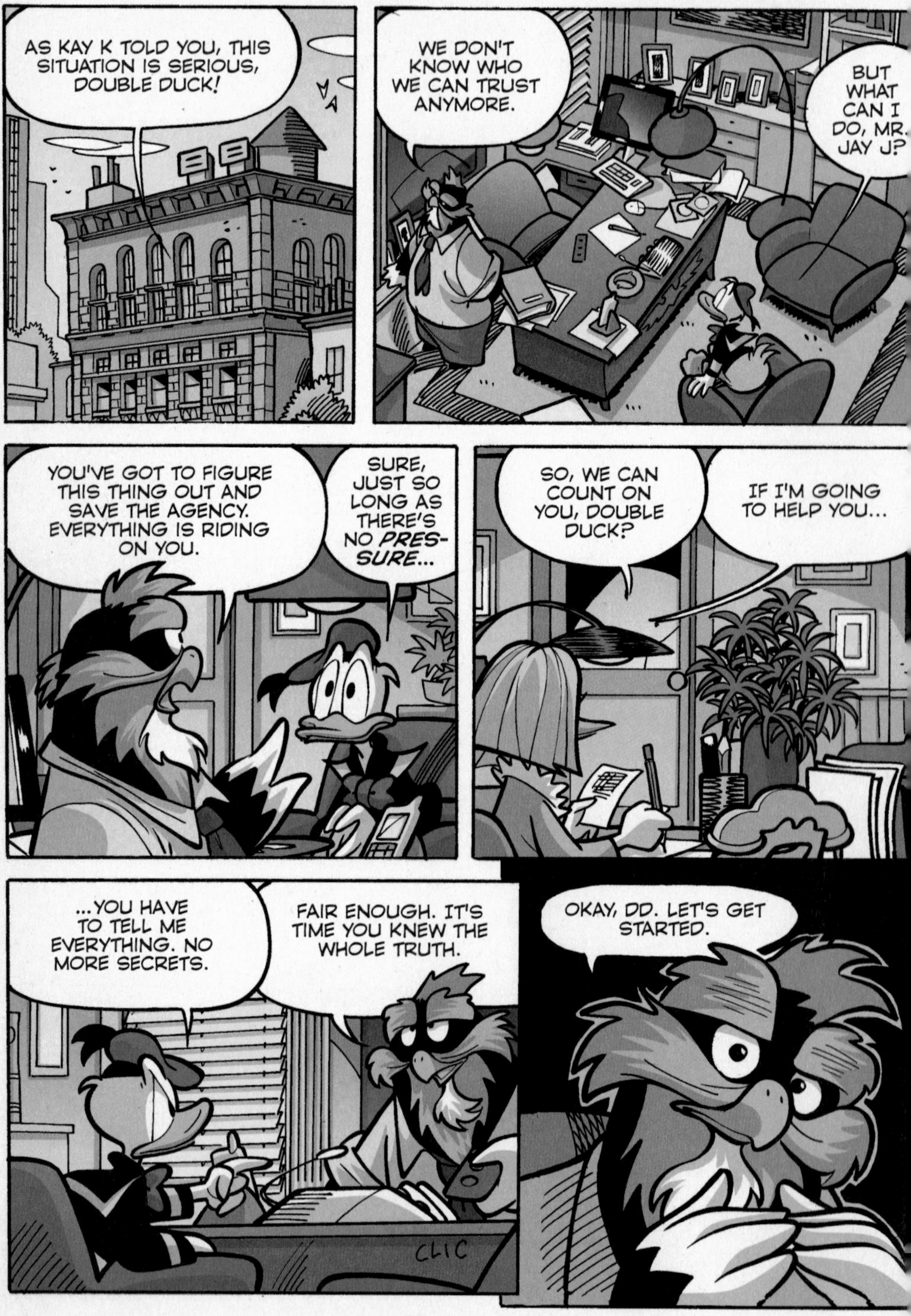
AS KAY K TOLD YOU, THIS SITUATION IS SERIOUS, DOUBLE DUCK!
WE DON'T KNOW WHO WE CAN TRUST ANYMORE.
BUT WHAT CAN I DO, MR. JAY J?
YOU'VE GOT TO FIGURE THIS THING OUT AND SAVE THE AGENCY. EVERYTHING IS RIDING ON YOU.
SURE, JUST SO LONG AS THERE'S NO *PRESSURE*...
SO, WE CAN COUNT ON YOU, DOUBLE DUCK?
IF I'M GOING TO HELP YOU...
...YOU HAVE TO TELL ME EVERYTHING. NO MORE SECRETS.
FAIR ENOUGH. IT'S TIME YOU KNEW THE WHOLE TRUTH.
CLIC
OKAY, DD. LET'S GET STARTED.

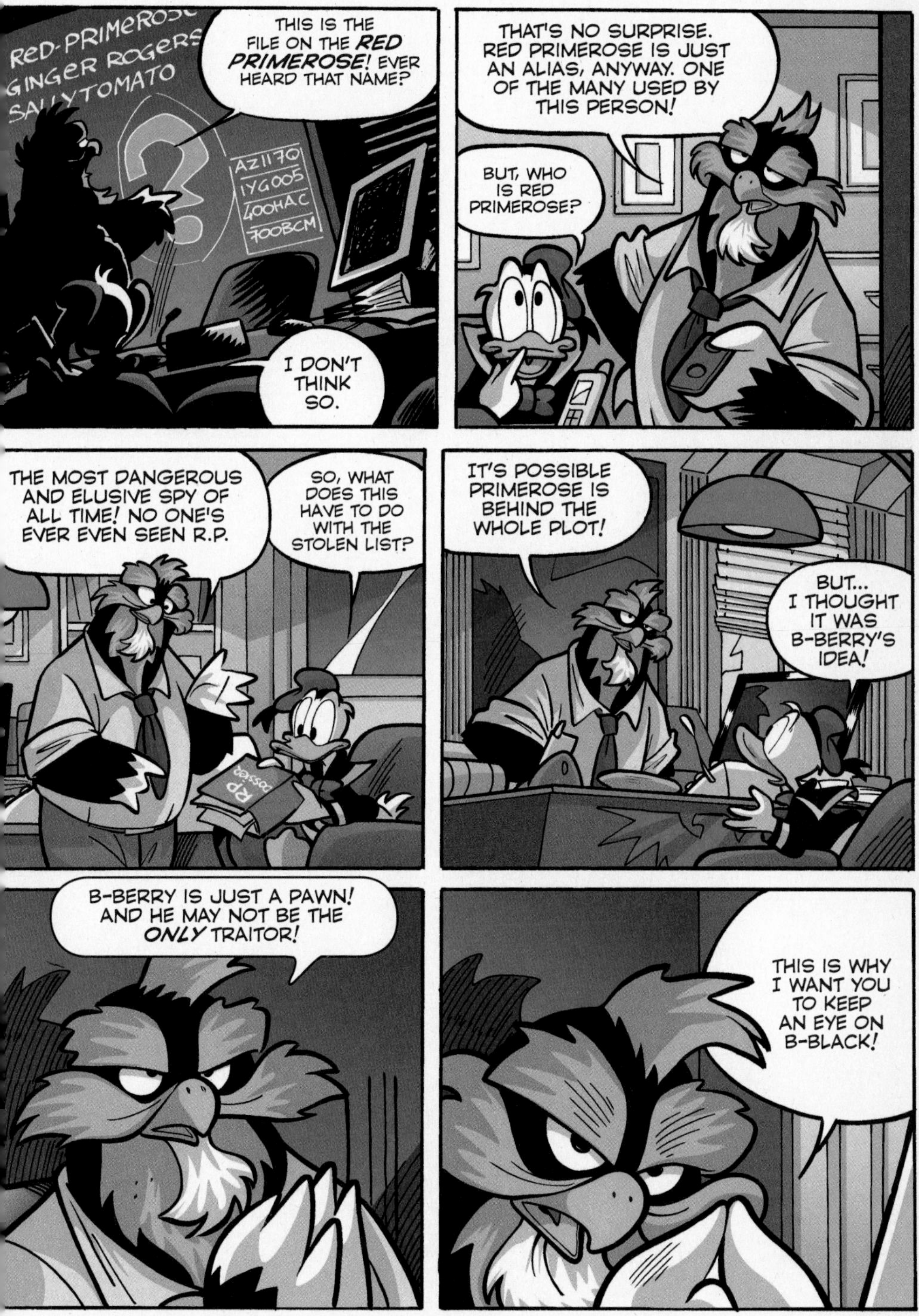
RED-PRIMEROSE
GINGER ROGERS
SALLY TOMATO
AZ1170
1YG005
400HAC
700BCM
THIS IS THE FILE ON THE *RED PRIMEROSE*! EVER HEARD THAT NAME?
I DON'T THINK SO.
THAT'S NO SURPRISE. RED PRIMEROSE IS JUST AN ALIAS, ANYWAY. ONE OF THE MANY USED BY THIS PERSON!
BUT, WHO IS RED PRIMEROSE?
THE MOST DANGEROUS AND ELUSIVE SPY OF ALL TIME! NO ONE'S EVER EVEN SEEN R.P.
SO, WHAT DOES THIS HAVE TO DO WITH THE STOLEN LIST?
RP DOSSIER
IT'S POSSIBLE PRIMEROSE IS BEHIND THE WHOLE PLOT!
BUT... I THOUGHT IT WAS B-BERRY'S IDEA!
B-BERRY IS JUST A PAWN! AND HE MAY NOT BE THE *ONLY* TRAITOR!
THIS IS WHY I WANT YOU TO KEEP AN EYE ON B-BLACK!

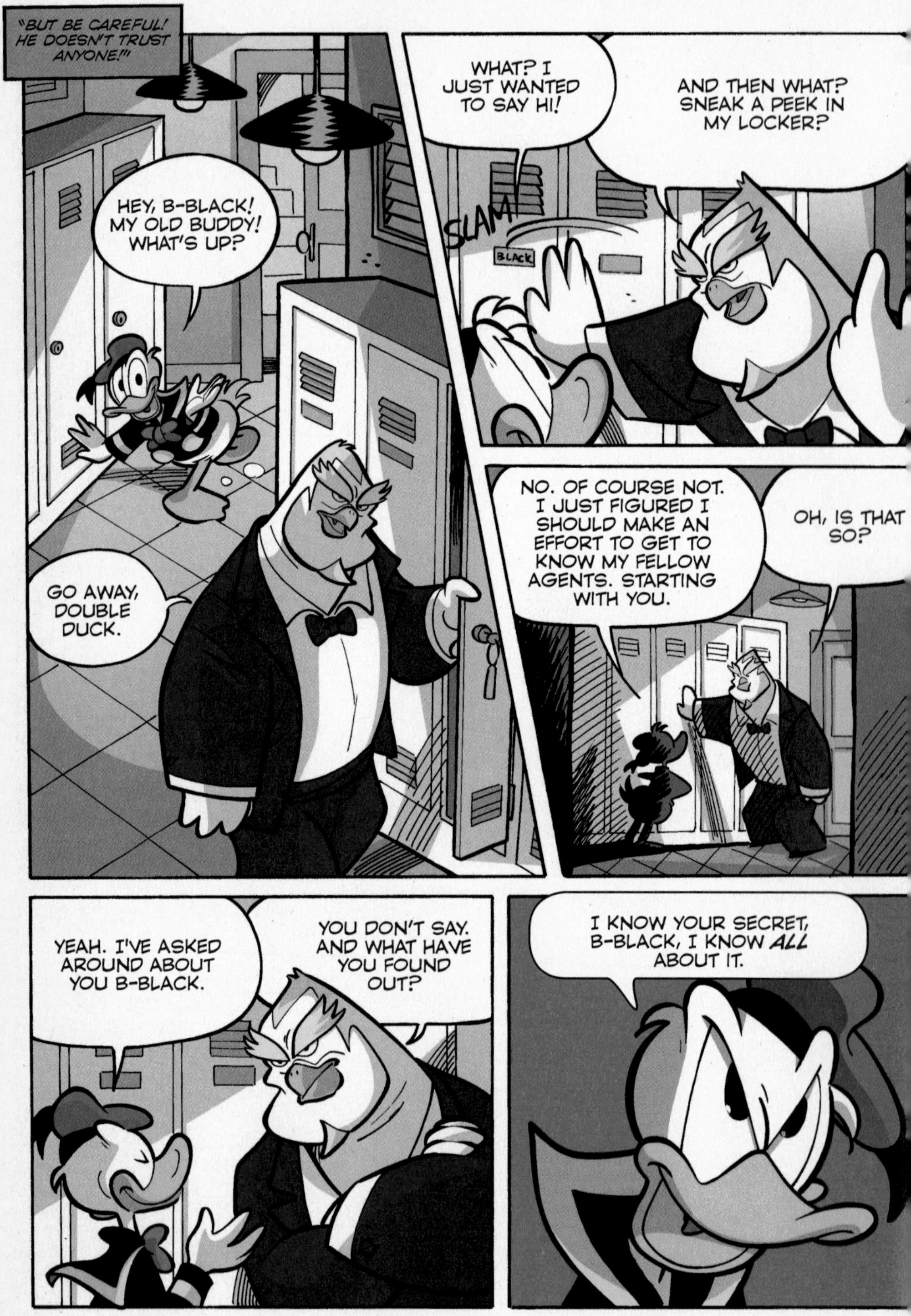
"BUT BE CAREFUL! HE DOESN'T TRUST ANYONE!"
HEY, B-BLACK! MY OLD BUDDY! WHAT'S UP?
GO AWAY, DOUBLE DUCK.
WHAT? I JUST WANTED TO SAY HI!
AND THEN WHAT? SNEAK A PEEK IN MY LOCKER?
SLAM
BLACK
NO. OF COURSE NOT. I JUST FIGURED I SHOULD MAKE AN EFFORT TO GET TO KNOW MY FELLOW AGENTS. STARTING WITH YOU.
OH, IS THAT SO?
YEAH. I'VE ASKED AROUND ABOUT YOU B-BLACK.
YOU DON'T SAY. AND WHAT HAVE YOU FOUND OUT?
I KNOW YOUR SECRET, B-BLACK, I KNOW *ALL* ABOUT IT.

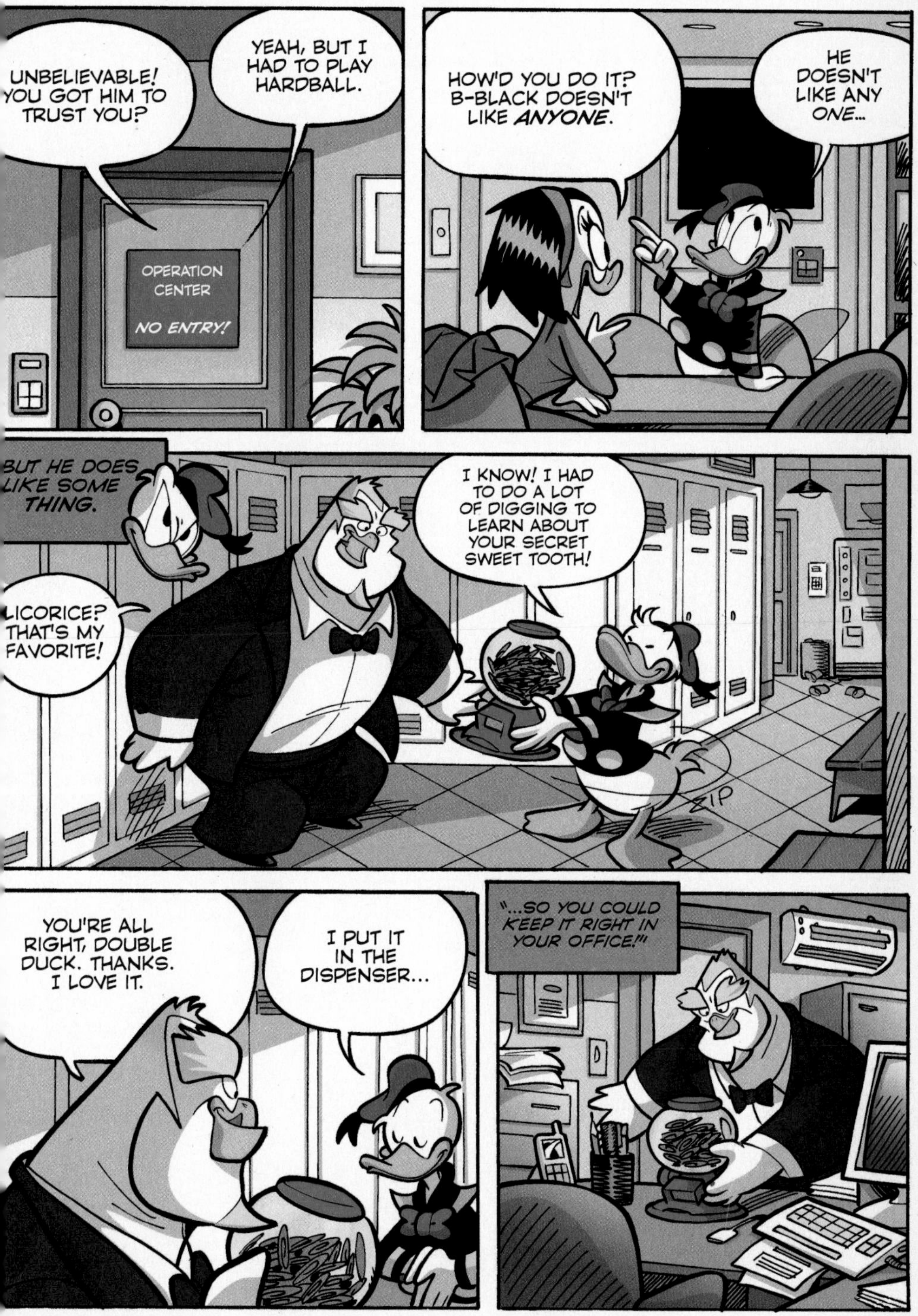
UNBELIEVABLE! YOU GOT HIM TO TRUST YOU?
YEAH, BUT I HAD TO PLAY HARDBALL.
OPERATION CENTER
NO ENTRY!
HOW'D YOU DO IT? B-BLACK DOESN'T LIKE ANYONE.
HE DOESN'T LIKE ANY ONE...
BUT HE DOES LIKE SOME THING.
I KNOW! I HAD TO DO A LOT OF DIGGING TO LEARN ABOUT YOUR SECRET SWEET TOOTH!
LICORICE? THAT'S MY FAVORITE!
ZIP
YOU'RE ALL RIGHT, DOUBLE DUCK. THANKS. I LOVE IT.
I PUT IT IN THE DISPENSER...
"...SO YOU COULD KEEP IT RIGHT IN YOUR OFFICE!"

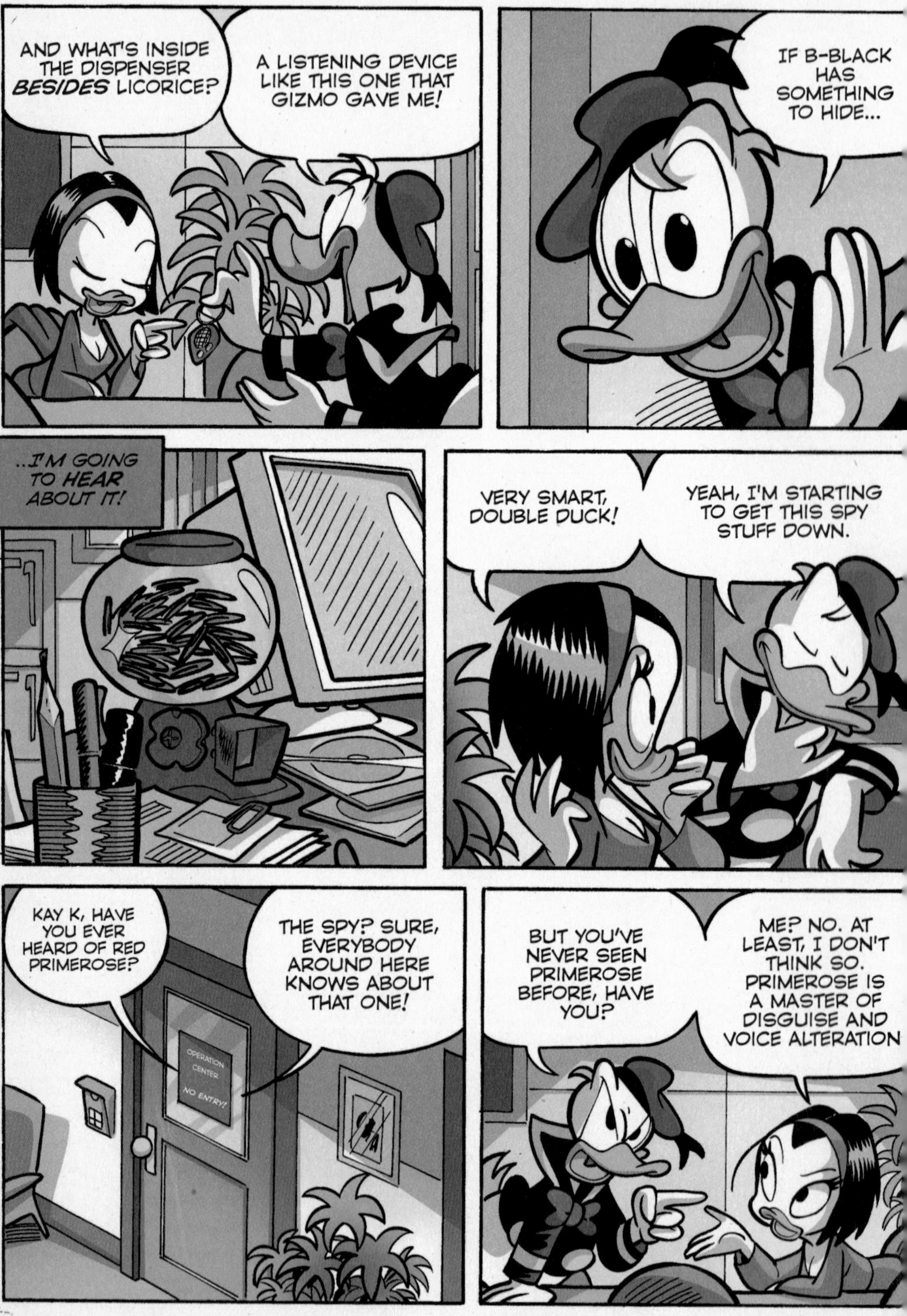
AND WHAT'S INSIDE THE DISPENSER BESIDES LICORICE?
A LISTENING DEVICE LIKE THIS ONE THAT GIZMO GAVE ME!
IF B-BLACK HAS SOMETHING TO HIDE...
...I'M GOING TO HEAR ABOUT IT!
VERY SMART, DOUBLE DUCK!
YEAH, I'M STARTING TO GET THIS SPY STUFF DOWN.
KAY K, HAVE YOU EVER HEARD OF RED PRIMEROSE?
THE SPY? SURE, EVERYBODY AROUND HERE KNOWS ABOUT THAT ONE!
OPERATION CENTER
NO ENTRY!
BUT YOU'VE NEVER SEEN PRIMEROSE BEFORE, HAVE YOU?
ME? NO. AT LEAST, I DON'T THINK SO. PRIMEROSE IS A MASTER OF DISGUISE AND VOICE ALTERATION

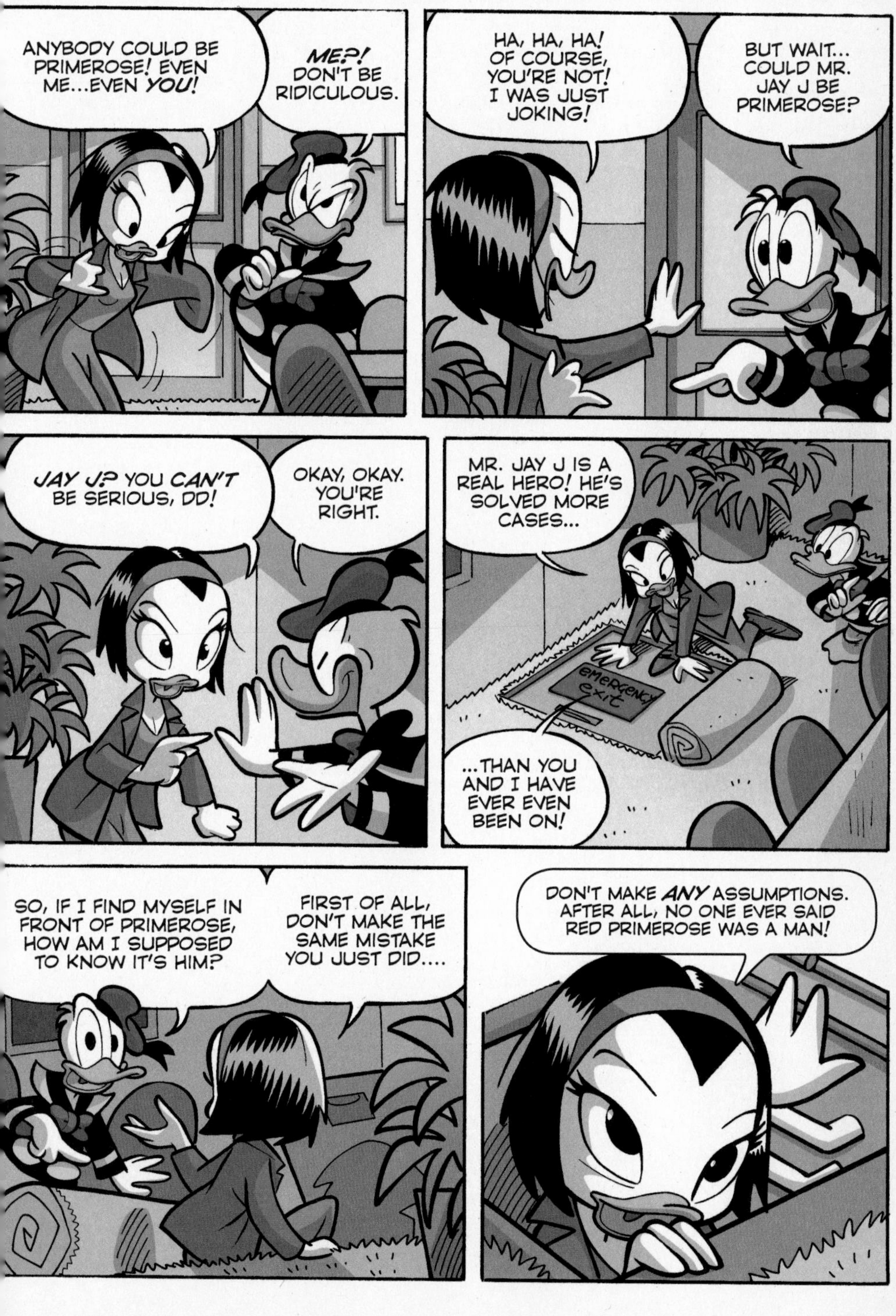

ANYBODY COULD BE PRIMEROSE! EVEN ME...EVEN YOU!
ME?! DON'T BE RIDICULOUS.
HA, HA, HA! OF COURSE, YOU'RE NOT! I WAS JUST JOKING!
BUT WAIT... COULD MR. JAY J BE PRIMEROSE?
JAY J? YOU CAN'T BE SERIOUS, DD!
OKAY, OKAY. YOU'RE RIGHT.
MR. JAY J IS A REAL HERO! HE'S SOLVED MORE CASES...
emergency exit
...THAN YOU AND I HAVE EVER EVEN BEEN ON!
SO, IF I FIND MYSELF IN FRONT OF PRIMEROSE, HOW AM I SUPPOSED TO KNOW IT'S HIM?
FIRST OF ALL, DON'T MAKE THE SAME MISTAKE YOU JUST DID....
DON'T MAKE ANY ASSUMPTIONS. AFTER ALL, NO ONE EVER SAID RED PRIMEROSE WAS A MAN!

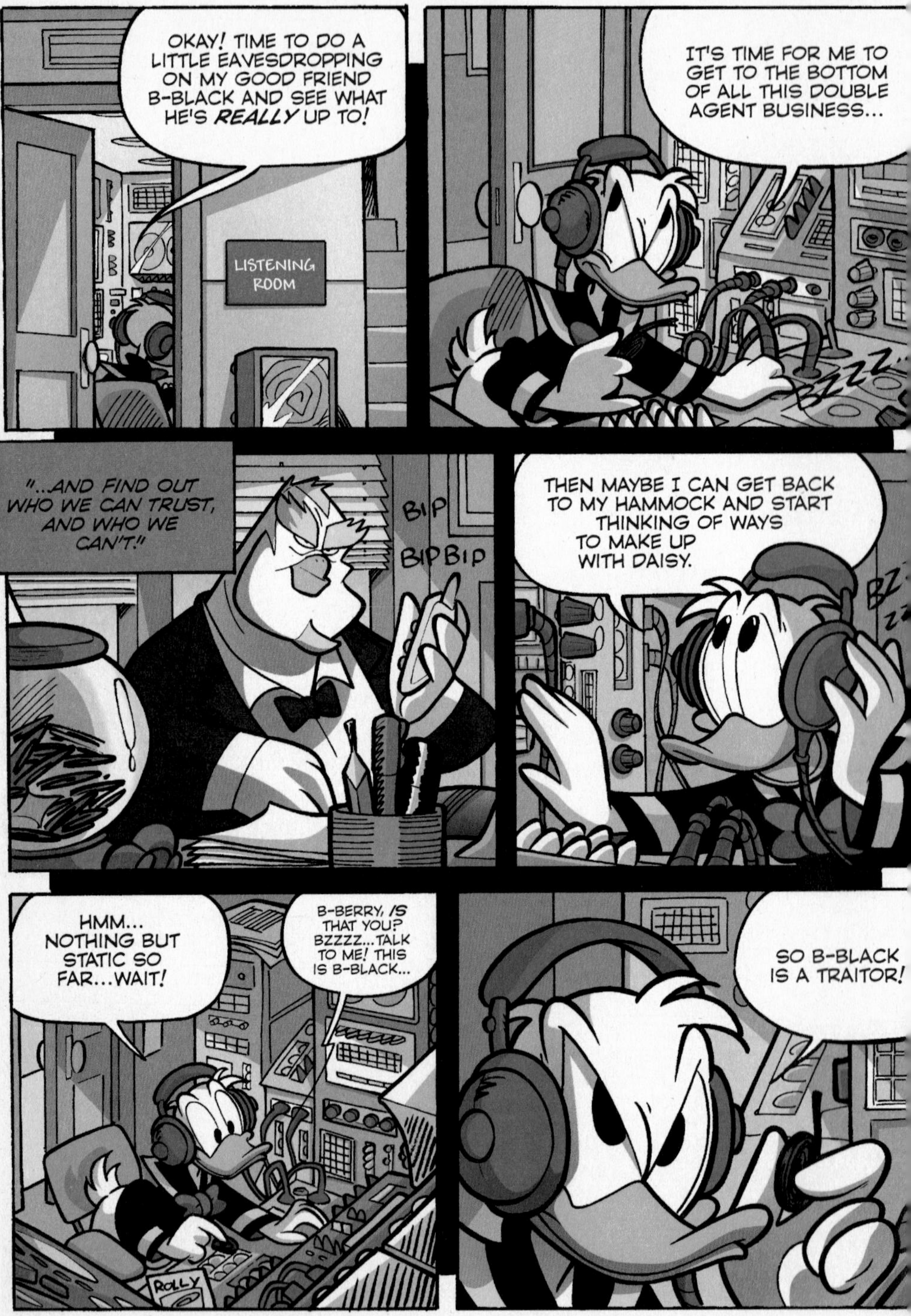
OKAY! TIME TO DO A LITTLE EAVESDROPPING ON MY GOOD FRIEND B-BLACK AND SEE WHAT HE'S *REALLY* UP TO!
LISTENING ROOM
IT'S TIME FOR ME TO GET TO THE BOTTOM OF ALL THIS DOUBLE AGENT BUSINESS...
BZZZ...
"...AND FIND OUT WHO WE CAN TRUST, AND WHO WE CAN'T!"
BIP
BIP BIP
THEN MAYBE I CAN GET BACK TO MY HAMMOCK AND START THINKING OF WAYS TO MAKE UP WITH DAISY.
HMM... NOTHING BUT STATIC SO FAR...WAIT!
B-BERRY, *IS* THAT YOU? BZZZZ...TALK TO ME! THIS IS B-BLACK...
ROLLY
SO B-BLACK IS A TRAITOR!

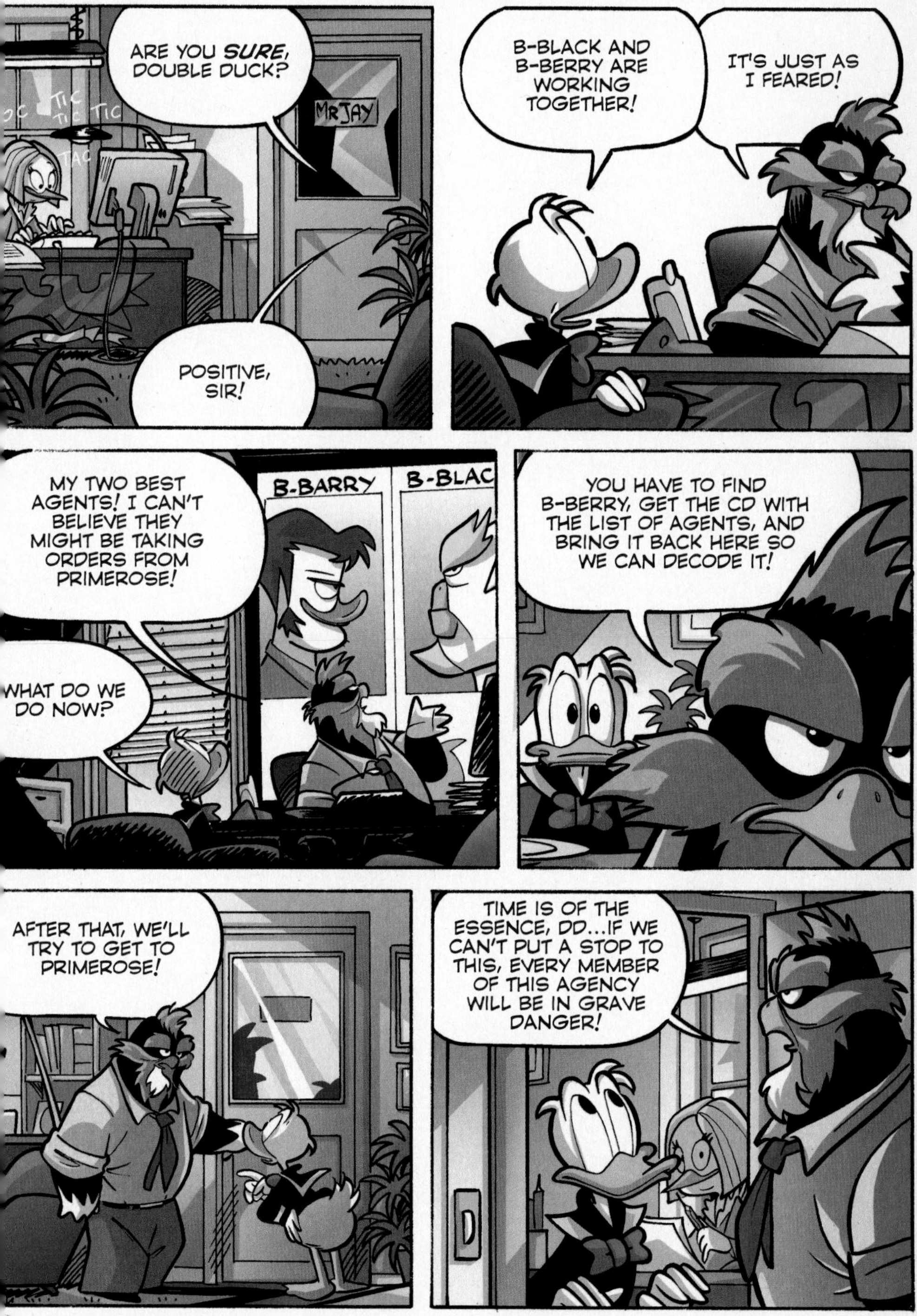
ARE YOU *SURE*, DOUBLE DUCK?
TIC TIC TIC
TAC
MR JAY
POSITIVE, SIR!
B-BLACK AND B-BERRY ARE WORKING TOGETHER!
IT'S JUST AS I FEARED!
MY TWO BEST AGENTS! I CAN'T BELIEVE THEY MIGHT BE TAKING ORDERS FROM PRIMEROSE!
B-BARRY
B-BLAC
WHAT DO WE DO NOW?
YOU HAVE TO FIND B-BERRY, GET THE CD WITH THE LIST OF AGENTS, AND BRING IT BACK HERE SO WE CAN DECODE IT!
AFTER THAT, WE'LL TRY TO GET TO PRIMEROSE!
TIME IS OF THE ESSENCE, DD...IF WE CAN'T PUT A STOP TO THIS, EVERY MEMBER OF THIS AGENCY WILL BE IN GRAVE DANGER!

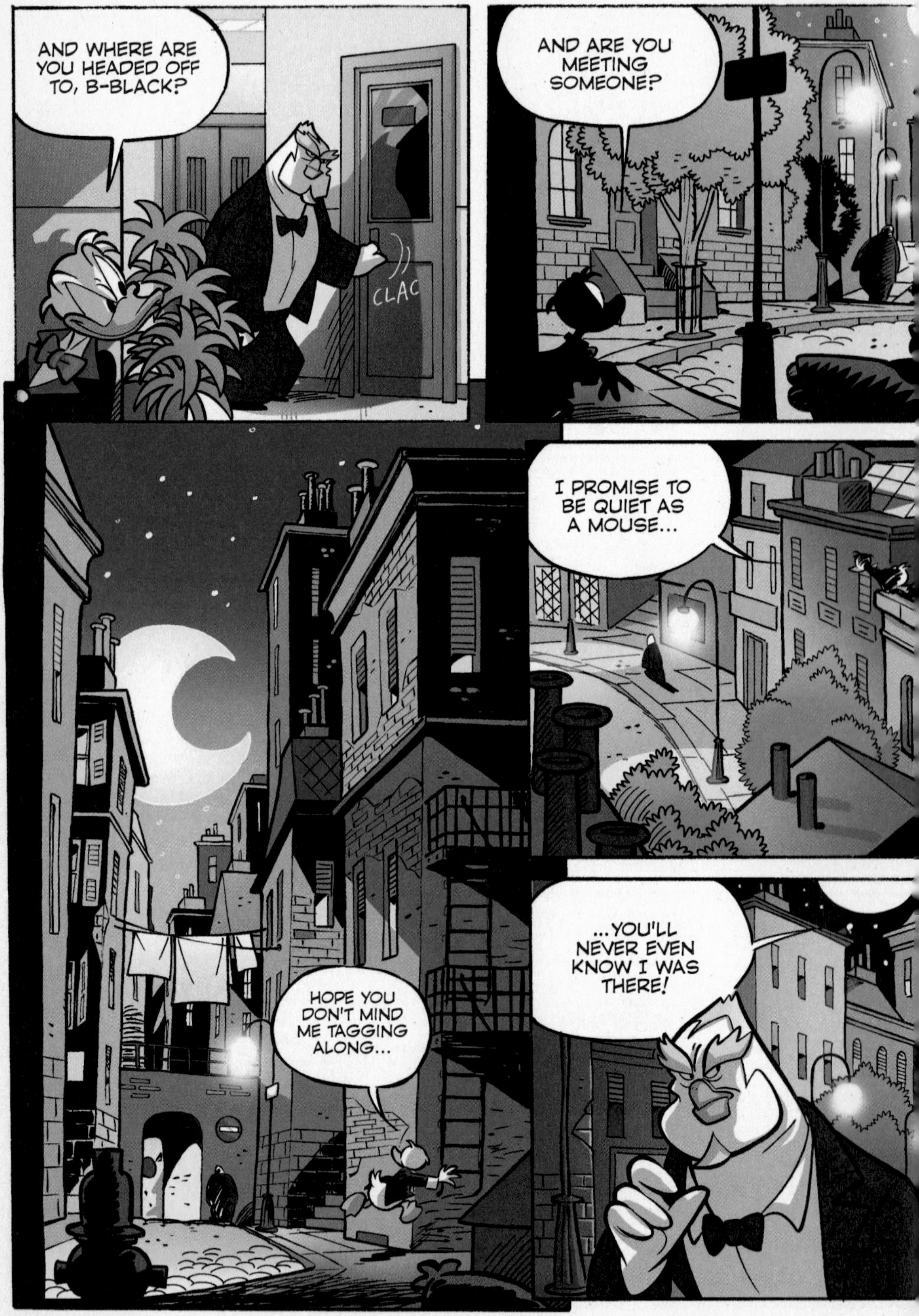
AND WHERE ARE YOU HEADED OFF TO, B-BLACK?
CLAC
AND ARE YOU MEETING SOMEONE?
HOPE YOU DON'T MIND ME TAGGING ALONG...
I PROMISE TO BE QUIET AS A MOUSE...
...YOU'LL NEVER EVEN KNOW I WAS THERE!

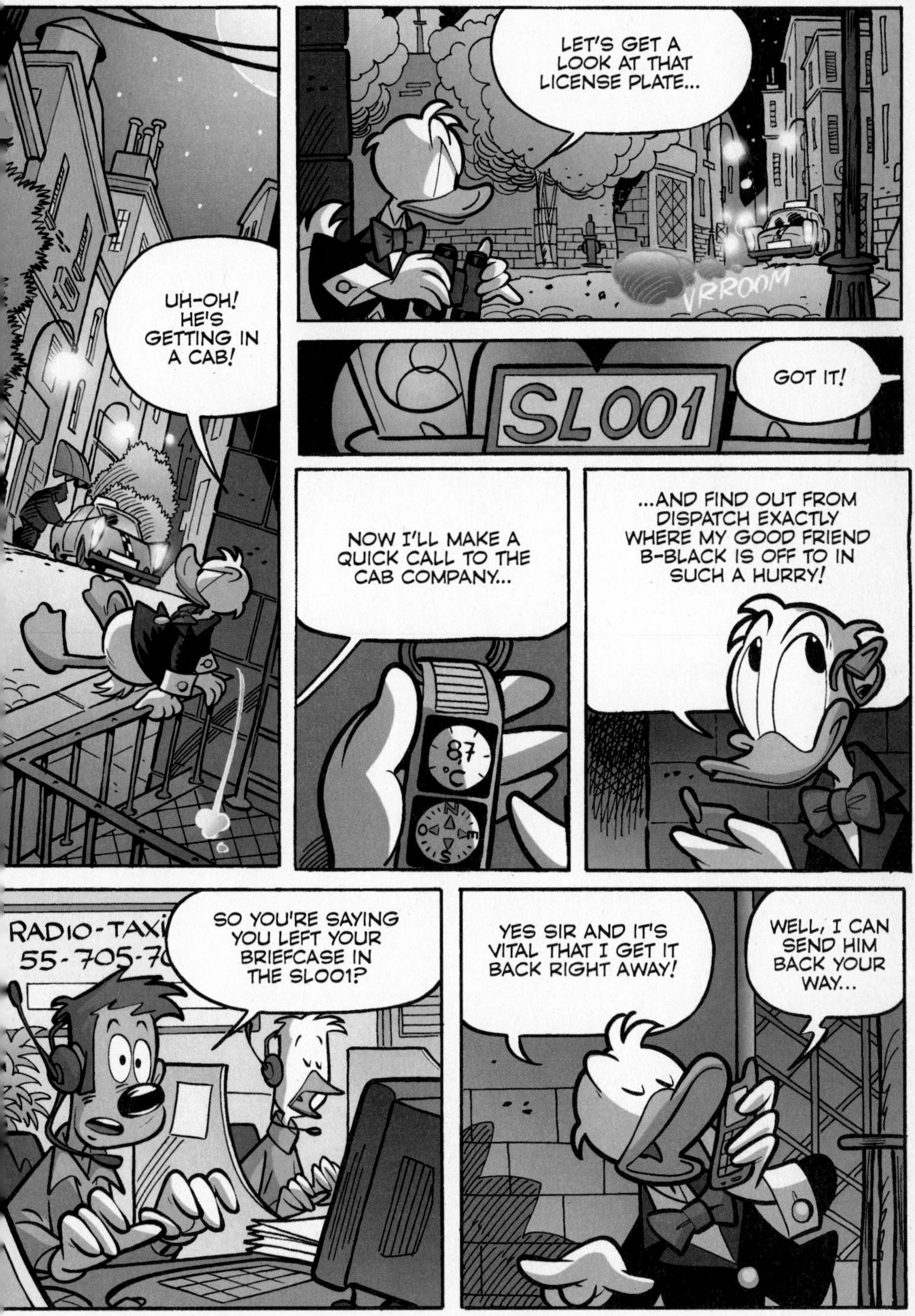
UH-OH! HE'S GETTING IN A CAB!
LET'S GET A LOOK AT THAT LICENSE PLATE...
VRROOM
SL001
GOT IT!
NOW I'LL MAKE A QUICK CALL TO THE CAB COMPANY...
87 °C
...AND FIND OUT FROM DISPATCH EXACTLY WHERE MY GOOD FRIEND B-BLACK IS OFF TO IN SUCH A HURRY!
RADIO-TAXI 55-705-70
SO YOU'RE SAYING YOU LEFT YOUR BRIEFCASE IN THE SL001?
YES SIR AND IT'S VITAL THAT I GET IT BACK RIGHT AWAY!
WELL, I CAN SEND HIM BACK YOUR WAY...

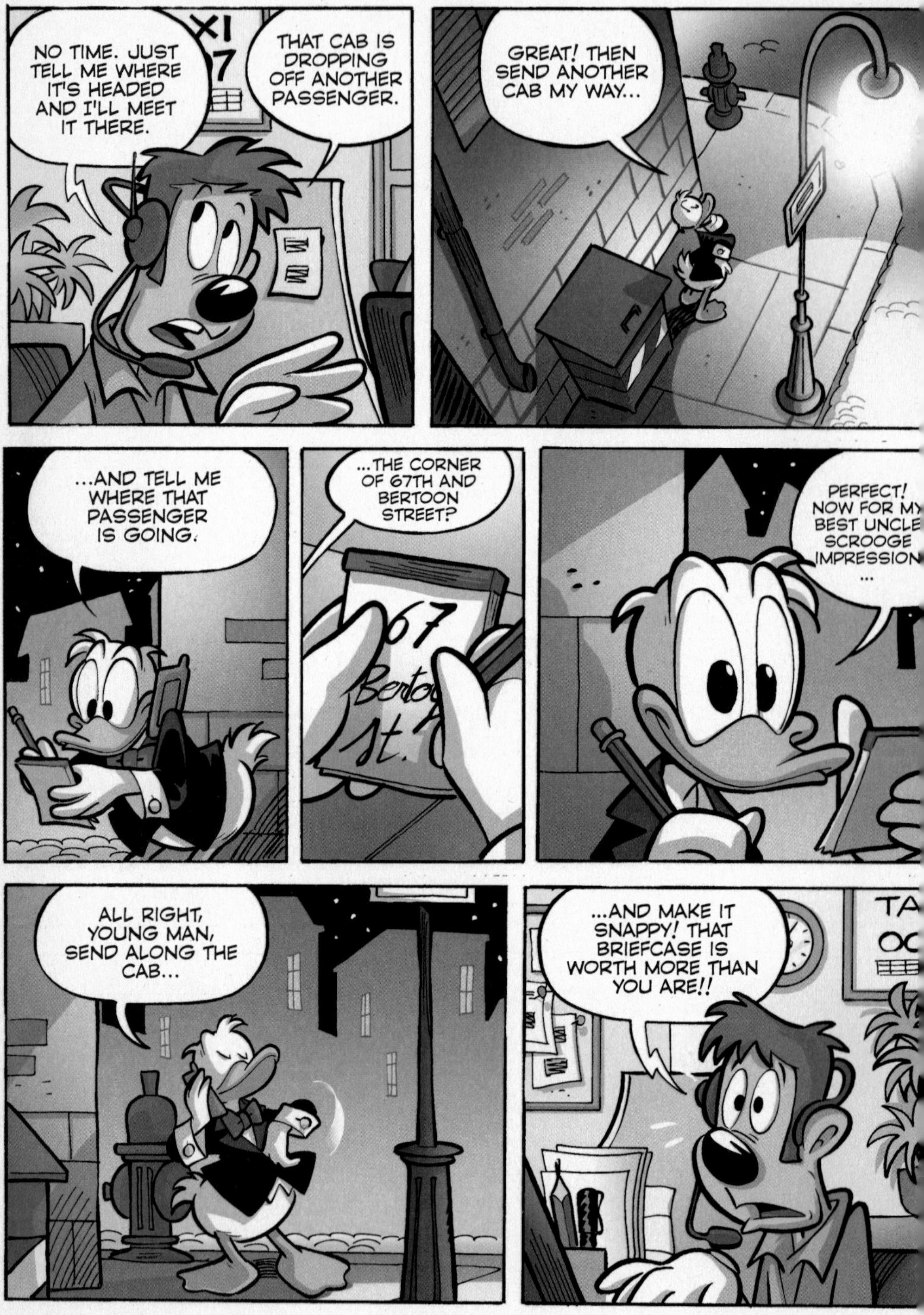
NO TIME. JUST TELL ME WHERE IT'S HEADED AND I'LL MEET IT THERE.
THAT CAB IS DROPPING OFF ANOTHER PASSENGER.
GREAT! THEN SEND ANOTHER CAB MY WAY...
...AND TELL ME WHERE THAT PASSENGER IS GOING.
...THE CORNER OF 67TH AND BERTOON STREET?
PERFECT! NOW FOR MY BEST UNCLE SCROOGE IMPRESSION...
ALL RIGHT, YOUNG MAN, SEND ALONG THE CAB...
...AND MAKE IT SNAPPY! THAT BRIEFCASE IS WORTH MORE THAN YOU ARE!!

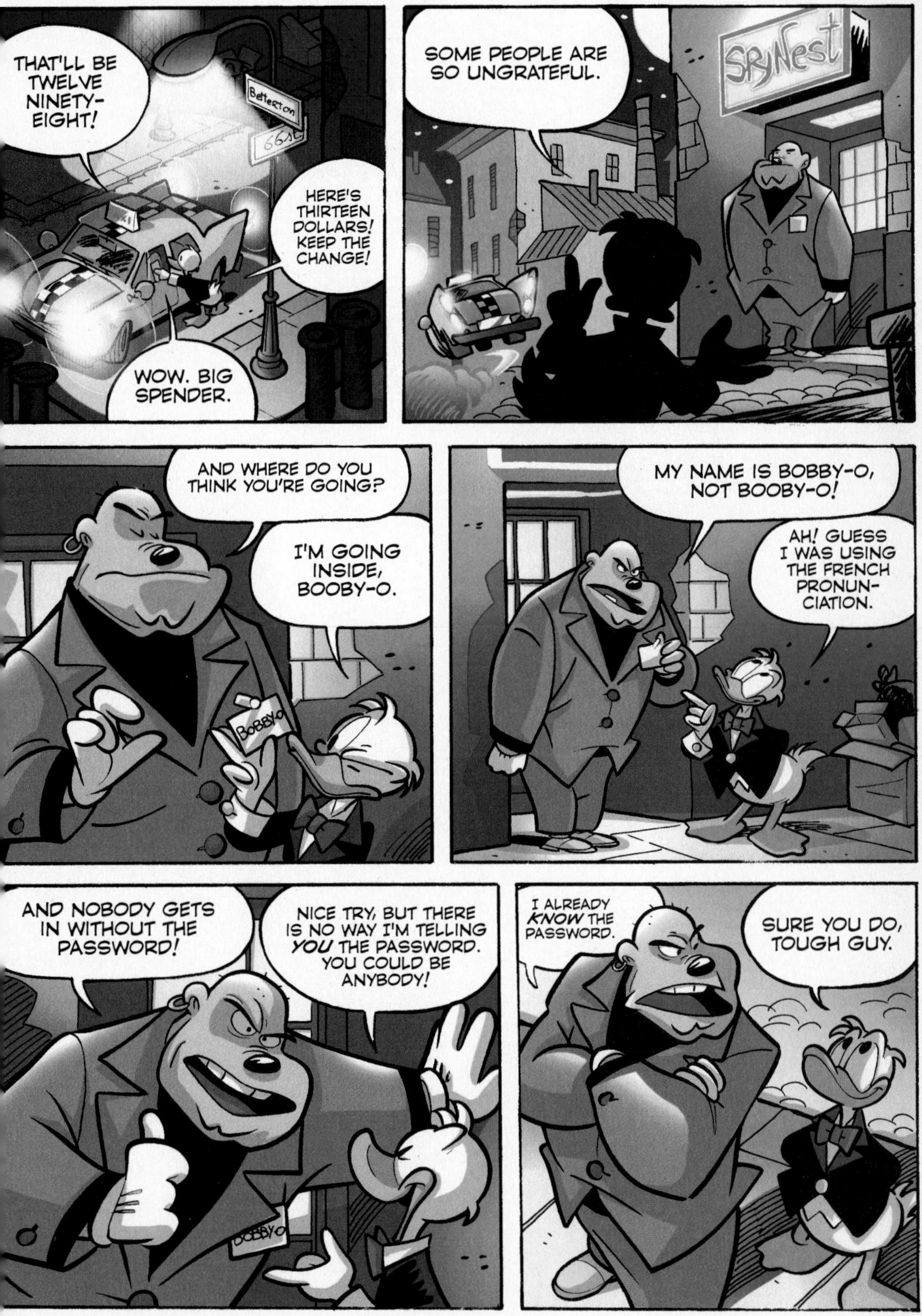
THAT'LL BE TWELVE NINETY-EIGHT!
Betterton
66st
HERE'S THIRTEEN DOLLARS! KEEP THE CHANGE!
WOW. BIG SPENDER.
SOME PEOPLE ARE SO UNGRATEFUL.
SPYNest
AND WHERE DO YOU THINK YOU'RE GOING?
I'M GOING INSIDE, BOOBY-O.
BOBBY-O
MY NAME IS BOBBY-O, NOT BOOBY-O!
AH! GUESS I WAS USING THE FRENCH PRONUN-CIATION.
AND NOBODY GETS IN WITHOUT THE PASSWORD!
NICE TRY, BUT THERE IS NO WAY I'M TELLING ***YOU*** THE PASSWORD. YOU COULD BE ANYBODY!
BOBBY-O
I ALREADY ***KNOW*** THE PASSWORD.
SURE YOU DO, TOUGH GUY.

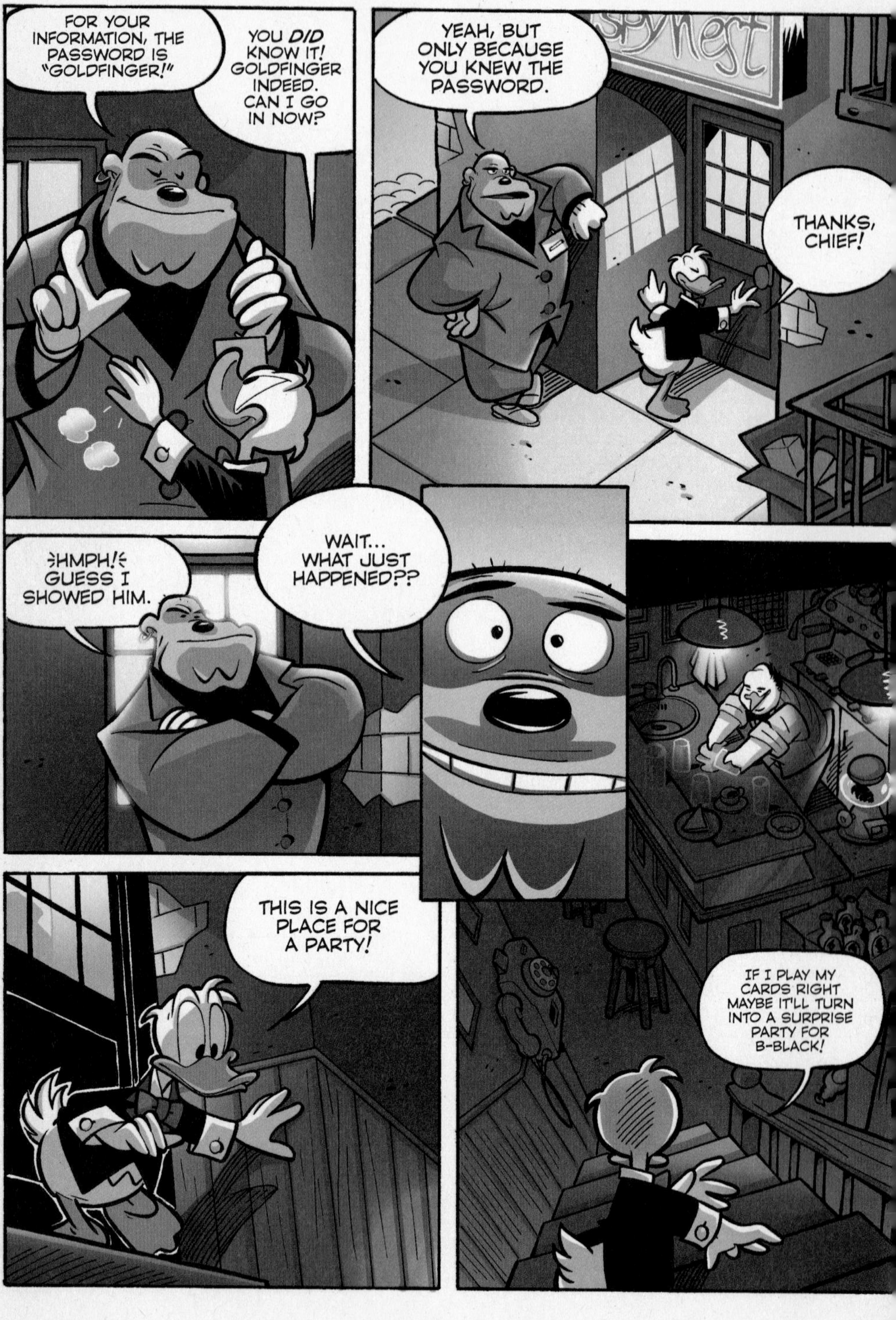
FOR YOUR INFORMATION, THE PASSWORD IS "GOLDFINGER!"
YOU DID KNOW IT! GOLDFINGER INDEED. CAN I GO IN NOW?
YEAH, BUT ONLY BECAUSE YOU KNEW THE PASSWORD.
spynest
THANKS, CHIEF!
HMPH! GUESS I SHOWED HIM.
WAIT... WHAT JUST HAPPENED??
THIS IS A NICE PLACE FOR A PARTY!
IF I PLAY MY CARDS RIGHT MAYBE IT'LL TURN INTO A SURPRISE PARTY FOR B-BLACK!

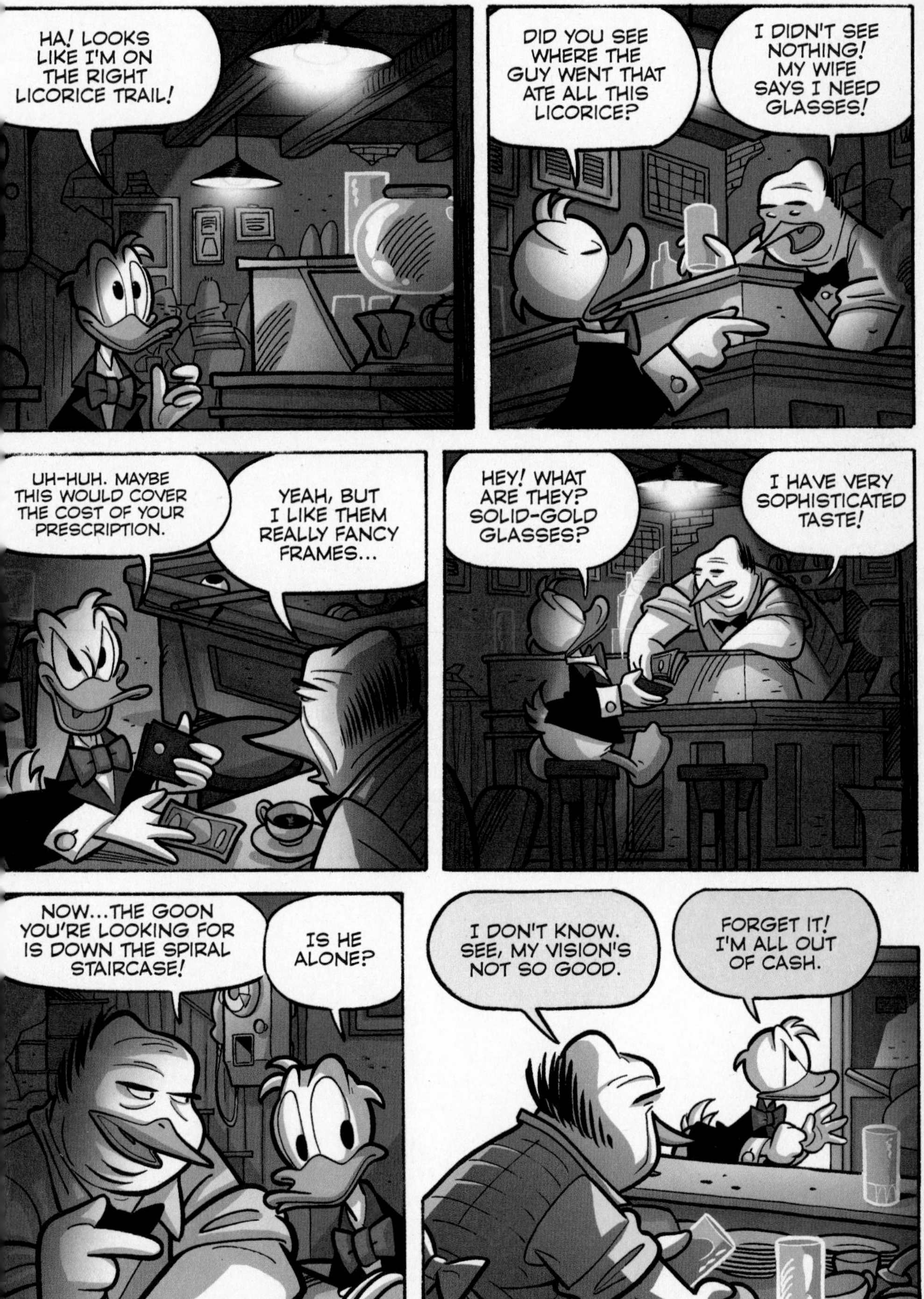
HA! LOOKS LIKE I'M ON THE RIGHT LICORICE TRAIL!
DID YOU SEE WHERE THE GUY WENT THAT ATE ALL THIS LICORICE?
I DIDN'T SEE NOTHING! MY WIFE SAYS I NEED GLASSES!
UH-HUH. MAYBE THIS WOULD COVER THE COST OF YOUR PRESCRIPTION.
YEAH, BUT I LIKE THEM REALLY FANCY FRAMES...
HEY! WHAT ARE THEY? SOLID-GOLD GLASSES?
I HAVE VERY SOPHISTICATED TASTE!
NOW...THE GOON YOU'RE LOOKING FOR IS DOWN THE SPIRAL STAIRCASE!
IS HE ALONE?
I DON'T KNOW. SEE, MY VISION'S NOT SO GOOD.
FORGET IT! I'M ALL OUT OF CASH.

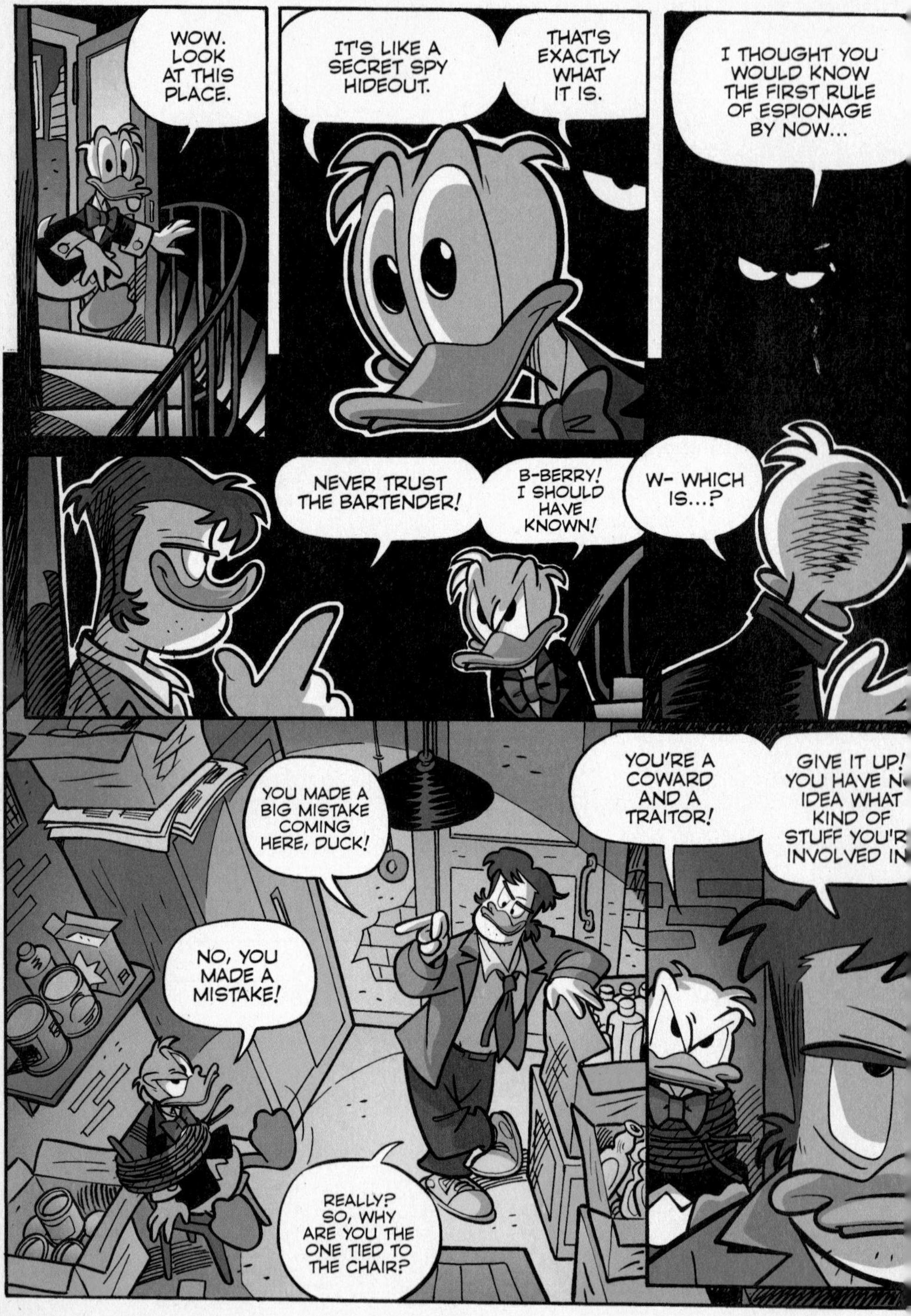

WOW. LOOK AT THIS PLACE.
IT'S LIKE A SECRET SPY HIDEOUT.
THAT'S EXACTLY WHAT IT IS.
I THOUGHT YOU WOULD KNOW THE FIRST RULE OF ESPIONAGE BY NOW...
W- WHICH IS...?
NEVER TRUST THE BARTENDER!
B-BERRY! I SHOULD HAVE KNOWN!
YOU MADE A BIG MISTAKE COMING HERE, DUCK!
NO, YOU MADE A MISTAKE!
REALLY? SO, WHY ARE YOU THE ONE TIED TO THE CHAIR?
YOU'RE A COWARD AND A TRAITOR!
GIVE IT UP! YOU HAVE N IDEA WHAT KIND OF STUFF YOU'R INVOLVED IN

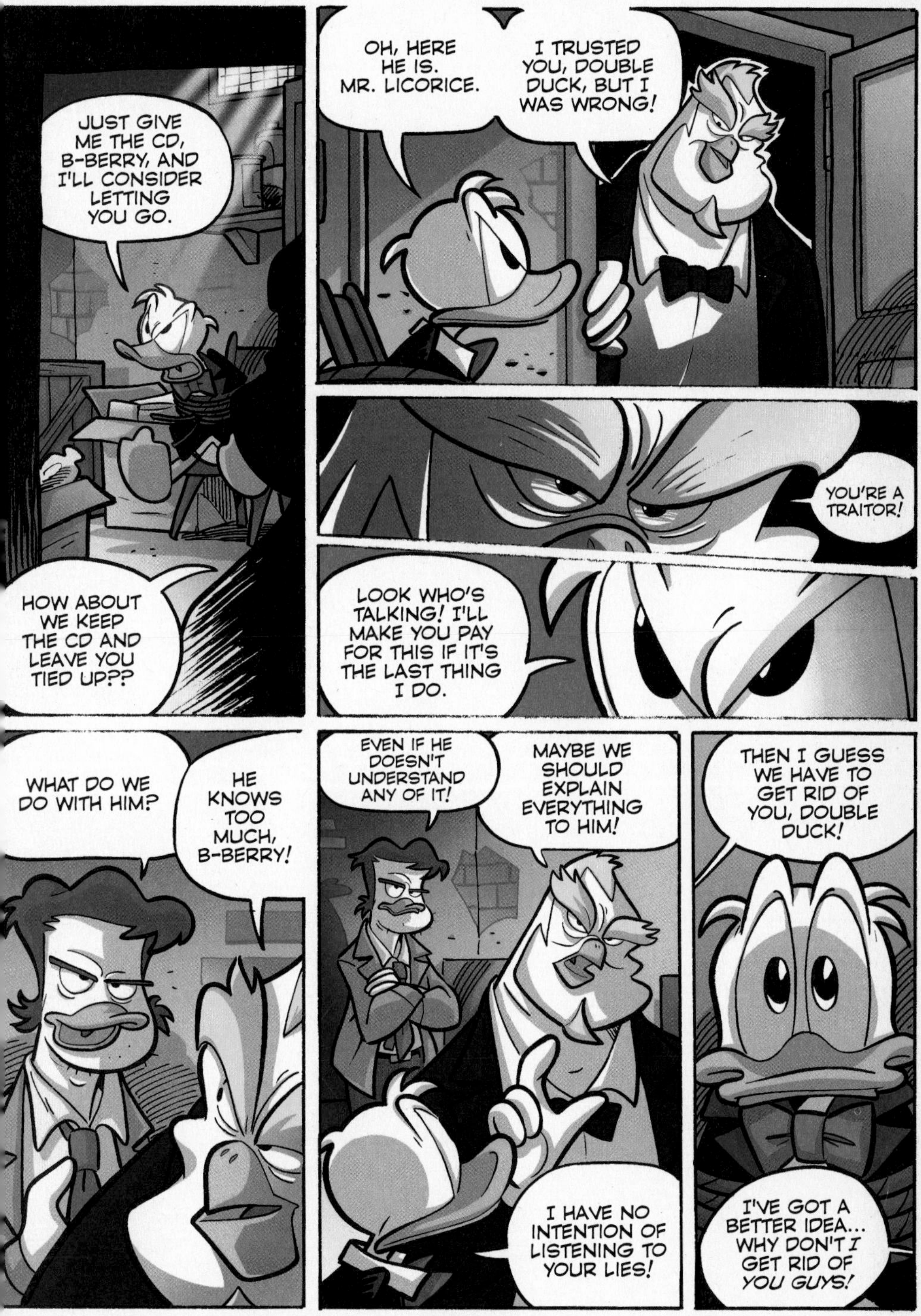
JUST GIVE ME THE CD, B-BERRY, AND I'LL CONSIDER LETTING YOU GO.
HOW ABOUT WE KEEP THE CD AND LEAVE YOU TIED UP??
OH, HERE HE IS. MR. LICORICE.
I TRUSTED YOU, DOUBLE DUCK, BUT I WAS WRONG!
YOU'RE A TRAITOR!
LOOK WHO'S TALKING! I'LL MAKE YOU PAY FOR THIS IF IT'S THE LAST THING I DO.
WHAT DO WE DO WITH HIM?
HE KNOWS TOO MUCH, B-BERRY!
MAYBE WE SHOULD EXPLAIN EVERYTHING TO HIM!
EVEN IF HE DOESN'T UNDERSTAND ANY OF IT!
I HAVE NO INTENTION OF LISTENING TO YOUR LIES!
THEN I GUESS WE HAVE TO GET RID OF YOU, DOUBLE DUCK!
I'VE GOT A BETTER IDEA... WHY DON'T I GET RID OF YOU GUYS!

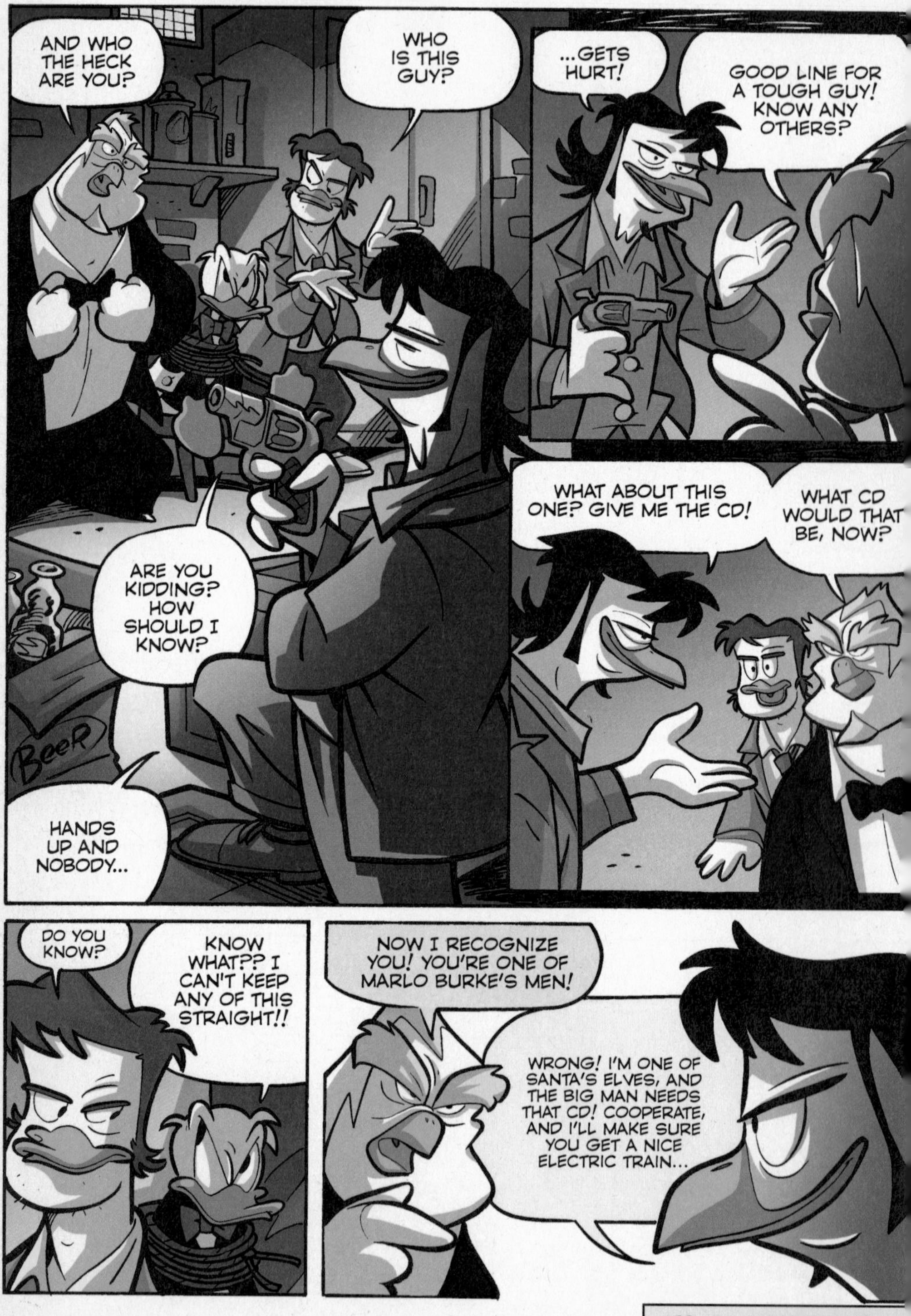
AND WHO THE HECK ARE YOU?
WHO IS THIS GUY?
ARE YOU KIDDING? HOW SHOULD I KNOW?
HANDS UP AND NOBODY...
...GETS HURT!
GOOD LINE FOR A TOUGH GUY! KNOW ANY OTHERS?
WHAT ABOUT THIS ONE? GIVE ME THE CD!
WHAT CD WOULD THAT BE, NOW?
DO YOU KNOW?
KNOW WHAT?? I CAN'T KEEP ANY OF THIS STRAIGHT!!
NOW I RECOGNIZE YOU! YOU'RE ONE OF MARLO BURKE'S MEN!
WRONG! I'M ONE OF SANTA'S ELVES, AND THE BIG MAN NEEDS THAT CD! COOPERATE, AND I'LL MAKE SURE YOU GET A NICE ELECTRIC TRAIN...
BEER

TO BE CONTINUED...

COVER GALLERY

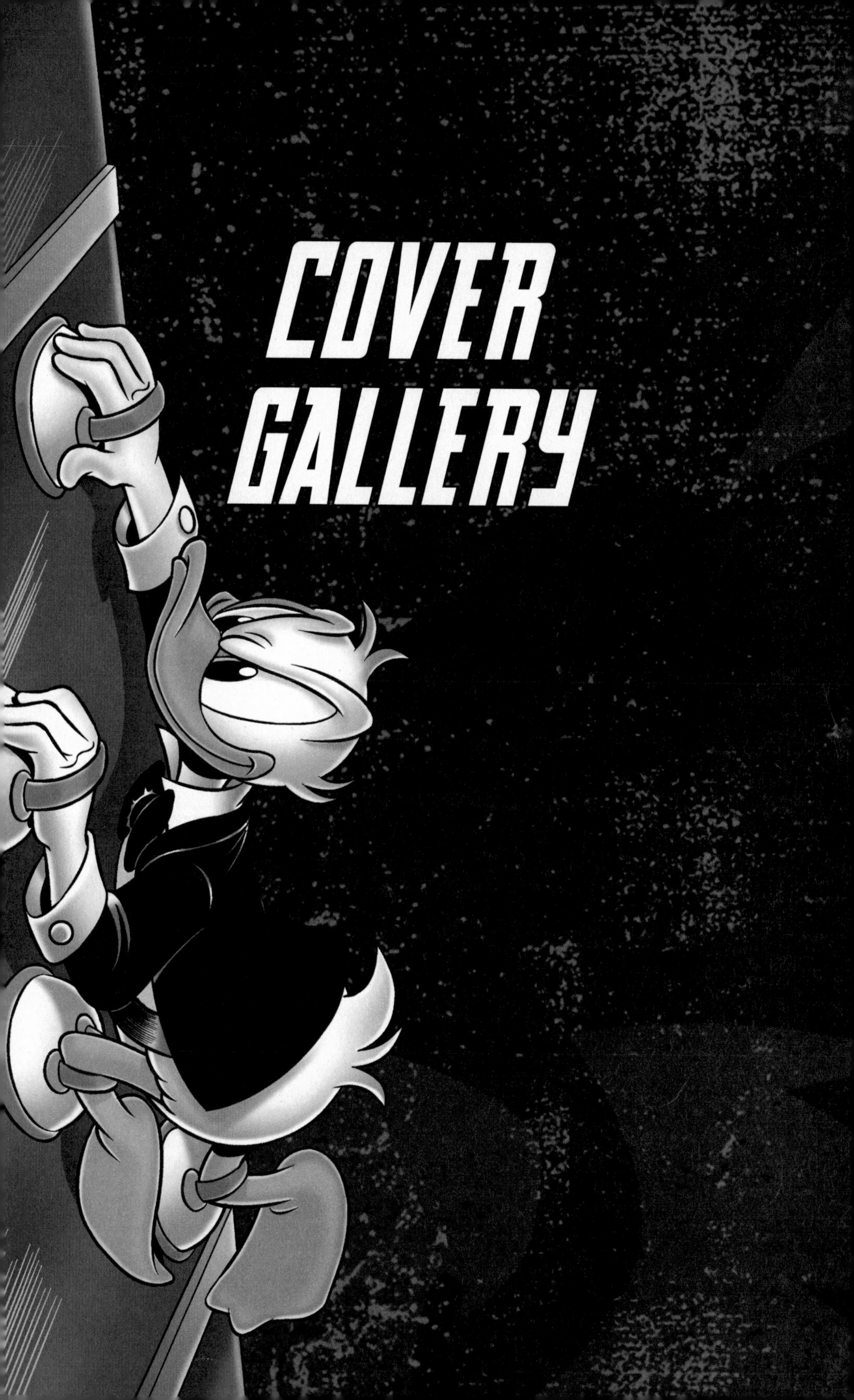

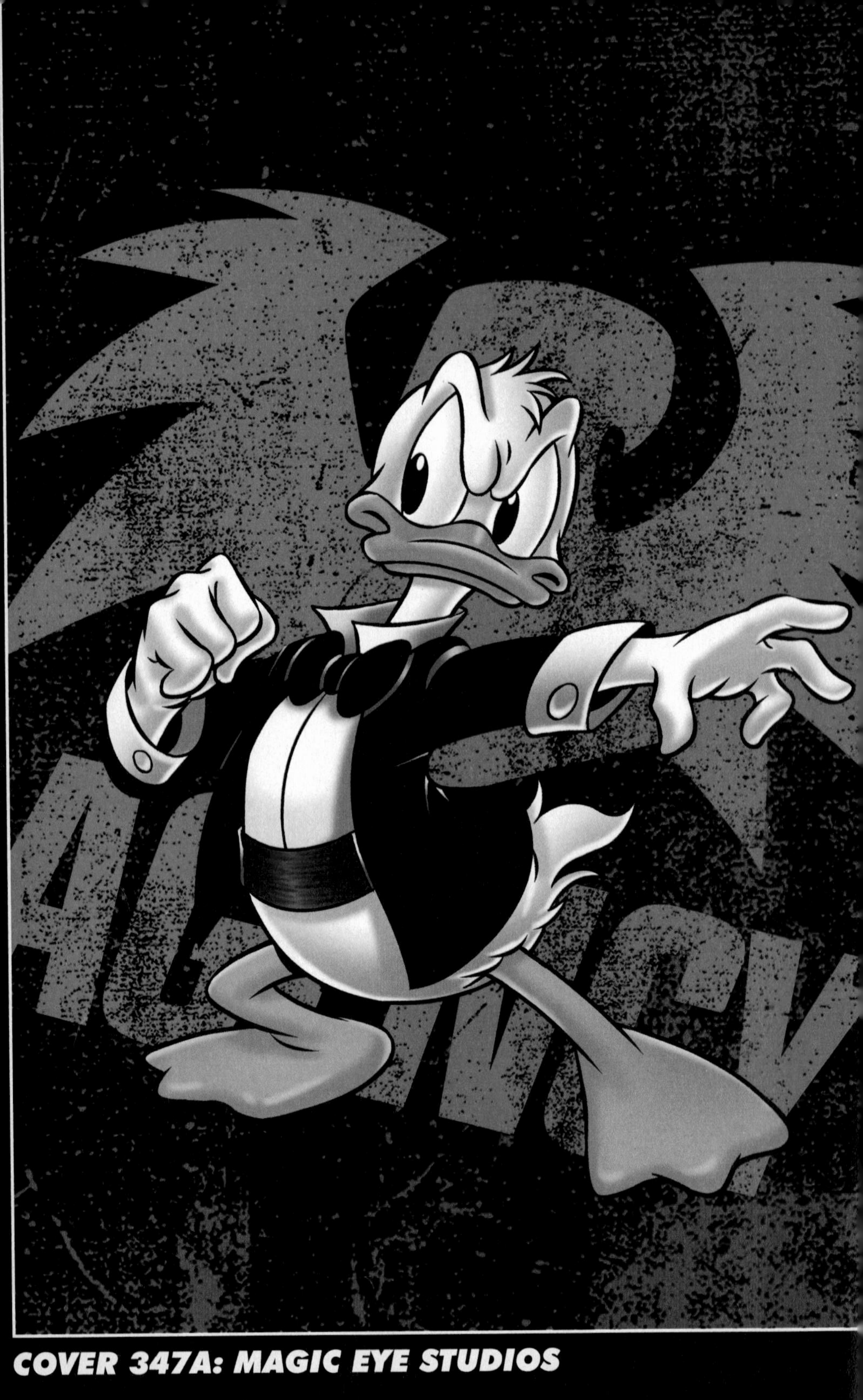

COVER 347A: MAGIC EYE STUDIOS

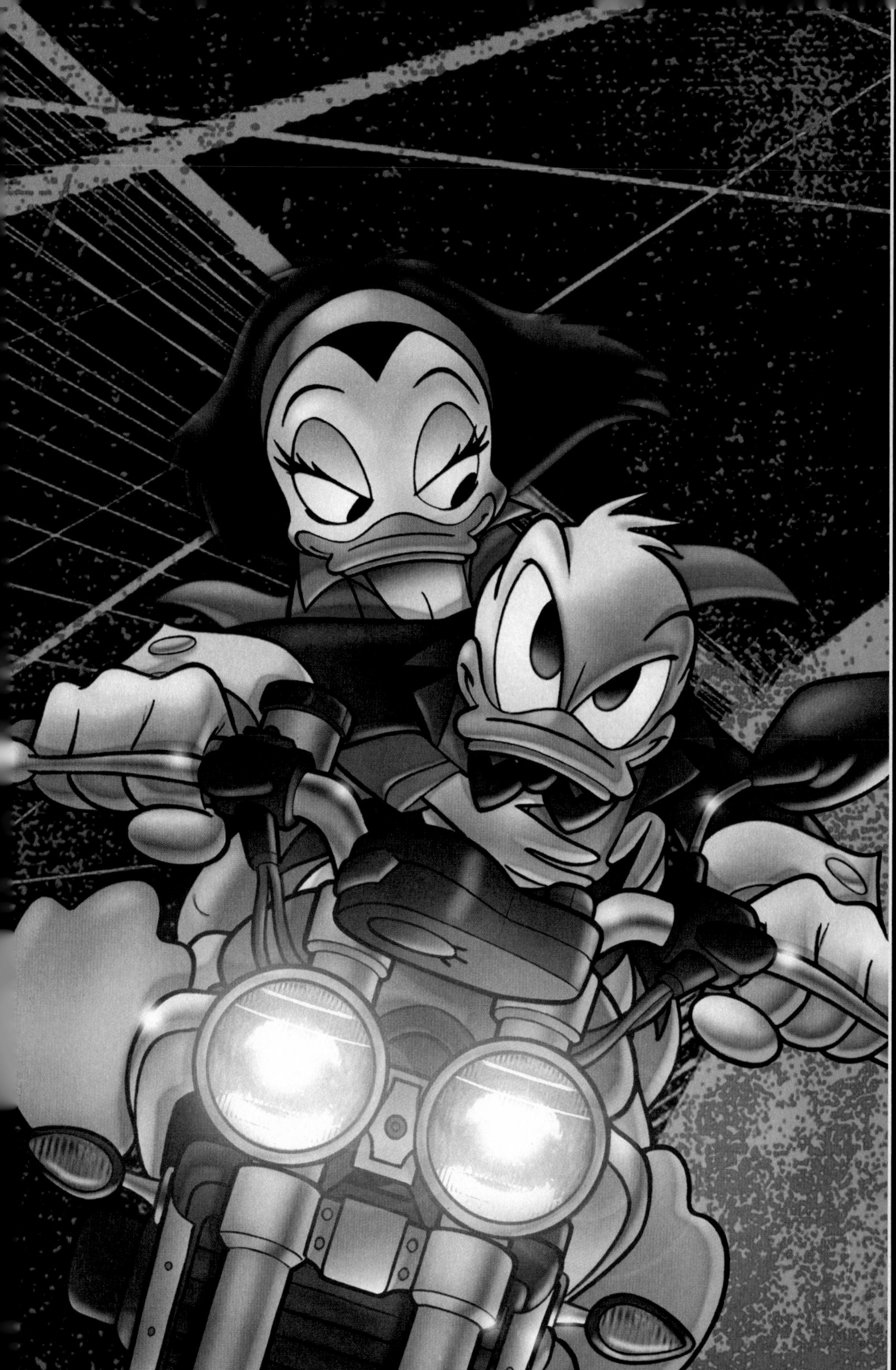

COVER 347B: ANDREA FRECCERO

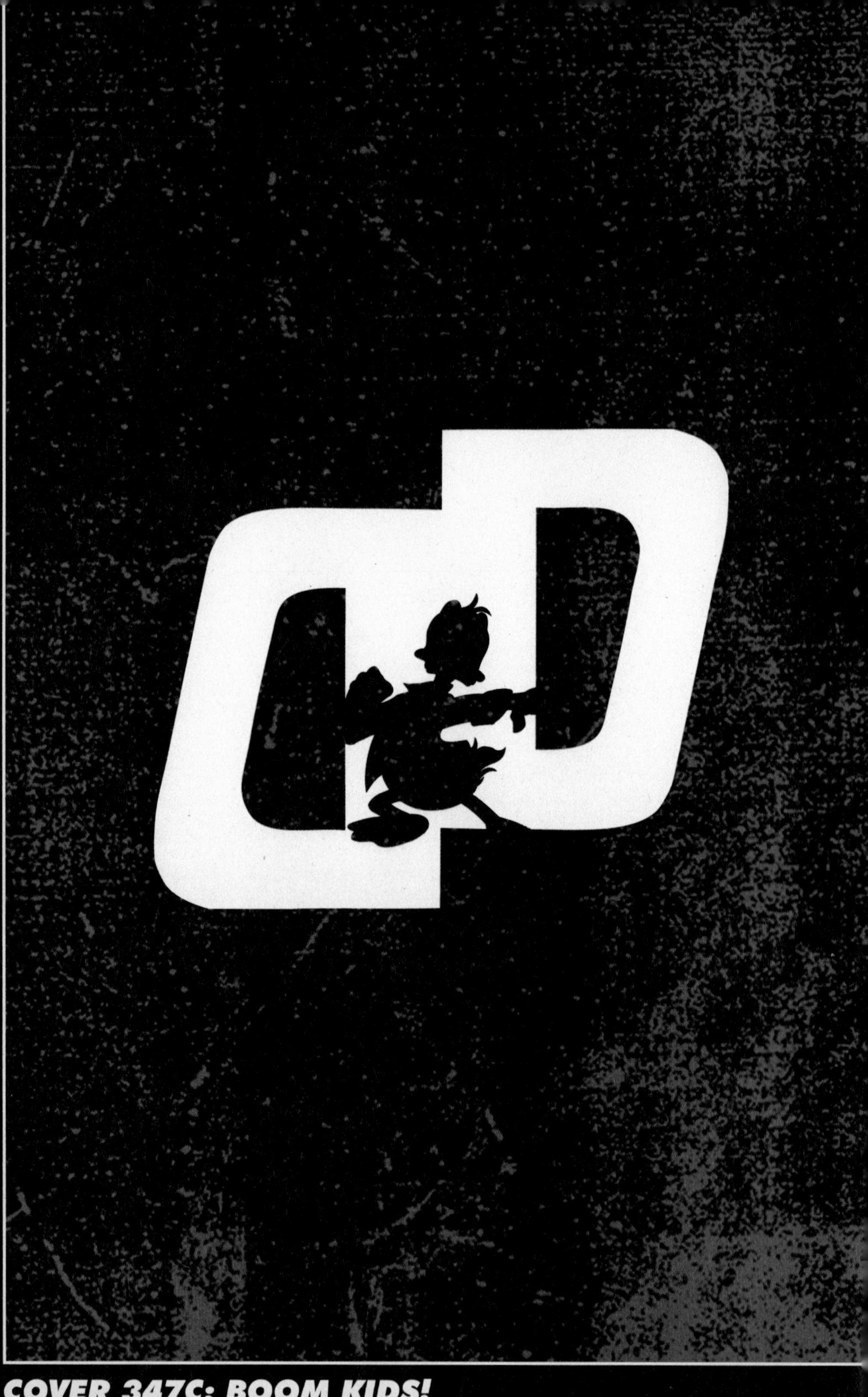

COVER 347C: BOOM KIDS!

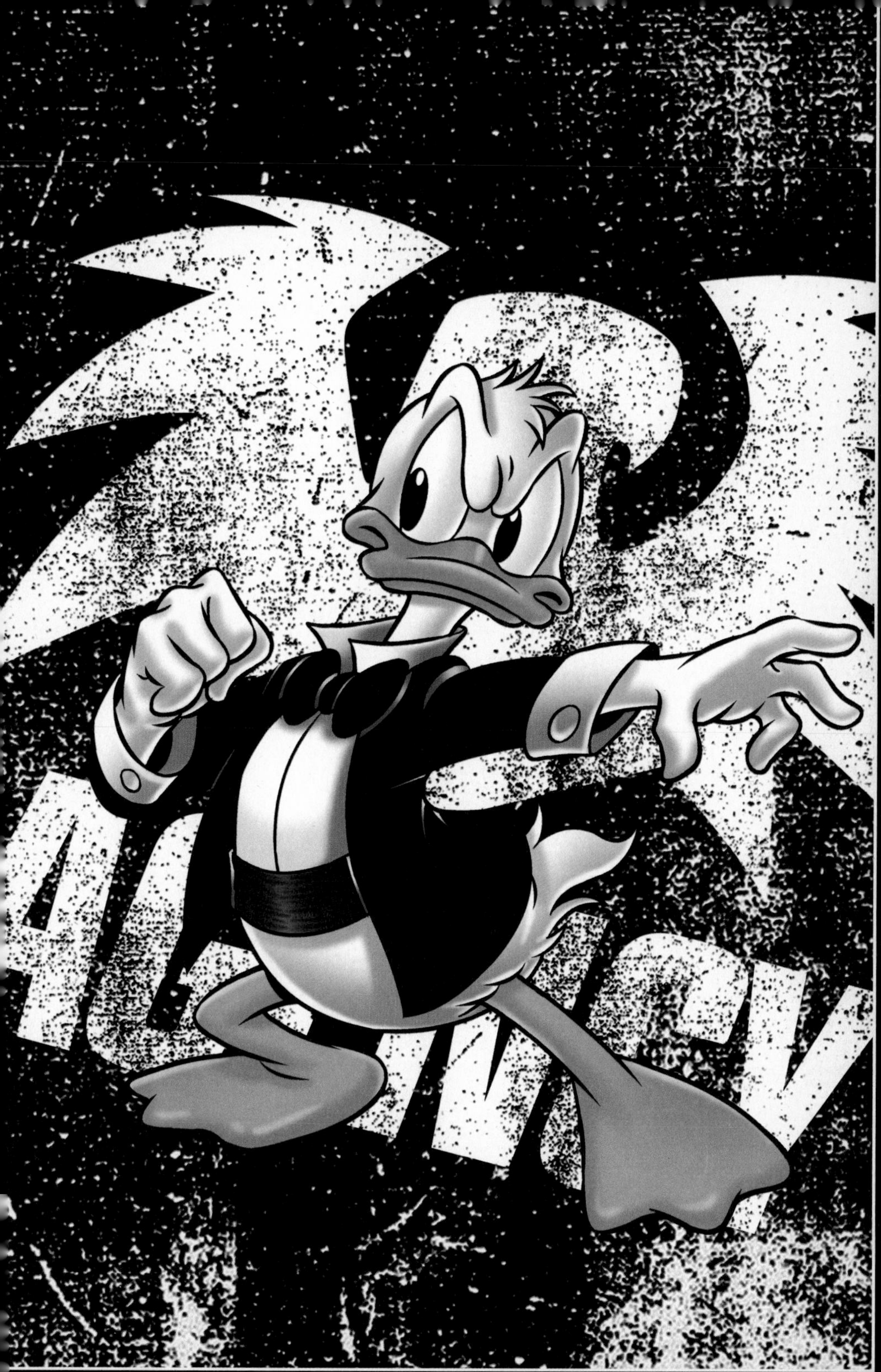

ISSUE 347 2ND PRINT: MAGIC EYE STUDIOS

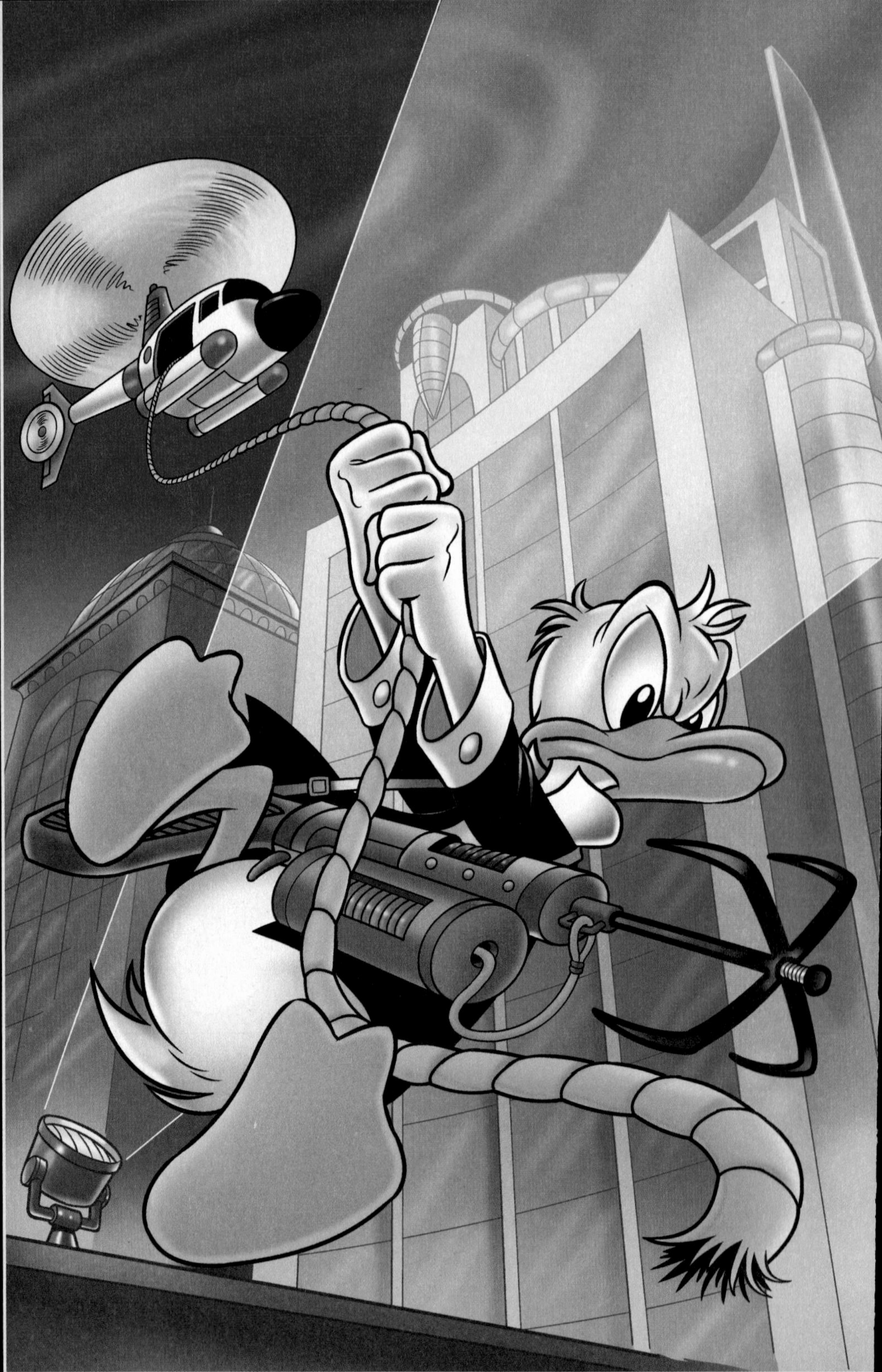

COVER 348A: MAGIC EYE STUDIOS

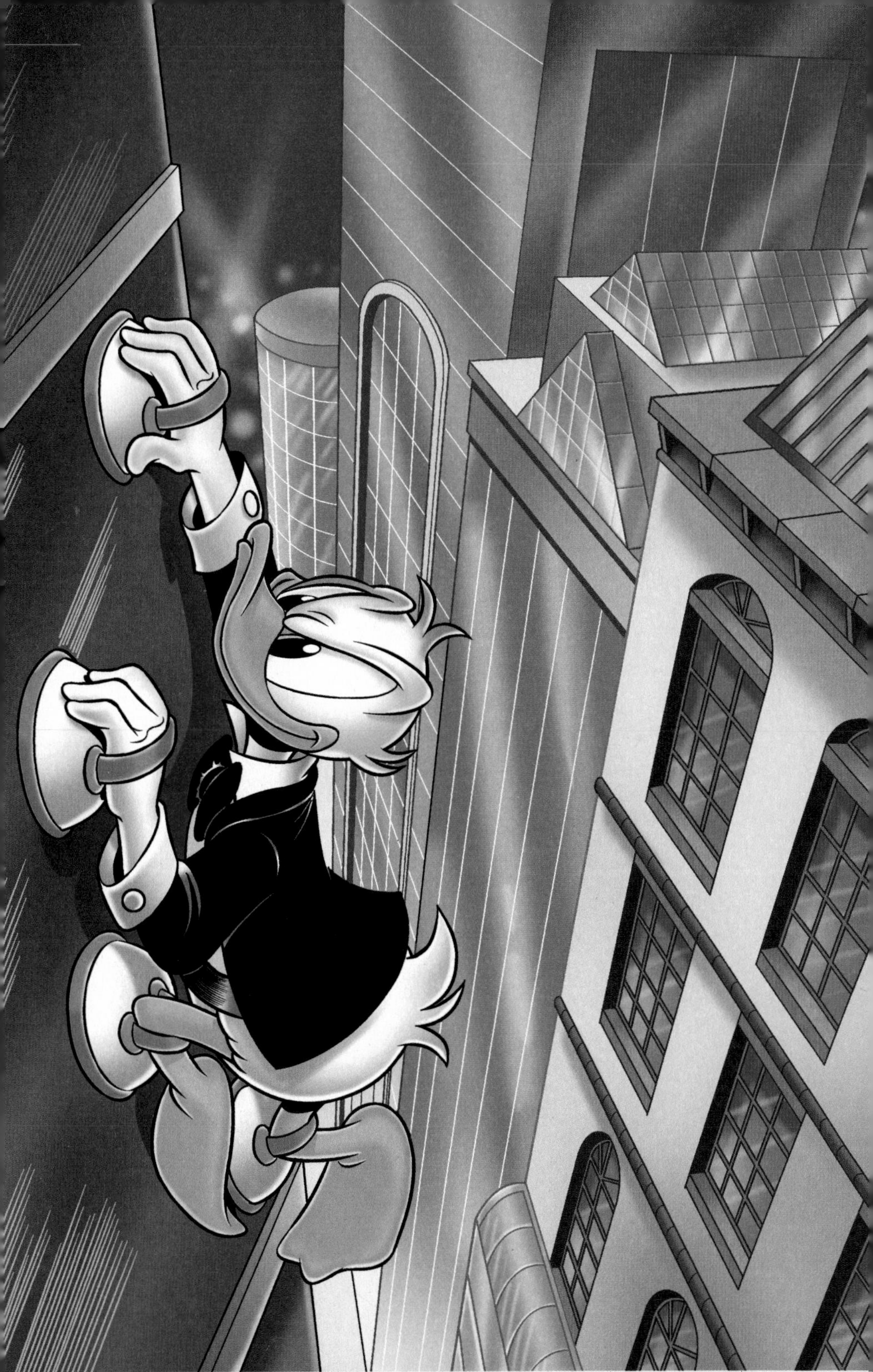

GIC EYE STUDIOS

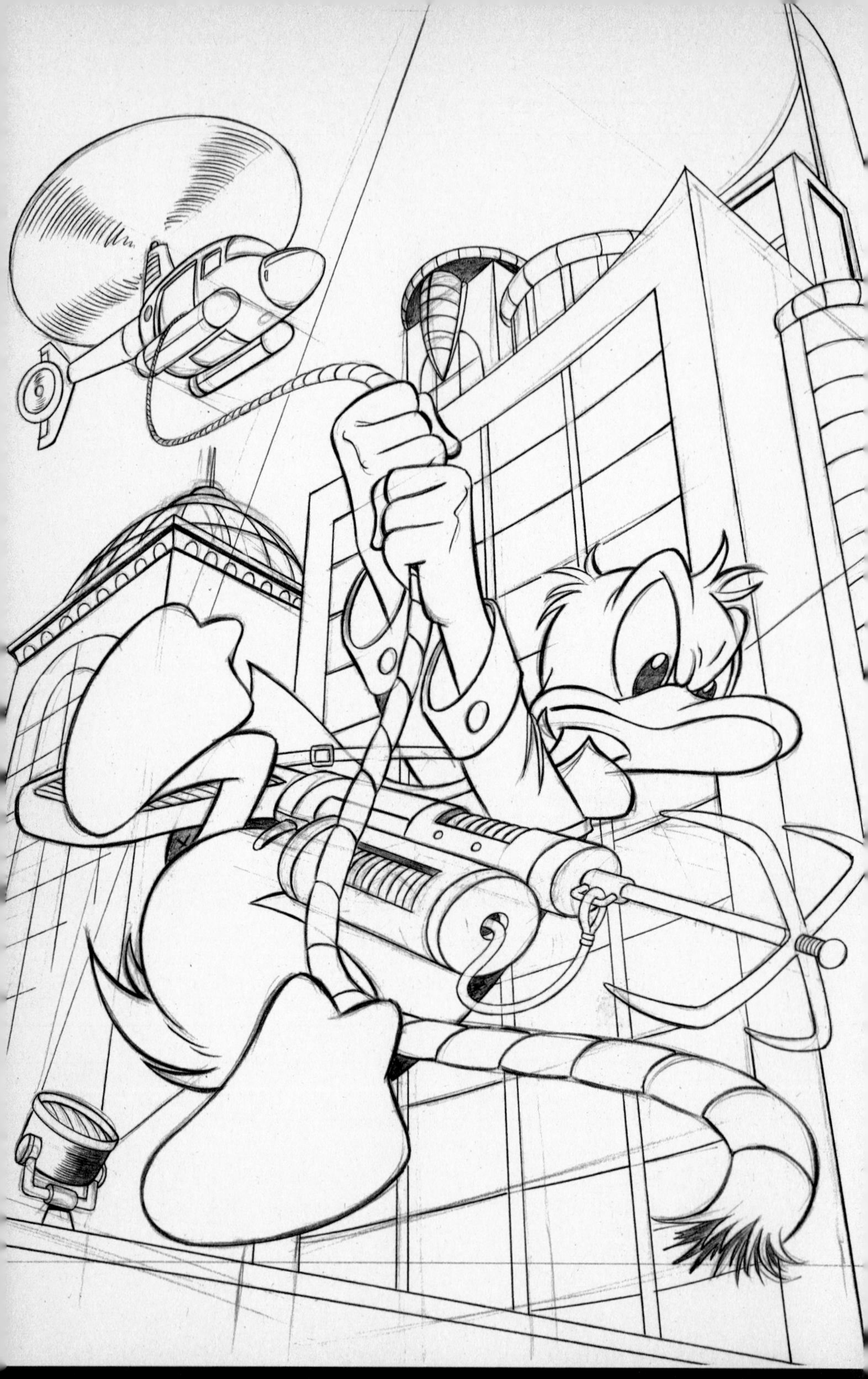

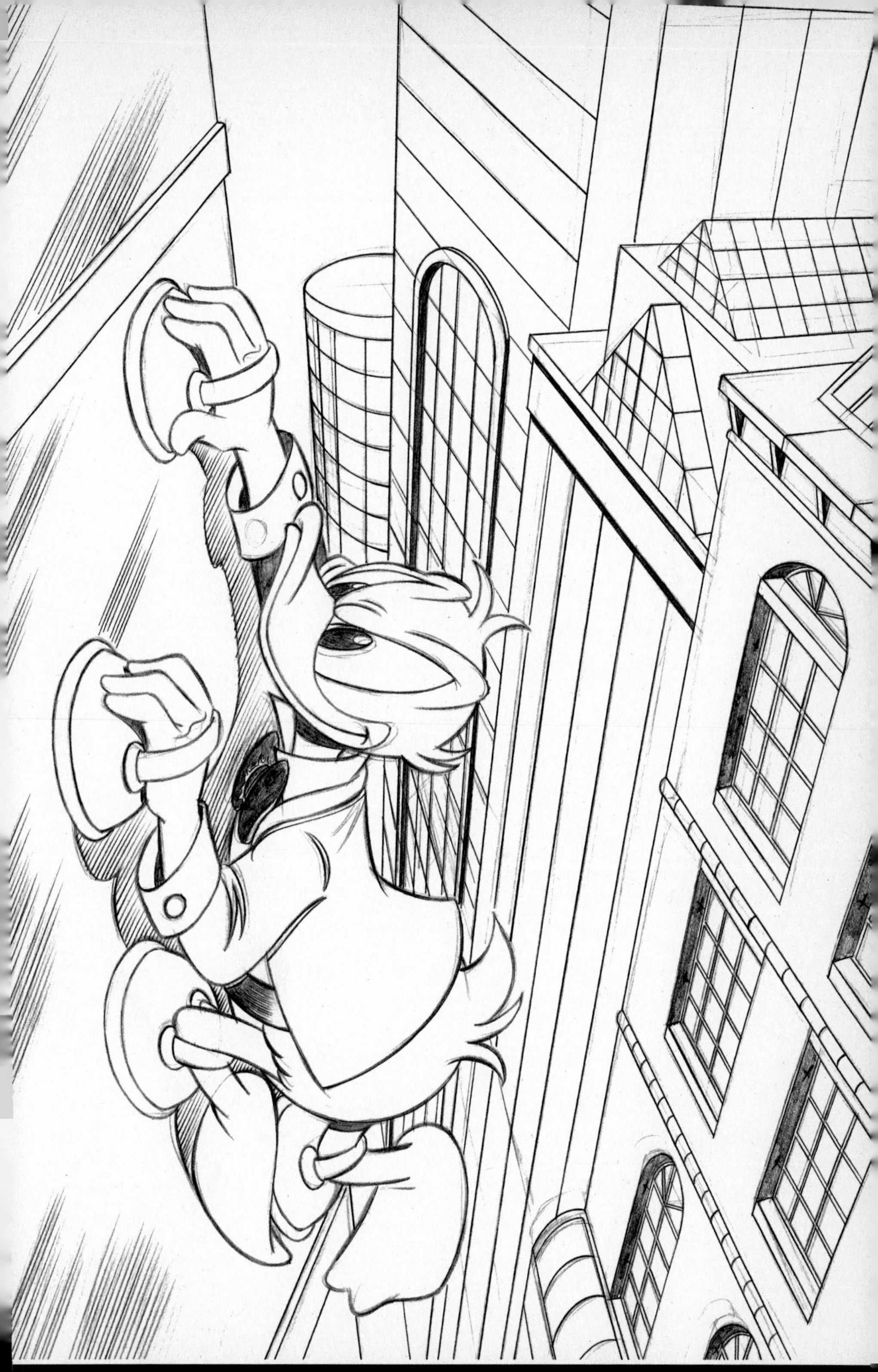

ISSUE 348 2ND PRINT: MAGIC EYE STUDIOS

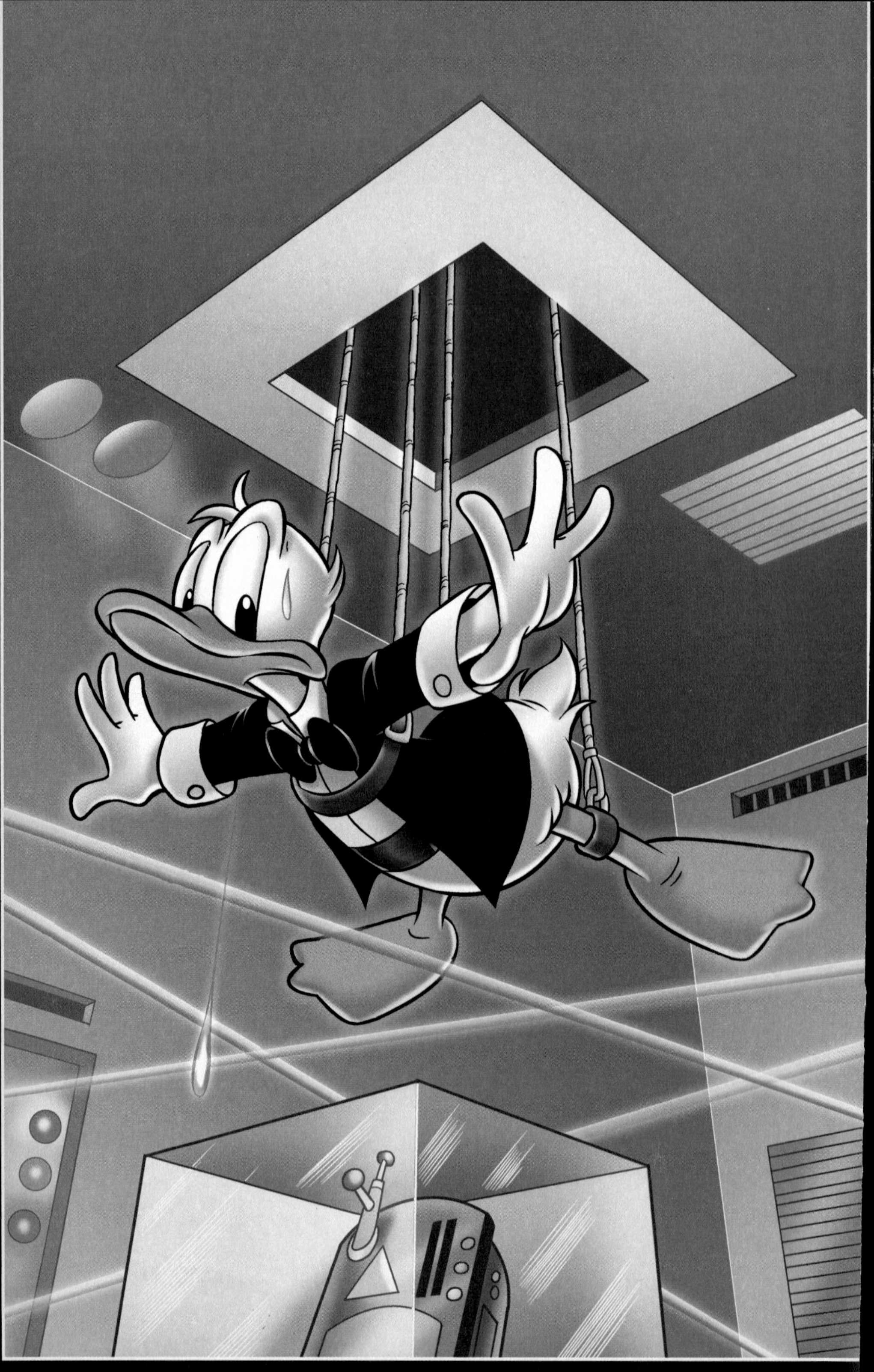

COVER 349A: MAGIC EYE STUDIOS

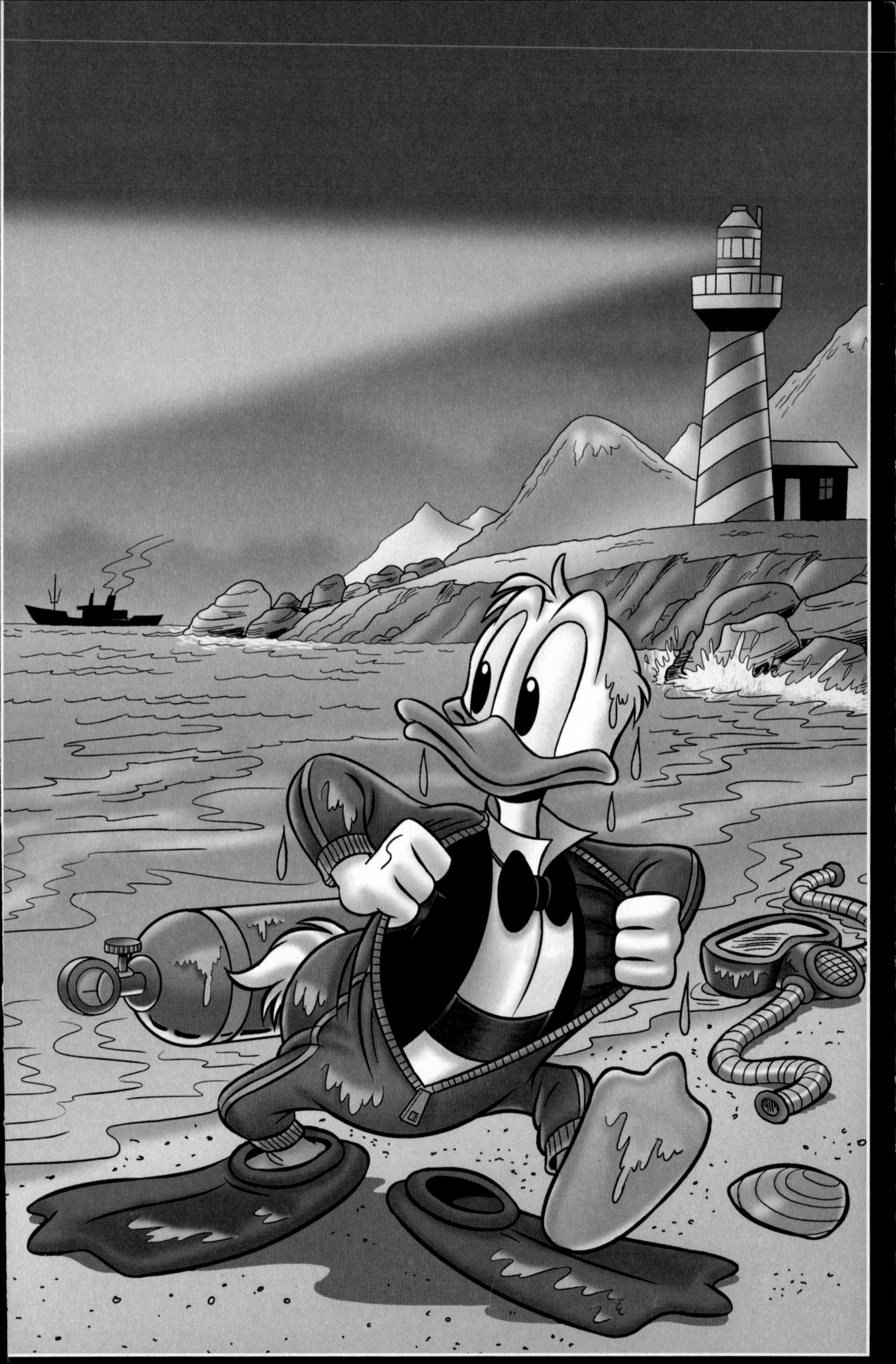

COVER 349B: MAGIC EYE STUDIOS

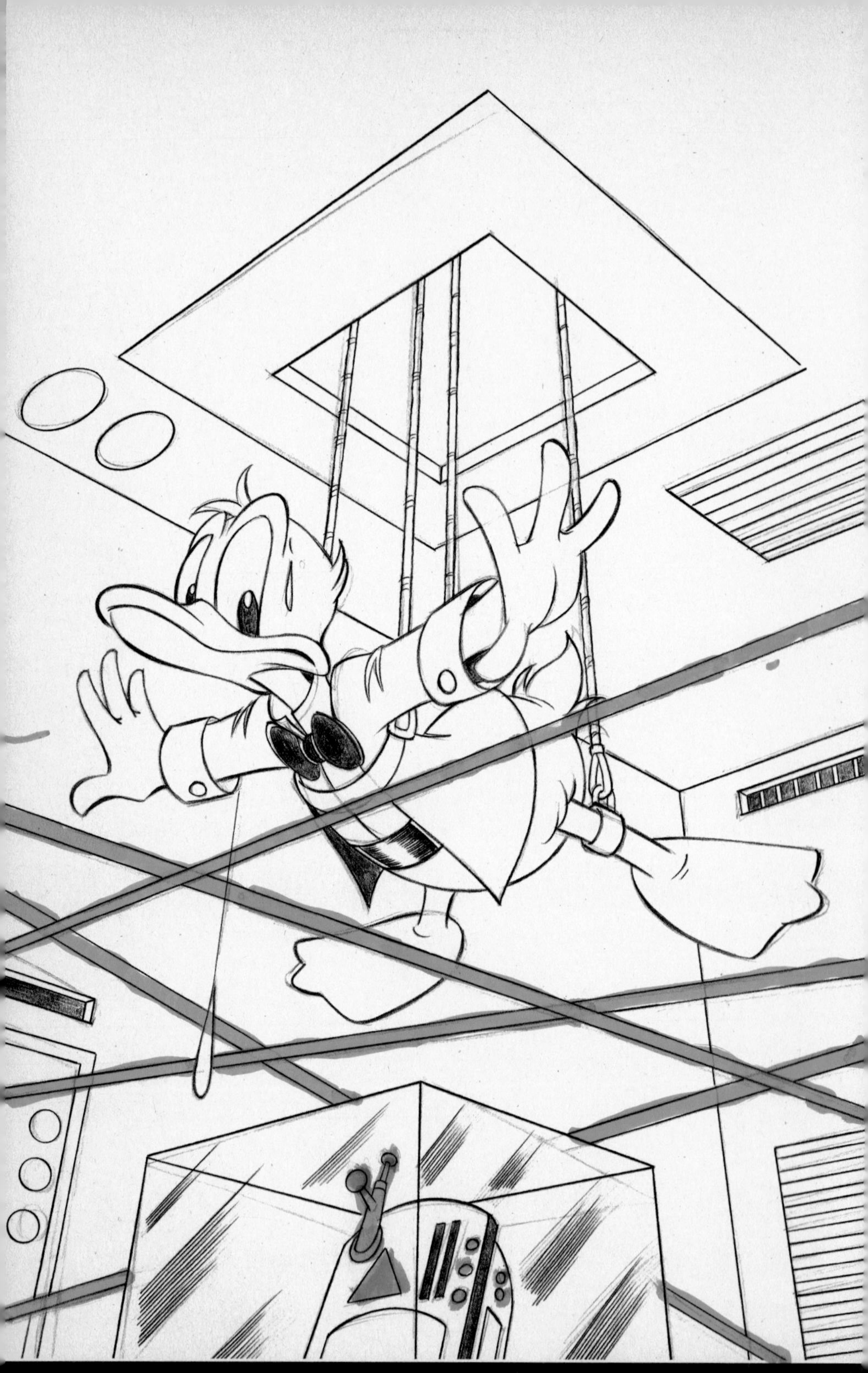

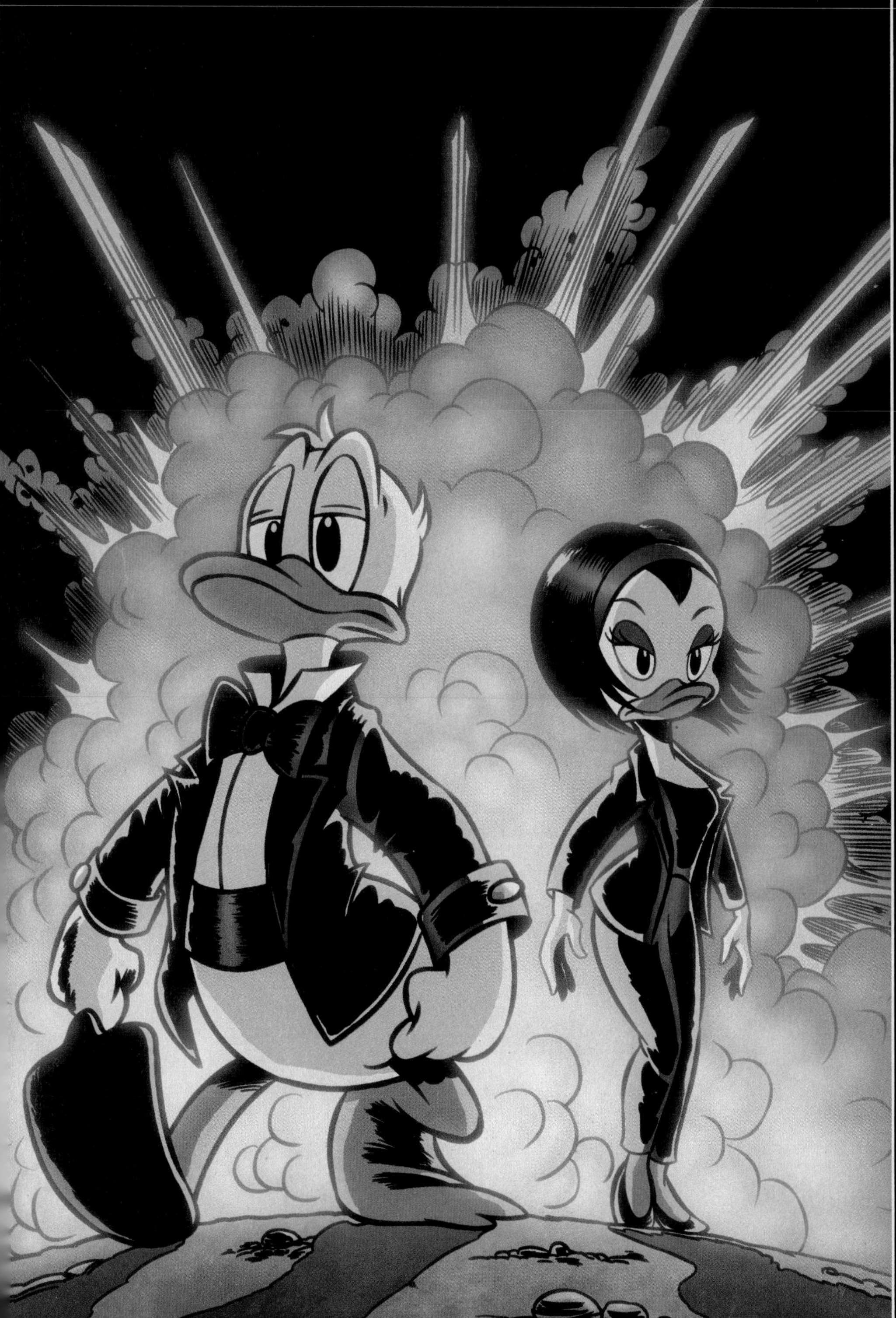

COVER 350A: MAGIC EYE STUDIOS
COLORS / ANDREW DALHOUSE

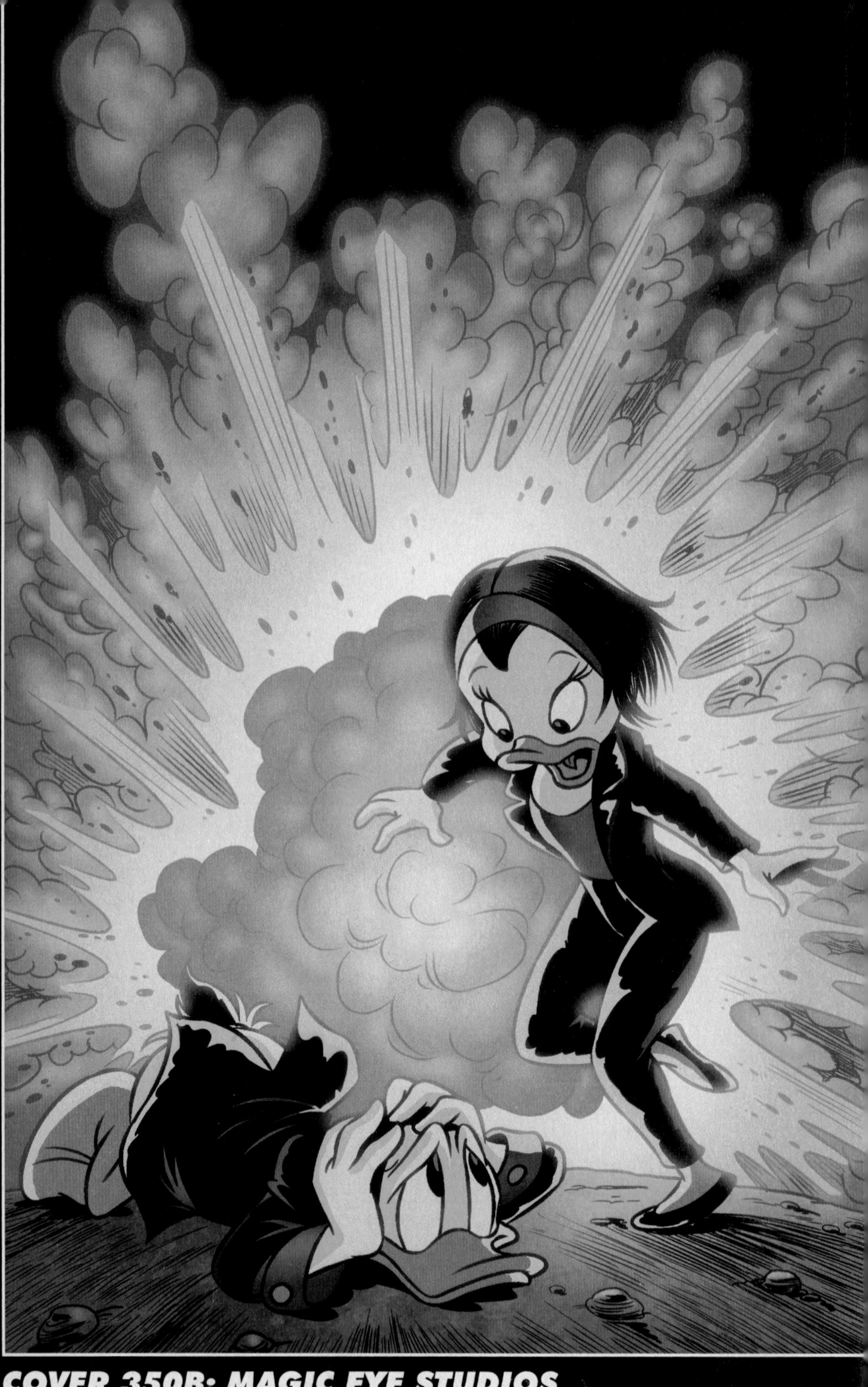

COVER 350B: MAGIC EYE STUDIOS
COLORS / ANDREW DALHOUSE

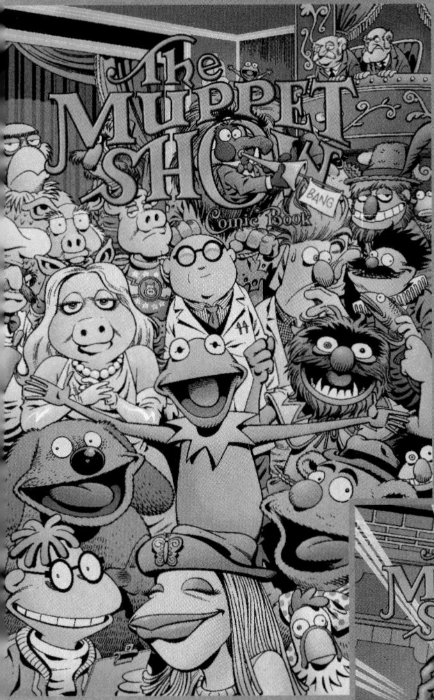
The
MUPPET
SHOW
Comic Book
BANG

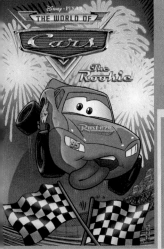

MEET THE MUPPETS
This hilarious trade collects the first four issues of THE MUPPET SHOW, written and drawn by the incomparable Roger Langridge! Packed full of madcap skits and gags, The Muppet Show trade is certain to please old and new fans alike!

THE TREASURE OF PEG-LEG WILSON
Scooter discovers old documents which reveal that a cache of treasure is hidden somewhere within the theater...and when Rizzo the Rat overhears this, the news spreads like wildfire! Can Kermit keep everyone from tearing the theater apart?

ON THE ROAD
With the theatre destroyed after the search for the treasure of Peg-Leg Wilson, the Muppets take their act on the road... but with two very familiar hecklers in every town, will the show be a hit, or will our Muppet minstrels be run out of town in tar and feathers? Also: Fozzie and Rizzo have plans for a big budget PIGS IN SPACE motion picture, but is Hollywood prepared?

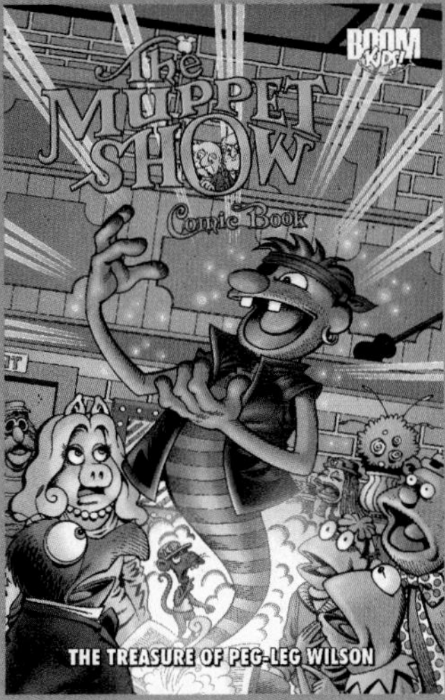
BOOM KIDS!
The
MUPPET
SHOW
Comic Book
THE TREASURE OF PEG-LEG WILSON

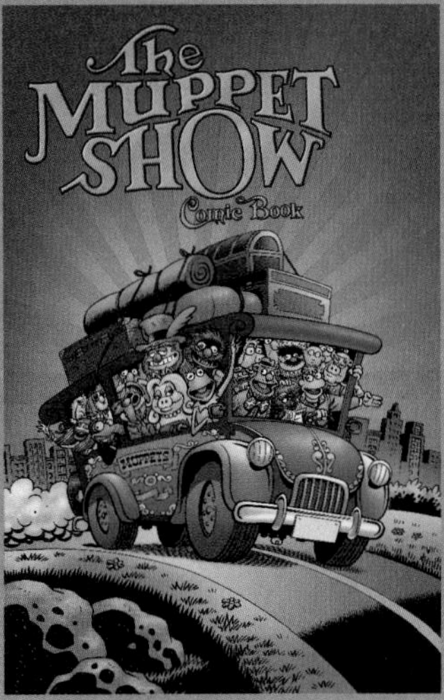
The
MUPPET
SHOW
Comic Book
MUPPETS

THE MUPPET SHOW COMIC BOOK: MEET THE MUPPETS
SC $9.99 ISBN 9781934506851
HC $24.99 ISBN 9781608865277

THE MUPPET SHOW COMIC BOOK: THE TREASURE OF PEG-LEG WILSON
SC $9.99 ISBN 9781608865048
HC $24.99 ISBN 9781608865307

THE MUPPET SHOW COMIC BOOK: ON THE ROAD
SC $9.99 ISBN 9781608865161
HC $24.99 ISBN 9781608865369

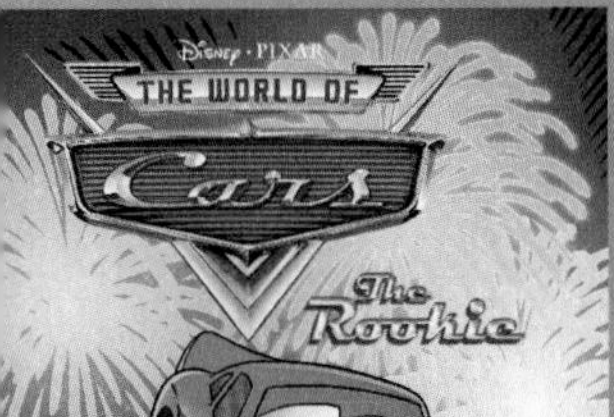
Disney • PIXAR
THE WORLD OF
Cars
The Rookie
Rust-eze
95

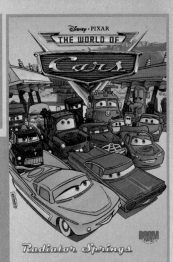

CARS: THE ROOKIE
See how Lightning McQueen became a Piston Cup sensation in this pulse-pounding collection! CARS: THE ROOKIE reveals McQueen's scrappy origins as a local short track racer who dreams of the big time...and recklessly plows his way through the competition to get there! Along the way, he meets Mack, who help McQueen catch his lucky break.

CARS: RADIATOR SPRINGS
From writer Alan J. Porter, this collection of CARS stories is perfect for the whole family! After his return to Radiator Springs, LIGHTNING MCQUEEN is hanging out with his friends at Flo's V8 Café when he realizes that everyone knows his story...but he doesn't know anyone else's! McQueen wants to know how his friends ended up in Radiator Springs...and more importantly why they decided to stay!

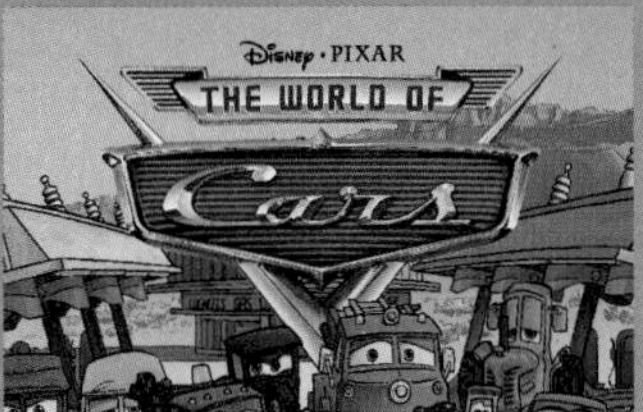
Disney • PIXAR
THE WORLD OF
Cars
BOOM KIDS!
Radiator Springs

CARS: THE ROOKIE
SC $9.99 ISBN 9781934506844
HC $24.99 ISBN 9781608865222

CARS: RADIATOR SPRINGS
SC $9.99 ISBN 9781608865024
HC $24.99 ISBN 9781608865284

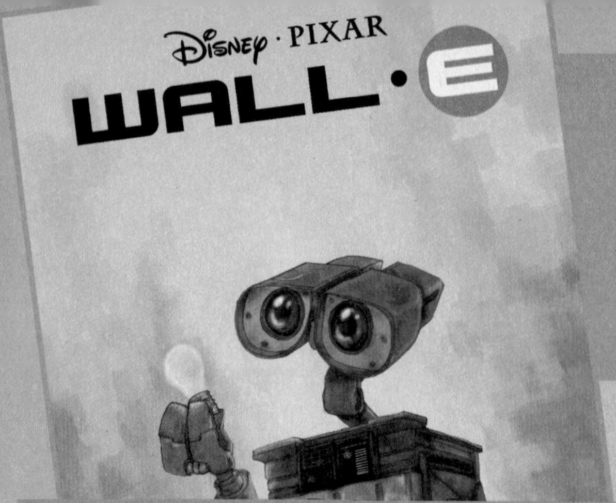
Disney · PIXAR
WALL·E

WALL-E: RECHARGE

Wall-E is not yet the hardworking robot we know and love. Instead, he lets the few remaining other robots take care of most of the trash compacting while he collects interesting junk. But when the other robots start breaking down, Wall-E must learn to adjust his priorities... or else Earth is doomed!

WALL E: RECHARGE
SC $9.99 ISBN 9781608865123
HC $24.99 ISBN 9781608865543

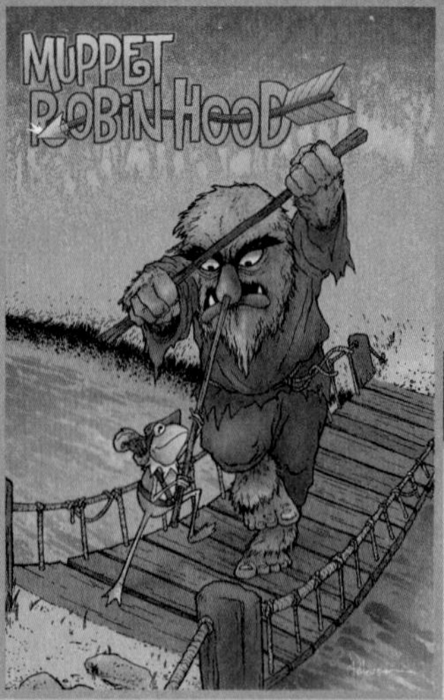
MUPPET ROBIN HOOD

MUPPET ROBIN HOOD

The Muppets tell the Robin Hood legend for laughs, and it's the reader who will be merry! Robin Hood (Kermit the Frog) joins with the Merry Men, Sherwood Forest's infamous gang of misfit outlaws, to take on the stuffy Sheriff of Muppetham (Sam the Eagle)!

MUPPET PETER PAN

When Peter Pan (Kermit) whisks Wendy (Janice) and her brothers to the magical realm of Neveswamp, the adventure begins! With Captain Hook (Gonzo) out for revenge for the loss of his hand, Wendy and her brothers may find themselves in a situation where even the magic of Piggytink (Miss Piggy) can't save them!

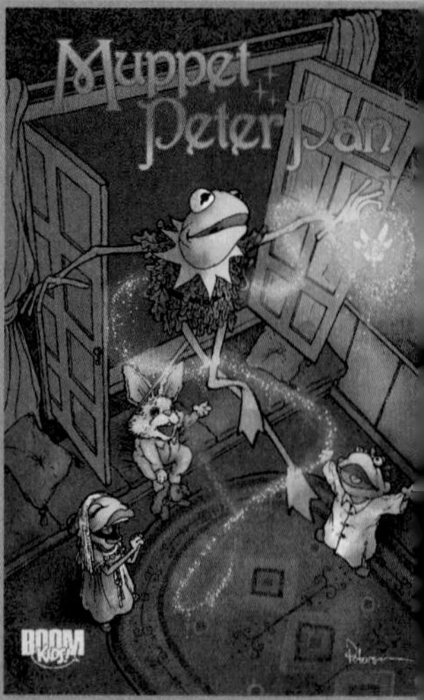
Muppet Peter Pan
BOOM KIDS!

MUPPET ROBIN HOOD
SC $9.99 ISBN 9781934506790
HC $24.99 ISBN 9781608865260

MUPPET PETER PAN
SC $9.99 ISBN 9781608865079
HC $24.99 ISBN 978160886531

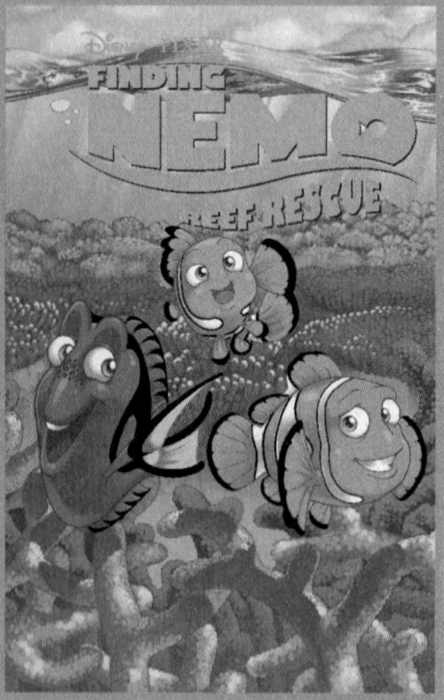
FINDING NEMO
REEF RESCUE

FINDING NEMO: REEF RESCUE

Nemo, Dory and Marlin have become local heroes, and are recruited to embark on an all-new adventure in this exciting collection! Their reef is mysteriously dying and no one knows why!

MONSTERS, INC.: LAUGH FACTORY

Someone is stealing comedy props from the other employees, making it difficult for them to harvest the laughter they need to power Monstropolis... and all evidence points to Sulley's best friend Mike Wazowski!

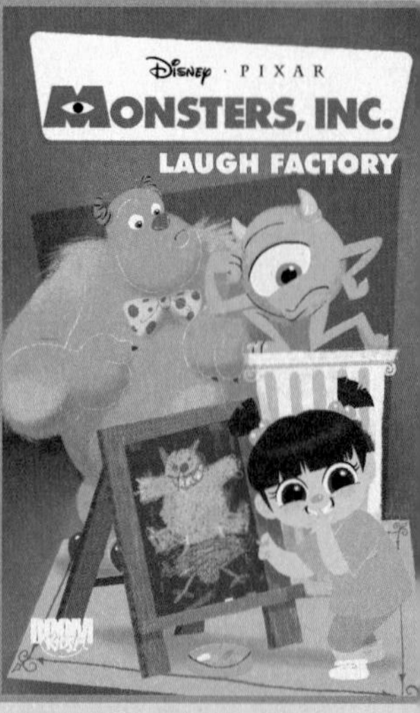
Disney · PIXAR
MONSTERS, INC.
LAUGH FACTORY

FINDING NEMO: REEF RESCUE
SC $9.99 ISBN 9781934506882
HC $24.99 ISBN 9781608865246

MONSTERS, INC.: LAUGH FACTORY
SC $9.99 ISBN 9781608865086
HC $24.99 ISBN 978160886533

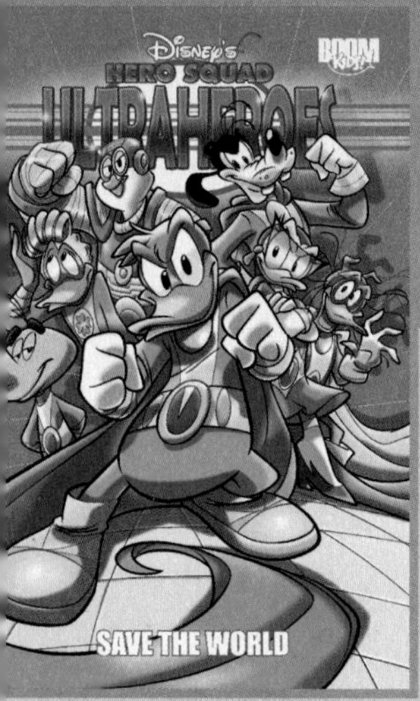
Disney's
HERO SQUAD
ULTRAHEROES
SAVE THE WORLD

DISNEY'S HERO SQUAD: ULTRAHEROES
It's the year 2734 and the only one standing in the way of earth's utter destruction is...Mickey Mouse?! Join the four-colored fun as Mickey Mouse, Goofy, Donald Duck take to the skies to save the world.

DISNEY'S HERO SQUAD: ULTRAHEROES
SC $9.99 ISBN 9781608865437
HC $24.99 ISBN 9781608865529

WIZARDS OF MICKEY: MOUSE MAGIC
Your favorite Disney characters star in this magical fantasy epic! Student of the great wizard Grandalf, Mickey Mouse hails from the humble village of Miceland. Allying himself with Donald Duck (who has a pet dragon named Fafnir) and team mate Goofy, Mickey quests to find a magical crown that will give him mastery over all spells!

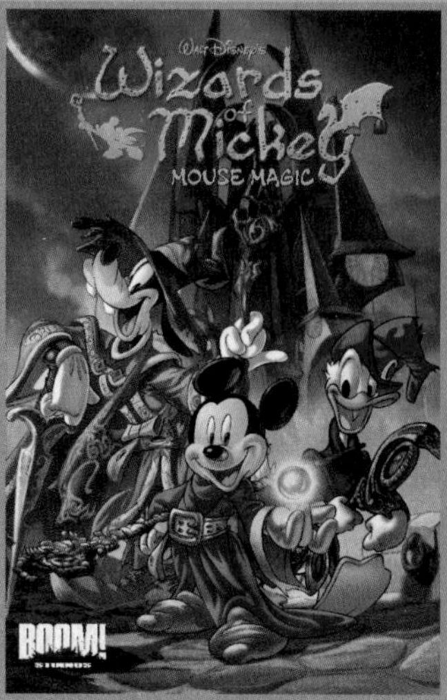
Walt Disney's
Wizards of Mickey
MOUSE MAGIC
BOOM!

WIZARDS OF MICKEY: MOUSE MAGIC
SC $9.99 ISBN 9781608865413
HC $24.99 ISBN 9781608865505

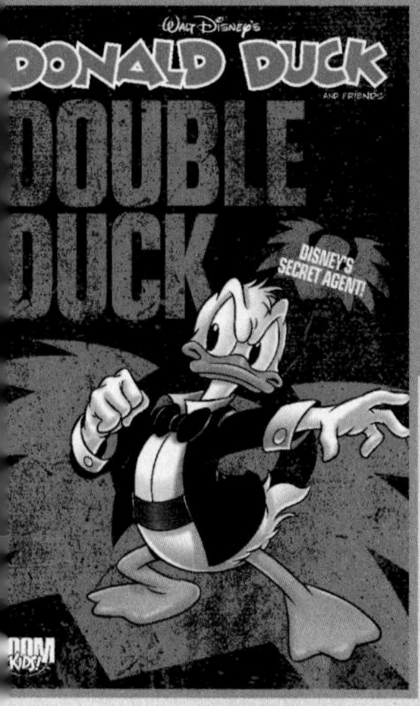
Walt Disney's
DONALD DUCK
AND FRIENDS
DOUBLE DUCK
DISNEY'S SECRET AGENT!

DONALD DUCK AND FRIENDS: DOUBLE DUCK
Donald Duck as a secret agent? Villainous fiends beware as the world of super sleuthing and espionage will never be the same! This is Donald Duck like you've never seen him!

DONALD DUCK AND FRIENDS: DOUBLE DUCK
SC $9.99 ISBN 9781608865451
HC $24.99 ISBN 9781608865512

UNCLE SCROOGE: THE HUNT FOR OLD NUMBER ONE
Join Donald Duck's favorite penny pinching Uncle Scrooge as he, along with Donald himself and Huey, Dewey and Louie embark on a globe spanning trek to recover treasure and save Scrooge's "number one dime" from the treacherous grasp of Magica De Spell.

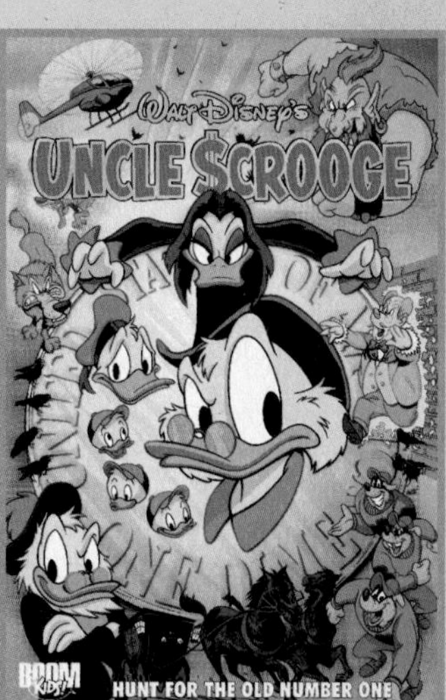
Walt Disney's
UNCLE $CROOGE
HUNT FOR THE OLD NUMBER ONE

UNCLE SCROOGE: THE HUNT FOR THE OLD NUMBER ONE
SC $9.99 ISBN 9781608865536
HC $24.99 ISBN 9781608865536

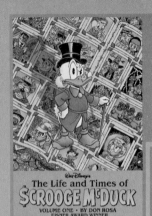

Walt Disney's
The Life and Times of
$CROOGE McDUCK
VOLUME ONE • BY DON ROSA
EISNER AWARD WINNER

THE LIFE AND TIMES OF SCROOGE MCDUCK VOL. 1

BOOM Kids! proudly collects the first half of THE LIFE AND TIMES OF SCROOGE MCDUCK in a gorgeous hardcover collection — featuring smyth sewn binding, a gold-on-gold foil-stamped case wrap, and a bookmark ribbon! These stories, written and drawn by legendary cartoonist Don Rosa, chronicle Scrooge McDuck's fascinating life. See how Scrooge earned his 'Number One Dime' and began to build his fortune!

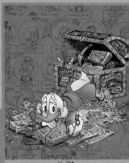

THE LIFE AND TIMES OF SCROOGE MCDUCK VOL. 2

BOOM! Kids proudly presents volume two of THE LIFE AND TIMES OF SCROOGE MCDUCK in a gorgeous hardcover collection in a beautiful, deluxe package featuring smyth sewn binding and a foil-stamped case wrap! These stories, written and drawn by legendary cartoonist Don Rosa, chronicle Scrooge McDuck's fascinating life.

Walt Disney
The Life and Times of
$CROOGE McDUCK
VOLUME TWO • BY DON ROSA
EISNER AWARD WINNER

THE LIFE & TIMES OF SCROOGE MCDUCK VOLUME 1 HC
HC $24.99 ISBN 9781608865383

THE LIFE & TIMES OF SCROOGE MCDUCK VOLUME 2 HC
HC $24.99 ISBN 9781608865420

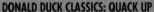

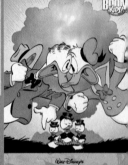

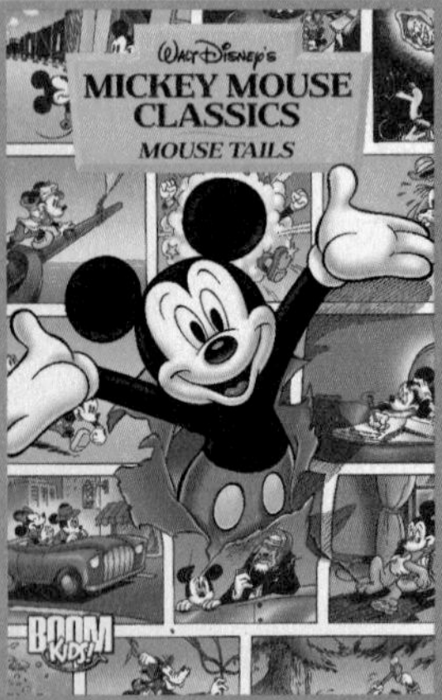

Walt Disney's
MICKEY MOUSE
CLASSICS
MOUSE TAILS
BOOM KIDS!

MICKEY MOUSE CLASSICS VOL. 1

See Mickey Mouse as he was meant to be seen! Solving mysteries, fighting off pirates, and just generally saving the day! These classic stories comprise a "Greatest Hits" series for the mouse, including a story produced by seminal Disney creator Carl Barks!

DONALD DUCK CLASSICS: QUACK UP

Whether it's finding gold, journeying in the Klondike, or fighting ghosts Donald will always have help with Huey, Dewey, Louie, his much more prepared nephews, by his side! Carl Barks brought Donald to prominence, and it's only fair to start off the series with some of his most influential stories!

BOOM KIDS!
Walt Disney's
DONALD DUCK
CLASSICS
QUACK UP

MICKEY MOUSE CLASSICS: MOUSE MAYHEM
HC $24.99 ISBN 9781608865444

DONALD DUCK CLASSICS: QUACK UP HC
HC $24.99 ISBN 9781608865406

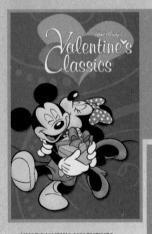

Walt Disney's
Valentine's
Classics

WALT DISNEY'S VALENTINE'S CLASSICS

Love is in the air for Mickey Mouse, Donald Duck and the rest of the gang. But will Cupid's arrows cause happiness or heartache? Find out in this collection of classic stories featuring all your most beloved characters from the magical world of Walt Disney! Featuring work by Carl Barks , Floyd Gottfredson, Daan Jippes, Romano Scarpa and Al Taliaferro.

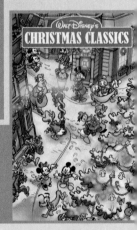

WALT DISNEY'S CHRISTMAS CLASSICS

BOOM! Kids has raided the Disney publishing archives and searched every nook and cranny to find the best and the greatest stories from Disney's vast comic book publishing history for this "best of" compilation.

Walt Disney's
CHRISTMAS CLASSICS

WALT DISNEY'S VALENTINES CLASSICS VOL 1 HC
HC $24.99 ISBN 9781608865499

WALT DISNEY'S CHRISTMAS CLASSICS VOL 1 HC
HC $24.99 ISBN 9781608865482

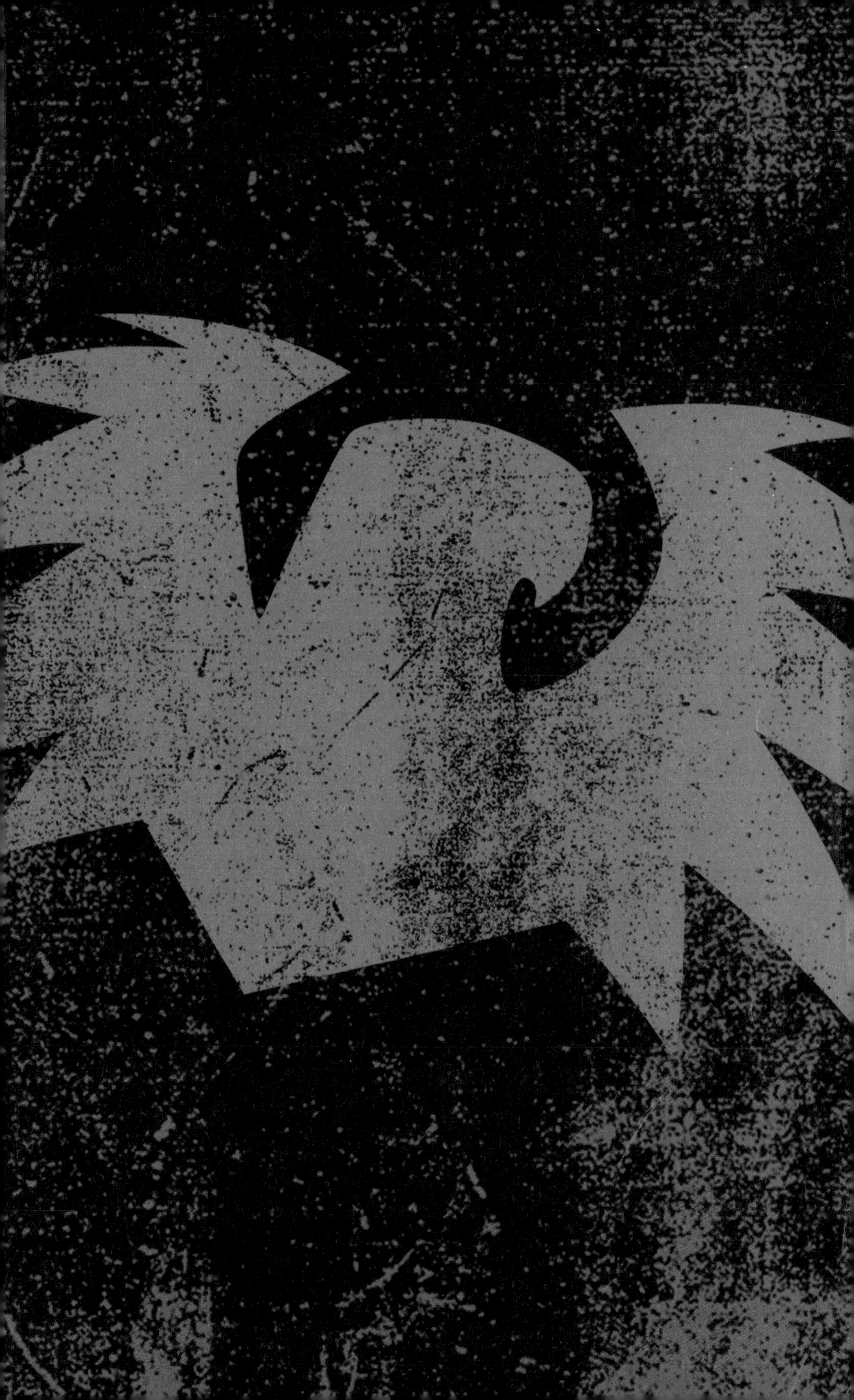

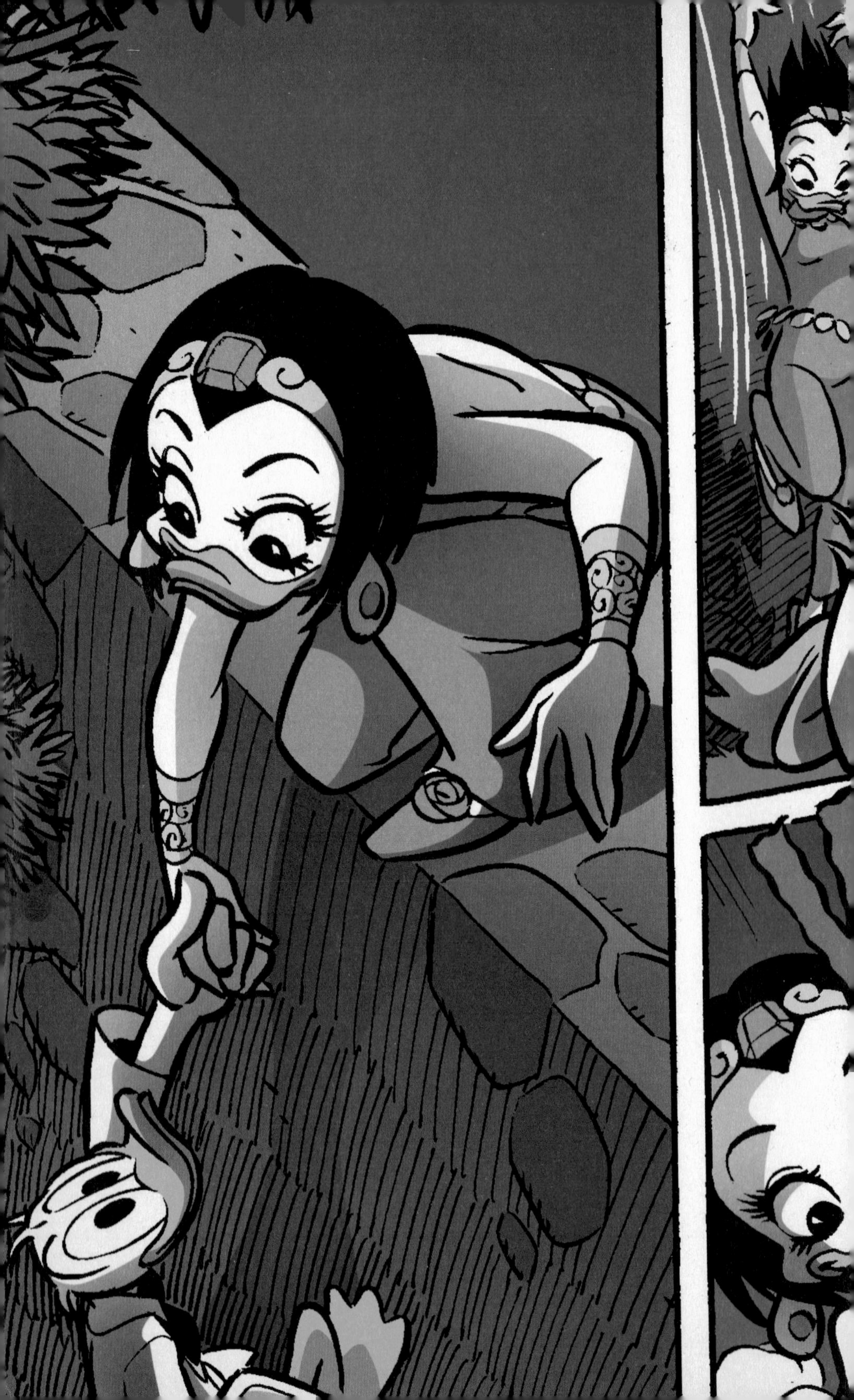